Praise for Chris Moriarty

and

SPIN STATE

Amazon.com Top 10 Editors' Pick for Science Fiction & Fantasy 2003
A *Kansas City Star* Noteworthy Book for 2003
***Library Journal* Pick for Best First Novel**

"*Spin State* is a spiky, detailed, convincing, compelling page-turner and the science is good too. Chris Moriarty is a dangerous talent."—Stephen Baxter

"Vivid, sexy, and sharply written, *Spin State* takes the reader on a nonstop white-knuckle tour of quantum physics, artificial intelligence, and the human heart."—Nicola Griffith

"Knife sharp. An amazing techno-landscape, with characters surfing the outer limits of their humanity, pulling the reader into a scary and seductive future. A thrilling high-end upgrade of cyberpunk!" —Kay Kenyon

"Action, mystery and drama, set against some of the most plausible speculative physics I've seen. This is science fiction for grown-ups who want some 'wow' with their 'what-if.' "—David Brin

"*Spin State* is an intriguing, fascinating, and totally engrossing— yet truly terrifying—look into the time beyond tomorrow, a time and place where an AI and a military officer face love, betrayal, and worse in a struggle over the shape of a future that already has full genetic engineering, bioengineered internal software, FTL communications and travel . . . and the age-old human weakness of greed and lust . . . and the love of power." —L. E. Modesitt Jr.

Also by Chris Moriarty

SPIN STATE

SPIN CONTROL

CHRIS MORIARTY

BANTAM BOOKS

SPIN CONTROL
A Bantam Spectra Book / July 2006

Published by
Bantam Dell
A Division of Random House, Inc.
New York, New York

ISBN: 978-0-7394-7270-5

Printed in the United States of America

For Ruth Isaacs, Barbara Gotchman, Viola Davis, Nancy Rolnik, Jim Russell, and James Winston Morris.

Most books—certainly most science fiction novels—only exist because the right teachers came into some child's life at the right time. For me, you were those teachers. The words "thank you" seem pretty inadequate, but they're the only words I have. So . . . thank you.

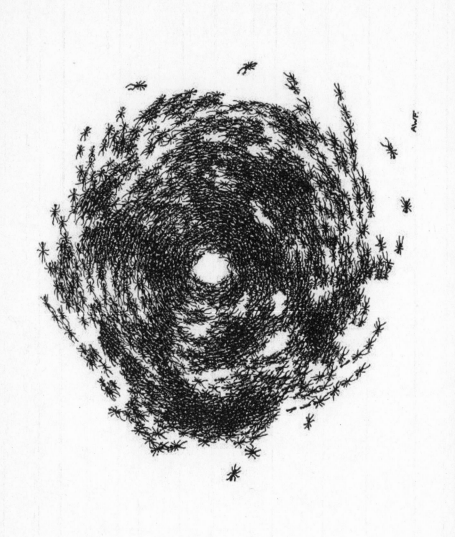

THE GOLEM

Monsters . . . are a state of mind.

—E. O. Wilson (1995)

S HE WAS PROBABLY NO MORE than thirty.

It was hard to tell with humans. They all looked old to Arkady, and they aged fast out here in the Trusteeships where people lost months and years just getting from one planet to the next.

This human looked like she'd lived harder than most. Her skin was ravaged by decades of unfiltered sunlight, her face lined by wind and worry, her features gaunt with the gravity of some heavy planet. Still, Arkady didn't think she could be more than a few subjective years beyond his twenty-seven.

"Act like you're picking me up," she said in a low husky voice that would have been sensual had it not been ratcheted tight by fear. She spoke UN-standard Spanish, but her flat vowels and guttural consonants betrayed her native tongue as Hebrew.

She flagged down the barkeep and ordered two of something Arkady had never heard of. When she gripped his arm to draw him closer, he saw that her cuticles were rough and ragged and she'd bitten her nails to the quick.

He bent over her, smelling the acrid fungal smell of the planet-born, and recited the words Korchow had taught him back on Gilead. She fed him back the answers he'd been told to wait for. She was pulling them off hard memory; her pupils dilated, blossoming across the pale iris, every time she accessed her virally embedded RAM. He tried not to stare and failed.

This is your first monster, he told himself. *Get used to them.*

He studied the woman's face, wondering if she was what other members of her species would call normal. It seemed unlikely. To Arkady's crèche-born eyes her features looked as mismatched as if they'd been culled from a dozen disparate genelines. The predatory nose jutted over an incongruously delicate jawline. The forehead was high and intelligent . . . but too flat and scowling to get past any competent genetic designer. And even under the dim flicker of the strobe lights it was obvious that her eyes were mismatched. The right eye fixed Arkady with a steel blue stare, while the left one wandered across the open room behind him so that he had to fight the urge to turn around and see who she was really talking to.

"Why did you come here?" the woman asked when she was satisfied he was who he said he was.

"You know why."

"I mean the real reason."

You have to ask for money, Korchow had told him during the interminable briefing sessions. He could see Korchow's face in his mind's eye: a spy's face, a diplomat's face, a manifesto in flesh and blood of everything KnowlesSyndicate was supposed to stand for. *You have no idea what money means to humans, Arkady. It's how they reward each other, how they control each other. If you don't ask for it, you won't feel real to them.*

"I came for the money," he told Osnat, trying not to sound like an explorer trading beads with the natives.

"And you trust us to give it to you?"

"You know who I trust." Still following Korchow's script. "You know who I need to see."

"At least you had the wits not to say his name." She glanced at the shadowy maze of ventilation ducts and spinstream conduits overhead to indicate that they were under surveillance.

"Here?" Arkady asked incredulously.

"Everywhere. The AIs can tap any spin, anytime, anywhere. You're in UN space now. Get used to it."

Arkady glanced at the sullen and exhausted drinkers around him and wondered what they could possibly be doing that was worth the attention of the UN's semisentients. These weren't humans as he'd been raised to believe in them. Where were the fat cat profiteers and the spiritually bankrupt individualists of his sociobiology textbooks? Where were the gene traders? Where were the slave drivers and the brutally oppressed genetic constructs? All he saw here were algae skimmers and coltran miners. Posthumans whose genetic heritage was too haphazard for anyone to be able to guess whether they were human or construct or some unknown quasi-species between the two. People who scratched out a living from stones and mud and carried the dirt of planets under their fingernails. Throwaway people.

Arkasha would probably have said they were beautiful. He would have talked passionately about pre-Evacuation literature, about the slow sure currents of evolution, and the vast chaotic genetic river that was posthumanity. But all Arkady could see here was poverty, disease, and danger.

The bartender slapped their drinks down hard enough to send sour-smelling liquid cascading onto the countertop. The woman picked up hers and gulped thirstily. Arkady just stared at his. He could smell it from here, and it smelled bad. Like yeast and old skin and overloaded air filters: all the smells he was beginning to recognize as the smells of humans.

"So." The woman used the word as if it were an entire sentence. "Who really sent you?"

"I'm here on my own account. I thought you understood that."

"We understood that was what you *wanted* us to understand." She had a habit of hanging on a word that gave it a weight at odds with its apparent significance and left Arkady wondering if anything in her world meant what it seemed to mean. "It wouldn't be the first time a professional came across the lines posing as an amateur."

Arkady played with his drink, buying time. *Don't explain, don't apologize,* Korchow had told him. Right before he'd told him what would happen to Arkasha if he failed.

"I'm a myrmecologist," he told her.

"Whatever the fuck that is."

"I study ants. For terraforming."

"Bullshit. Terraforming's dangerous. And you're an A Series. You reek of it. No one who counts ever gets handed that raw of a deal."

"It was my Part," he said reflexively before he could remember the word meant nothing to humans.

"You mean you *volunteered*?"

"I'm sorry." Arkady's confusion was genuine. "What is volunteered?"

Her right eye narrowed, though the left one remained serenely focused on the middle distance. An old scar nicked the eyebrow above the lazy eye, and for the first time it occurred to Arkady that it might not be a birth defect at all, but the product of a home-brewed wetware installation gone wrong. What if it wasn't internal RAM she was accessing but the spooky-action-at-a-distance virtual world of streamspace? What was she seeing there? And who was paying her uplink fees?

A movement caught Arkady's eye, and he turned to find a lone drinker staring at him from the far end of the grease-smeared bartop. He watched the man take in his unlined stationer's skin, his too-symmetrical features, the gleam of perfect health that bespoke generations of sociogenetic engineering. They locked eyes, and Arkady noticed what he should have noticed before: the dusty green flash of an Interfaither's skullcap.

You were supposed to be able to tell which religion Interfaithers hailed from by the signs they wore. A Star of David for Jews; two signs Arkady couldn't remember for Sunnis and Shi'ites; a multitude of cryptic symbols for the various schismatic Christian sects. He gave the Interfaither another covert glance, but the only sign he could see on him was a silver pendant whose two curving lines intersected to form the abstracted shape of a fish.

The Interfaithers scared Arkady more than any other danger in UN space. It had been Interfaithers who killed an entire contract group right here on Maris Station and mutilated their bodies so badly that all their home Syndicates ever got back were diplomatic apologies. The rest of the UN had made peace with the Syndicates—if you could call this simmering cold war a peace—but the Interfaithers hadn't. And when anyone asked them why, they used words like *Abomination* and *Jihad* and *Crusade*—words that weren't supposed to exist anymore in any civilized language.

Arkady glanced at the bar-back mirror, trying to reassure himself that he fit in well enough to pass safely. What he saw didn't reassure him at all. Korchow's team had broken his nose and one cheekbone, a precaution that had seemed barbaric back on Gilead. But it took decades at the bottom of a gravity well to get the lined and haggard look of the planet-born. And it would have taken a lifetime—someone else's lifetime—to mold Arkady's frank and open crèche-born face into the aggressive mask most humans wore in public.

Arkady gave the Interfaither another surreptitious glance, only to find the man still staring at him. Their eyes locked. The Interfaither turned away, still holding Arkady's gaze, and spit on the floor.

"Creature of magicians," the woman muttered, "return to your dust!"

"What?" Arkady asked, though he knew somehow that the words were a response to the Interfaither.

"It's from the Talmud." Again that black inward gaze as she tapped RAM or slipped into the spinstream. *"Then Rabbah created a man and sent him to Rabbi Zera. Rabbi Zera spoke to him but received no answer. Thereupon he said to him: 'Creature of the magicians, return to your dust!'* That's how the first golem died."

"What's a golem?" Arkady asked.

"A man without a soul." Her laugh was as hard-bitten as everything else about her. "You."

Arkady heaved a shaky breath that ended in a bout of coughing. He was running a fever, his immune system kicking into overdrive to answer the insult of being stuck in a closed environment with thousands of unfamiliar human pathogens. He hoped it was just allergies. He couldn't afford to get sick now. And he didn't even want to think about what the UN's human doctors would make of his decidedly-posthuman immune system.

He lifted his glass and sipped cautiously from it. Beer. And not as bad as it smelled. Still, he didn't like the cold skin of condensation that had already formed on the glass. It was a sure sign that the station was underpowered and overpopulated, its life-support systems dangerously close to redlining. A Syndicate station whose air was this bad would have been shutting down nonessential operations and shipping its crèchelings to the neighbors just to be on the safe side. But people here were carrying on as usual. And on the way to the meet Arkady had passed a group of completely unsupervised children playing dangerously far from the nearest blowout shelter. You could spend years listening to people talk about the cheapness of life in human space, but it didn't really come home to you until you saw something like this . . .

You were wrong, Arkasha. They're another species. We're divided by our history, by our ideology, by the very genes we hold in common. All we share is the memory of what Earth was before we killed it.

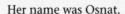

Her name was Osnat.

Hebrew? German? Ethiopian?

Arkasha would have known which half-dead language had spawned such a name. It was exactly the kind of thing Arkasha had always known. And exactly the kind of thing Arkady had never learned for himself because he'd always thought Arkasha, or someone like Arkasha, would be there to tell him.

Osnat guided him through the back passages of the station as sure-footedly as if she'd been born there. When she finally ducked into the shadowy alley of a private dock, the move was so unexpected that Arkady had to backtrack to follow her.

The gate's monitor was either broken or disconnected. Outside the scratched porthole a dimly lit viruflex tether snaked into the void. At its far end, looking as if it had been cut out with scissors and pasted against a black construction paper sky, floated the impact-scarred hulk of an obsolete Bussard-drive-powered water tanker.

Osnat palmed the scanner. Status lights flickered into life as the gate began its purge and disinfect cycle.

"No one said anything about getting on a ship," Arkady protested, though it was far too late to back out or demand answers.

"So your employers don't seem to be keeping you too well informed. What do you want me to do about it?"

Arkady didn't answer, partly because she was right . . . and partly because he was wracking his faded memories of pre-Breakaway history trying to figure out what *employers* were.

The purge and disinfect cycle ended. The airlock irised open and a bitter breeze wafted over them, smelling of space and ice and viruflex. Arkady peered down the long tunnel of the tether, but all he could see were scuffed white walls curving away into darkness.

Osnat put a hard hand to the small of his back and pushed him into the dazzling spray of the gate's antimicrobial cycle. By the time he blinked the stinging liquid from his eyes she was in the tether with him, riding its movements with the ease of an old space dog. It took Arkady a curiously long time to notice the gun in her hand.

"You're a piss poor spy, pretty boy."

"I'm not a—"

"Yeah yeah. Ants. You told me. Well cheer up. You'll get plenty of ants where we're going."

"Where *are* we going?"

"Just suit up. They *did* teach you how to use your NBC gear, didn't they?"

The nuclear-biological-chemical suit was supposed to be just for allergies, according to Korchow. Which had seemed reassuring until Arkady actually stopped to think about it. He pulled the unit out of his pack and tried to activate it. His fingers fumbled on the unfamiliar controls. Osnat shifted from foot to foot impatiently, cursed under her breath, and finally grabbed it from him.

He thought briefly of grappling with her now that her hands were occupied. He imagined himself disarming her and slipping back through the airlock into the relative safety of the station. But one look at Osnat's hard body and strong hands was enough to discourage him.

She slipped the mask over his face and demonstrated the filter's workings with quick gestures of her ragged fingers. "This line connects to an auxiliary air tank if you need one. The tank clamps on here and here. You brought spare filters?"

He checked. "Yes."

"You'll need 'em. You're not engineered to survive where we're going."

"Are you?"

She squinted at him, lips pressed together in a bloodless line. Somehow the question, as ordinary to him as asking about the weather, had offended her.

She shrugged it off. "Guess you could call it that. Few million years of the best engineering no money can buy. What about the shots we told you to get?"

There'd been dozens of shots, starting with a bewildering array of antiallergens and intestinal fauna, and ending with cholera, tuberculosis, polio, yellow fever, and avian influenza. Arkady had spent hours in his bare white room on Gilead Orbital—a prison cell for all intents and purposes, though there was no lock on the door and he would never have thought to call it a prison before Arkasha—trying to guess where he was going from the shots Korchow had given him. But no immigration authority anywhere in UN space required that battery of inoculations; if such a hellhole existed in the vast swathe of the galaxy that still belonged to humans, they were ashamed enough to keep it secret.

"Good," Osnat was saying. "An allergic reaction doesn't mean sniffles and a runny nose down there."

"Down where? Where are we going? Please, Osnat."

"Haven't you figured it out yet?" She sighted down the barrel of her gun at him, and the smile that drifted across her face was as thin as the clouds in a terraformed sky. "We're going to run you through the blockade, golem. You're going to Earth."

Three men waited in the heavy rotational gravity of the freighter's bridge. Two were just muscle. The third, however, was quite the other thing.

Slender, sharp-eyed, professorial in wire-rimmed glasses. The olive skin and the close-cropped black beard could have placed him in any number of ethnic or nationalist enclaves along the MedArc of Earth's orbital ring. But the army surplus shorts, the wrinkled T-shirt, and the thick-soled sandals worn over white athletic socks were so perfectly Israeli—and so exactly what Korchow had told him to expect—that Arkady knew he could only be looking at Moshe Feldman.

Captain Feldman, Korchow had called him. But it had became clear in the course of what Korchow liked to call their "conversations" that the former Captain Feldman of the Israeli Defense Forces, was now Security Consultant Feldman of the very private and very profitable GolaniTech Group.

It had begun. The Israelis had snapped Arkady up like the raiding front of an army ant swarm snapping up a beetle. And once they had determined he was edible, they would pass him along from worker to worker and mandible to mandible, all the way back up the raiding column to the swarm's soft stomach.

First, however, he would have to get past Moshe. And Moshe didn't look like an easy man to get past.

"Well if it isn't the clone who came in from the cold," Moshe said in the deliberate cadence that hours of tape in the KnowlesSyndicate language labs had taught Arkady to recognize as the mark of Israel's Ashkenazi intellectual elite. "Let's see now. Arkady stands for A-18-11-1-4. Which makes you a RostovSyndicate A series, from the eleventh geneline approved by your home Syndicate's steering committee. And tells us that the first run of your geneline was detanked in crèche one in Syndicate Year Four? Have I got that more or less right, Arkady?"

"Perfect."

"No, Arkady." Moshe smiled, showing pink gums and straight white teeth small enough to belong in a child's mouth. "You're the one who's perfect. I'm only human."

Arkady couldn't think of anything to say to that, so he said nothing.

"So," Moshe said, putting the same vast volumes of meaning into the syllable that Osnat had—and making Arkady marvel at how the dry patterns from the training tapes came alive in Israeli mouths. "What do I need to know?"

"What do you need to know about what?" Arkady asked.

Moshe crossed his arms over his chest. He was small, even by human standards; but his legs were hard and sunburned, and with every movement of his hands Arkady saw corded tendons slide under the skin of his forearms. "First, it would be reassuring to know that you are who you say you are." Another flash of the childish teeth. "Or at least that you are *what* you say you are."

A flick of Moshe's fingers brought a lab tech scurrying over with a splicing scope and sample kit. The sampling was ungentle, and it required the removal of the mask and filter—a risk that Osnat muttered darkly about and Moshe shrugged off philosophically.

"He's for real," the tech finally announced in Hebrew.

"How sure are you?" Moshe asked.

The man spread his hands.

"And what would it take to be completely sure?"

"I'd have to run it by Tel Aviv."

"Then do it. I'm not taking any chances this time."

This time?

The tech retrieved his scope and sampling gear and retreated to the streamspace terminal. Then, to Arkady's surprise and dismay, they waited.

It should have taken days of queuing and relaying for the sample to reach Earth's Orbital Ring. And then it should have taken weeks for it to be cleared for import by the ossified bureaucracy tasked with enforcing the Controlled Technology Addendum to the Kyoto Protocols. Instead, Arkady watched with growing unease as the tech fed his samples into the terminal and keyed up a streamspace address that began with the fabled triple *w*.

The implications of those three letters made Arkady catch his breath. Earth was offstream under the Tech Addendum. If Moshe could talk directly to Earth—let alone teleport tissue samples for analysis—then he must have a portable Bose-Einstein terminal and a secure source of entanglement outside the UN's network of entanglement banks and BE relays. Only a handful of private entities in UN space had the financial means to maintain private entanglement banks: the largest multiplanetaries; the UN bureaucracy itself; the richest AIs and transhumans. And of course the constant wild card in UN politics, a type of entity so archaic that its very existence provoked horrified amazement among Syndicate political philosophers: Earth's nation-states.

They're animals, Arkady had protested back on Gilead when he'd first understood he might be dealing with nationalists. *Worse than animals. What can we possibly have in common with them?*

There's an old Arab saying, Korchow had answered from behind that unfathomable KnowlesSyndicate smile: *The enemy of my enemy is my friend. And a thousand idealistic General Assembly resolutions can't change the fact that Earth has her hand on the Orbital Ring's water tap.*

But Moshe didn't look much like the nationalists in Arkady's old sociobiology textbooks. And he certainly didn't look like he planned to turn the water off on anyone unless he was logically convinced that he was going to reap some benefit from their ensuing thirst.

Arkady blinked, feeling an ominous stinging sensation behind his eyes, and realized that his nose was filling. He sniffed surreptitiously and looked around hoping no one had noticed.

"Have a tissue," Moshe said.

Arkady took the thing reluctantly, wondering how he was supposed to use it. Then, to his horror and humiliation, he sneezed.

"Go ahead. Blow your nose."

"May I be excused for a moment?"

"Why? We're savages, remember? No need for your fine Syndicate manners here."

Then he saw it. Moshe had set the trap, and he'd walked into it without a backward glance and ended up just where Moshe wanted him: more worried about sneezing in public than about doing the job Korchow had sent him to do.

He blew his nose—something he hadn't done in public since he was six or so—then stood there holding the used tissue and not knowing what to do with it.

Moshe smiled.

"He's clean," the tech announced from behind his terminal.

Everyone in the room must have been holding their breath, Arkady realized; he heard a collective sigh of relief at the news.

"Right, then." Moshe sounded like a professor leading his lecture group into difficult theoretical territory. "Now that we know you're perfect, why don't you tell us to what we owe the pleasure of your perfect company?"

"I told you," Arkady said, still following the script Korchow had laid down for him. "The Syndicates—"

"Yes, yes, I know the spiel by heart. The Syndicates have developed some kind of mysterious genetic weapon and they're planning to use it against us. But as an ethical evolutionary ecophysicist you can't abide the thought of wiping out Earth's wonderful genetic diversity. So you've defected in order to do your modest little bit toward making the universe safe for humans." He gave Arkady a quizzical look. "You don't *look* stupid. Did you really think we were going to swallow such bunk?"

Korchow's last warning echoed in Arkady's mind: *Absalom is the sharpest blade you have. Far too sharp to unsheathe unless you're quite sure you can put it away again without cutting off your own fingers.*

Was he sure? No. But if he failed through an excess of caution, it would be Arkasha who paid the price. He took a quick, nervous breath. "There's more," he said, "but I'll only tell the rest to Absalom."

"Absalom, indeed." Moshe's voice was soft, almost pleasant. He could have been discussing the weather. "And who told you to dangle his name in front of me?"

"No one."

"I wouldn't exactly call Andrej Korchow no one."

Arkady's eyes snapped to Moshe's face, but all he could see in the glare of the bridge lights were the two flat reflective disks of his glasses.

"Of course it was Korchow who told you to ask for Absalom." Moshe made it sound trivial. Not a lie. Just a practical joke between friends. "He wants us to think Absalom's back in the game again. He wants us to be so busy worrying about whether Absalom is playing us for fools that we forget to worry about whether you're doing the same."

"I don't know what you're talking about."

The first blow knocked Arkady to his knees. As he tried to stand, Moshe hooked his feet out from under him and delivered a flurry of surgically precise kicks to his stomach and kidneys.

Osnat laughed. But it sounded like a laugh of shock and surprise, not amusement. Arkady even thought he sensed a recoiling in her, a flush of pity under the soldier's hard loyalty. Or did he just want to sense that?

"Get up," Moshe said in the bored tones of a man for whom violence was a job like any other.

Arkady tried to stand. He only managed to kneel, head spinning, hands splayed on the cold deck.

Moshe crouched beside Arkady, his face bent so close that his breath caressed the skin of Arkady's cheek. "I can't let you lie to me, Arkady. You can see that, can't you?"

A waiting silence settled over the bridge. Arkady realized that Moshe expected an answer to this apparently rhetorical question.

"Yes," he gasped. Just the effort of speaking made him feel like he was going to throw up.

"How many Arkadys do they detank a year?" Moshe asked. "Fifty? Five hundred? Five thousand?"

The real number was probably on the high end of Moshe's guess. But Arkady had never asked about the actual numbers. He'd never even thought of asking. And for the first time in his life he wondered why. "I don't know," he answered at last. "A lot, I guess."

"A lot, you guess." A cold edge crept into Moshe's voice. "You're a piece of equipment, Arkady, as mass-produced as sewer-pipe sections. And if we can't get what we need from you, we'll throw you away and order a replacement part. Just like your Syndicate's already done. Or do you want to tell me I've got that wrong and you weren't condemned meat from the second they shipped you out here?"

Osnat stirred restlessly. "Oh, for fuck's sake, Moshe. Give him a break. Can't you see he doesn't know anything?"

"He told you that, did he? And you believed him? Or did you just take a look into those big puppy-dog eyes and decide to trust him?"

Osnat flushed to the roots of her hair. Arkady felt the rest of the room freeze. What had Moshe done to make them so frightened of him? But perhaps a man like Moshe didn't need to *do* anything to frighten people.

Moshe dropped back into Hebrew, speaking with quiet but unmistakable anger. Arkady struggled to understand, but the unfamiliar words spilled past too quickly. That it was a dressing-down was clear, though; Osnat absorbed the rebuke with the immovable stoicism of a soldier on parade ground.

Was she a soldier? Had he already been drawn so deep into the tangled web of Israeli Intelligence that he was dealing with government agents and not hired corporate muscle? If so, then which stray thread of the web had quivered in response to Arkady's carefully choreographed offer of defection? And how much did the success of his mission—and with it Arkasha's freedom—depend on his guessing correctly?

What if they're Mossad?

The question spooled across his mind accompanied by old spinfeed of bombings and assassinations. He pushed the images aside. All Mossad agents couldn't be vicious killers, he told himself, any more than their opposite Palestinian numbers could be the peace-loving posthuman sympathizers that Syndicate propagandists insisted they were. And as long as he kept Korchow happy, it didn't much matter what the truth was.

Moshe turned back to Arkady, his voice cold and academic again. "Listen, Arkady. I have no personal grudge against you. I'm not some little boy pulling the wings off flies during recess. But the road to Absalom goes through me. And if you cross me, if you lie to me, if you so much as quiver in a direction that makes me nervous, I'll kill you. The police won't blink. My superiors won't even give me a slap on the wrist. It'll be like killing a dog as far as they're concerned. Less than killing a dog; with a dog there's always some schlemiel ready to call the animal protection society. And trust me, Arkady, there *is* no golem protection society."

They stared at each other, Arkady sweating and panting, Moshe as calm as he'd been before the surreal outbreak of violence. "Do you remember my last question?" Moshe asked.

"Whether Korchow told me to ask for Absalom."

"Good."

"But I—"

"Don't answer now. You're leaving in the morning. I won't see you until we're both on the other side of the blockade. And meanwhile I'd like you to spend the trip thinking about the difference between what Korchow can do for you once you're on Earth and what I can do for you."

The freighter had been built in what Arkady thought of as the White Period of UN jumpship design.

For ten or twelve years, in one of those inexplicable emergent phenomena of fashion, white viruflex had come into style simultaneously on all the far-flung UN colonies that habitually sold their obsolete driveships to the Syndicate buyers. Everything that could be made of viruflex was made of viruflex, and every piece of viruflex that could be white was white. White deckplating. White walls. White ventilation grills, white water and power and spinstream conduits. And, hovering in the fading shadows above them, white ceilings with glimmering white recessed-lighting panels.

As Osnat led him through the ship, Arkady remembered with a twinge that he had used just this rather silly example of emergence to explain how ant swarms worked in his first real conversation with Arkasha. Arkasha hadn't cared for the metaphor. And now, in the face of all this merciless whiteness, Arkady saw why.

The whole ship looked like a euth ward.

It looked like an empty euth ward whose patients had all shut themselves into their rooms and taken their terminal doses. He imagined cold white cells behind all the cold white doors, and cold white beds containing cold white bodies whose limbs and faces betrayed terrible deformities. Or, worse, bodies whose physical perfection hinted at even more horrifying deviations of mind and spirit.

Osnat stopped, tugging at his arm like an adult shepherding a crècheling through a pressure door, and led him into a room that was mercifully empty and ordinary. A battered viruflex chair stood beside a bed made up with square military corners. The blanket on the bed was wool, something Arkady had never seen outside of history spins. He could smell it all the way across the room: a faint animal smell, at once dry and oily.

"Bathroom." Osnat pointed. "Washing water. Drinking water. Mix 'em up and you'll be sorry. Recyclables disposal. Biohazards disposal. And biohazards include anything that touches your body until you clear your Syndicate-side flora. You need anything else, press the call button by the door. But only if you really need it. Moshe's not a patient man." Her eyes flicked to the corner of the tiny space and she frowned. "Sorry about the ants, by the way. I'll bring some roach spray if I can find any."

Arkady followed her glance and saw a gleaming rivulet of amber carapaces that he'd at first mistaken for a crack in the laminated viruflex flooring. "Pharaoh ants," he said, intrigued by the unexpected discovery. "Is the ship infested?"

"If only it were just the ship. They're taking over the fucking universe."

"They've always owned it." He corrected her without a second thought now that he was back on familiar territory. "Vertebrate biomass was negligible compared to ants, even before Earth's ecological collapse. And as far as any biogeophysical cycles are concerned—"

He stopped, sensing Osnat's stare.

"This isn't one of those Syndicate suicide missions, is it?" she asked abruptly. "A . . . what do they call it . . . a gifting of biological property?"

"Right. I mean . . . yes, that's the word. But no, I don't think it is one."

"You don't *think* so? You mean they can order you to die without even telling you ahead of time?"

Who was this *they* she was talking about? And could humans still "order" each other to die the way they ordered meals at restaurants? But surely that was impossible, even on Earth. He must have misheard her.

"What about Novalis?" she pursued. "Was Novalis a suicide mission?"

He froze, forcing himself to wait a beat before looking into her eyes. This was the first time anyone had said the planet's name. And hearing the familiar word on Osnat's lips reminded him abruptly that she worked for Moshe.

"Fine," Osnat said after a silence long enough to make his skin itch. "I was just asking."

"How is Moshe going to get me through the UN's Tech Embargo?" Arkady asked.

"I don't know. The Americans are handling that part. We didn't want to bring them into it, but no one else on Earth is still crazy enough to go head-to-head against UNSec."

America! The mere name was enough to make Arkady catch his breath. The land where Audubon had seen the last legendary flights of the passenger pigeons. The land where de Tocqueville had walked through virgin forests so dense that uprooted oak trees hung in the surrounding branches and crumbled to dust without ever touching the earth. The land that had spawned the great twentieth-century myrmecologists, from Wheeler and Wilson to Schnierla and Pratt and Gordon. The country whose scientists had taken the first halting steps toward modern terraforming theory . . . even as the engines of their industry were shredding the fragile web that made man's continued life on Earth possible.

"Don't worry," Osnat reassured him, misinterpreting his dazed expression. "We're not actually *going* there. I can't promise we won't accidentally get you ripped limb from limb by a mob of religious fanatics, but it's not Plan A."

"Religious fanatics? In America?"

Osnat gave him a quizzical look. "How much do you actually know about Earth, Arkady?"

"Um . . . I know a lot about the ants."

"Great. Well, just don't talk to anyone. And by anyone, I mean particularly Americans and Interfaiths. Which should be easy since they're usually the same people. And while I'm handing out free advice, you want to back off a bit with this Absalom business. Keep tossing that name around and you might just piss Moshe off so badly he decides no amount of intelligence value is worth the aggravation."

"Why?"

Her good eye fixed him with an incredulous stare.

"You don't even know who Absalom is," she said finally. "It's just a name to you. Korchow didn't give you a clue what you were walking into. Un*fucking*believable."

He didn't answer, and after staring at him for another acutely uncomfortable moment she muttered, "Like a goddamn lamb to the slaughter," and stalked out of the room.

The first thing Arkady did when Osnat left was walk across the room to examine the wool blanket. It was warm to the touch, as if it still remembered the heat of the animal it had come from. He ran his hand over the rough surface, feeling the hairs—or were they called furs?—prick the skin of his palm.

He went to the sink and poured himself a cup of water. It tasted stale, as if the tanker was limping to the end of a long slow time run and her tanks were overdue for scrubbing. It also had a salt-and-copper tang that turned out to be the taste of his own blood.

He washed his face and prodded at his teeth until he was sure nothing had been knocked loose. He wasn't surprised. Moshe had worked him over so expertly that even in the midst of the pain Arkady had had a perversely comforting feeling of safety; if he just submitted and lay still, some instinct had whispered, no real harm would come to him.

Maybe that had been the real purpose of the beating. If so, Moshe had pounded the point home pretty effectively.

Arkady leaned over the sink and inspected the face staring back at him from the mirror. He hadn't shaved since he'd reached UN space, and the black shadow of a beard pooled in the angles and hollows of a face sucked thin by gravity. It made him look hungry and breakable . . . and disconcertingly like Arkasha.

He covered his broken nose and warped cheekbone with the palm of one hand and looked at the pieces of his face that were still recognizable after Korchow's hammer job. There were the dark eyes, so like Arkasha's eyes; the fine-featured Slavic face, so like Arkasha's face; the pale skin, so like Arkasha's skin.

And the soft doubtful uncertain mouth that had never been anything like Arkasha's mouth, even before Novalis.

He curled his upper lip in the mocking half smile that had always been Arkasha's first line of defense, and tried to summon the illusion that kept him going. The trick to making it work was not to ask for too much. He couldn't imagine Arkasha in his arms. That was far too obviously impossible. But he could call up his hoarded memories of his pairmate: all the moments and movements that he'd never quite paid enough attention to as they slipped by. The intent curve of Arkasha's back as he bent over his splicing scope. The fine-boned hands, nervous in idleness but precise and graceful when they turned the pages of a book, or mounted samples, or handled a splicing scope. The mercurial combination of strength and fragility that had called forth a devotion Arkady had never thought himself capable of feeling. Sometimes he could convince himself that the face looking back at him in the mirror was real and that Arkasha was safe. Far away—perhaps too far away for Arkady to ever hope to see him again—but alive and well and, most important, happy. That wasn't too much to imagine. And it made sleep possible. It made everything possible.

Arkady sighed and dropped his hand. He crossed the room to the narrow bed, slipped under the unnerving blanket, and whispered the lights off.

Nothing happened.

He got up and circled the room looking for a manual switch, but there was none. He reached for the door, acting on reflex, intending to open it and find the switch in the corridor outside.

It wouldn't open.

He rattled it, yanked at it, slammed his shoulder against it, feeling a thrumming panic start to build in his gut.

And then he understood.

They'd done something no one had ever done to him in his life. Something there wasn't even a word for in Syndicate-standard English. Something he'd never heard of anyone doing except in the most ancient and appalling tales of human cruelty. They had locked him in.

He backed away from the door. His fingers stung from wringing at the unyielding metal latch. He was panting like an animal, and he made a conscious effort to slow his breath. Had Osnat done this? Did human beings do such things to each other and not just to constructs? And if so, then why hadn't Korchow warned him?

Arkasha would have known, he caught himself thinking for the thousandth time. Arkasha with his insatiable fascination with humans. Arkasha with his history books and his political philosophy and his ancient literature. Arkasha could probably even have come up with some explanation crazy enough to make sense of such a crime.

So why am I here instead of you, Arkasha? And what has Korchow done to you?

He wrapped the blanket around his shoulders and paced back and forth trying to tire himself out, but the mere thought of the locked door made his guts churn. He tried the latch again, working at it systematically, hoping he'd just failed to understand the proper way to open it. But no. It was locked after all.

Finally, out of options, he did what he should have done in the first place and sat down on the floor to watch the ants.

There were perhaps three hundred of them. They emerged from the narrow crack between wall and deckplating, wound across the floor in the classic branching and puddling fractals of a colonizing swarm, and disappeared into a facing crevice just as lightless and impenetrable as the first. They were a river, a living stream of thoraxes that glittered like spilled oil under the sickly gleam of the shipboard lighting. They shouldn't have been here. They were pests. No one had ever meant to bring them into space. And yet here they were, welling from the ship's intestines like blood from an open wound: poor ravaged Earth wreaking her revenge through these, her smallest foot soldiers.

Arkady dipped a finger into the flood and let the tiny minor workers swarm onto his hand so he could get a closer look at them. He felt a mild sting as one of them took an experimental bite out of him. He blew the ants off his hand—brushing them off might have crushed delicate legs and antennae, and he'd never been able to bear hurting ants avoidably. He rubbed at the bite pensively and forced his mind back to the same question that had obsessed him since that first meeting with Andrej Korchow.

Why Arkady? What made him different from all the thousands of other Arkadys on the half dozen Syndicate orbital stations and surface settlements? Why had Korchow extended his miraculous offer of clemency to Arkady and Arkasha? Arkady had spent his whole life studying ecosystems and biospheres: mapping the complex web of interlocking energy cycles that drove the metabolism of a living planet. It was only natural for him to apply these skills to his current situation. But all his attempts to construct a coherent picture of Novalis and its aftermath had failed miserably. Whatever confidence he'd had in his ability to grasp the underlying structures of his own life, it had vanished into Novalis's impenetrable jungle.

He shuffled back to the sink, poured a fresh glass of water, and entertained himself by sprinkling it in the swarm's path. A few solitary foragers responded, dipping into the spilled water and marching back to their companions with miniscule droplets glittering between their raised pincers like diamonds set in amber. But the main body of the swarm flowed on, too firmly in the grip of the swarm-colonize pheromone to turn aside even for life's ultimate necessity.

Arkady kept up the attempt for a while, wishing he had his collecting gear. He searched for the telltale elongated thorax of an ambulatory queen, trying to recall whether colonizing Pharaoh ants took their supernumerary queens with them or sequestered and assassinated them.

Then he just sat, numb with exhaustion, and watched the ants hurtle from one darkness to another in search of a moveable idea called home.

ARKADY WOKE WITH A START, knowing, though he couldn't have said why, that he wasn't alone.

He rolled over and saw Moshe sitting in the chair beside his bed, bathed in the secondhand starlight refracted off the tanker's solar collectors.

"We need to talk," Moshe said.

Arkady sat up, pulling the rough blanket around his nakedness. "What time is it?"

"Early. Or late, depending on how you want to look at it. But then I guess people who grow up in space don't get station lag. You want to get dressed, go ahead."

He got up and put his clothes on. Moshe's eyes tracked him across the room.

"Can I use the toilet?"

"No one's stopping you."

He went into the bathroom, shut the door behind him, blew his nose, and went back out again.

Moshe was still in the chair, but now the lights were on. "Have a seat," he said, gesturing Arkady back to the bed.

The bed that had seemed so hard when he was trying to fall asleep now felt too soft. He couldn't sit up straight in it. And there was something ignominious about slumping in the ruins of his crumpled sheets while Moshe sat on his chair as neat and straight as a toy soldier.

"It seems my superiors have gotten cold feet, Arkady. They've decided to make me decide whether we should run you through the Embargo or just dump you back into the pond to be snapped up by the next fish that happens by. In other words they've figured out how to put my ass on the line for decisions they're getting paid to make. Do they promote self-serving incompetents in the Syndicates too? Or have you people evolved beyond that sort of thing?"

"Uh . . . not quite yet."

"Well, I guess that should make me feel better." He cocked his head as if he were taking the measure of his feelings. "It doesn't. By the way, Arkady, we're on spin. Is that a problem for you?"

"Would it make any difference if I said it was?"

"No. But I thought I'd ask. My mother raised me to be polite. You *do* know what a mother is, don't you?"

"I've seen dogs have puppies," Arkady said doubtfully.

Moshe gave him a hard unfriendly look. "Novalis," he said after a moment. "Start from the beginning. Tell me everything. Tell me about the survey mission. Tell me about this genius, Arkasha, and his brilliant discovery. That's what you're selling, isn't it? Some genetic weapon this Arkasha person discovered?"

"Not a weapon. An antidote."

Moshe snorted. "If you think there's a difference between the two, then you've grossly misunderstood the last five hundred years of human history."

Arkady blinked and cleared his throat. This line of conversation felt dangerous; technical knowledge was one thing, but Moshe could read him far too well when they strayed into broad-brush ideological debates. "Arkasha didn't discover it. I told you. The UN spliced it and tried to use it against us in violation of the Treaty provisions. Arkasha just isolated a sample. I'm willing to trade it to you."

"In exchange for what? And don't give me some candyass speech about genetic diversity."

"For Arkasha's safety."

"Keep talking." Moshe's face remained impassive. "I'm listening."

Arkady collected himself and tried to pull the story together in his mind the way Korchow had told him to tell it. But it was like giving a shape to water. And Korchow wasn't the one who was going to have to face Moshe's fists and feet if he was caught out in a lie.

"Novalis wasn't just a survey mission," he began tentatively. "It was more of a survey and a terraforming mission all in one. Novalis was selected based on unmanned probe telemetry. We're looking for the same thing everyone's looking for: abandoned Evacuation-era terraforming starts. Bare branch colonies are the best, of course, but synthetic biospheres are tricky. If something killed off the original colonists, there's always the chance it could still be around to kill you."

"What do you mean, killed off?" Moshe interrupted. "Like . . . predators?"

"Uh . . . no." Was that a joke? "More like mold. Anyway . . . what we do isn't really all that different from what UN terraformers do. We just do it with a smaller team."

And a smaller safety margin. But there was no reason to tell Moshe about that. God knew what he'd make of it. Probably file a report about how the Syndicates were so desperate they were throwing terraformers away like soldier ants.

"But you guys are a hell of a lot better at terraforming than humans are," Moshe prompted.

"Well, half the planets on the Periphery were terraformed by corporate-owned constructs. And some of them came over in the Breakaway. We have a lot of expertise. And we don't have the evolutionary baggage humans have. We don't try to treat synthetic biospheres as if they were Earth before the ecological collapse. We've shaped our entire social organism to respond to the ecophysical realities of postterrestrial . . ."

Moshe shifted restlessly. "Okay. Let's start with the team members. How many of you were there?"

"Ten."

"Home Syndicates?"

"Two from Aziz. Two B's from Motai. Then the two Banerjees and us four from Rostov."

"Why four team members from Rostov? Was Rostov commanding the mission?"

"I'm not sure what . . ."

"I mean did Rostov have some kind of final say on mission-critical decisions?"

"No." Arkady grimaced. "The Aziz A's did." That had been the first fatal error the joint steering committee had inflicted on them.

"And what's the communications lag between Novalis and the nearest Bose-Einstein relay?"

Arkady looked at Moshe, thought about lying, and decided it wasn't worth it. "Six hundred and twelve days if you hit the short trajectory launch window."

"Which would mean the closest BE-relay has to be . . . let's see, somewhere offshore of Kurzet's star? Don't worry," Moshe said in reply to Arkady's stricken look. "I'm sure UNSec would care, but we don't tell them everything. Actually, we don't tell them shit unless they really lean on us. Still, I would have thought the Syndicates were seeding thicker out there."

"Bose-Einstein relays cost money. And the kind of people who are willing to sell to the Syndicates want cash."

"Thought you clones were making money hand over fist since peace broke out."

"Not BE-relay kind of money."

Moshe acknowledged this truth with a rueful nod that made Arkady realize tech poverty must be a daily fact of life on Earth, just as it was in the Syndicates. "So you guys were real old-time explorers, huh? Alone in the Deep with no one on the other end of the comm but a two-year-gone ghost. What was supposed to happen if you ran into real-time trouble?"

"We had a tactical unit on ice we could wake up. If we had to."

"And you were going to keep them under for three years plus travel time? Haven't you people ever heard of fair labor practices?"

Arkady guessed this must be a joke, so he smiled.

"Seriously, though. Why didn't you thaw them out as soon as things started to go sour?"

Arkady repressed a shudder. "You've never met tacticals."

"Weren't the Ahmeds tacticals?"

"The Ahmeds are A's. Military, yes. But not tacticals." Not by a long shot. And the fact that Moshe could confuse the two things suddenly seemed like a measure of the profound hopelessness of ever coming to an understanding with humans.

Moshe must have sensed Arkady's dismay, because he backed off suddenly. When he spoke again his voice was casual, almost companionable.

"Do you mind if I ask a personal question? It's silly, really. But let's just say I'm curious."

"Okay," Arkady said cautiously, the memory of the last time he'd failed to answer one of Moshe's little questions still throbbing in his gut.

"Why is Korchow so ugly? By Syndicate standards, I mean. By human standards he's perfectly decent-looking."

"Dishy," Osnat drawled.

Arkady practically jumped out of his skin. When had she come in? And how in God's name had she done it without his seeing her?

She looked like she'd just woken up. She'd swapped her civilian clothes for a faded but carefully ironed T-shirt, desert drab fatigues, and brown leather paratrooper's boots. The boots were run-down at the heel, but they had that glassy sheen that can only be achieved by years of spit and parade wax. And the short sleeves of her T-shirt rode up over her biceps to reveal a tattoo on one arm that Arkady hadn't seen before: a flying tiger, its bared fangs and unsheathed claws neatly framed by long-pinioned eagle's wings.

"The Knowles A's are meant to look human," Arkady explained, speaking to both of them. "It makes their work easier."

"But it must make life difficult for them back home."

"No. They . . . they look the way they're meant to look. A Knowles construct who looked any other way would be norm-deviant."

Moshe laughed. "And what about you, Arkady? How do you norm out? You're quite the pretty boy. Osnat's been making calf eyes at you ever since she marched you through the airlock. Was Arkasha a pretty boy too? Or was he a deviant?"

"Arkasha's *not* a deviant!"

"Then how come Korchow threw him in a euth ward? Because he tried to defect, like you? Let's face it, Arkady, the only Syndicate constructs who defect to UN space are spies, perverts, and deviants. Which one was Arkasha? And which are you?"

But Arkady couldn't answer. Moshe's first sentence had raked through his mind and left it too raw and tattered to comprehend the rest.

"Who told you . . . how do you know that Arkasha's in a renorming center?"

"Come on, Arkady. You know I can't tell you that."

"Then at least tell me how old the information is. You can tell me that, can't you?"

"Our last news from your side of the Line is about a month old."

"Then we have to hurry," Arkady said urgently. "You have to make up your minds fast."

"Why? It's not like Arkasha has a date with the hangman. All he has to do is act normal and he's out. And even if he can't do that . . . well, what about that famous poet, what's his name? People can sit on the euth wards for years."

"Arkasha won't."

"Why not?"

"Because he told me if he was ever sent for renorming again he'd kill himself."

Moshe made a sceptical face. "Very convenient. I start to balk and you pull a potential suicide out of your hat to make sure I gulp down the bait without taking the time to look at it too closely. Nicely done . . . for an amateur."

"I'm not making it up! And I wasn't ordered here either, if that's what you're suggesting."

"Don't play word games with me, Arkady. You people don't have to be ordered to throw away your lives. That's why you're the next step on the evolutionary ladder, isn't that right? That's why you're going to wipe us out and usher in a brave new world without humans."

"We don't want to wipe you out," Arkady whispered. "We just want to be left alone."

Moshe stood up, circled the room, went to the porthole, and stared out at the sharp silver night. "Did you fight in the war, Arkady?"

No need to say which war. The struggle between the UN and the Syndicates had subsided to a lethal simmer, but it was still the axis along which every other conflict lined up. Even on lonely backward Earth.

"I was too young."

"Too young to remember it, or just too young to fight in it?"

Visions of burnt-out crèches. Visions of the once-vibrant rings of ZhangSyndicate gutted to hard vac. Visions of shooting stars that were dying ships and pilots . . . but, hush, don't tell the crèchelings. "Just too young to fight," he said at last.

Arkady had been six when the shooting started. The official fighting between the UN and Syndicate armies had been bloody beyond the imagination of a spacefaring age, but the riots had been worse. Posthuman populations all along the Periphery had revolted, whether because they supported the Breakaway or merely because it thinned out the omnipresent UN Peacekeepers enough for them to make a bid for their own independence. The UN had met violence with violence, and Peacekeepers had fired on demonstrating crowds in eight of the fifteen trusteeships. The shootings touched off riots throughout the Periphery, forcing the UN to fight a war on two fronts . . . a war that many people had come to see not as a political conflict but as a struggle to the death between two species battling for possession of the same ecological niche.

Arkady eyed Moshe, taking in the clever resolute face, the thin yet strong body. "Did *you* fight in the War for Independence?"

"If you're going to talk about it to humans, you might want to consider calling it something else. But no, I didn't. Earthers aren't required to make troop contributions for off-world Peacekeeping missions." Moshe sat down again and leaned forward to stare at Arkady. "But I saw the war on the evening spins. You fought like ants. You died and died and died until the Peacekeepers had nervous breakdowns from having to shoot so many of you. What do your officers threaten you with to make you fight like that?"

"We have no officers."

"Then what are you afraid of? People only fight like that when they're faced with something that scares them worse than dying."

Later Arkady would see this moment as a turning point. Before it, he had managed, just barely, to keep Moshe guessing. After it, Moshe and Osnat both knew in their guts what he really was . . . even if it took their brains a while to catch up with the knowledge.

"Some things are stronger than fear," he whispered.

"Name one."

He hesitated, acutely aware of Osnat's gaze boring into his back. There were plenty of safe words he could have chosen. Duty. Honor. Gene loyalty. Genetic gifting. If he'd latched on to any of those abstract concepts he could have kept up the lie. He could have remained the empty vessel that Korchow wanted him to be: a vessel into which Moshe could pour his own beliefs and desires without ever touching on the real truth of what had happened on Novalis.

Instead, Arkady uttered what seemed to be the only word left inside his rattlingly empty skull:

"Love."

NOVALIS

The Spirit of the Hive

Sex is an antisocial force in evolution. Bonds are formed between individuals in spite of sex and not because of it. Perfect societies, if we can be so bold as to define them as societies that lack conflict and possess the highest degree of altruism and coordination, are most likely to evolve where all of the members are genetically identical.

—E. O. WILSON (1973)

ARKADY WOKE TO THE SMELL of curry.

No solid food for twelve hours before the coffin: that was the rule for all cold shipping on the Syndicate's creaking fleet of Bussard-drive-powered interstellar ships. It was rumored that this precaution had been rendered obsolete by the newest generation of UN-built jumpships. But that kind of wishful rumor, fueled by privation, envy, and cryophobia, was always winging its way through the vacuum between the various Syndicate orbital stations. And given the fact that Arkady felt as if he'd fasted through every day of the long months of slow drift from Gilead to Novalis, the extra twelve hours hardly seemed significant.

He sat up, rubbing at skin raw with freezer burn and fighting his way out of the bruised haze of jump hangover. There was a thrumming, flickering whisper in the air, below and beyond the normal shipboard noises, as if quick fingers were tap tap tapping along the ship's hull out there in the starless dark.

A dust field? Please let it only be a dust field.

They were running ahead of the charts now, flying half-blind on spectrometry that was years out of date before it ever reached them, with only the skill of their superbly spliced and trained pilots standing between them and hull breach. In its wake the ship shed a maelstrom of astronomical and navigational data that would guide later ships on the same journey. But up ahead there was only the razor-thin spin-stream from the unmanned probes. And though space was empty, it wasn't so empty that you could jump off the edge of the map and be sure you weren't going to hit something.

Arkady's clothes lay in the hold-all beside his coffin, neatly folded in an airtight insectproof flatpack: orbsilk shirt and trousers that hung loose on his dehydrated body and still smelled faintly of the sweet clean air of KnowlesSyndicate; soft stationside shoes whose soles and uppers blended into each other with a seamlessness that went a long way toward explaining why hand-thrown orbsilk had become the Syndicate's number one cash crop since the Trade Compact with the UN worlds; the little rucksack, neither indecently large nor puritanically small, that contained all the moveable property he held separately from RostovSyndicate's communal stores.

Someone had left a sweater beside the rucksack: a thick rollneck with the soft hand and deep rippling color that only the most carefully spliced and cosseted worms could produce. It was a "think of me" if Arkady had ever seen one: the kind of beautiful luxury object that might be passed to a crèchemate setting off for a distant assignment with the ritual words: "think of me when you use it." And it was just the thing for a body still in the shivering grip of cold sleep.

He stood up and felt the sharp tug of the ship's .4 gs on muscles raised in microgravity. The retrofitted lab and ark modules of the ship would be in the old zero-g cargo bays—places that the human designers had never meant to be shirtsleeve working environments but that were the closest thing to home the retrofitted UN ship could provide for its new passengers. In contrast, the cryobay, bridge, and crew quarters had all been designed to provide humans with the rotational gravity their skeletons and immune systems required. The Syndicate crew, who needed fake gravity not at all, would just have to live with the sore muscles and broken equipment.

Arkady had to squeeze past the tacticals' still-active coffins to reach the corridor. He slid past with a shudder, trying not to look too closely at what slumbered beneath the backlit viruflex. He hadn't seen a tactical since the UN invasion . . . and he hoped never to see another.

The corridor hugged the outer hull of the ship, and sure enough the rustling whisper was louder there. He peered through the nearest viewport. White hull plunging away into blackness. And out on the edge of darkness something so strange that it took him several stunned moments to identify it.

They were flying through a forest.

Leaves pattered on the hull like raindrops. Twigs and branches rasped down its length like fingernails scrabbling for purchase. A mulberry leaf tumbled past, and the shipboard running lights flashed on the bright tracery of veins that had exploded into ice crystals when they hit hard vac. The leaf was followed by an orbsilk cocoon, its priceless golden worm dead inside it. Then a woman's hairbrush, turning lazily end over end, its momentum so close to the ship's own that it seemed to slide sternward at little more than strolling speed.

This was the ship they'd been sent to overtake, hurtling along their same trajectory, its hull open to the void, its silk gardens shredded by decompression, its little ark of living treasures cast upon the deep. Arkady tore his eyes away from the viewport. He had known, they had all known, that another ship had tried to reach Novalis before them and failed. But it was one thing to know it. It was another thing to hear the lost lives picking at the hull like hungry ghosts.

There are so very few of us, he whispered to the gods of the void, if there were any. *I can stand dying. But not for nothing. Let Novalis be the home we need so badly. Who knows how many more chances we'll have?*

Arkady had spent only four hours on the ship before going into cryo, so the smell of the curry led him more surely than his vague memories of the hab module's configuration. The ship seemed smaller and harder-used than he remembered it. A trick of perception; in point of fact, it had barely been used at all during the two years they'd spent in cold sleep. And it was just the right size for the ten members of the survey team, most of whom were already in the dayroom, nursing their cryo hangovers and watching Novalis slowly stealing real estate from the black void on the wall monitor.

They'd put the dayroom in one of the old UN-designed zero-g lab modules on the theory that if you were going to relax, you might as well be comfortable. But it still had the oddly cramped look that so many UN-built ships did; as if the humans who designed them had never quite grasped that there were no ceilings in free fall. And the survey team were all sitting at the table on the "floor" side of the room rather than lounging comfortably around its various corners the way they would naturally have done in a Syndicate-designed room.

Arkady scanned the faces around the table, but he didn't see the one familiar face he most wanted to see. His pairmate *had* arrived, hadn't he? Surely they wouldn't have launched without the mission's head geneticist?

"Hair of the dog?" someone asked, proffering a squeezeball of beer.

The entire ten-person survey team had agreed, in a deal brokered by the two Banerjees, to use half their personal weight allowances for brewing supplies. Arkady had taken the agreement as a good omen for the people who would be his only companions for the duration of the mission.

He took a sip and blinked in surprise. "Hey, that's actually *good*!"

One of the Banerjee A's grinned. "Pride of the Banerjees," he said in the noble but slightly pompous tones that crèchelines learned young to associate with the Heroes of the Breakaway.

"Plates, food, forks," one of the Ahmeds said, pointing.

Arkady crossed the room, aware of half a dozen pairs of eyes weighing and measuring him. He bent over the simmering pot. "Fantastic," he said in his best fitting-in voice. "Three cheers for AzizSyndicate."

"Actually, we didn't cook it," the other Ahmed admitted. "You can thank your sib for the feast."

"That would make him the first Arkady I've ever met that could cook worth a damn." Arkady looked at the curry with renewed suspicion, tasted it, and had to admit it was good. "And where *is* this marvel of culinary talent?"

He turned around just in time to see the two Ahmeds exchange a cryptic glance.

"Working?" one of them hazarded. And already there was that little something in his voice that should have been a warning.

Someone ruffled Arkady's hair, and he turned around to the welcome sight of another Rostov face. "Aurelia, right?"

"Right."

"And where were you when I woke up?"

"Hey, don't look at me. I'm the rock doctor, not the people doctor."

"I see." Arkady took a closer look at her; as the team's single geophysicist she might well be working closely with him, depending on what they found on Novalis. "I'll make sure to bring you any sick rocks I stumble over."

"I'm the people doctor," said the other Aurelia from down at the far end of the table. "You met me an hour ago. You just don't remember it.

I've been sitting up with you since they popped your top, but I thought I'd let you do your last little bit of waking up in private."

Functioning within Syndicate society required a good dose of what Keats had once famously called negative capability: the ability to hold two conflicting ideas in your head at the same time. On the one hand you had to learn to recognize individual constructs for the purposes of work and social interaction; the human brain, however profoundly reengineered, couldn't be entirely freed from the individual consciousness that had powered the first four hundred millennia of its evolution. On the other hand, the structures and customs of Syndicate society were all geared toward eliminating distinctions between individuals in the same geneline. A Syndicate was a family, with the same consanguinity between its various genelines that welded together human families. But your sibs, the fellow members of your own geneline, were more than family. They were *you*. And the individual body you inhabited—the lone physical organism inside its prison of skin and skull—was no more a whole person than an ant was a whole swarm. Geneline names reflected this. Each individual construct had a dossier, compiled over the course of his or her life by docents, professors, crèchemates, steering committee representatives; but the dossier filing number was as unreal as paperwork. On a day-to-day basis, from the moment he or she was detanked, every one of the thousands of Arkadys was simply Arkady, every Bella, Bella; every Ahmed, Ahmed; every Aurelia, Aurelia.

If you wanted to single out one of your sibs in normal conversation, you were reduced to ad hoc nicknames or to complicated formulations like "the year seven who led the mission to Karal-20," or "the year five who spent last year planetside working on the arctic core survey," or "the one who told that awful joke about the dog," or "the one who wrote the paper on cryogenesis in amphibians."

Or, in the grammatical construction that had fueled more grief, joy, strife, and passion than any other in all of Syndicate history: "the one I love."

Arkady instinctively thought of his new crewmates as geneline members first and individuals second. First—the phrase *pari inter pares* came somewhat sarcastically to mind—came the two AzizSyndicate Ahmeds. Their Syndicate name reflected its founder's North Indian heritage, as did their tall soldierly frames and square-jawed faces. Arkady had met both Ahmeds briefly before launch, and had privately dubbed them

"Laid-back Ahmed" and "By-the-Book Ahmed." Laid-back Ahmed was a full centimeter taller than Aziz-8135 gene-norm, and had adopted a habitual slouch to disguise the deviation. Something about the combination of the slouch and his levelheaded self-deprecating manner promised to Arkady that he might be that rare treasure: a pilot who was tough enough to command a ship in the Deep, but modest enough to back off after planetfall and let the scientists do their jobs. By-the-Book Ahmed, on the other hand, was a cold fish and a bit of a martinet . . . the last kind of personality Arkady would have assigned to command a crew full of science track Rostovs and Banerjees.

But perhaps he was just stereotyping. One of the Ahmeds' older cogenetics was a wildly popular spin star. His sex- and violence-laden adventures were one of the great guilty pleasures in a society that had been increasingly cold and austere and rationed since the UN invasion. No one could look at any Ahmed's muscular frame and commanding features without thinking of their famous sib, and the manly virtues that AzizSyndicate embodied in the Syndicate collective consciousness. Or that it was supposed to embody, anyway. Arkady certainly hoped that this particular pair of A-8s would bring the strengths of their phenotype to the mission at hand, rather than its failings. Because if either of them acted with the kind of impetuous arrogance their spin star sib displayed on-screen, then the whole survey team was headed for heavy weather.

After the two Ahmeds came the two Bellas, also both present. And how typical of MotaiSyndicate to send two B series constructs. Had that really been a purely technical decision—the need to put together a workpair with the right mix of skills for the mission—or was it a subtle transhuman dig at the older Syndicates' resistance to caste-based series design?

Other than the fact that they were B's, the most remarkable thing about the two Bellas was their eerily perfect resemblance to each other. Normal constructs differed from their sibs almost as much as natural twins did. They might look identical to human eyes, but they could always tell each other apart by little variations in features, height, coloring— even cowlicks, as Arkady had reason to know. But the MotaiSyndicate B's weren't twins; they were living, breathing mirrors. And the massive in vitro and postpartum culling that MotaiSyndicate used to achieve such perfection was almost as controversial among the older Syndicates as their caste-based genelines.

It was all ideologically impeccable, of course: a ruthlessly elegant expression of the highest and purest principles of sociobiology. But it still made Arkady's stomach curl. What would it do to a person to know that his place in life had been preordained while he was still under the splicing scope in a hierarchy as inflexible as the most rigid human class system? What would it mean to have not one or two repressed memories of culled playmates, but dozens? And what would it mean to know that at every cull you were more likely than not to fail the cut yourself?

He saw no answer in the two Bellas' faces—only a pale and polished beauty that didn't even make the usual ritual nod to humanity. His first sight of those violet eyes, rimmed round with the delicate filigree of the MotaiSyndicate logo, was enough to make Arkady decide that transhumanism, for all its much-vaunted political purity, was an evolutionary step toward a future he didn't want to live in.

The Aurelias, on the other hand, were balm to Arkady's homesick soul. They were Rostovs, like Arkady and his pairmate. Lean and tall, with long-fingered surgeon's hands, and long noses, and long narrow faces that would have been forbiddingly severe if not for their humorous, sensible, intelligent expressions. They loafed elegantly at the far end of the table like a matched set of wolfhounds, leaning against each other with a casualness that made Arkady suspect they were already old friends or lovers. One look at Aurelia the surgeon was enough to tell Arkady that she must have spent her schooldays sitting in the front row, hand permanently raised, eager to prove she knew the answer to everything. One look at her sib left him equally sure that she'd spent her time in the back row passing notes and throwing spitballs and looking forward to soccer practice. The geologist was particularly recognizable at the moment because she had a little more of a tan than her cogenetic. But even when the tan faded it would be easy enough to tell those two strong personalities apart.

They were from RostovSyndicate's A-12 series, and as the numbering suggested they had a high rate of genetic overlap with Arkady's own A-11 line. A higher rate than was normal, in fact; it was quite unusual for newly spliced genelines to be cleared for large-scale production two years running, and it had happened under the auspices of a now-legendary design team. Looking down the table at them, Arkady felt a swell of possessive pride at the phenomenal quality of his fellow Rostovs' work—a pride that was enhanced, rather than reduced, by the fact that he would never know their names or be able in any way to distinguish them from their thousands of cogenetics.

The final workpair was represented by only one of its members—the other one presumably being on bridge duty at the moment. Both the Banerjees on the Novalis mission were astrophysicists with a secondary specialization in engineering that allowed them to cover for the Aziz pilots during the in-flight portions of the mission. Ranjipur . . . and Shrinivas, wasn't it? Arkady found it very difficult to remember individual names. He couldn't begin to imagine how humans managed the trick. But Banerjee was one of the original pre-Breakaway Syndicates, and it took pride in not using the post-Breakaway naming conventions. It also took pride, like RostovSyndicate, in resisting the newer Syndicates' move toward caste-based genelines. So all the Banerjees, no matter what bizarre letters their names might start with, were A's.

"All right," said Laid-back Ahmed when the introductions had wound down and Arkady had begun to make some inroads into his curry. "On to important things. Like who's going to make breakfast tomorrow?"

"I actually like cooking?" one of the Bellas said in a voice so hesitant it sounded like a question.

Arkady had already given up on telling the Bellas apart. Now he realized that the one speaking was standing holding a dish towel in her hands and apparently getting ready to do everyone's dishes. The Motai Bs *couldn't* be thinking that the others expected them to clean up after them, could they? That wasn't just series specialization. It was rank *humanism*!

"On the other hand," Bella went on, "Arkasha does seem to have started off very well. . . ."

"*Arkasha?*" Laid-back Ahmed was grinning incredulously at her. "The rest of us haven't even exchanged a full sentence with him and you're already on a nickname basis?"

"He's nice. . . ."

"You think everyone's nice," her sib said, making a sour face. Suddenly Arkady realized that it wasn't going to be at all hard to tell the two Bellas apart.

"Well, he *is* nice." Shy Bella—as Arkady was already privately calling her—twisted the dishrag between her pale hands and appealed to Arkady for support. "Isn't he?"

"Uh . . . I've never met him, actually."

Six pairs of amazed eyes turned to stare at Arkady.

"Shit," Laid-back Ahmed said. "On a three-year mission? That takes balls."

"Well, we were supposed to meet first. But his last assignment ran over. And then there was something about a delayed surface-to-station flight. And then . . . well . . ."

"Sounds like the beginning of a bad romance novel," scoffed Aurelia the surgeon.

"Don't listen to her!" her sib cried. "There *is* no such thing as a bad romance novel. Besides, he's cute, Arkady. A little skinny but really, really cute." She winked conspiratorially. "Not that I'd know what boys think is cute, of course."

"Oh, leave him alone, you two, he's turning red as a beet!" Laid-back Ahmed gave Arkady a reassuring clap on the shoulder. It felt like being hit by a cargo hauler. "They're just being silly women, Arkady. Arkasha's a hard worker and a good pre-citizen in every way that counts. It'll be fine. I'm sure it will."

"You're sure what will be fine?" said a voice Arkady knew like his own skin.

Arkasha—though it would be weeks before Arkady actually began to call him that—had paused in the doorway to take stock of the room before entering, just as Arkady himself had. But where Arkady had hovered hesitantly on the threshold, smiling and looking for answering smiles, his sib lounged against the door frame eyeing his crewmates with the cool detachment of a designer evaluating preculls for conformity to geneline norms.

"Uh, nothing," Ahmed covered. "The curry's fantastic, by the way. We were just talking about whether you might be willing to share cooking duty with Bella here."

"I might. The sweater looks good on you, Arkady."

Syndicate children learned very early not to say the words *my* or *mine* in polite company. *Our* was socially acceptable, as long as it was never applied to any group smaller than the whole geneline. But the singular possessive was beyond the pale. Still, there was a way of saying *the* that meant *my*. And that was the way Arkasha had just said it.

Arkady felt a hot flush creeping up his face. "Oh. Um. It's very warm. Thank you."

"Too warm for me." Arkasha gave him a measuring look, squinting and tilting his head to one side. "And you fill it out better across the shoulders. You should keep it."

Before Arkady could think to thank him, Arkasha slung his wiry frame onto the bench next to Laid-back Ahmed and started haggling over what scut work he and Bella could get out of in exchange for cooking. He adopted a sly, self-mocking tone that soon had Bella laughing and blushing and Ahmed threatening to take up cooking himself if it was that advantageous.

Meanwhile Arkady took advantage of the momentary distraction to covertly ogle his new pairmate.

He saw a slighter, slenderer, more refined version of himself. Arguably a little too refined; but beyond that quibble he was as perfectly norm-conforming as any A-11 Arkady had ever met. And of course he had the sleek, dark, classic Rostov hair instead of the chaotic whirl of cowlicks that greeted Arkady in the mirror every cycledawn. Aurelia had been right. Arkasha was very handsome. But he was also . . . unsettling.

Arkasha looked up and caught Arkady eyeing him. Then he glanced at Arkady's heaping plate and raised an eyebrow. "The condemned man ate hearty."

"I'll probably throw it all up in half an hour," Arkady answered. "But the body wants what the body wants."

"It certainly does," Arkasha acquiesced. "And speaking of the body, for what sins were you sent here?"

Arkady choked. "Uh . . . I do ants."

"Well, that's certainly grave. But I suppose we can forgive you."

Shy Bella giggled again.

"What about you?" Arkasha asked her. "What obese, wrinkled, and importunate steering committee crone did you refuse to sleep with in order to achieve the dubious honor of this assignment?"

"I didn't. None of them asked. Just grilled me on ideology so they wouldn't have to admit they knew less about terraforming than a lowly B. Come to think of it I've never slept with an A." She cocked her head prettily—a move that had a visible effect on her sib. "Should I be insulted, do you think?"

"Well," Arkasha announced magnanimously, "I'm always available if you'd like to broaden your repertoire."

And everyone laughed the nervous, keyed-up, self-conscious laughter that always accompanied the mention of the ultimate taboo.

"You should be more careful what you say," Arkady told Arkasha when they were finally alone together in the relative privacy of their cabin.

That hadn't come out the way he meant it to, he realized. He'd meant it to sound . . . well, how had he meant it to sound? What the hell had he been thinking, actually?

He cleared his throat nervously. "Top or bottom bunk?"

"I'd prefer the top if that's all right with you."

"Okay."

But neither of them moved toward the bunks. Instead, Arkasha seemed to be taking cautious stock of his new pairmate; and Arkady took the opportunity to get another look at the man who was going to be the most important person in his life, for good or bad, for the next two years.

He saw him with a crèchemate's well-trained eye. He passed over the things a stranger would have noticed first: the graceful proportion of hip and shoulder; the refined intellectual's face that spoke so clearly of their geneline's unique character and talents; the clean planes of jaw and cheekbone and temple; the slight Cupid's bow of the upper lip that the Rostov designers had settled on as the perfect compromise between beauty and manliness.

Instead, he saw the little details that crèchemates learned early to take heed of. That his new pairmate carried a good five kilos less than their crècheyear average, a sure sign of a nervous disposition. That he had a habit of balancing on his toes as if he were perpetually expecting the unexpected, and had learned from experience that the unexpected was usually unpleasant. That his narrow face radiated intelligence and character, but also a wounded reserve that did not bode well for Arkady's personal life over the course of the next two years.

The sardonic façade was just that, Arkady realized. A defensive weapon honed to a sharp edge in order to keep others off-balance and at a distance. Except that a Syndicate construct had no more reason to keep his crèchemates at a distance than a human child had to keep his own brothers and sisters at a distance.

Arkady's first impression of the man had been right; he was about as safe and predictable as an unexploded bomb.

Arkasha grinned suddenly. "That's some set of cowlicks you've got there. Classic fuzzy 18 defect. Some poor slob at the splicing scope must have caught an earful of misery over that screwup."

"Gee, no one's ever said *that* to me before."

"Scarred for life, were you?" The grin broadened. "Children can be such monsters."

"It wasn't that bad," Arkady lied.

"Then your crèche must have been a kinder, gentler place than mine was."

Arkady cleared his throat. "You're from Crèche Seven?" he asked, trying to paper over the silence with small talk.

"That's right."

"I had a pairmate from Seven, uh, let's see . . . the assignment before last? A glaciologist. Big guy, seventy kilos easy, played goalie for the Crèche Seven team. Ring any bells?"

"Not that I can hear."

"Most of the Arkadys from Seven are above height norm," Arkady babbled on. "At least in our year."

The grin faded to a sardonic smirk. "They put in a special order for big and dumb our year."

"Good footballers too." He assessed the lean but well-muscled frame of the man in front of him. "You play?"

"Alas, I'm not temperamentally suited to team sports."

"Me neither, actually. Not that I don't like the company. But I suppose when it really comes down to it, I'd rather be poking around under dead logs looking for ants."

This elicited a broader smile from Arkasha—but no answering confession.

"I read your articles on the *Aenictus gracilis*," Arkasha said. He fixed Arkady with an intense stare, as if he were trying to send or decipher some vital secret message. "It's extremely fine work. As good as anything I've seen in years. I particularly liked your paper on the adaptive value of dissent in collective decisionmaking. It was . . . thought-provoking."

Arkady's academic advisory committee had thought that paper was thought-provoking too. And a few other less complimentary things that had earned Arkady a friendly but still highly unnerving visit from a renormalization counselor. He hadn't exactly abandoned his dissent research after that . . . but he'd certainly been more circumspect in the words he used to write about it. Ants had such overwhelming symbolic value in Syndicate society that people were apt to make overheated comparisons. Metaphor creep could twist even the most solid science into politics. Sometimes Arkady envied the pre-Evacuation human entomologists who had done the pioneering work on social insect societies. They'd been able to draw much bolder conclusions than he could . . . mainly because the moralists of their day and age had been too busy pestering the beleaguered primate researchers.

Now Arkasha was saying something about multivalent superstructure, whatever that was. "You were careful not to cite it, of course, but surely the reference to Kennedy on Althusser is implicit?"

"They're just ants," Arkady said, falling back on the same formula that had always gotten him out of trouble before.

"You don't write about them as if you thought they were just ants."

They stared at each other. Arkasha seemed to be searching for something in Arkady's face and not finding it. Finally he sighed and settled back on his heels a little. When he turned away there was a sad little slump to his shoulders. "Oh well," he murmured. "The work's still good. That's the main thing. And I certainly won't give you anything to complain about in that department."

"Listen," Arkady stammered. "I didn't mean to offend you earlier. What I said about Bella, about watching what you say . . . it came out all wrong. I just meant that . . . well, sometimes it's better to be a little careful at the beginning of an assignment when you don't know everyone yet. Some people can't tell the difference between a joke and reality."

Arkasha squared his shoulders and set his sardonic mask firmly back in place. "What makes you think you offended me?" he asked. "And for that matter what makes you think it was a joke?"

That was when Arkady really began to panic.

"Uh . . . top bunk you said? I'll just leave this stuff here on the bottom then, and . . . er . . . uh . . . I really need to get down to the lab now and make sure everything got on board in one piece and—"

"Relax," Arkasha said, with that same mocking little smile lingering on his lips. "My perversions aren't nearly that simple."

Later Arkady would hear the seed of Arkasha's sickness in those words. He would parse them, shuffle them, turn them over like a fortune-teller's cards, looking for the first misstep on the long slide toward exile.

But in that moment he saw only the face that was his and not his; the eyes that were his and not his; and the soul behind the eyes, as complex and intractable and miraculous as a living planet.

A POLITICALLY USEFUL TOOL

Although it may take several decades for the process of transformation to unfold, in time, the art of warfare . . . will be vastly different than it is today . . . the distinction between military and commercial space systems—combatants and noncombatants—will become blurred . . . advanced forms of biological warfare that can "target" specific genotypes may transform biological warfare from the realm of terror to a politically useful tool.

—*Rebuilding America's Defenses: Strategy, Forces, and Resources for a New Century. A Report of the Project for the New American Century.* (SEPTEMBER 2000)

ALL ARKADY EVER KNEW FOR certain about running the blockade was that he was drugged into dazed half-consciousness for most of the trip.

He remembered the ship; the stretched, surreal claustrophobia of jump dreams; an interlude of bright refracted sunlight slicing through the mirrored canyons of Ring-side skyscrapers; the hard eyes and sunburned faces of the security guards at the El Al boarding gate. Then he was waking up and his fellow passengers were bursting into the chorus of *"Heveinu Shalom Aleichem"* and the shuttle was streaking over impossibly blue water toward the white rooftops and glittering solar panels of Tel Aviv.

Ben Gurion International Airport was a marvel of architectural design, but it had been built a century before the Evacuation and the artificial ice age. By the time they'd been on the ground for five minutes, Arkady's fingers were aching with cold.

Osnat dove down the concourse, pulling Arkady along in her wake. People hurried past, jostling and pushing. There were so many faces, each one shockingly different from every other, and all hardened by the grim battle of all-against-all that seemed to constitute normal life for humans.

"Who's that?" Arkady asked, pointing to a vast, grainy photograph that filled most of the wall above the Departures and Arrivals board.

"Theodor Herzl. And don't point. People are jumpy here."

Two girl soldiers strode by, automatic weapons held at the half-ready. A man with the reddest hair Arkady had ever seen elbowed between him and Osnat, practically tripping him. While Arkady was still flailing for balance, a raucous group of women barreled into him, several of them with screaming children in tow. They all had the same blond curls and freckled skin, and there was a faint but reassuring similarity to the shape of their faces. Not the clear, clean melody of a single geneset, but something at least approaching the harmonious chord of a Syndicate's component genelines. The group enveloped Arkady, carrying him along in their wake. When Osnat backtracked to rescue him, he turned to stare over his shoulder, reduced to openmouthed amazement by his first sight of a "family."

And then came the ads.

There were no visibly wired people in the crowd—ceramsteel filament was Earth-illegal because it had to be manufactured in microgravity—but the airport itself was still on-grid, and the air overhead crackled and glittered with publicity spins.

NORAM-ARC JEWS FOR PEACE NOW said one banner that popped alarmingly into midair just over Arkady's head. A second ad plunged him into a sunlit grove of frost-resistant oranges populated by smiling kibbutzniks who urged him to "exercise your Right of Return right now" by buying from Kehillot Tehilla Realty. A third spin, which perplexed Arkady enough to bring him to a standstill, proclaimed j-cupid.com "the number one Jewish singles dating and matchmaking service" and advised him in a perky voice that fertility/virility stats on all registered singles were just one click away. "Don't you deserve someone special?" the voice-over asked in a tone that seemed actually to imply that "special" was a good thing.

Then the thing he had been afraid of from the moment he set foot in UN space finally happened.

"Arkady!" a woman called out in a voice sharp enough to stop him in his tracks.

The woman was short, muscular, probably Korean. She was a soldier out of uniform; he read it in the cut of her hair, the set of her shoulders, the decisive moments of someone who actually knew how to hit people. She was also, quite unmistakably, a genetic construct. But no

Syndicate design team would produce a face so functional and so un-aesthetic. And no crèche-raised construct would speak so sharply or stare out at the world through such hard, uncompromising, self-sufficient eyes. This woman was a pre-Breakaway construct, spliced and tanked and raised to serve humans. And if she really was the soldier she appeared to be, then she'd chosen to kill for humans too.

The man with her, on the other hand, was anything but a soldier. He slouched elegantly behind his companion, as if he could barely be bothered to pay attention to Arkady. Yet there was a taut, poised, abstracted quality to the beautiful body that set Arkady's teeth on edge. This wasn't a person, whispered some atavistic instinct. It was a living doll operated by an unseen and supremely skilled puppetmaster.

Then Arkady remembered that the proper word for it was *shunt*. He'd just met his first Emergent AI. And if his grasp of basic cognitive theory was correct, then he was now being laughed at by the closest thing he'd ever see in his entomologist's life to a sentient ant swarm.

"Arkady," the woman repeated. "We thought you were dead."

"Don't let her frighten you," the AI drawled with a smile that would have looked perfectly at home on Korchow's face. "I'm sure she doesn't mean *dead* dead."

Arkady stared at the machine-man, torn between horror and fascination. The AI watched him through wide hazel eyes, a faint shadow of that mocking smile still hovering at the corner of its lips. Somehow Arkady was quite sure that the smile belonged to the machine, and not to the human into whose shunt-suppressed body it had poured some incomprehensible distillation of its component selves. It was a clever, changeable, humorous smile. A smile that would be easy to love but impossible to trust . . . even if there were anything but a teeming chaos of semiautonomous agents behind it.

"I—I don't think I know you," he said, speaking both to the woman and the machine.

"But Korchow—"

The woman fell silent as abruptly as if someone had interrupted her. The AI cocked his head like a dog listening for its master's voice, and Arkady had the sense that some shared thought had just passed between them in streamspace.

"Oh," the woman said. "Of course."

She turned on her heel. Her coat flew open, and the blaring orange of an El Al security seal winked at Arkady from the trigger guard of a holstered pistol. Then they were gone, swallowed by the swirling human tide as quickly as they'd emerged from it.

Osnat frowned nervously at him. "You okay, Arkady?"

"I think so."

"Was that who I think it was?"

"I don't know. Who do you think it was?"

"Well, it looked like—no, never mind. That's crazy. He wouldn't have the nerve to show his face here. Any of his faces. You sure you're okay? You look like shit."

"I'm fine."

But he wasn't fine. They'd *known* him. They'd known his series name, even if they'd mistaken him, as humans so often did, for another Arkady. And they'd thought he was dead.

Dead how? Dead where? What had happened to that other Arkady before he died?

And what did Andrej Korchow have to do with it?

OHEN LOOKED OUT THE WINDOW of the Ben Gurion–Jerusalem bus and told himself he needed a new body.

It was impossible to go anywhere quietly in this one. That Hoffman girl had been on the edge of recognizing him. Even the nice boy at El Al Security had waved him to the front of the line far too obviously for discretion. It had been one thing when he'd still been able to travel under his French passport, but the Tel Aviv fiasco had put an end to that and left him with no claim to citizenship or humanity except the one his long-dead inventor's religion gave him.

And then, of course, there was the irksome detail of being a ghost.

"Why do they keep calling you that?" Li had asked the first time someone did it in front of her. "It's creepy. Like they actually think you're him instead of you."

"It's just a formality. No one takes it seriously except the religious nuts."

But Li had been less interested in theological niceties than in the soldierly virtue of loyalty. "Has it ever occurred to you that if they really were your friends, they'd have gotten the hell over it sometime in the last four centuries?"

"Well, they have a point. Technically, I'm only a Jew because Hy Cohen's mother was one. And it isn't like he was observant, trust me—"

"I'll remind you of that self-righteous tone next time I catch you eating oysters."

"—but some Orthodox rabbi ruled that digitally reconstituted personalities are ghosts, not golems, and therefore entitled to all the rights and privileges of their originals under Halakhic law."

Never mind the absurdity of trying to argue that the vast virtual universe of coevolving neural networks, affective loops, and expert systems called "Hyacinthe" was even remotely the same person as the Hy Cohen who had uploaded the memories of his failing body into the long-junked original hardware.

And never mind that even Hyacinthe was only one of the thirty-four separate sentient and quasi-sentient synthetic entities (this week's head count) currently enjoying the somewhat debatable benefits of Israeli citizenship under Cohen's Toffoli number.

And never mind the problematic thirty-fifth wheel: one very sentient and only partially synthetic Catherine Li, formerly of the UN Peacekeepers.

She was sleeping now, caught in the intense, lying web of dreams that still had the power to shock Cohen after half a dozen lifetimes among humans. She slept with her arms crossed over her chest and her boot soles braced on the seat in front of her. Looking at her clenched fists and frowning face, at the faint tracery of ceramsteel snaking under the brown skin, Cohen thought: *Even in sleep she defends herself.*

Meanwhile the dusty blue-and-white Egged bus rattled up onto the plateau of the Jordan floodplain, and half of Cohen's associated selves looked out the window or worked on unrelated projects, while the rest eavesdropped on Li's intermittent dreams and scrambled to keep his Ring-to-Earth connection ticking along at the massive bandwidth required to knit borrowed body and far-flung souls together.

He stretched, appreciating, as he always did, the elastic grace of Roland's young and exquisitely well tended body. Humans took the pleasures of health and youth for granted—something that was a little harder to do once you'd survived dying of multiple sclerosis. But then taking things for granted seemed to be wired into the human gene pool.

Cohen looked around, taking stock of his fellow passengers in realspace. A smattering of Ring-side tourists and business travelers, conspicuous for the cranial jacks that revealed Earth-illegal wetware and psychware. Young aggressively secular Israelis, whose tanned good looks hinted at weekends spent windsurfing off Tel Aviv's fashionable beaches—and whose skin-hugging outfits looked like the kind of goods that only slipped through the Embargo because Ring-side customs was too busy fighting real violations to worry about youth fashion. A rickety old Ashkenaz reading the *Ha'aretz* sports section—*Maccabi Tel Aviv Smites Haopel Jerusalem 77–49*. Well, at least someone at the *Ha'aretz* sports desk still had a sense of humor, which was more than you could say for the Op-ed page. A large-eyed and unnaturally silent family of Hasidim huddled along the back bench where the ride was always roughest. The usual disturbingly large number of caps and chadors in the dusty green of the Interfaithers. And of course the impossibly young Israeli Defense Force soldiers whose rumpled uniforms made Cohen imagine mothers leaning over balcony railings all over Israel shouting, *You're-going-out-in-public-like-that?*

The only thing missing was the Palestinians. Before the war they would have been here on the student passes that were a mere formality during the long peaceful generations of the open border. Laughing with their Israeli friends. Kissing their Israeli girlfriends to the abiding and roundly ignored horror of the ultraorthodox. Locked at the hip, like their two countries—and too young and idealistic to realize that the peace they took for granted was just a pause for station identification.

Li was waking up.

Cohen could feel her all around him, stirring, shifting, running the day's events through her half-waking mind in a rapid-fire succession of half-formed dreams that cut in and out like the nightly newspin on fast forward. He tried to catch on to the tail of a few dreams as they passed, but he couldn't make sense of them. And she was aware of him as a vague, alien presence in her mind, though she hadn't yet awakened enough to identify the intruder.

Spying on her, she called it. And there'd be hell to pay if she caught him at it. He untangled himself from her, erasing his retreating footsteps and feeling hurt, as he always did, that she made him sneak and steal to get what he would have given her for the mere asking.

She twisted, murmuring, and brushed ineffectually at a lock of hair that had fallen over her forehead. He reached out cautiously and pushed it back.

She opened her eyes.

He took his hand away.

"You need a haircut," he told her.

"I know." She stretched, yawning and he felt a pang of desire so strong it made his jaw hurt. "Things were so crazy before we left, I forgot. How's your connection?"

"Fine."

Not a lie. Just a nonrandom sampling of the available data.

He was wardriving—stealing streamspace time from unsecured local access points instead of going through Kyoto-legal channels. He and Li had argued heatedly about this. But he didn't want UNSec eavesdropping on some of the Earthside errands he was planning to take care of this trip. There was nothing they'd like better than to slap an expensive corporate felony charge on him, if only for the PR value. And, as he'd pointed out in answer to Li's objections, if he was going to give someone the power to pull the plug on him, he'd rather hand it to the warchalkers than to either General Nguyen or the boys on King Saul Boulevard.

He'd also pointed out to her (though much good it did) that the worst problems of interfacing on Earth had nothing to do with secrecy and everything to do with bandwidth. He had to resort to scattershot prefetching just to be able to carry on a normal conversation. And prefetching, though it always made you look like an idiot sooner or later, was hardly a safety issue in normal circumstances.

Still, she was worried. And he didn't like to worry her. So he was doing his best to limit the technical complications to his side of the intraface.

<So what's Arkady doing here?> Li asked onstream. <And am I crazy, or did I get the impression that you knew the woman he was with?>

The question flashed across his networks with the up/down, either/or, black-and-white clarity of the spin states that encoded it. And even before she hung the flesh of letters and syllables on the thought, he could feel the twist of strung-up nerves and vague worst-case-scenario visions that drove the question.

<I don't think she recognized me,> Cohen answered.

<I didn't ask whether she recognized you. I asked whether you recognized her.>

"Old friend from the office," Cohen said, going offstream because it was so much easier to be evasive in realspace. "There's a file on her somewhere or other. Router/decomposer can't access it at the moment."

Li groaned internally. <Is this going to be another one of those trips where you decide to pack light and end up forgetting to bring the one database you actually needed?>

"Anyway," he said, changing the subject, "you're assuming it really was Korchow's Arkady we ran into. I'm not convinced that was an act back there."

"Neither am I," Li said aloud, "but I've never gotten burned by being too suspicious. And I don't believe in coincidence. Not that kind. We're here for—" She glanced around and stopped talking, but he heard the rest of the thought just as he heard all her thoughts. At least all the ones she let him hear. <We're here to bid on a piece of Syndicate tech some alleged defector brought across the line, and suddenly we run into an A Series we last saw in the company of Andrej Korchow? If I let that kind of 'coincidence' slide, we'd both be dead by now.>

<There's more than one Arkady. It's not like running into a human. You ought to know that.> He glanced at her symmetrical construct's features and decided not to pursue that line of thought. <Anyway, you worry too much.>

And then, with an almost humanly malicious sense of timing, they passed onto a new grid of his access point map, router/decomposer lost the most recent open node and failed to locate a new one, and the bottom fell out of streamspace.

The bus and its passengers drained away around Cohen as if someone had pulled the plug in a bathtub.

What the hell? Cohen queried his routing meta-agent. But if the other AI heard him, he wasn't answering.

Cohen dialed through the virtually stacked grid coordinates of the local nets, passing over the endless sea of **O**'s and triple slashes that marked closed nodes and danger points. He toyed briefly with two high-bandwidth nodes chalked with the legends KIND WOMAN TELL SOB STORY and RELIGIOUS TALK WILL GET YOU FOOD. He dropped them both; access with a data trail, however faint, was as bad as no access at all.

The next block was a government system full of high-security data holes (NOTSAFE).

Then the Border Police (BIG DOG—MOVE ON QUICKLY).

He skittered across the spinstream, feeling all contact with Earth slipping away from him. The bandwidth requirements for running a full-body shunt were inconceivable by the standards of human data-pushers—and human tolerances were all that most Earth-to-Orbital hardware was built to handle.

<Hold for contact,> he messaged to Li's Ring-side postbox across the low-bandwidth, high-surveillance Orbital–Surface routers, but he might as well have been shouting down a well for all the good it did. If anything went wrong down there while he was offstream, there was nothing he could do for her.

And then he saw it, gleaming through the haze of low-bandwidth static like incoming tracer fire: Two inverted brackets bellied up to each other to form the inverted capital I that marked the unpatrolled entrance ramps to Earth's wide-open post-Embargo information freeway:

][
OPEN NODE SKY'S THE LIMIT

He was back.

He slipped back into the sensory feed from Roland's cortical shunt like a diver sliding into blood-warm water. The bus and the passengers and the city all took shape around him. Most important, he felt Li's reassuring presence interpenetrating the edges of his own composite consciousnesses:

HELLO WORLD

He sent the letters blinking across their shared work space in archaic LED green.

<What the hell was that?> she asked.

<Nothing. Old programmer's joke.>

<Jeez, be serious for once, can't you?>

"Okay. Sorry about the road bump."

"I'm sorrier. I thought I was about to be stuck making small talk with Roland for the next two weeks."

"I thought you liked Roland."

"A little of Roland goes a long way." She gave him a sly sideways glance, seemed about to say something, then obviously thought the better of it.

"It's your fault, anyway." Cohen stretched coquettishly. *"I* wanted to be a girl for this trip."

"We're in the land of the Interfaithers and the ultraorthodox, Cohen. One of us needs to be able to pass as a member of the master sex. Besides, if I'd let you shunt through a girl on this trip, any last hope of making you pack sensible shoes would have gone straight out the window."

"Sensible shoes are bad for the soul," Cohen kvetched. He ducked his head into the curve of her neck, tasting her familiar skin and the rich musky dust of Earth.

She shrugged him away.

It was barely a shrug. No outsider would have noticed the gesture, even if they'd been looking for it. But to Cohen it was unmistakable.

"Penny for your thoughts?" he asked after a moment.

Li's generous lips compressed into a tense line. "Why pay for what you can get for free?"

And there it was, the truth Li could neither change nor live with. The two of them formed a hybrid creature whose realspace body was just the tip of the streamspace iceberg, and Cohen wrote the rules in streamspace. They ran on his networks. They navigated his gamespace. They depended on his processing capacity, which exponentially exceeded anything a mere organic could field—even an organic as heavily wired as Li.

Cohen had the power to go anywhere, see everything, do anything, take anything. Li only had the power to walk away. Not much for a woman who had commanded battalions and led combat drops. Not enough, Cohen was beginning to think.

Cohen's routing meta-agent interrupted with a message that he'd sorted out the routing bug and was working on a patch for it. It was of course completely unnecessary for router/decomposer to bring such a message to Cohen's conscious attention. Nor was it necessary to deliver it on a general access spinstream. But router/decomposer had sided with Li on the wardriving issue, and he had a point to make.

Router/decomposer had originally called himself just plain decomposer. And a decomposer was exactly what he was: a fully sentient massively parallel decomposition program supported by a vast Josephson Array currently holding in a low lunar orbit carefully calculated to keep its spin glass lattice operating at a crisp refreshing twenty-seven degrees Kelvin. But when Cohen's last communications routing meta-agent had decamped in protest over Li's arrival, decomposer—albeit with endless grumbling over being dragged away from his beloved spin glass research—had also taken over management of Cohen's ant-based routing algorithms.

When his job changed, decomposer had quite logically changed his name: to router/decomposer, or, among friends, 01110010 01101111 01110101 01110100 01100101 01110000 01011100 01100100 01100101 01100011 01101111 01101101 01110000 01101111 01110011 01100101 01110010.

Functional nomenclature didn't appeal to Cohen any more than the personality architecture that normally went with it. But router/decomposer was fabulously good at his job, fully sentient, and eminently capable of spinning off into his own autonomous aggregation. No other Emergent AI came close to matching the seamless integration and dizzying processing speeds Cohen could achieve thanks to router/decomposer's elegant spinstream routing solutions. And router/decomposer would have applied for his own Toffoli number and gone into business for himself long ago if it were not for what he cogently termed his "low tolerance for the social friction costs of dealing with assholes."

Needless to say, Cohen tried very hard to keep the social friction costs of dealing with Cohen to a minimum.

<Do you have any idea how much processing space I'm blowing on your little spy games?> router/decomposer queried.

<Where's your sense of adventure,> Cohen joked, <and you just a young whippersnapper of a hundred and fifteen?>

Router/decomposer demonstrated his sense of adventure by sending an extremely rude chaotic attractor flickering across the hidden layers of their shared Kohonen nets.

"Tell him to get a real name, will you?" Li said, having caught the tail end of router/decomposer's dirty joke.

"Tell him yourself," Cohen answered.

"I would, but he seems to not be speaking to me at the moment."

"What? Why?"

"Hell if I know."

<What's that about?> Cohen asked router/decomposer on the root-only stream.

<She keeps asking to access data you've made me firewall. It's embarrassing. Actually,> router/decomposer suggested slyly, still on the root-only stream, <it would save a lot of RAM if you'd stop making me lie to her.>

<It's *not* lying!>

<Sure. Whatever lets you sleep at night. The point is, our current associative configuration is highly inefficient. And detrimental to your relationship with her.>

<Oh really? If you know so much about humans, why don't you stop backseat driving and get your own?>

<Nah,> router/decomposer said placidly. <I'm more the heckling-from-the-sidelines type than the do-it-yourself type. Besides, I tried shunting once. It was . . . squishy. A little bit of human goes a hell of a long way. That's why I like Li. A little human, but not *too* human. Now if you'd just take my advice and—>

<Don't you have *anything* useful to do right now?>

<Not until you fuck up again.> An affective fuzzy set drifted downstream and dispersed across Cohen's neural networks like the icy plume of a mountain river mingling with the sea. It "felt" like all router/decomposer's algorithms: as cold and complicated and inhuman as his beloved quantum spin glass. But the emotion that the set expressed was all too human: smug self-righteousness. <Seriously, though. I still think you need to back off and give Li a little more space.>

<That's not the way the Game works. As you damn well know.>

<Bet I could figure out how to tweak the Game so you could do it.>

<Tweak my soul, you mean.>

That earned Cohen another rude attractor. <Souls are just obsolete social engineering for monkeys. And even if you get some perverse kick out of pretending to believe in such fairy tales, the Game is not your soul. It was a damn sloppy piece of code when Hy wrote it three hundred years ago, and it hasn't improved with age. Code is written to be rewritten, and this piece is long due for an overhaul. Seriously, Cohen, do you see *me* chasing after humans like a codependent golden retriever?>

"So how did you get him to stop talking to you?" Cohen asked Li out loud. "And can *I* do it?"

But Li was laughing too hard to answer. And when he probed her thoughts across the intraface the only coherent words he could get out of her were <Down, Fido, down!>

It was too bad, but there it was.

If you wanted to get from Ben Gurion International Airport to modern Jerusalem, you had to go down the Jaffa Road. And if you went down the Jaffa Road, you had to go past the Line.

Every year there was talk of moving the road or building a new highway that would swing out to the north and away from the dirty zone. But every year the planning board put it off until next year . . . mainly because building a new road would mean admitting that the war wasn't just a passing inconvenience but a permanent fixture on the landscape. It was the same kind of mentality you saw in every low-level, multigenerational civil war: Lebanon, Ireland, Iraq, America. On the one hand, no one wants to be on the losing side of sectarian violence. On the other hand, no one was foolish enough to think that anyone could "win" such a war. And since no one quite understood how or why peace had disintegrated into bloodshed, most people still nursed a vague hope that a reverse process might occur (Cohen thought of it as a kind of sociopolitical phase transition) in which the chaos of war would spontaneously reorganize itself into peace.

Years went by like this, with people schizophrenically dividing their time between waiting for peace to break out and trying to schedule the war around the weddings and brises and bar mitzvahs and funerals that *will* keep happening even when there's a combat zone around the corner. And in the meantime, the streets weren't getting fixed, and the real estate market was crashing, and the plumbing was getting iffy . . . and Jerusalem was starting to look more and more like a city whose back had been broken on the rack of civil war.

Nowhere was the disintegration more visible than in the spreading no-man's-land that leached out from the Line toward the southern suburbs of Jerusalem. Biohazard signs began to sprout on street corners like poisonous mushrooms. The divided highway deteriorated into a rough two-lane strip of pavement as it approached the last habitable houses. Then even the two-lane died of a slow bleed, giving way to mortar-pocked dirt, sporadically bulldozed to smooth out what was left of the roadbed.

As the Line got closer the passengers got tenser. A screaming match broke out at the back of the bus between a paunchy middle-aged ultra-orthodox man and a scantily dressed young woman whose skimpy T-shirt had ridden up to expose what Cohen at first assumed was a charmingly old-fashioned bit of cosmetic scarring.

"What's she saying?" Li asked, her spinstream-assisted Hebrew completely unequal to the fast and furious pace of the argument.

"She asked him to close the window. He refused."

The young woman was now actually pulling up her shirt and pointing to her stomach while the ultraorthodox averted his eyes in horror. And the scars weren't cosmetic at all, it turned out; they were old shrapnel wounds.

"Then," Cohen translated on the fly, "he told her to cover up her arms if she was cold. So she told him to fuck off. So he told her get on the next Ring-bound shuttle if she didn't want to be a real Jew. And now she's shouting about how she spent two years on the Line and she doesn't have to take this shit from some schmuck ultraorthodox draft dodger and how would he like to see her scars. All of them." He grinned, caught between pride and embarrassment. "Welcome to Israel."

"The Line," Li said when the screaming match in the back of the bus had finally subsided. "As in the Green Line?"

Cohen nodded absently, craning out the window for his first view of what was left of the Old City.

"That girl was an *Enderbot*?"

As if summoned into existence by the word, a squad of soldiers crossed the road in front of them, forcing the bus to a grinding halt. It wasn't a checkpoint; these soldiers were coming off the Line, smeared with red dirt and dressed in bulky desert camouflage NBC gear.

Without stopping to think whether it was a good idea, Cohen reached out across streamspace and sampled the squad leader's spinstreams. Red flags must be going up all over EMET headquarters; but if he could hack their spins that easily, then whoever was handling security over there richly deserved to be hauled onto the carpet.

Besides, he told himself, it was as good a way as any to let Didi know he was coming.

As the squad dropped off the far side of the roadbed, one of the soldiers looked back. Her eyes were startlingly green, and the coin-shaped derm marks of long-term cortical shunt use were dead white against the sun-browned skin of her temples. She was Sephardic, of course; the well-heeled children of the Ashkenazim were back in the EMET programming bunkers running the AIs, not under shunt and facing live fire and land mines. A few leftist politicians had suggested rotating reservists through the Line on regular intervals, but it would have cost too much to install even the low-grade IDF shunts in such numbers.

And what politician really wants to send his campaign contributors' kids home in body bags? So the privileged children of the Ashkenazim sat under full-spectrum lights in the IDF programming bunkers and pampered and debugged and lied to the tactical AIs. And the children of Iraqis, North Africans, and Ethiopians collected the combat pay and the bullets and the genetic damage.

"So that's EMET." Li's voice was flat and expressionless.

"Yep. EMET meet Catherine. Catherine meet EMET, the latest and allegedly greatest stage in the evolution of military-applications Emergent AI. You want a war, EMET can run it for you from the lowest private to the fattest general. And Israel's just the field trial. If little EMET runs this war well enough, he'll put soldiers out of business permanently . . . except for the shunt-controlled cannon fodder."

Li glanced after the soldiers. She looked sick. "Was that girl under shunt?"

"I can't tell," Cohen lied.

But of course he could. And even for him it was hard to imagine that there was anything even remotely human behind those blank killer's eyes. Was that what Li saw when she looked at him? The thought sent a shudder through Roland's body that router/decomposer's best buffering algorithms couldn't suppress.

"You couldn't pay me enough to go under shunt in combat," Li muttered.

"The casualty rates are a lot lower when the AIs run things."

"Some things are worse than dying. To wire yourself into a semisentient . . ."

"They're not semisentients. EMET's component AIs are fully sentient, right down to the individual squad member level."

Li snapped around to stare at him. "So every one of those soldiers is being run by a fully sentient Emergent?"

"Of course. Human consciousness is an operating system for the human body. Any AI that can operate a human body well enough to take it into combat has to be at least as self-aware as the average human." More so, in practice; AIs didn't have the armature of instinct, autonomic reflexes and hormones that humans had to fall back on.

"But how do they get past the termination problem?"

It would be called a suicide problem, Cohen thought bitterly, if it were humans instead of AIs killing themselves. The termination problem had been the stumbling block of every attempt to automate land combat since the dawn of Emergent AI. It turned out that Emergent AIs who were sentient enough to handle real-time nonvirtual ground combat were also sentient enough to suffer from most of the psychiatric disorders that afflicted human soldiers. And since AI identity architecture was far more brittle than the human equivalent, the result was suicide. Hard on the public stomach. And even harder on the AI programmers, who had an unfortunate tendency to get attached to their lab rats.

In the course of their long war, carried out in punctilious observance of the letter of Embargo law, the Israelis and the Palestinians (the Palestinians had their own version of EMET too, of course) had worked through every variation and iteration of the termination problem.

At first EMET's AIs had full real-time interface with the Line: helmet-mounted digital cameras, roving RPVs, real-time SyWO and SpySat feed. The result had been a rash of synthetic psychiatric disorders and self-terminations.

Next they tried running the Line with semisentients. Total carnage. Skyrocketing human casualty rates. Peace marches. Demonstrations. Shoving matches in the Knesset. The IDF backed off the semisentients faster than you could say "preterm election."

Then they'd developed EMET.

EMET was a recursive acronym for EMET Military-Applications Emergent Tactical Systems. But the real significance of the acronym was as much mythic as technological. EMET—*truth* in Hebrew—was the word Rabbi Loew of Prague carved on his golem's forehead in order to bring dead clay to life. And when the golem's work was done, the Rabbi had simply erased the first letter of truth from its forehead, making it MET: dead.

And that was exactly what the IDF did to EMET. When one of EMET's AIs realized that the game wasn't a game and the blood was real, they hard booted it and wiped its memory banks. Just like the original golem, EMET contained both truth and death separated by a single breath. But while truth had given life to Rabbi Loew's golem, for EMET's AIs discovering the truth of who they were and what they did was a death sentence.

"They *kill* them?" Li asked, grasping the essence of EMET in as little time as it took Cohen to think about it.

"It's nice to know you see it that way."

"Of course I do!" Li snapped, conveniently forgetting that no court in UN space would charge killing an AI as murder. "That's the most hypocritical . . . how can you *work* for these people?"

Cohen resisted the urge to squirm, even though he knew perfectly well that Li would interpret Roland's unnatural stillness as exactly the overcompensation it was. "That's complicated. Actually, it's not complicated. It's my country."

<That's the most complicated thing of all,> she said instream.

He probed her feelings about EMET. Not pushing, just throwing out the merest suggestion that he was there and listening. Half a dozen vague associations swirled through the phase space in which he "saw" her cortex's neural burst patterns. They traced a series of chaotic attractor wings that encoded the continuous shaping and reshaping of memory both humans and AIs called consciousness. Relief that she had gotten to be a real soldier instead of a zombie . . . no matter how badly it had ended. Memories of all the times she had fought her way out of cold sleep after a combat jump wondering what she'd forgotten this time, and whether she'd lost it to randomly decohering spins or UNSec memory washing. Fear at the way that memories long lost to her conscious mind could still twist her emotions. One memory that retained all its raw emotional power despite the invasive UNSec memory washing: standing under the deep blue sky of Gilead watching Andrej Korchow bleed out in a steaming pool of blood and coffee. And permeating all the rest—grooving itself into the older memories so that it would always be associated with them—a cold panic at the thought of the Enderbots struggling toward sentience only to be pushed back under by the cold hand on the keyboard.

"I hate it too," he said, knowing she would understand all the chaotic and contradictory feelings behind the words. "But what can I do?"

Li reached over and set her hand lightly on Cohen's.

He could "see" through the link between them that she was watching Roland's hands, the skin around his eyes, the corners of his mouth—all the little telltales she used to divine Cohen's feelings through the veil of another person's flesh. Over the years her relationship to Roland's body had settled into a placid affection that she half-consciously associated with her few fragmented memories of her own parents' marriage. That was what he felt in her now as she put her arms around him.

"I love you," she said, and meant it.

A human lover would have been happy.

But Cohen wasn't human. And inside he could feel her letting go even as she held him. Drifting away, not with anger or resentment but with a kind of dull resignation.

She loved him more than she had ever imagined she could love anyone. But she was going to leave him anyway. And if there was anything he could do to stop it, she couldn't tell him what it was because she didn't even remember why she was leaving.

T HE LEFT-BEHIND BOMB EXPLODED at eight in the morning on Easter Sunday of 2049.

"Democracy of the bomb, twenty-first-century style," Osnat told Arkady as their chopper thundered over the Line just high enough to be out of range of any locals crazy enough to take potshots at them. "Some maniac from Hoboken decided the Rapture wasn't getting here fast enough, and he had to do his little bit to help Armageddon along. The cleanup stalled out after Phase One: the Old City and the Temple Mount. Now the UN keeps whining about funding and asking for new environmental impact reports. And meanwhile they're offering state-subsidized tank babies to anyone who'll emigrate."

"But why would the UN want you to emigrate?" Arkady asked, bewildered by the welter of unfamiliar terminology.

Osnat looked at him as if he'd said something almost comically stupid. "Water," she said, as if that was all the answer his question demanded.

Arkady nodded, less to indicate understanding—he understood almost nothing that came out of Osnat's mouth—than in the hope that a nod might elicit some more information that would make sense of what came before.

It didn't, but he was learning to live with being terminally confused.

The Left-Behind Bombing had been the last poisonous shot fired in the War on Terror. An angry young man had stolen a genetic weapon designed to lower Sunni birthrates in Iraq without affecting neighboring ethnic groups. The targeting hadn't quite lived up to the defense contractor's hype, and the explosion had single-handedly wiped the most holy sites of Islam, Christianity, and Judaism off the political map.

"It really is green," Arkady breathed, staring down at the burgeoning wilderness of the Line. "It's *alive*."

"Chernobyl Effect," Osnat explained. "Contamination's bad, but humans are worse. The Line's just about the healthiest real estate in the Middle East these days as long as you don't happen to be human."

Arkady caught his breath at a fluid and briefly glimpsed dun-and-gray form passing under the scattered trees along the canal bank. "Is that a *horse*?"

"Wild donkey," Osnat answered. She was staring down at the Line too, her eyes gone so pale in the weak winter sunlight that from where Arkady sat they seemed to be transparent. "Horses are extinct now. Even on the Line."

"Wild," Arkady said, picking up on the earlier word. "You mean naturally reproducing."

"Yeah." Her voice sank to near background noise as she craned her neck out the far window to keep the donkey in her line of vision. "Those early genetic weapons were pretty unpredictable. Mostly they boiled down to dumping massive loads of pesticides and synthetic estrogens and heavy metals and hoping that the combined toxin load would do the job. The Temple Mount bomb scrambled horse, human, and songbird DNA beyond repair. Donkeys, on the other hand, are still breeding like rabbits. Actually, rabbits are still breeding like rabbits, come to think of it. And I'm sure I don't have to tell *you* how well the ants are doing." She sighed—a sigh that was all out of proportion with the not-very-serious problem of too many ants. "On the other hand, the bombing *did* scare us into three centuries of peace. I guess that counts for something."

"What started up the war again, Osnat?"

"Hell if I know. It was like everyone just woke up one morning and decided to flush it all down the toilet."

She frowned down at the treetops while the silence (a relative notion in the ear-shattering roar of the helicopter) stretched to uncomfortable lengths.

"You must remember the open border," Arkady ventured finally.

"I grew up with it. I was already in college when the war started."

Arkady had read about the open border, a fact of life in Israel and Palestine during the centuries of shocked peace that followed the Left-Behind Bombing. The whole concept of the border—of any border—had seemed impossibly theoretical until now, as incomprehensible to Syndicate eyes as everything else about the human notions of countries and national loyalties. Now, watching the shadow of their chopper flicker over the hills and valleys, Arkady could finally match words to reality.

There were fences down there. And the only fences Arkady had ever seen in his life were the ones crèchelings put up at the back of playing fields during field trips to Gilead to stop stray balls from rolling away. They really meant it, he realized, looking at those fences. The idea of "owning" a piece of a planet might seem as quaint as witchcraft to him, but these people were willing to kill each other over it.

"Did you know any Palestinians before the war?" Arkady asked Osnat.

"My first boyfriend was Palestinian. My parents loved him. Thought he was a good influence on me." She smirked. "I was *not* a well-behaved adolescent."

Arkady blinked, taken aback by the sheer number of unthinkables in that reply. "And what's he doing now?"

Her smile shut down like an airlock slamming closed. "He's dead. All those nice boys I grew up with are dead. On both sides." She gave a bitter laugh. "And for what? So we can listen to the bastards in the Knesset make patriotic speeches."

She lit a cigarette and smoked it, hunched over the little flame like a dog trying to keep someone from stealing its bone.

"This used to be the most beautiful country," she said finally. Arkady would hear those words, or some version of them, so many times over the coming weeks, and from so many people on both sides of the Line, that they would come to seem like an epitaph for the Jerusalem Osnat's generation had grown up in. "I wish you could see what it was like before the war. They were even talking about opening up the cleaner parts of the Line and turning them into an international peace park." She turned away and stubbed out her half-smoked cigarette as if she'd lost the stomach for it. "Ah, fuck, I don't know why I'm even telling you."

Arkady made a helpful face but Osnat was staring out the window, seeing only the past and its long-buried dead.

"Oh well." She sounded almost friendly for a moment. "Not your problem. Just dodge the mortars for a few weeks and you're out of here."

"And you?"

"And me what?"

"Why don't you leave?"

She jabbed a nicotine-stained finger toward him abruptly enough to make him flinch. "Bingo. Just the question I ask the bitch in the mirror every morning."

"And?"

"And you'll be the first to know if I ever get a straight answer out of her."

Arkady must have fallen asleep after that. When he woke the city was gone and they were flying over empty desert.

Waves of sand ran away to the horizon under towering dust-brown thunderheads that the pilot seemed to be flying into at every moment. The sun shone feebly through the enveloping haze, though Osnat's sunburned face testified to its destroying power.

Arkady shifted uncomfortably. He'd hoped that flying would relieve the constant ache of full gravity. But, flying or earthbound, he was still sucked onto this spinning rock like a bug in a wind tunnel, every joint popping and aching until it was hard to believe his ancestors had survived long enough to make it off the planet.

Night was falling, and suddenly he identified something that had been pricking at the edge of his mind for several minutes.

"There are lights down there!"

"What?" Osnat had dozed off too, judging by the soft, bleary-eyed face she turned toward him. "Sure. No big deal. Someone's got a generator."

"But . . . aren't we still over the Line?"

She glanced at her bulky wristwatch. "Yep."

"People *live* down there?"

She cocked her head, turning her good eye on him. "What, you thought all that prime real estate was empty just because of a piddly few birth defects?"

"Who are they?"

"They're called *Ghareebeh*. Arabic for *stranger*."

"So they're Arabs?"

"Some of them. Some of them are the children of Jewish settlers who refused to leave. Some of them are just poor schmucks born in the wrong place at the wrong time."

"But how do they *live*?"

"Let's just say they don't drink the water if they can afford not to. Like I told you, those were the wild frontier days of genetic weaponry." Her voice took on a more sarcastic edge than usual. "Now we're more environmentally responsible."

"Osnat?"

"What?"

"Can you answer a question?"

"Ask it and I'll let you know."

"Who's Absalom?"

"It's a code name." She sounded as flatly objective as if she were summarizing the results of a peer-reviewed scientific study. "Most people on this side of the Line think the man behind the code name was Gavi Shehadeh."

"A Palestinian."

She wrapped her arms across her chest and huddled into the corner of her seat. "Half-Palestinian. His mother was Jewish. I don't know the whole story. Just that he was some kind of war hero back in the days when the soldiers on the Line were real soldiers, not Enderbots. And then he went into AI work. Or maybe he was already doing it before the war started, I don't know. Anyway, he was working on EMET when the Mossad tapped him for counterintelligence work. Just compsec at first, but he didn't stay stuck there for long. Didi Halevy moved him into counterintelligence. And then . . . he climbed. And not just by riding Didi's coattails. No one ever accused Gavi of not being good at his job."

"And what did he do to make Moshe hate him so much?"

"He turned traitor."

"So he's in . . . prison?"

"No." She looked like she wanted to spit. "Maybe he had a horse—that's what we call it when someone has a friend in high places to protect him. Or maybe it was just too embarrassing for the people who promoted him and trusted him. All I know is he's still alive."

Arkady digested the staggering implications of that statement. "You mean you still *execute* people?"

"Of course not. We're not the *Americans,* for God's sake. But you can always arrange a nice clean traffic accident."

They set down on a gritty landing strip hacked out of the same straggling scrub oak and juniper that Arkady could have found on almost any of the terraformed planets he'd worked on in the last decade. The pilot flew in low and fast and lifted off again before they'd even cleared the rotor wash.

Osnat hustled Arkady across the tarmac to a small half-track whose paint had been scoured so clean by wind and sand that Arkady couldn't read its markings.

"I'll have to ask you to get in the back," she said. "Sorry."

The back of the half-track was unlit and smelled strongly of biodiesel and some unclean animal that he gradually identified as human. He climbed in and found a blanket to sit on.

"Just keep your mask on," Osnat told him, "and remember this is for your own safety too. There are a lot of people around here who'd kill you on sight if they knew what you were. And they don't all work for the UN." Then she rolled the steel door down with a clatter, leaving Arkady in darkness.

The truck stopped so many times that Arkady lost count. The first few stops were at traffic intersections, he thought. Another two were at checkpoints. But though he heard the border police checking the truck over, they never opened up the back or asked him for his papers.

Other stops had no obvious purpose. The truck would simply pull over to the side of the road, gravel crackling under the wheels, and wait. Sometimes Osnat and the drivers got out, sometimes they didn't. Sometimes they waited for a minute, and sometimes they waited for what felt like hours. Once, very late into the night, he heard Osnat's voice:

"Look at that! Back a day and I already have a mosquito bite. How can you get a mosquito bite in the middle of a fucking desert in the middle of a fucking ice age?"

One of the men said something in Hebrew too riddled with slang for Arkady to make sense of.

"Not unless you pay better than the army does," Osnat said succinctly, and everybody laughed again.

Eventually Arkady dropped off to sleep, only jolting awake when the engine shuddered to a halt again. He heard voices, footsteps. Then the steel door rattled up to reveal Osnat flanked by two powerfully built young men, both gripping snub-nosed carbines in their broad farmer's hands.

"Out," Osnat said.

They hurried him across a dark parking lot toward a low shed that was the only building Arkady could see anywhere this side of the undulating desert horizon. Despite the visible weapons, Arkady had the feeling that discipline had relaxed here. What was the point of theatrics, after all, when he didn't stand a chance of crossing the waterless waste that surrounded them?

The shed turned out to be the top end of a flight of stairs that plunged down three stories without a single door opening off it in any direction. The stairs bottomed out in front of a steel fire door. The fire door opened on a cramped room with nothing in it but a ratty couch and a dilapidated workstation. Sitting on the couch, sipping Turkish coffee with his sandaled feet up on a crate of RPG rounds, sat Moshe.

He raised his glass to Arkady. "Good news. The first round of the auction kicks off the day after tomorrow at the King David Hotel."

"Auction?" Arkady asked, confused. "What auction?"

"Oh right. You slept through all that. Turns out—excuse me." Moshe rummaged in his pockets, pulled out a frayed and crumpled handkerchief, and blew his nose with loud abandon. "Turns out Israel's not interested in your genetic weapon after all. My betters have decided to put you back on the market and see if they can make back the money we blew getting you here."

"But I defected to *Israel*. I never agreed to—"

"You're right. It's not very nice of us." Moshe had been wearing his usual shorts and T-shirt when they'd arrived, but now the guards were rattling up and down the stairs bringing in supplies from the half-track, and a cold wind whistled down the stairwell. Moshe fished a sweater out from between the frayed cushions of the couch and pulled it over his head so that his next words were muffled. "You want to call the whole thing off and go home?"

"I can't go home." Arkady let all the fear and uncertainty and isolation of the past weeks well up in his voice. "It's too late for that. *They'll kill me.*"

Moshe straightened his glasses and hunched forward to stare at

Arkady. "I wish I knew whether it was your skin or your career prospects you were really worried about. The thing is, Arkady, we might be willing to help . . . but you haven't given us any reason to take much of a chance on you."

"But Arkasha's work—"

"Wake up and smell the coffee. Your so-called genetic weapon is for the public in front of the curtain. If someone's willing to pay for it, we're happy to take their money. But if you want us to commit to you, you're going to have to bring something better than cloned bugs to show-and-tell."

"Like what?"

Moshe gave him a level stare. "Like Absalom."

"And if I give you Absalom?"

"Political asylum. Guaranteed. For you and Arkasha. In Israel, not some corporate black hole where they'll pull your fingernails out just to make extra sure you're telling them everything."

"I don't know if—"

"It's a take-it-or-leave-it deal, Arkady. And it's all I got. So do yourself a favor and take the time to think about it."

"How long do I have?"

"Until the auction. Oh, and did I mention Korchow was going to be there? What's the matter, Arkady? You look a little nervous. Not so eager to see your old friends again?"

NOVALIS

Ground Truth

While the human species, as a mechanical going concern, has become organized into a social whole, the motivation that keeps it going has not undergone the same thoroughgoing reorganization, but continues to be in a great measure individualistic in type. Social ends are achieved through appeal to individual selfish instincts. Our present industrial system operates by way of a *mutually selfish bargain*, in which each party to the transaction seeks his own advantage, regardless of the gain or loss to the species as a whole. The system works tolerably well . . . at least so it seems to those accustomed to the system.

But . . . the future evolution of our race may proceed in a direction that shall ultimately ease the conflict between man and man, and between man and the world at large.

—ALFRED J. LOTKA (1924)

T HE FIRST SIGN OF TROUBLE on Novalis was the detailed volatiles inventory. Theoretically, the nonsensical DVI numbers were a purely scientific issue. In practice, however, the DVI crisis turned out to be less about science than about culture and social skills. And the ensuing flurry of questions, arguments, and recriminations made Arkady begin to worry that the Novalis survey might turn into the kind of spectacular disaster that provided fodder for mission-planning manuals.

The DVI was Aurelia's baby—Aurelia the rock doctor, not Aurelia the people doctor. Both Aurelias had become Arkady's fast friends before he'd even scrubbed away the last remnants of freezerburn. He'd worked with other Aurelias before, and the Aurelias on the Novalis mission had their geneline's typical character and attitudes. They worked hard, even by Syndicate standards. They gave short shrift to fools and hypocrites. They expected perfection from themselves and others. They were tactless, abrasive, aggressive, impatient, and generally impossible if you got in their way. They were also loyal, affectionate, and profoundly kind if you were lucky enough to have earned their friendship.

As often happened on new assignments, Arkady and the current pair of Aurelias benefited from past goodwill. Arkady had been close friends with other Aurelias and was hoping to be equally close to the new A-12 workpair. The Aurelias had fond memories of past Arkadys and were primed to make friends with their new A-11 colleagues. Arkady slipped into the ready-made friendship as comfortably as a duck hopping into a familiar pond . . . which was a good thing considering the distinctly uncomfortable nature of what should have been a much closer friendship: the one with Arkasha.

Not that he had a lot of time to think about that. Everyone was racing so frantically to get the prelanding work done before the ship fell into orbit around Novalis that they barely had time to sleep and eat, let alone worry about their social lives.

The DVI was central. The count on free volatiles would tell them whether the planet was geophysically capable of supporting plant and animal life. It was the DVI more than any other single set of numbers that the Aziz A's would be looking at when they decided whether or not to greenlight the mission and transfer the team to the landing module. And when the DVI went south, so did all hopes of making planetfall on schedule.

The crux of the problem was Bella—and, in a more general way, the very presence of Aziz and Motai constructs on what was supposed to be a purely scientific mission.

The Novalis mission was a one-shot sprint-style expedition: fast and cheap, but by definition shorthanded. Each team member had to be capable of assisting with, or if necessary taking over, mission-critical tasks outside their normal areas of specialty. Indeed, one of the main arguments for including the Aziz A's and the Motai B's instead of four more scientists was that they had the generalized practical expertise to take up the slack for the life-sciences teams.

Things hadn't quite worked out that way.

The two Aziz A's, with all the goodwill in the world, lacked the training and technical skills even to serve as lab assistants. And the Bellas . . . well, the Bellas were turning out to be complicated.

As Arkady had predicted, they were quite easy to tell apart despite their uncanny physical resemblance. By the second day out of cold sleep, Arkady had privately dubbed them "Shy Bella" and "Bossy Bella." Shy Bella barely spoke unless spoken to, and when she did screw up the courage to get a few words out you had to strain to hear them. Arkasha and Laid-back Ahmed both claimed she had a wicked sense of humor, but they were the only two crewmembers besides her pairmate that she was comfortable enough to joke with. And frankly Arkady wasn't sure how comfortable she was with her pairmate.

By Syndicate standards, Bella's diffidence verged on social deviance. Arkady had wondered how a construct with such a personality fault had made it through the MotaiSyndicate's famously stringent culls . . . until he saw her at work in the orbsilk garden. At that point the mystery of why she'd been spared culling gave way to the mystery of why such a supremely gifted silk thrower had been exiled to the social backwater of a long-term survey mission. No matter. Whatever the reason, at least on this trip they wouldn't have to worry about defective solar sails or hab ring seal blowouts.

Bella's pairmate, on the other hand, could have used a healthy dose of shyness. Bossy Bella was that rare thing in Syndicate society, and space settlements generally: a truly rude person. Watching her in action, Arkady could only conclude that socialization in MotaiSyndicate crèches involved a lot fewer lectures about consideration, politeness, and Lotka-Wilsonist ideals, and a lot more of the aggressive jockeying for social dominance that was supposed to have vanished with the abolition of class oppression and private genetic property. He got the distinct impression that Bossy Bella was used to reigning over her fellow Motai B's from the top of some primitive pecking order and was now working out just how far she could push her bullying in a group of science-tracked A's who weren't used to taking orders or deferring to anyone.

So far Bella's pushing had worked pretty well. By-the-Book Ahmed liked her. Laid-back Ahmed tolerated her. The Rostov and Banerjee A's were either blissfully blind to social nuance or too busy to notice.

But now Bella had let her social jockeying bleed into Aurelia's DVI. And Aurelia, being an Aurelia, was out for blood.

Technically, what modern Syndicate ecophysicists did wasn't terraforming at all. Certainly it had little to do with the sledgehammer-style "planetary engineering" that early human terraformers had attempted when they hurled the first unmanned seed probes out of their solar system.

Most Evacuation-era terraforming starts had gone belly-up, leaving nothing behind but impact-scarred wreckage interesting only to historians. But where luck and skill had been with the original terraformers, their remote seeders had created impact craters in which the precious free volatiles collected and life could eventually thrive. The original terraformers had called these chains of isolated island ecosystems "oases." Syndicate terraformers, none of whom had ever seen Earth's oases, just called them "potholes."

The pothole worlds (Gilead had been one when the first generation ship fell into orbit around it) were not terraformed but merely potentially terraformable. Each pothole evolved as its own separate planet, separated from its neighbors by sterile highlands lashed by lethal dust storms and solar radiation. Most of them flared into brief unstable life, then crashed. As Arkady's first biogeography teacher had pointed out, knowing that isolated population fluctuations took the form of undamped oscillations around a stable equilibrium was small consolation if a downward oscillation dropped the population of a critical organism below zero. But some potholes survived. And a few, a very few of them were still there when the first-generation ships arrived: the scattered seeds of viable planet-spanning biospheres.

All but a handful of human colonies failed anyway, even where they were lucky enough to land on pothole worlds. The number of ways colonists had found to choke, drown, starve, or poison themselves was awe-inspiring. In most cases, however, the ultimate cause of death was startlingly basic: failure to adapt.

Dead colonies—including the genetically nonviable colonies of walking ghosts that the Treaty euphemistically called "bare branches"— died for one of two reasons. Either they refused to retool Earth-born customs and expectations to fit the unforgiving fragility of synthetic biospheres, or they refused to accept the invasive genetic engineering humans needed in order to survive anywhere but on their native planet. Colonies that survived only did so by facing up to the cold equations of life after Earth's ecological collapse. They gave up the dream of building a second Earth. Or they gave up the dream of staying human. Or they died.

The Syndicates had given up on both those dreams. And in doing so, they had earned the privilege of working miracles. Which meant that the new worlds, the worlds out in the Deep beyond the treaty lines, were theirs for the taking.

Novalis was a typical Syndicate terraforming mission. It unfolded in four phases, only the last of which involved launching a manned driveship toward the target planet. Or rather, the presumed planet. For when the first remote probe launched, its target wasn't a planet at all but merely a suggestive infrared excess in the spectrometry of a distant star.

The first probe swooped around Novalis on its subluminal flyby and found planets, two of them in orbits that were at least theoretically compatible with the presence of liquid water.

A second probe arrived eight months later, its launch window carefully scheduled to give the RostovSyndicate ecophysicists time to chew on the first round of raw data. In a maneuver that was always touch-and-go in terms of fuel conservation, it fired its onboard thrusters in order to translate into the plane of the most promising satellite: a more or less Earth-sized planet, blessed with a more or less Moon-sized moon that had the geophysicists whispering hopeful little phrases like "satellite stabilization" and "mild Milankovitch cycles."

Translation was successful. The flyby happened—a spectacular display of interstellar sharpshooting at a mere seventy thousand kilometers above the target planet's cloud-shrouded surface. The probe dropped seven automated landers before it hooked around Novalis's yellow sun and shot off on its final voyage into the unsounded Deep.

Four of the landers vanished without transmitting any data at all.

The fifth lander made it most of the way down before succumbing to a damaged heat shield segment, and it sent back infrared and microwave soundings of an ocean (an ocean!), whose scatterometry produced a marine wind field map that Banerjee's chief oceanographer pronounced promisingly reminiscent of Earth's southern oscillation.

The sixth lander reached the surface and sent back a wealth of intriguing and frustratingly inconclusive readings before it drove over a cliff, to the spluttering humiliation of its design team, and shattered its solar collector.

The seventh lander caught an ant.

An ant whose DNA, when crushed and sequenced and cross-checked and cataloged, proved her to be the many thousandth great-granddaughter of a cloned ponerine queen boosted into space in 2031 on one of the European Space Authority's venerable *Ariane* rockets and still covered by a perpetual, though obviously unenforceable, patent originally held by a Delaware corporation with the unlikely name of Monsanto.

With the discovery of one humble ant, all hell broke loose in the skies over Gilead. Scientific teams zipped back and forth from Syndicate to Syndicate. Aziz and Banerjee planners hammered out launch windows and crew and cargo manifests. The infamous "annoyance questionnaires" began to circulate among potential payload and mission specialists, a sure sign that not only was a long-range mission being planned, but that it would be a sprint mission: a desperate direct throw of the bare minimum of personnel and equipment needed to stake a claim to the target planet. Good luck, happy sailing . . . and we'll deliver logistical support if you survive long enough to need it.

A third unmanned probe was dispatched, this one sleek, heavy, expensive, and freighted with a weight of scientific equipment worth the gross annual product of some of the smaller Syndicates. Two years behind the third probe—these things take time, after all—RostovSyndicate launched the ship whose arboretum they had just flown through at a speed that precisely measured the technical advances in interstellar propulsion made in the six years that separated the two ships' launch dates.

And now, in a matter of days, the survey team would swing into orbit around Novalis . . . and begin the real work for which each of them had been training ever since they'd opted for the sciences track at sixteen and tested into geophysics, genetics, engineering, astrophysics, oceanography, zoology, genetics, molecular biology complex systems study, chaotic systems control, and all the other manifold specializations that the science-cum-art of terraforming demanded.

Arkady was at once awed and inspired by the sheer weight of history that lay behind each step of a preterraforming survey. Every reading, every sounding, every measurement they would use to establish the baseline condition of Novalis's biosphere represented the life's work of generations of engineers and scientists before them. Even so simple a task as taking the temperature of the ocean's surface from orbit embodied a trajectory of technological evolution that began with the first primitive infrared sounding devices NASA engineers invented back in the twentieth century to explain the subtle color shifts that entranced the first astronauts to see Earth's oceans from space.

Each member of the survey team—Arkady with his ants, Aurelia with her exacting measurements of the planet's geophysical processes, Arkasha with his DNA samples—was part of an endless cycle of trial and error and recalibration that spanned two sentient species, several dozen planets, and a millennium of scientific investigation. And at the end of all their work lay the same thing their forebears had faced, a term coined by the first geophysicists on Earth but still a fertile part of the terraformer's working vocabulary all these centuries later:

Ground truth.

Ground truth was the final judge from whose verdict there was no appeal. Ground truth was what you found when you finished your measurements and plans and preparations and took your heart in your hands and landed on your target planet. Ground truth was what you found when you sampled the soil, when you physically dropped a sounder into the ocean, when you walked through the forest or grassland or tundra you had surveyed from orbit and dissected and sequenced the specimens you collected there.

And this was the second source of Arkady's endless fascination with his chosen field. In a very real sense every expedition to a new planet retraveled in miniature the long evolution of the discipline that humans called terraforming and Syndicate scientists called ecophysics. Syndicate survey teams might be armed with technical and theoretical tools that would have appeared near-magical to pre-Evacuation humans; but each new planet, even if every living thing on it was earthly in origin, presented an entirely new set of experimental parameters. Those parameters inevitably produced results that confirmed prior theory . . . and results that pointed out the limitations of trying to generalize about the largest complex nonlinear dynamic system anyone had yet encountered based on a sample size of one. Every unsurveyed planet was, quite literally, a new world. And nothing in all the wide universe said that the next planet wouldn't blow the lid off every prior theory.

Which was exactly—though it was hard for Arkady to bring himself to believe such a thing could be happening—what Bella's DVI numbers would do.

If they were real.

"You want her to learn on the *job*?" Aurelia was asking incredulously when Arkady walked into the hastily called formal consult over what the Ahmeds were calling the DVI situation. "She was supposed to know her job before we launched. People who can't do a simple job right belong on a euth ward, not on a deep-space survey mission!"

"I *did* do the job right the first time!" Bossy Bella protested. Bella had been assigned, after much covert maneuvering and insistence that she was too busy (she wasn't, and wouldn't be until it was time to establish the food cycle systems in the dirtside habitat module), to help Aurelia with data collection for the all-important DVI. The two of them had already developed a cordial dislike for each other . . . and when something went wrong, the inevitable happened.

"So now you know my job better than I do?" Aurelia asked coldly.

"My numbers are right," Bella insisted.

Her sib stirred beside her. "Perhaps . . ."

"Perhaps nothing! If you'd been helping me instead of wasting time staring into space, we wouldn't *be* in this mess!"

Shy Bella bowed her head submissively, but judging from the dark shadows under her eyes Arkady seriously doubted she'd been slacking. In fact, she'd lost several kilos since they came out of cryo, and she and her sib were now worrisomely easy to tell apart even before they opened their pretty mouths.

Someone jogged his elbow: the other Aurelia. She was worried about her sib, and her usually confident face showed it. "What does Arkasha think about the numbers?" she asked Arkady in a nervous whisper.

He cast a furtive glance at Arkasha, who was sitting at the other end of the consult table, his shoulders turned away just enough to isolate himself from the rest of the group, flicking through a sheaf of densely inked printouts.

"How should I know?" he said bitterly. "I haven't exchanged twenty words with him since we woke up. I couldn't have seen less of him if he'd been ducking out of airlocks to avoid me."

"I've been around a while," Bossy Bella was saying when Arkady turned back to the general conversation. She'd been detanked two years before her pairmate and three years before the Ahmeds, Arkadys, and Aurelias. In her place, Arkady would have been embarrassed about being dropped behind his age group, but Bella predictably treated the age difference as a reason to pull rank on the rest of the crew. "I was on the Kuretz-12 survey while you all were still waiting for your year nineteen cull. And no one has ever found any problems with the work *I* do—"

"I, I, I, I, I!" Aurelia burst out, exasperated. "If you thought a little less about your precious self and a little more about *our* job out here—"

"How dare you accuse me of—"

"No one's accusing you of anything," Laid-back Ahmed said soothingly.

But Aurelia wasn't willing to let it slide. And if you put half the energy into working that you put into slinging malicious gossip—"

"I refuse to allow this consult to degenerate into personal attacks," By-the-Book Ahmed said, predictably rising to Bella's defense. "If you don't have the leadership skills to manage the people under you—"

"That's humanist crap!" Aurelia burst out. "I don't need leadership skills! I'm not a goddamn sheepdog! And it's not my Part in life to chase down people who won't put in an honest day's work unless they're nagged and nattered at!"

"Listen," Arkady began, knowing from late-night drinking sessions that once Aurelia started in on her ideological objections to caste-based genelines things could only go downhill. Not that he disagreed with Aurelia on either count. Ever since that first night she'd let her sib do her dishes, Bossy Bella had shown a formidable talent for being nowhere in sight whenever there was work to do. And as to the caste nonsense . . . well, just look at the current situation.

His interruption did no good, though; Aurelia had gotten the bit firmly between her teeth.

"And speaking of nagging and nattering," she went on, "I've about goddamn well had it with the so-called shipboard duty schedule. Are we grown-ups or crèchelings?"

"Collective job lists are inefficient," By-the-Book Ahmed said in his usual categorical tones.

"Not as inefficient as pissing people off by treating them like galley slaves instead of pre-citizens!"

"Shipboard duty rosters *work*," Ahmed insisted. "It's proven."

"By AzizSyndicate studies!" Aurelia said contemptuously. "Studies done on B's and C's. Well, we're not B's and C's, in case you hadn't noticed. And if your so-called leadership skills are limited to bossing around worker drones sociogenetically programmed to swallow your counterrevolutionary humanist bullshit—"

"Look," Laid-back Ahmed said in his usual levelheaded tone. "Let's just focus on the problem at hand. We can't solve everything today. And none of the rest matters worth a lick if we can't get to the bottom of the DVI situation."

"Why not just redo the DVI readings and make a fresh start on the problem?" Arkasha said. It was the first time he'd opened his mouth since the consult started.

There was a momentary silence while everyone considered his

proposal. Arkasha had acquired an unofficial and nebulous authority over the past week as his crewmates—one by one, and without ever admitting they'd done it—downloaded his public dossier. The long string of publications, citations, and discoveries attached to the dossier had subtly shifted not only their views on Arkasha but their assumptions about the entire mission. Arkasha was the closest thing the anti-individualist culture of the Syndicates had to an academic superstar: one of the best theoretical geneticists of his generation in a society where genetics was the undisputed top of the scientific food chain. Naturally his articles were published under his geneline name. But you only had to see that all-important first footnote to understand how many articles he'd written, and how influential his work had been on other geneticists. Arkasha's presence on the mission signaled the magnitude of what the joint steering committee expected them to find on Novalis. And without doing or saying anything to demand the position—in fact he barely even talked to anyone except poor little Shy Bella, who was the farthest thing imaginable from a social power broker—Arkasha had become the de facto lead scientist on the survey.

Bossy Bella, however, was conspicuously uninterested in Arkasha's academic qualifications. She and Arkasha stared at each other, locked in a private battle of wills. "If you've got something to say," she told him, "why don't you have the guts to say it? Or would you rather come creeping around my quarters again making your nasty insinuations?"

"There's no need to jump down his throat!" Aurelia snapped, interrupting whatever had been going on between Arkasha and Bella and foreclosing any chance at finding out what Arkasha's "nasty insinuations" had been. Arkady smothered a sigh. He dearly loved Aurelias in general, and these Aurelias in particular . . . but their "help" in a consult was a burden he wouldn't wish on his worst enemy.

"Don't browbeat me!" Bella cried, her attention momentarily deflected from Arkasha.

"*Browbeat* her?" Aurelia's sib muttered for Arkady's ears only. "I wish we could horsewhip her."

"Come on, people." Laid-back Ahmed again. "Let's focus on solutions, not fault finding."

Arkady took a deep breath and plunged in. "Maybe the best solution really is just to check the numbers again. I'll redo the DVI if Bella doesn't have time. It's no problem. Honestly."

Laid-back Ahmed gave him an eloquently grateful look. The idea that doing a little extra work yourself was better than letting the social gears get squeaky was one of the many things Arkady and the big Aziz A had already discovered they saw eye to eye on.

"I don't need you looking over my shoulder for mistakes," Bella snapped at Arkady. She cast a venomous look toward Arkasha's end of the table. "And don't think I don't know who put you up to this!"

"No one put me up to anything," Arkady said, wondering what Arkasha could possibly have said to provoke such animosity. "I just meant that I have a little extra time and if you're too busy to be able to go over the numbers again, I could . . . uh, help you." Arkady did his best to make the offer sound supportive and unthreatening. Inside, however, he was having counterrevolutionary thoughts about whether some of those bad old repressive human political systems had found a way to make sure the decent hardworking people didn't get the short end of the stick . . . and the bullies, prima donnas, and manipulators didn't rise to the top like scum on milk.

Bella's sib leaned over to whisper something in her ear. Whatever it was Bella didn't like it much.

"Why are you doing this to me?" she cried. "Why are you turning against me?"

"I'm not. I just—"

"It's not fair! Why isn't anyone asking if it's Aurelia's analysis and not my readings that are wrong? Why are you all so ready to believe her and turn against me? Because she's an A and I'm a B, that's why!"

"Because she knows her job and you don't, you moron," Aurelia's sib muttered—thankfully too softly for anyone but Arkady to hear.

"She has a point," By-the-Book Ahmed said. "Why *aren't* we considering the possibility that the numbers are good and the, uh . . . what did you call it just now, Arkady? . . . the ground truth is different than what we thought it would be?"

"Because . . ." Aurelia said, and trailed off helplessly.

Arkady and every other science track A sitting around the table knew what that "because" stood for. Because the numbers Bella had come up with were flat-out impossible. Because we didn't come all the way out here to run a basic ecophysics course. Because we all have too much work to do to waste our collective time explaining to Bella why if she knew her ass from her elbow she'd know her numbers were wrong.

But of course the Ahmeds knew even less about terraforming than Bella did. All they knew was that they had a bunch of temperamental techs and scientists at each other's throats. And in the absence of technical knowledge, they could only fall back on their knowledge of their fellow crewmates. By-the-Book Ahmed sided with Bella because she flattered and deferred to him and was the only crewmember who didn't display "lack of motivation" by bridling under his beloved shipboard duty roster. Laid-back Ahmed followed his basic philosophy—fair in most disputes but disastrous in this case—of trying to get the combatants to split the difference and compromise.

"I agree," Laid-back Ahmed said. "I mean there's no reason not to consider every possibility, is there?"

The science track A's greeted this with stunned silence. One of the Aurelias coughed. Arkasha fidgeted.

"The thing is," one of the Banerjees said cautiously, "that if these numbers were right, it would mean we were looking at a planet that already had large contiguous regions of its surface in a state of biogeological climax."

Both Ahmeds looked blank. Could they really have so little insight into what the survey and terraforming team was supposed to be doing once they hit planet surface? If so, they were going to be deadweight as soon as the team made planetfall. Worse than deadweight if they began meddling in survey decisions they didn't understand. Something had gone very wrong in the mission preplanning, Arkady realized. And he felt a bitter little seed of resentment over the planning failures lodge somewhere close to his heart.

"So what you're saying is that Bella's numbers are better than we thought they'd be," By-the-Book Ahmed said. "What's wrong with that?"

"It's not a question of better or worse," the other Banerjee began.

"Then what *is* it a question of? Why can't we get straightforward answers out of you people?"

"Because we don't have them. This isn't calculating a launch window or the bearing strength of an I-beam. There's no simple answer."

"Then how do you know Bella's wrong?"

"Because . . ."

"I don't think you're hearing us," Aurelia said. "This planet shouldn't be here."

"Then where should it be?" Laid-back Ahmed asked blandly.

"I meant—" Aurelia began. And then she saw the joke. "Oh for God's sake, Ahmed, be serious!"

"I am serious. I just think we're getting a little overheated. No one's trying to put you on the hot seat. Just give us the general picture in laymen's terms."

But of course Rostov A's were not used to dealing with people who needed to be given the general picture in laymen's terms . . . and for the first time in his life Arkady was beginning to see that in the wrong circumstances the very strength of the Rostov genelines might be a liability.

"For instance," Laid-back Ahmed said, "how do these numbers compare to Gilead?"

"Basically," Arkady said, "they don't."

"So it's further along than Gilead? Is *that* impossible?"

"No . . . um . . . Gilead's not a useful comparison."

"Why not?"

"Because . . . well . . . Gilead gives you large contiguous areas of 'terraformed' surface. But they're all being artificially held away from ecological climax in order to keep boosting the volatiles. That gives you a very recognizable volatiles profile, especially in the free nitrogen. Gilead is a textbook-perfect best-scenario case of terraforming on the numbers. But the numbers Bella's getting for Novalis aren't that at all. They're . . . well, they're nonsense. There *are* no comps for those numbers."

Something moved in Arkady's peripheral vision.

Arkasha.

He was sliding his thick stack of printouts across the table toward the Ahmeds.

"Yes, there are," he said. "Right here."

By-the-Book Ahmed grabbed the printouts and squinted at them. "Is this another one of your practical jokes?" he asked accusingly. He and Arkasha had already come dangerously close to locking horns twice—both times over what By-the-Book Ahmed referred to as Arkasha's "too smart to follow the rules" attitude.

Arkasha's only answer to Ahmed's question was a dismissive shrug.

Arkady craned his neck to read the heading on the printed page across the table. When he finally managed to decipher it, he decided that Ahmed was right. It *must* be a joke. It said:

EUROPEAN SPACE AGENCY WHITE PAPER
Results of DISTRIBUTED VOLATILES INVENTORY performed for
the Climate Change Baseline Project, authorized pursuant to
Sec. 17 of the Beijing Addendum to the Kyoto Accords,
May 15—April 3, 2017

"All Bella's numbers are fluctuating within two points of this DVI," Arkasha said flatly.

"Could, uh, this be a coincidence?" Laid-back Ahmed asked in a hollow tone that made Arkady quite sure he had understood what Arkasha was leaving unsaid.

"Not unless Novalis actually *is* Earth, complete with a two-hundred-year-old planet-spanning fossil-fuels economy and some serious CFC contamination."

"I don't have to take this!" Bella exclaimed, standing up.

"Sit *down*!" Laid-back Ahmed said in a tone that knocked Bella's knees out from under her.

Don't say it, Arkady pleaded with his sib. *Just let the Ahmeds handle it. She's not the kind of person you want to make into your enemy.*

But Arkasha wasn't going to let it go. He was going to try to be nice. And he was going to do it in a way that only deepened Bella's humiliation.

"I don't want to cast blame," he said, keeping his dark eyes carefully fixed on the table. "This is a failure at the steering committee level, not the individual level. A great deal of early training in the sciences involves learning not to panic when your numbers look wrong. And the numbers often look wrong in complex systems work. Throwing someone with a purely technical background into this kind of situation without real supervision more or less guarantees panic. And someone without a really solid grasp of ecophysics might well look at the relatively advanced flora and fauna the landers picked up on Novalis and make the mistaken assumption that a planet so far along in the ecopoietic curve might look the same on the numbers as Earth did when it was on its way down."

Arkasha had spoken deliberately, so that everyone around the table had time to understand what he was accusing Bella of: cribbing the numbers from the Earth DVI when her own readings didn't look right.

Twelve pairs of eyes shifted furtively toward Bella, who sat staring at her hands and breathing hard.

Arkasha's eyes flicked once toward Bella, then dropped away. "There's no shame in not being perfect. As long as you're honest. A lot of people's lives could depend on our honesty. Starting with our own. We need to redo the DVI. We can do it with no questions asked. I think that's the way we should do it. But it would be extremely helpful to have your notes of the original readings."

No one spoke for a long moment. The two Banerjees both stared resolutely out the nearest viewport. By-the-Book Ahmed was fuming, while his sib had no readable expression at all on his handsome features. Arkady looked sideways just in time to see Aurelia glance back and forth significantly between him and Arkasha and raise an eyebrow at her own sib.

"Bella?" Laid-back Ahmed said. "Can we have your notes? Please?"

"I gave them to you!" she snapped. And pointed to the neat printout of her final measurements she had circulated at the beginning of the consult.

But those weren't notes. Even the Aziz A's knew enough to understand that.

Ahmed and Arkasha looked at each other, obviously reaching some kind of understanding.

"Okay," Ahmed said, "I see the problem. If there was a problem, which I'm not saying there was. And I propose that we just, uh, decide how to handle the DVI on a forward-going basis." Ahmed looked around the table but no one contested his analysis. "Any thoughts? Anyone?"

Everyone in the room knew what was supposed to happen next. They'd spent half their lives sitting around tables or in childhood crèche circles, mastering the slow, courtly, circular procedures of consensus decisionmaking. They all knew that the script called for a series of tentative summings up; carefully structured and only vaguely purposeful statements that would begin with self-effacing phrases like "If I understand what's been said so far," or "I'm hearing from Bella that . . ." or "We might consider investigating the possibility of . . ." and would allow the group to arrive at a decision without actually forcing any single person openly to declare his or her positions and allegiances.

But once again Arkasha wasn't willing to follow the script.

"I say we land," he announced, tossing the naked proposal out like a duelist flinging his glove at an opponent's feet. "Enough probes and flybys and extrapolations. We need a good dose of ground truth. And trust me, if the question is whether or not Bella's DVI numbers are right, we'll know that the minute we open the airlock."

"Unacceptable," By-the-Book Ahmed snapped. Why did he always have to sound as if he were lecturing children when he was talking to the mission specialists? "Too much risk involved."

"Too much risk to the mission?" Arkasha retorted, "or too much risk that you can't cover your ass if things go wrong?"

"I'm responsible for the safety of this ship and crew," Ahmed said sententiously. "I'm not willing to put us down on a planet *you* can't even give me reliable numbers on."

Arkasha opened his mouth and shut it again. He and the other Rostovs had all bridled under Ahmed's heavy-handed assertions of authority ever since the mission started. But what could they do, really? The Ahmeds were the ship's pilots. There might be arguments once they were all planetside about relative authority, but as long as they were in space they were essentially captives.

"I see Arkasha's point though," Laid-back Ahmed said, tactfully directing his comment as much to his sib as to Arkasha. "Perhaps we can find a middle ground? What if we agree to spend a predetermined amount of time check—uh, redoing the DVI, and then meet again and make a firm decision on how to proceed? That'll give us a deadline for one thing, so the DVI doesn't turn into too much of a time sink."

Arkasha shrugged—but this time the movement had none of the dismissive quality with which he'd mocked By-the-Book Ahmed before.

"It's just a question of minimizing the uncertainties, really. Does that make sense to everyone?"

Nods all around the table.

"Would a week be enough time to minimize the uncertainties? What do you all think? I know it's a tight schedule for some of you, but does a week work for everyone?"

It seemed a week did work for everyone.

"Arkady, would you work with Arkasha and Aurelia to put together a plan of attack?"

"Absolutely." Arkady accepted for all three of them before Arkasha or Aurelia could stir up any more trouble.

"Is tomorrow evening too soon for us to look over your plan together? No? Good. I'll look to go over it with you tomorrow evening.

And then I'll go around and get feedback from the individual teams before we finalize the schedule."

It was neatly done, Arkady realized, with a newfound admiration for the big Aziz A. A potential conflict had been avoided. Everyone's opinion had been solicited, but in a way that gave no one the chance to complain about his or her colleagues or foment bad feeling. The main dissenter had been co-opted by being put in charge of administering the very decision that had been taken over his head. Arkady had been inserted into the vendetta between Arkasha and Bella so that there was no reason for the two of them to have to deal with each other until they cooled off a bit. And all potential for conflict had been siphoned off into "individual consultations" in which Ahmed's considerable charm could be deployed to head off any potential acrimony.

But underneath the neat managerial tricks, Arkady had the sense that he'd just watched a tectonic realignment of continents. Bella, who had been jockeying with the equally assertive Aurelias for social dominance, had been publicly shamed. By-the-Book Ahmed had broken fast out of the gate, then fallen behind in the backstretch. Laid-back Ahmed, despite his easygoing affability, had emerged as the real leader of the expedition. And though he clearly neither wanted nor sought the role, Arkasha had replaced By-the-Book Ahmed as the unacknowledged second-in-command.

As the rest of the team stretched and shuffled their papers and began getting back to the real business of the day, Arkady glanced at Bella. She was still in her chair, sitting up quite straight, with her hands resting in her lap and her beautiful face set into a mask of nobly wounded dignity. But her violet eyes were fixed on Arkasha as if he were the only other person in the room. And one look at their expression left no doubt in Arkady's mind that his sib had just earned an implacable enemy.

Night cycle.

No moon lit the sky. Novalis loomed overhead, visible only as a darker blackness in the surrounding void.

A brush fire raged across the invisible curve of the northern continent's central grasslands. On the ground the killing fields must cover thousands of kilometers, but from here the fire was just a pinprick in the surrounding blackness: a reminder that life itself was fire, and that all life devoured other life just as surely as the flames licking across Novalis's gravid belly.

Arkady's feelings toward the planet had changed subtly over the last few days. His impatient excitement had given way to an apprehension bordering on fear. Eve of battle nerves, he told himself, brought to an uncomfortably high pitch by that distasteful nonsense over the DVI numbers. But a voice inside him whispered that he could die down there, and if he died Novalis would eat his flesh and mulch his bones, and not one molecule of the water or volatiles or trace metals he was made of would ever go home to RostovSyndicate. He stared up at the planet, desperately homesick, and asked himself if he was strong enough to face *that* ground truth. The only answer was the swirl and flicker of the flames.

He shuddered and turned back into the bright cocoon of the ship. The bridge seemed safe and familiar, a last glimpse of home before the long fall into the gravity well. Status chimes rang soothingly. In the kitchen alcove off the navigator's station the hum of the refrigerator competed with the splutter of the coffeemaker.

Arkady floated over to the table, feeling liquefied with exhaustion and privately cursing whoever had drunk all the coffee and left the machine empty. He watched the drops of coffee seep into the spherical carafe and wander around until they finally bumped into the container's viruglass shell and stuck there like caffeinated amoebas. Which he supposed made him what? A decaffeinated amoeba? That sounded about right.

The main bridge door cycled open.

"Oh, good," the newcomer said. "Coffee's on."

Bella. But which Bella? He squinted at her and decided with a distinct lowering of spirits that it was Bossy Bella.

"What a week!" She sighed, settling next to Arkady in a flowing rustle of orbsilk. Arkady repressed the urge to move away from her. When the coffee finally spluttered to the end of its cycle he pushed off with alacrity. "Can I get you some?"

"Thanks," she said. She made no effort to track down milk or sugar.

"Just look at that sink," she said. "What a mess! But of course everyone's too busy and important to do the dishes around here."

This was pretty rich considering that Bella was undoubtedly the least busy person on board. Which gave her plenty of time to poke her sharp little nose into other people's private lives, Arkady thought, and then repressed the thought as petty.

"Don't you agree with me?" she asked.

"Sure," he said, settling cravenly for the path of least resistance.

"I blame the Ahmeds," she continued. "We would never have allowed things to go this far in *my* home crèche. They're too soft, too inexperienced—"

"Oh, I don't know about that."

"*I* do. I may not be an A, but I do know enough to see when things need to be put back on track. A little constructive criticism—"

"I hardly think it's worth calling a group critique session over a few dirty dishes, Bella."

"Well . . . no . . . of course not. But it's the *idea,* you understand."

Arkady gave the Motai B a sideways glance, wondering once more what it would do to a person to grow up under MotaiSyndicate's harsh normalization regimes. He tried to count up the crèchemates from his own year—very few of them, it had to be said in Rostov's defense—who had mysteriously vanished after fifth- and eighth-year norm testing. It wasn't easy. The docents firmly discouraged any discussion of culled crèchemates. And as always when you tried to separate the individual from the geneline, names became cumbersome. But he remembered his feelings about culled crèchemates with painful clarity. Fear. Insecurity. Gratitude to the docents who had approved and promoted and protected him. The panicky need to believe that the vanished children were deviants, and that he could avoid their fate if he just worked a little harder at being normal and well-adjusted. And, worst of all, the first dark suspicion that while most people soon learned to hate the suffering that came with culls and critique sessions, others learned that enforcing "normality" could be a source of pleasure and power.

He thought he knew which kind of person he was. And he was starting to get a pretty good idea which kind Bella was.

Meanwhile she was watching him, her beautiful features alert and hungry-looking. "I've noticed that your sib and my sib seem to be pretty friendly with each other," she said.

Arkady had noticed too. He hadn't thought much of it. After all, he spent nearly all his free time with the two Aurelias. There was nothing strange about it. The opposite sex was refreshingly . . . well, opposite. And you could be friendly to them without worrying about the awkward misunderstandings or sexual tensions that complicated relationships between crèchemates.

"So how are you and Arkasha getting along?" Bella asked.

"I have nothing to complain about," Arkady said evasively.

"That's not exactly ringing praise."

"Well what do you want me to say? He's smart . . . hardworking . . . uh, clean . . ."

They stared at each other. Arkady could feel a furious blush spreading across his face.

"Are you sleeping together yet?"

"I . . . uh . . ."

"I thought not."

"Not everyone jumps into bed with his pairmate the first week of an assignment," Arkady protested—and then could have kicked himself for the implicit admission. "He's not deviant, if that's what you're implying."

Bella smiled like a cat who'd just made a kill. Why hadn't Arkady noticed that sleek, predatory complacency before?

"Deviant!" she said in a voice that was patently insincere yet somehow impossible to challenge. "I only meant that his behavior seems a bit selfish. But you're his pairmate after all. If you've started wondering . . . and now that you mention it, he did make that odd joke the first night. And, really, the way he looks at my sib sometimes . . . don't tell me you haven't seen it?"

Arkady hadn't seen it. Arkady didn't want to see it. Though of course now that Bella had put it into his head, he *would* see it. That was the problem with this kind of talk. Once someone had put the revolting idea in your mind, nothing could get it out. And you could never look at the person again without that little niggling blister of doubt rubbing at you.

In fact, Arkady did manage to put Bella's insinuations aside for a few days, not so much through force of will but because the mission itself hit a long-overdue patch of smooth running.

The new DVI numbers were low enough to make sense but still high enough to reassure the Ahmeds. And from the moment the landing was greenlighted, the mission seemed to be running on rails. Site selection and GPS seeding went as smoothly as the most elementary training sim. Even the choice of a landing site went off with only nominal conflict. Arkasha argued for the southern tip of the larger continent, which jutted conveniently toward the equator. The Ahmeds, on the other hand, wanted to land in the temperate zone along the eastern flank of the continent. Arkasha stated his case: higher rates of evapotranspiration would translate into higher species richness, making their field time more efficient; they had a far better baseline for tropical ecosystems than for temperate ones, and so forth. But as Arkady had predicted, Arkasha had resolutely avoided doing anything since the last consult either to patch things up with Bella and By-the-Book Ahmed or cement his alliances with the other science track A's. So while Arkady and (to everyone's surprise) Shy Bella supported Arkasha's preferred site, the rest of the team rapidly reached a consensus for the Ahmeds' chosen site. To Arkady's surprise, Arkasha backed down without a confrontation—and they settled on a likely-looking base camp site in the coastal flatlands of the main continent.

Ahmed was the first to the door when they made planetfall. He stepped up to the porthole and peered through the viruglass, gauzy white with decades of impact scratches—and caught his breath sharply enough to send a stab of fear coursing through Arkady's body.

"What is it?" someone asked.

"Come see."

The team bunched together in the airlock, staring up at the distant sky like miners peering out of the depths of a pit shaft. The Ahmeds had set the lander down in a broad open area that Arkady would have called a pasture had Novalis possessed any grazing animals, or any mammals at all for that matter. There was a river not far off, and it might have been visible from the landing site during what passed as winter on Novalis. At the moment, however, the line of sight extended for about sixty meters downhill and ended abruptly in a tangled, spiky, completely solid wall of greenery.

Arkady and the rest of the survey team stood in staring amazement. These were not the straggling scrub oak and cottonwoods of the Periphery's terraformed planets, including Gilead. The trees—if you could call such giants trees—towered overhead for fifteen, twenty, forty meters. Even on a first, casual inspection Arkady counted some two dozen different species. He couldn't begin to imagine the intricate network of interlocking water, air, and chlorophyll cycles it must take to maintain this world-girdling symphony of greenery.

Shy Bella was the first one to get her breath back and summon up words when they saw what was waiting for them outside the airlock.

"What *is* that?" she whispered.

Arkady craned his neck backwards, feeling like he was looking up out of a well, his ears full of a roaring like the sound of waves beating on a rocky shore.

"I think it's a forest."

THE ALMOST INFINITE DISTANCE
BETWEEN A CAUSE AND
ITS EFFECT

In war, more than any other subject, we must begin by looking at
the nature of the whole . . . and . . . the vast, almost infinite
distance there can be between a cause and its effect.

—CLAUSEWITZ (1780–1831)

THE REAL PROBLEM WITH CHESS, in Cohen's opinion, was that the options for any given world state were so limited. What fun was it, after all, to intuit your way through a game that you could beat into submission by brute processing power?

Not that chess lacked historical and aesthetic interest. In fact, he was currently running a simulation of the Deep Blue–Kasparov match—worthwhile if only for the opportunity to admire the angels-on-pinheads acrobatics of the old-time code jockeys. But Cohen had been built with a bigger game in mind.

Life, if you wanted to call it that.

And every ant algorithm and Kohonen net in his far-flung systems was telling him that this moment—here under the tall sky of Earth, sitting in an outdoor café on the treacherous edge of the International Zone, waiting for a man who was going on forty-two minutes late by Cohen's favorite, albeit hopelessly inaccurate, wristwatch—was one of life's dangerous moves.

They'd waited while dawn burnished the Dome of the Rock and pressed her ice-age-cold fingers into the crooked squares and narrow alleys of the Old City. By the time the first real sun of the morning set the dust motes dancing over their table, early-rising Hasidim were returning from the Wailing Wall and the automated *muezzin* was wafting the call to prayer through the Temple Mount's loudspeakers, reminding the faithful that there was no god but God and prayer was sweeter than sleep.

The streets swelled with a rising tide of early-morning commuters. Metal shutters rattled up on shop fronts. Shopkeepers called to each other in the archaic, Arabic-inflected Hebrew of the Jerusalemites.

"It's so quiet," Li said.

Cohen didn't have to ask what she meant. To posthuman ears, the morning cacophony was overwhelmed by the absolute silence where all the accompanying streamspace chatter of a busy commercial street should have been.

Cohen threw out a hand to encompass the whole crooked, claustrophobic tumble of the Old City. "Behold the Great Unwired, brought to you by a multigenerational coalition of SUV-driving Americans and self-serving orbital corporations and a UN General Assembly whose environmental watchword is not-in-my-backyard!"

The technological embargo had been imposed in the late twenty-first century, when Earth was in ecological free fall and the rats were just starting to realize that they didn't have another ship to jump to. By then the only people left on the planet were the Exempt Populations—aboriginals and major world religions—and the rogue nations. The aboriginals hadn't caused the problem and thus, in a brilliant display of what router/decomposer liked to call human illogic, weren't given a say in solving it. The fundamentalists just wanted to kill each other in peace without tripping over any stray Peacekeepers. And the rogue nations (a polite way of saying America) had parted ways so decisively with the UN by then that no one even bothered to ask if they wanted to participate.

America resisted, of course. But economies can't survive indefinite solitary confinement any more than people can. Doing business with America soon became bad business as well as bad politics. The American juggernaut sputtered to a slow crawl, crippled by climate change, economic isolation, and a massive multigenerational brain drain that was gleefully encouraged by Ring-side immigration policy.

Meanwhile the technological gap between Earth and the Ring got wider with every new advance in AI design or microgravity manufacturing. The generation ships lifted off from every overpopulated and impoverished corner of the globe. And the Embargo, ostensibly a simple moratorium on sale of space-based technology to Earth, began to achieve its true purpose: the reduction of Earth's human biomass to a level that the crippled planet could sustain.

It worked. Suburbs were swallowed up by weedlot wilderness. Trees and plants—albeit only self-pollinating ones—replaced concrete. Frogs were gone. So were butterflies, non-genetically-modified honeybees, most large mammals, and the migratory songbirds whose flocks had blackened Earth's skies in a time beyond the reach of even Cohen's earliest stored memories. But their ecological niches had been filled in, more or less, by other species. The world might not be as complex or as beautiful as it had been before man's Industrial Age, but it worked. In fact, it worked well enough that people were even starting to talk about loosening the Embargo.

People on Earth, that is.

No one Ring-side wanted to hear a word about it.

The humans who imposed the Embargo had meant it to be temporary. Industrial activity would be shut down until the planet's biogeological functions righted themselves. And when the environmental remediation was complete, everyone would move back downstairs and get back to life as normal. After all, Earth was home.

But Earth wasn't home to the 18 billion humans and posthumans who now inhabited the Orbital Ring. To them, Earth was just another moon. But a moon with a difference: a moon that had something they desperately needed.

Water.

Earth was dry and getting drier. The Ring was thirsty and getting thirstier. And every human who wasn't born on Earth meant a few hundred thousand extra liters of drinkable water for the Orbital Ring. So the UN offered Earth's few remaining humans a Solomonic choice, wrapped in the neutral language of the Tech Embargo: stay on Earth and accept the overwhelming odds against ever producing live offspring, or emigrate to the Ring and enjoy all the benefits of modern genetic engineering. And in the poisoned Holy Land, where one could go days on end without seeing a single child, that choice was as stark as the choice between life and death.

A pair of Legion fighter jets flashed overhead, wreathed in a virtual mist of encrypted spinstreams.

"Stop looking at your watch," Li griped. "It's always slow, then you get the wrong time in your head, and I catch it from you, and it screws with my wetware."

"That sounds fun," Cohen quipped. "Can we try it when we get back to the hotel?"

A squadron of Legionnaires walked by, their faces young and hard behind mirrored sunglasses, the creases in their uniforms sharp enough to threaten innocent passersby with paper cuts. As they passed the café one of the young men skipped a step, bringing himself into marching rhythm with his companions with the naturalness that only comes of long training.

"The real problem," Cohen said, returning to the subject of the watch, "is that I can't take it to Geneva for revision anymore. No one knows how to clean a real watch properly anymore. No one has the patience."

"Just waiting for the barbarians, are we?" Li said in a voice of patently fake sympathy.

"Yes, darling," Cohen drawled, "but who are the barbarians these days? There are so many people lining up for the job it's getting hard to pick a winner."

Li smiled, but her mind was only half on the banter. She was back at work again; Cohen could feel her on the other end of the intraface, scanning the approaches, converting the three-dimensional world into a relief map of lines of fire and points of cover and potential kill zones. "If I were this late," she muttered, "it would only be because something was wrong. Or because I was planning to make something *go* wrong."

A lone Israeli man settled at the table behind them, *shalomed* politely, ordered a cup of black coffee, and opened up the weekend section of the *Ha'aretz*. A moment later two camera-toting NorAmArc pilgrims sat down at the next table over and began a high-decibel argument about whether the cog railway ran to the Dome of the Rock overlook on Saturdays. Cohen goggled at them, only to realize that his friendly *Ha'aretz* reader was doing the same. Their gazes crossed, and the two men shared a moment of anonymous amusement.

"You watch," Li muttered. "The contact's not going to show up until after lunch. And meanwhile we're goddamn sitting ducks."

"Relax, Catherine."

"If you wanted relaxed, you shouldn't have brought me. Speaking of which, why the hell are we here anyway?"

"My country calls and I answer," Cohen quipped.

"Your country called all right. But they don't seem to give enough of a shit about you to provide bandwidth for the return call. Sometimes I could just strangle Hy Cohen for saddling you with this baggage."

"He probably never thought twice about it. He could be a bit lacking in subtlety sometimes. And he never could get his brain around the idea that Israel wasn't perfect." Cohen grinned sheepishly. "Not all of my pig-stubborn loyalty is the Game's fault. Some of it I come by honestly."

Li stopped scanning the approaches and actually turned in her chair to stare at him. "You know that's the first time I've ever heard you admit he wasn't perfect?"

"He was anything but perfect. He slept around behind his wife's back for one thing. I hated that. Not the adultery so much as the lying." Cohen felt the familiar flutter of self-loathing stir somewhere near the pit of what would have been his stomach if he had one. "I despised the lying."

"But you never told her."

Cohen stared into the middle distance, seeing the face of the first woman he had ever loved . . . and who had slipped away from him just as Li was now slipping away. "She didn't want to know," he said at last.

"And you always give the players what they want, don't you?"

He reached out for her instream, ran into a wall, and stared into her eyes only to find that they were equally unreadable. "Not you," he whispered. *"I love you."*

At that instant their contact stepped out of a narrow alley between two restaurants, glanced at them—so briefly that Cohen only caught the look when he replayed Li's spinfeed—then looked quickly away.

Li settled in her chair, shifting her weight forward, sliding her feet farther apart. Her face was expressionless, but onstream she radiated a profound and wordless satisfaction that Cohen suspected was pretty close to what you'd get if you tapped the neural feed of a cat who'd just found a nice fat mouse to play with.

The contact turned out to be a woman, and a woman who had the history of Israel written on her face. She could have stepped straight out of a 1950s kibbutz harvest photo or a grainy black-and-white movie about the Warsaw Ghetto uprising. The rawboned farmer-turned-soldier body. The tousled fair hair and the hawklike face. The steel-blue eyes—one of them dark with the stain of an old injury.

<Shrapnel?> Li asked. <Or did she have a rifle blow up in her face?>

<Love tap from a grenade. Sayeret Golani training exercise.>

<Ah. So you *do* know her.>

<I told you, I don't want you having any contact with people from the Office unless it's absolutely necessary. I thought we agreed about that.>

<No. I just stopped arguing about it so router/decomposer wouldn't have to waste his time playing magical moving files for you.>

Cohen ignored the jibe. Li could complain all she wanted to about unequal file-sharing protocols, but he wasn't going to drop the firewall he kept between her and the boys on King Saul Boulevard as long as he had a choice in the matter. She could think up enough ways to get herself killed on her own without his help.

<So what should I know about her that you're actually willing to tell me?> Li asked.

<Let's just say that Tel Aviv might not be the most tactful topic to raise.>

The woman stopped in front of their table, crossed her arms over her chest, and threw her head a little back and sideways in order to get her good eye on them. "Oh, so it *was* you back in the airport. You could have said so. Or don't you remember me?"

"Of course I remember you, Osnat. I just didn't know you'd gone private sector."

"Lot of people's careers went down in flames after Tel Aviv. Can't complain. Could have been worse. Could have ended up with a bullet in the head."

The fury radiated off her like a bomb blast. Well, Cohen couldn't blame her. They'd known each other very slightly. As far as she was concerned he was Gavi's friend, end of story. And Osnat had special, complicated, and intensely personal reasons for hating Gavi.

"I heard Gur died," Cohen said. "I'm sorry."

"Everybody's sorry."

She pulled the empty chair free of the table and sat down in it. No one spoke for a long and extremely unpleasant moment.

"When do we get to talk to the sellers?" Li asked finally.

Osnat ignored her. "You were supposed to come alone," she told Cohen flatly, "not bring a golem of your own."

Li made her move so fast that even Cohen missed it. One moment she was on the far side of the table from Osnat. A blink later, she had her hand around the other woman's wrist and was squeezing hard enough to drain the blood from her face.

"Being a golem has its uses," she said in a companionable tone. "Also, the only way to ALEF is through Cohen, and the only way to Cohen is through me. So the next time I talk to you, you'll look me in the eye when you answer."

Osnat gave her a pale hostile stare. Then she did what every well-trained infantryman does when pinned down by enemy fire; she called for air support. And she called for it, of all places, from the next table.

Cohen followed Osnat's glance just in time to see the *Ha'aretz* reader put down his newspaper and smile politely at them.

"May I join you?" he asked. He folded his newspaper into precise halves, picked up his drink, and walked over to sit next to Osnat. "Moshe Feldman," he said. "Pleasure to meet you. Can I buy you coffee?"

A waiter they hadn't seen before appeared before Moshe had even raised his hand, carrying a filigreed coffee service. He deposited it on their table, poured out two eggshell-sized cups of cardamom-flavored coffee, produced a bottle of mineral water and two glasses from his apron pocket, and left.

Cohen reached for the water.

Moshe reached for Cohen's hand.

Li reached for her gun.

"Please," Moshe said. "Drink your coffee first."

Li picked hers up, drank, grimaced.

<Are you all right?> Cohen asked anxiously.

<God, that's shitty coffee!>

<Is that a yes or a no, Catherine?>

<Yeah, I'm fine.> But as she set the cup back in the saucer he felt a chilly little quiver of pain and shock run across the intraface.

All her systems, biological and synthetic, natural and artificial, kicked into overdrive to identify the attack and tally up the damage. Cohen could feel the churning, chaotic, complicated process unfolding as clearly as if he were inside her skin and not sitting in his own chair with two feet of air between them. Eventually she identified the cold prick of pain as the point of a needle sliding into the web of skin between thumb and forefinger. <It's fine,> she told him a moment later. <DNA sampler.>

<He's a suspicious bastard, isn't he?>

<Unless he has some reason to mistrust us that you're not telling me about?>

As he picked up his own cup and felt the needle slide into Roland's flesh, Cohen decided that the implied question in that statement was one he'd rather leave unanswered.

It took Moshe an hour to do the genetic work.

"Well," Li asked when he finally returned, "are we who we say we are?"

"Apparently. Even Cohen's . . . er . . ."

"Face," Cohen prompted.

"Right. Even the, er, face is who you told us he would be." Moshe paused uncomfortably. "How do you acquire your bodies, by the way? Do you grow them?"

"Good heavens, no! We're not the Syndicates. He's a real person. Parents, passport, bank accounts. Bank accounts that are substantially better funded since he started working for me."

Cohen crossed his arms, realized the gesture looked defensive, and asked himself whether deep down inside he might not have something to feel just the tiniest bit guilty about. Hadn't Roland been meaning to put himself through medical school back when they first met? When was the last time he'd heard anything about that? Was Li right, God forbid? Did he just sort of . . . *swallow* people? He pushed away that unwelcome thought, telling himself that he'd ask Roland how med school was going next time they saw each other.

"And how much does it cost to . . . what's the right word . . . rent someone?"

Cohen grinned. "If you have to ask, you can't afford it."

"And it's legal, is it?"

"Well, mostly." Cohen felt Li's smirk tickling at the back of his mind. "As my associate has just pointed out, it's easier to bend the rules when you're filthy stinking rich."

"Mmm." Moshe's expression sharpened. "Speaking of bending the rules, I understood that ALEF would send one representative to the bidding. And that it would be someone we could vet beforehand to make sure they didn't pose any security risks." His eyes touched briefly on Li, then skittered away again. "But now here you are with one of the, uh, least vettable individuals in UN space."

<He could talk to me about it,> Li said. <What the hell's wrong with these people, anyway?>

"You could talk to her about it," Cohen repeated, mimicking her annoyed tone with such painstaking precision that only someone who hadn't grown up surrounded by the twenty-four-hour hum of spinstream traffic could have mistaken the words for Cohen's.

Moshe turned to face Li. "I have no problem with talking to you. Or with your genetics. Or your enhancements. Or your status under UN law, Jewish law, or any other law. What I do have a problem with is trusting a former Peacekeeper with information that we most assuredly do not wish to share with the Controlled Technology Committee."

"The operative word there is *former,*" Li said. "I lost my commission three years ago."

Moshe's eyes flicked to Li's throat and wrists. "But you didn't lose your wetware. What assurance can you give me that everything you see and hear isn't feeding straight into UNSec data banks?"

A slow smile spread across Li's face. "I'm not a very subtle person, Moshe. If you've got something to say, you'd better say it."

"Just that I wonder why they didn't reclaim your wetware. And how it could have taken your superiors eleven years to get around to prosecuting you for shooting those prisoners."

"I bought my wetware by signing my pension back to the government. Any soldier's entitled to do that, and most do, if only to avoid the surgery. As for the rest . . . you're spinning fairy tales. The court-martial proceedings were public. Man on the street knows as much about it as I do. Just look at the spins."

"Spins can be faked. Anyone who's worked on EMET knows that."

Li stared across the table, her face calm, her eyes level. This must be costing her, Cohen realized, but he had no idea how much. Three years after the court-martial they'd still never talked about it. And even his most cautious attempts to cross that particular no-man's-land had been violently rebuffed.

"Unfortunately," Li said when he'd just about decided she wasn't going to say anything, "those particular spins don't seem to have been faked."

She and Moshe stared at each other, locked in one of those testosterone-fueled battles of will that Cohen, three centuries removed from his only unmediated human memories, was beginning to find increasingly incomprehensible.

Finally Moshe leaned forward in his chair, the flimsy metal creaking under his weight. "The thing is, Major, I just don't trust you."

"You want ALEF as a bidder, you'll have to trust me."

Moshe pursed his lips.

"Do you need to talk to someone?" Li asked. The question came off of a collective work space shared by Li, Cohen, router/decomposer, and a gaggle of chattering semisentients, but it seemed politic to let Li ask it. Moshe had clearly slipped into the trap of treating the two bodies in front of him as separate entities . . . and you never knew when that sort of misconception might work to your advantage.

"No. I have discretion." He hesitated for another instant. "All right then. We go forward. For now. But we may require additional *bona fides* after the next meeting."

"You may not be the only one," Li retorted. "We still have nothing more than your word that the seller's genuine. What about his *bona fides*?"

"That's between you and the seller." Moshe got to his feet, left the paper on the table, and dropped a few shekels on top of it. "I just open the cage and crack the whip. Whether the bear decides to dance for you or eat you is your problem."

SEX, WATER, GOD

The individual's enhancement of his or her reproductive chances
never happens in a void but only in relation to the reproductive
chances of other members of the species.
Just as corporations seek to externalize their costs of production,
individuals inevitably seek to externalize their costs of
reproduction, enhancing the value of their own genetic property
by reducing the value of their neighbors' genetic property.
When twentieth-century existentialists sipped coffee in Parisian
cafés, or twenty-first-century shoppers flocked to Wal-Mart for
cheap consumer goods, they were both participants in a global
economy whose ultimate evolutionary effect was to shift the
means of reproduction (high protein diets, high standards of
living, paid child care, etc.) to the Consuming Nations, while
shifting the limiting factors on reproduction (war, poverty,
pollution, etc.) to Producing Nations. . . .
Viewed in this light, Earth's ecological collapse can be seen as the
logical, even inevitable conclusion of four millennia of human
evolution. Earth died not because humans strayed from the path of
"nature" or "instinct," but because individual humans obeyed their
natural instincts far too well for their own collective good. . . .

—INTRODUCTION TO SOCIOBIOLOGY (APPROVED FOR THE SIXTH-YEAR
CURRICULUM BY KNOWLESSYNDICATE STEERING COMMITTEE, YEAR 11,
ORBIT 227)

THEY HELD THE FIRST BIDDING session on the dangerous but neutral ground of the International Zone.

Arkady and Osnat crossed through the Damascus Gate checkpoint at just past ten in the morning, elbow to armpit with a sweating crowd of religious pilgrims, under the hard watchful eyes of the Legionnaires. By the time they cleared the checkpoint and plunged into the Old City, Arkady had already realized that this was a different city from the one they'd walked through before reaching the great gate. Where the lines at the checkpoint had been dominated by pilgrims and commuters, the actual streets of the Old City were dominated—at least to Arkady's Syndicate-bred eyes—by beggars. It took him a while to understand that they actually were beggars. They didn't ask for money. They just sat slumped along the stone walls lining the narrow streets, looking like they'd been there so long they'd given up even hoping for money. Arkady's instinctive response was impatience. Why didn't they just go to collective supply, take out what they needed, and get on with life? But of course there was no collective supply here. And when he looked more closely at the beggars he saw that many of them were crippled or deformed or obviously crazy.

"It's a *euth ward*," he said wonderingly.

"They try to chase them away," Osnat said with a fatalistic shrug, "but there are only so many cops around."

"But there must be some kind of renormaliza—er, rehabilitation program."

She gave him an incredulous look out of the corners of her eyes. "If someone in the Syndicates has figured out how to rehabilitate people from being poor, they ought to apply for the freaking Nobel Peace Prize."

Arkady stared at the crumpled forms, trying to take the measure of the people inside the rags, but none of them would meet his eyes. And they weren't the only ones.

There was a special quality to the gaze in the International Zone, a quality of nonlooking, nonseeing. The Legionnaires wore their mirrored sunglasses like body armor and did their level best to pretend not to speak any language but French when anyone had the effrontery to ask them questions. Hasidim hurried along under their dreary hats, assiduously shielding their eyes from any contact with the godless present. NorAmArc Christians lumbered through the stations of the cross, eyes glued to their spincorders, doing their best to turn a real living city into a theme park. Muslims glared into the near distance as if they thought some Sufist act of will could make the hordes of unbelievers vanish from their holy sites. Even the crazy people—and there seemed to be a great many of them—shouted through you instead of at you. The only people who actually looked at anyone were the Interfaithers . . . and the way they looked at you made you realize that being ignored was far from the worst thing that could happen to you.

"Why are there so many Interfaithers?" Arkady asked.

"Open your eyes. *Why* is right in front of your nose."

He looked. He saw bored Legionnaires, sullen locals, dusty walls crumbling in the ozone haze of a warm fall afternoon, six thousand years of history surrounded by sandbags and reinforced concrete. "I don't see it."

"That's 'cause you're not pointing your nose the right way."

He glanced at her in confusion, then followed her hiked thumb skyward and finally saw it.

The Ring. Strung out along the declination of the equatorial belt some 35,786 kilometers overhead, it was faintly visible today through one of those quirky contrapositions of star and satellite that physics teachers throughout UN and Syndicate space set their frustrated students to calculate. The Ring wasn't an actual ring, of course; just the area of space that contained all of Earth's stable geosynchronous orbits. But it had been packed so full of residential and manufacturing habitats and commsats and solar collectors and offshore tax shelters, that by now it was as visible and clearly defined as the rings of Saturn.

The Ring's traffic control and dynamic stabilization requirements were so impossibly complex that they had been the primary driving force behind the evolution of Emergent AI over the course of the last three centuries. The Ring was also—because of the sheer volume of reflective metal whipping around up there—one of the thousands of complex mutually interacting causes of the artificial ice age. A little reduced insolation here; a little increased albedo there; a gentle nudge of the coupled water transport systems of ocean and atmosphere. Arkady, terraformer that he was, appreciated the subtlety of the system: controlling chaos by the flutter of the butterfly's wing rather than the fall of the sledgehammer. And of course the Ring's terraformers, prodded onward by the unmitigated disaster they'd inherited, had done what station designers on the thinly populated Syndicate planets had never had to think about doing: They had crafted an orbital Ring that was so perfectly integrated into the biome of the planet below it that Ring and planet could almost be thought of as a single organism.

Still . . . he didn't think Osnat was suggesting that the ice age had caused the Interfaithers.

"We're poor," she said in answer to his questioning look. "And the Ring is rich. And we have to watch Ring-siders being rich every night on the evening spins. Knowing that we'll never have what they have. Knowing that our children, if we're lucky enough to have any, won't live nearly as long or as well as their children. Knowing that everything that counts in our lives is decided up there by people who think Earth is just a sponge they can squeeze the water out of. That kind of thing makes you hate, Arkady. And no one's ever invented a better excuse for hate than God. The Americans figured that one out a few centuries ago, and now we're all catching their new religion."

"You speak as if the Interfaithers had taken control of America."

"Not officially. Unofficially . . . well, just look at all those freaky Constitutional amendments they keep passing. And they haven't had a president or even a member of Congress in living memory who wasn't a member of the Interfaith."

"But they can't *do* anything, can they? They have no power. They're not UN members. They have no modern technology. . . ."

"They have oil. And they have an army. And they're willing to burn both. That gives them power."

"They're not going to bid on the weapon, are they?"

"I'm sure they'd try to if they knew about it. And all they have to do to get a foot in the door is threaten to tattle to UNSec. That's the game we're all playing. We want your little bauble for ourselves, but if we can't keep it to ourselves, then better our next-door neighbor should have it than the UN getting hold of it. After all, if the Palestinians or even the Americans get hold of a genetic weapon, they *might* use it, or they might just threaten to use it in order to get a bigger water allowance. But if the UN gets hold of it, you can bet your life they'll use it sooner or later. They're not afraid to fight dirty. Look what they did to ZhangSyndicate." Arkady caught his breath at that name and had to force down a nauseating surge of panic. "In the end," Osnat continued, either not noticing or misinterpreting his silence, "the only number the UN cares about is the one we all try not to talk about: Every person born on Earth represents an eleven-million-liter lifetime allowance of water that can't go to the Ring. It's all about water, Arkady. Everything on this planet comes down to sex and water."

"And God," he said, glancing at yet another passing Interfaither.

"Oh, you poor sap. Haven't you figured it out yet? God's just a way to pump up your ethnic group's birth rate so you can demand a bigger share of the water."

"You seem to have a lot of theories," Arkady said politely. "Do you have an interest in sociobiology? Have you ever thought about studying it?"

She stared at him for a moment, her mouth hanging open. Then she laughed. "Don't tell me you had me pegged as the hooker with the heart of gold. Sorry to disappoint you. My brother's a comp lit professor at Tel Aviv University. I'm practically considered a half-wit because I quit school after my master's degree. In polysci. Which is the closest thing we have to what you call sociobiology in the Syndicates."

"Then how . . . ?"

"How did a nice girl like me go so terribly wrong? What, you thought only poor people joined the army? This is Israel. And I'm not an Enderbot. I'm a real soldier. Or haven't you figured out the difference yet?"

The house hunched over Abulafia Street like one of the weathered old men who shuffled down the International Zone's crooked streets and loitered in its shabby coffeehouses. All you could see of it from the street was a high windowless wall whose stone bones were covered with a tattered skin of plaster. The only opening in the wall was a monumental wooden door, its planks so broad and long that Arkady would have been sure they were composite if he hadn't touched them with his own hands. In one corner of the door, so small it was almost lost in the shadow of the lintel, hung another smaller door. It opened to Osnat's knock, and they stepped through it into a tall courtyard.

The courtyard had been built for a hotter climate. Its fountain was turned off for the winter already, its rusted pipes tilting forlornly over tiles streaked yellow with *khamsin* dust. Even the roses reminded Arkady less of plants than of construction site scaffolding: two stories of stem and thorn and leaf thrown up against the sagging balconies just to point a few anemic blossoms at what little sun trickled over the encircling roof tiles.

It was a house out of time. The flow and chatter of the street faded away as soon as the gate fell to on its hinges. Even Earth's stupendous sky was reduced to a precise blue square, as completely submitted to the spare geometry of the building as if it were the roof of the house and not the roof of the whole world.

Osnat stopped, looked around the courtyard, and sneezed. She took a tissue out of her pocket and scrubbed at her nose with it while Arkady averted his eyes politely. "My God, I wish it would rain," she muttered. "The fucking dust is killing me."

They waited, though Arkady had no idea what they were waiting for. A water seller passed by in the street outside, calling his wares, but it might have been a voice from another planet. A single petal fell from one of the high rose blossoms and fluttered to the ground, the only moving thing in the visible universe. Then the gate opened behind them, and the most perfect human Arkady had ever seen stepped through it.

Her face possessed such flawless bilateral symmetry that Arkady had to look a second and third time before he decided she wasn't a genetic construct. Only the subtle blend of race and ethnicity, so different from the distinct ethnic phenomes of the Syndicates, identified the woman as what she was: a member of the heavily genetically engineered Ring-side elite that biogeographers were beginning to describe as a new posthuman quasi-species in its own right. And thinking back to Korchow's briefings, Arkady had no trouble putting a name to the woman:

Ashwarya Sofaer. Ash to her friends . . . not that she has any. She's the closest thing to pure ambition you'll ever see; a walking cost-benefit analysis of mammalian dominance drives. Ex-Mossad of course, like all the higher powers at GolaniTech. She shouldn't even be allowed to live on Earth, but she's grandfathered in under one of their endless loopholes. She spent three years in the Ring as the UN-Mossad liaison, then back to Israel and through the revolving door to GolaniTech. Now that Gavi Shehadeh's out of the way, she's probably Didi Halevy's most likely replacement if and when his enemies succeed in toppling him. As they say on King Saul Boulevard, the revolving door spins both ways. And it's not out of the question that the lovely Miss Sofaer might be interested in using you to give the proverbial door a good hard push. . . .

Ash had the Ring-sider's clothes to go with her Ring-sider's body: a sleek white suit programmed to hug every curve of her lean body; high-heeled vat leather shoes that made her long legs seem even longer than they were; impeccably styled hair slicked back from an impeccably made-up face that gave away absolutely nothing of the person behind it.

Ash and Osnat shook hands. Osnat looked stubby and flyblown next to the other woman.

"Captain Hoffman," Ash said.

"Colonel." Osnat gave the word a parade ground lilt that suggested respect entirely unalloyed by personal affection.

"Moshe said you'd come over to us," Ash said. "How did he convince you to make the jump?"

"He told me the grass might be greener on your side of the fence."

"It is." Ash eyed Osnat speculatively. "As green as you want it to be. We should talk sometime."

"Sure," Osnat said, obviously not meaning it.

A frown of irritation compressed Ash's beautiful lips for a moment, then vanished before Arkady could even be sure it had been there.

Briefly, she explained to Osnat that the room was being readied, that the bidders were still arriving, that she would make the introductions.

"And then what?" Osnat asked.

"And then we'll see."

Ash shook hands with Osnat again and swept off into the house without having so much as glanced at Arkady. Osnat stared after her with a troubled expression, rubbing the palm of her right hand on her pant leg as if she were trying to rub off the smell of the other woman.

Arkady, child of a world born only two years before his own birth, had never seen any place like the room he was eventually ushered into. Even the smell . . . the smell of wood and wool and furniture wax and all the other priceless things that were rare and inconceivable luxuries to the space-born. He tried to focus on the other people in the room, to match their faces with Korchow's descriptions. But his eyes kept floating to the whirling ceiling fans, the shivering ladders of light and shade cast by the slatted shutters, the cedar and sandalwood shadows under the high rafters, the complex patterns of rugs and drapery, the nuanced colors of walls and windowsills and floor tiles, the endless tumble of old and incomprehensible objects scattered over the polished tables and sideboards.

When he finally picked out Korchow, slouched in the shadowy depths of a leather wing chair, he saw that the KnowlesSyndicate A was laughing silently at him.

"Poor Arkady. You look even loster than you are."

Arkady started toward him, stopped, looked at Osnat.

"Go ahead," she said, lenient in Moshe's absence.

Korchow put an arm around Arkady's shoulders and gave him the traditional kiss of greeting. The sight of the Knowles A, after the weeks of isolation among humans, nearly unmanned Arkady. Back on Gilead, Korchow had seemed more than half human. Now he looked like home.

"I can't begin to tell you how glad I am to see you safe and sound, Arkady." Korchow had affected the avuncular air of an older series speaking to a younger member of his own geneline, but his smile remained as bland and carefully rationed as ever. It was the same smile Korchow had worn during the tense weeks of interrogation, and Arkady still sensed that Korchow's every move was part of an act played out not for its apparent audience but for the unseen watcher behind the camera.

Arkady returned Korchow's kiss. "May we do our part," he said, taking refuge in formality and formula.

"Your part?" For a moment the diplomat's mask gave way to a look of disdain and anger. Or was that merely another mask, just as calculated as

"Are you so sure of that? My offer's still open—"

"Catherine," the machine interrupted, "why are you even talking to him?"

"—I could get you on a Long March Rocket out of Guangdong Province next week. You'd be on Gilead within a month."

"The last person you made that offer to's dead," Li pointed out.

"Yes." Korchow agreed placidly. "But she put her hand up the wrong skirt. And humans are so touchy about that sort of thing."

"Just drop it," the machine said, looking hard at Korchow. "She's not interested."

"My, things *have* changed." Korchow looked back and forth between the two of them. "The Catherine Li I remember never needed anyone to tell people what she thought."

"If you two are done socializing," Ash said, striding in on the heels of two hard young men whose skin was marked by the subdermal filigree of Earth-illegal wetware, "perhaps this would be a convenient moment to make the introductions."

"Assuming all the bidders have arrived?" Korchow asked, letting the question hang in the air unanswered for a moment before he retreated to the shadows of his wing chair.

It seemed that all the bidders had indeed arrived. And when Arkady had sorted out the bidders from the coteries of bodyguards that he was starting to suspect were a routine cost of doing business in Jerusalem, there seemed to be three of them.

First the machine and his companion.

Second an elderly Palestinian man whose suit looked like something from a pre-Evacuation history book, and whose immaculate cotton headdress gleamed like a pearl in the dusky light that threaded through the shutters. Arkady had no trouble recognizing this bidder either: Shaikh Yassin, spearhead of the Palestinian hard religious right . . . and not at all the man Korchow had hoped the Palestinians would send.

"At last," Yassin said when Moshe introduced Arkady to him. "Abu Felastineh, blessed be his children, and his children's children, sends his greetings."

That wasn't a name, Arkady remembered from Korchow's briefings, but an honorific used to protect the anonymity and physical safety of the president of Palestine. *Abu Felastineh*. The Father of Palestine. And by now Arkady knew better than to begin to try to guess what any title that contained the word *father* really meant to humans.

The Palestinian bowed courteously and extended a hand to Arkady. Arkady stepped forward to shake it . . . and ran into a solid wall of muscle as the man's grim-faced bodyguards surged around him.

"Forgive the boy." Korchow had stepped up behind Arkady so smoothly that it was impossible to say when exactly he'd left his chair. Now he slipped a hand around Arkady's arm and drew him back a few cautious steps. "We in the Syndicates lack the institution of political assassination. We are, as I like to say, a too-trusting people."

"A too-trusting people," Yassin repeated. He made it sound as if the words were his and not Korchow's. He made it sound as if he were the man who had invented the very idea of words.

"Exactly so." Korchow bowing yet again and drawing Arkady back to safety under the unblinking gaze of the bodyguards.

"So how's the water business?" Catherine Li interrupted.

It took Arkady a moment to realize she was speaking to Yassin—largely because she spoke in a casual, almost confrontational tone that had nothing to do with the way every other person in the room had spoken to him.

The Palestinian turned slowly to face her. Then he looked past her at Cohen. "I am always delighted to see the ghost of my grandfather's friend. Your young associate seems to have been sadly misinformed, however. My family has no ties to the water trade, and I should be most sorry to think that you should have overheard any unfounded and malicious rumors to the contrary."

"My dear fellow," the machine murmured, patting the air with both hands as if he were smoothing down the hackles of a possibly dangerous dog. "Not at all. Nothing of the sort. My, er, associate is a bit over-emotional. Young people, you know."

"He sells *water*?" Arkady whispered to Korchow.

"Absolutely not," came the answer, whispered like his question from mouth to ear. "Shaikh Yassin is a perfectly respectable arms merchant."

"Arkady," Ash said. "Come here."

Arkady wheeled around—and found himself face-to-face with the final bidder.

"This," Ash announced, "is Turner."

Arkady searched his mind for some memory of the exotic-sounding name and found none. What kind of a name was Turner anyway? And why hadn't Korchow told him about this bidder?

He tried to take stock of the man, but all he could glean was a series of piecemeal impressions. A wrinkle-resistant button-down shirt stretched over an incipient potbelly and a weight lifter's muscles; a soft-palmed hand that had never done the hard work of surviving on a Syndicate space station, but still had the strength nearly to crush Arkady's fingers; freshly laundered hair combed precisely over a pink, smooth, wrinkle-free face and the coldest blue eyes Arkady had ever seen.

"Good to know you!" Turner said in a voice that took possession of the room just as aggressively as his big body did.

"Good to know you," Arkady repeated, assuming this was some unknown human-style formal greeting.

Turner laughed loudly. He seemed to be a man who did everything loudly. "Hear you're here to sell us something, Arkady. You got the goods, or are we gonna not be friends in the morning?"

"Um . . ."

"Just kidding!" He dealt Arkady a staggering blow on the shoulder. "No hard feelings, hey?"

"Uh . . . sure." Arkady rubbed at his shoulder.

Ash, meanwhile, had been watching this exchange with a vaguely amused expression on her smooth features. "Shall we begin?" she asked.

One of the guards dragged a heavy plush velvet armchair into the center of the room and positioned a standing lamp beside it so that the light would shine directly on the face of the unfortunate person sitting in it.

"Arkady?" Ash said pointedly.

Arkady hesitated, then walked obediently over to the chair and sat down.

As he did so the bidders sorted themselves onto the chairs and sofas which had already been placed around the edges of the room.

Their eyes turned to Arkady. He licked his lips and cleared his throat and shifted in his chair. He glanced around the circle of expectant faces and thought that they looked like wolves watching a hamstrung caribou. He glimpsed the flickering pinprick of a black box status light behind Catherine Li's left pupil—another new thing in a day full of new things—and wondered what other watchers on what distant planets were hearing his tale. Then he looked down at his hands and kept his gaze there, knowing that he was going to have to lie and that he would lose the thread of the lie if his concentration faltered.

"My survey team was assigned to evaluate Novalis for terraforming and settlement—" he began.

"Hang on," Li interrupted, leaning forward in her chair with an intent, predatory expression. "There's no Novalis on any UN charts. What star does it belong to? What are the old Astronomical Survey coordinates? Where is it in relation to the treaty lines?"

Arkady began to glance at Korchow, then stopped the movement and looked instead toward Ash.

"That information will be provided in the stage-two bid package," Ash answered. "After we've received your initial financial commitments."

"Based on what, an initial blind bid?"

Ash nodded.

"What are the payment arrangements?"

"A hundred thousand. Twenty up front, eighty on the day."

"Delivery on the day?"

"Naturally."

Li shrugged. Arkady took it as permission to continue.

"There were ten of us," he resumed. "Arkasha was the geneticist, and of course it's his notebooks we're talking about here. I was the biogeographer. Then there were the Ahmeds—"

"That's AzizSyndicate's biggest run A series," Korchow interjected. "It's a line whose main applications are military. They'd be familiar to Major Li from the last war"—he nodded politely in her direction—"but I doubt any of the rest of you would ever have seen one. Since the recent and, ahem, insufficiently anticipated outbreak of peace, the central joint steering committee has been trying to find alternative applications for them in the survey and terraforming missions. Sorry, Arkady. Go on."

"Well, the Aziz A's were the command team, pilot and navigator. They had the final word on all mission-critical decisions. Then we had the two Bellas, MotaiSyndicate B's. One of them was an entomologist, like me, but a specialist in orbsilk worms. The other—"

"Hang on a minute." Turner was taking notes, one muscular calf slung over the other knee to support his pad and pencil. "I'd like to get full names on these folks."

"I'm sorry?" Arkady said.

"Those are their full names," Korchow answered. "Arkady can't give you anything else. Ahmed. Bella. Even Andrej"—Korchow smiled infinitesimally—"are merely geneline designations. Though Arkady here may know intuitively that one Ahmed isn't the same as another, his language, his upbringing, and his convictions all tell him that the organism is nothing and the superorganism—the geneline—is everything."

"But some of them have their own names. This Arkasha person—"

"Arkasha," Korchow interrupted smoothly, "is the exception that proves the rule."

"Are you saying he's a political dissident?" Li interrupted.

"Let's not indulge in morally loaded terminology, Major. Arkasha is merely . . . an atavism. Whether he is an atavism with some useful evolutionary role to play is a decision for the RostovSyndicate steering committee to make. Not for me. And certainly not for you."

And so it went, just as he and Korchow had mapped it out back on Gilead, Arkady leading his audience down the twisting path—so close to the truth in almost every way—that Korchow had concocted for him.

"And what are we to make of this?" Shaikh Yassin said when Arkady finally reached the end of the story and fell silent. It was the first time he had spoken since the meeting began.

"What you make of it is your concern," Ash answered. "Needless to say, your conclusions will largely determine the price you are willing to pay."

"But what are we paying *for*?" Li again. She seemed to be the point man by consensus, and the others seemed content to hang back and see what game she managed to flush. "I mean, are we buying this so-called genetic weapon? Or Arkady? Or Arkasha's notebooks? Is Arkasha himself for sale, for that matter?"

"That's partly for you to determine," Ash answered smoothly. "You have discretion to put together your own bid. Tell us what you want. Tell us what you're willing to pay for it."

"And what does it mean that we're dealing with your charming self?" Yassin asked Ash. Beneath the courteous language, his voice sounded sharp as razors. "Can we infer from GolaniTech's involvement that Arkady has already been interrogated by Israel, and we're merely being offered their leavings?"

"You can infer whatever you like," Ash said—and the room fell silent while each of them tried and failed to stare the other down.

"My problem is still with the story itself," Li said, breaking the silence. "How do we know Arkady's not just making it all up as he goes along?"

"You know because of what he is." Ash gestured toward Arkady with one immaculately manicured hand. "An unaltered Syndicate construct, pure as a freshly detanked babe. No internal wetware. No stored spinfeed. No hard files. Nothing that can be edited, altered, or erased. What he remembers is what happened to him, pure and simple."

Across the room, Yassin was nodding contemplatively. The two ALEF bidders sat utterly still, though something in their expressions convinced Arkady that they were speaking to each other in the nebulous parallel universe of streamspace. Turner merely sat, one thick ankle crossed over the knee of the other leg, his pale eyes flicking back and forth between Arkady and Korchow as if he were calculating the angles and momenta of a targeting problem.

"People can lie," Li insisted.

"Not perfectly. Not under drugs. Not under . . . educated questioning. And once we work out the escrow arrangements, you'll each have the chance to question Arkady in the time and place of your choosing."

"But for how long? And with what limitations?"

Korchow started to answer, but Ash interrupted him. "I think discussing limitations as to duration and interrogation techniques in Arkady's presence would be counterproductive at this point."

"That's pretty damn cold," Li muttered.

"Yep," Turner said. "But it works."

Korchow cleared his throat and unfolded his slender stationer's frame from the leather depths of the wing chair. "It seems to me that this would be the moment at which Arkady and I might most appropriately make our exit."

As they left the room, Arkady glanced back and met Turner's stare, as coldly blue as the cloudless sky over Novalis's polar ice sheet.

I T WAS UNREAL. AN IMPOSSIBLE, glorious, inconceivable violation of all the rules and restrictions that had pressed in on Arkady since that first fateful meeting with Osnat.

He and Korchow walked side by side across the courtyard and through the narrow door into Abulafia Street. No one stopped them. No one asked Korchow where he was taking Arkady. No one even followed them that Arkady could see. And ten minutes later they were in the thronging heart of the Arab Quarter.

"I have some errands to run," Korchow told him. "You don't mind tagging along, do you?"

Korchow's "errands" stretched through the afternoon. He guided Arkady through the crowded streets, winding past beggars and water sellers, weaving through roving packs of pilgrims, and ducking into an endless series of antique stores and art galleries and rare book dealers.

At every store Korchow would go through the same incomprehensible ritual. He would introduce himself—under a different false name each time—and begin to look through the dealer's collections. He seemed to have a taste for antiquities, and in particular portable ones. He would greet the first four or five or eight items the dealer presented with polite lack of interest. The dealer would respond accordingly, and the prices being bandied about would rise dizzyingly. Korchow, however, would remain placidly unmoved . . . both by the prices and by the *objets d'art* being presented for his inspection. The dealer would begin to hem and haw about export restrictions and end user certificates. Korchow would smile and nod and pronounce what Arkady assumed were the proper noises of reassurance . . . at which point they would stop even talking about prices.

The dealer would brew the sweet hot tea that everyone in the Old City seemed to live on and usher them out of the public showroom and into a discreet back room that Korchow referred to, with an amusement that Arkady found utterly incomprehensible, as "the high rollers' room."

The high rollers' rooms were always soundproofed and spintronically deadwalled. And for good reason. For even Arkady could see that the objects presented for sale in these rooms had no business being anywhere outside of a museum, and certainly no business being shipped off-planet for private bidders.

Within the space of three hours Arkady watched Korchow conclude negotiations for a Saffavid Dynasty miniature of the assassination of some prince whose name Arkady forgot two minutes after Korchow told it to him; two David Grossman first editions ("Have you read *The Smile of the Lamb*? No? You really must. One of those human masterpieces in which one can feel the breath, the promise, of posthumanity."); and a portion of the True Cross encased in an exceptionally gaudy twelfth-century Byzantine reliquary ("The real value is in the packaging, Arkady. There's a lesson there. Remember it.").

Each time they stepped through the sonic curtain into the next high rollers' room and sat together, encased in a cocoon of artificial silence, while the dealer fetched the next illicit treasure for Korchow's delectation, Arkady expected the KnowlesSyndicate A to broach the real subject of interest between them. And each time Arkady was disappointed yet again.

Only between the third and fourth stops on the shopping tour—by which time Korchow had dropped a sum of money that would have provided a year's worth of air, food, and water for all of RostovSyndicate—did Arkady succeed in picking the two stolid-looking young Israelis out of the crowd.

"Are they *following* us?"

"Don't stare, Arkady. It's embarrassing."

He glanced surreptitiously at the young men while Korchow threaded along the narrow stone street ahead of him. Was it only those two, or was there another team as well? And was he completely crazy for thinking that the buxom schoolgirl bouncing along the opposite sidewalk was the same person as the frumpily dressed housewife who'd trudged by not five minutes ago pulling a wheeled grocery cart?

"They don't look embarrassed," he told Korchow.

"Who said it was *them* you were embarrassing?"

"Sorry," Arkady began—and then he rounded a corner in Korchow's wake and ran smack into absolutely the last face he ever expected to see on Earth.

The face stared down at him from a billboard the size of a house. The eyes were shadowed with the sorrow of hard experience. The square jaw was set in a frown of heroic determination. The perfectly balanced musculature of the bare chest was a paean in flesh and blood to the technical mastery of its AzizSyndicate designers.

There was a caption below the picture, though Arkady didn't need to read it to know what spin the image came from:

see AHMED AZIZ in
THE TIME OF CRUEL MIRACLES

"Ahmed *Aziz?*" Arkady mouthed.

"Well," Korchow said mildly, "humans watch art spins too. Though I've been told they recut the endings before they release Syndicate spins for UN audiences. Apparently humans don't find lovers' suicide pacts quite as romantic as we do." He squinted up at the billboard, arms crossed thoughtfully. "Our Ahmed's better-looking than the one who stars in the spins, don't you think?"

The possessive was hard enough for Arkady to parse that it took him a moment to understand who Korchow was talking about and draw the obvious connection.

Korchow sighed patiently. "I handled his debriefing too. I would have told you, if you'd ever trusted me enough to ask."

"Anyway, he's not better-looking," Arkady said. "He's just nicer. It makes him seem better-looking."

He looked over to find Korchow grinning indulgently at him.

"What?"

"You're an idiot, Arkady. But you're a sweet idiot. I'll say that for you. How you survived four months in Arkasha's back pocket I'll never fathom."

Only at the fifth stop did Korchow finally begin to show his cards. This store's street front consisted of one windowless door tucked behind a sweating stone buttress in the angle of an alley so narrow that Arkady wondered if the sun ever shone on the place. The brass sign advertised "antiquities" in French, English, Hebrew, and Arabic; but the lettering was so small that Arkady had to stoop to read it.

Walking into the place was like walking into a cave. The windows were hermetically sealed and the closed shutters blocked out what little light might have trickled through the smeared glass. The shop's single room seemed to fall away unevenly into the shadows, as if the cobweb-infested ceiling and the carpet-lined floor drew closer together the deeper you penetrated into the building's entrails. The man behind the counter was as oddly built as his shop. Only when he stepped out from behind the counter to greet them could Arkady make sense of his un-usual proportions; he was a dwarf, and he'd been standing on a pile of carpets half a dozen deep. Indeed, the farther back in the shop you went, the deeper the carpets got, until in the back of the place they were stacked up in slithering chest-high piles, fragrant with the perfume of mothballs and long-dead sheep.

But the carpets, however impressive they were, turned out to be a mere sideline. Once they were settled in the back room, slightly shabbier than the ones preceding it, and had suffered through the same tea and the same honeyed cakes and the same desultory small talk, the dwarf be-gan to shuffle across the mounded carpets in a pair of frayed and faded bedroom slippers, extracting curious little flat boxes from corners whose very existence Arkady had not suspected. And from the boxes, handling the pages with infinite delicacy, he began to produce his miniatures.

"Yes, yes," Korchow said to the first painting the dwarf presented, an ornate illustration of the Prophet—or at least Arkady assumed that was who it was; his face was completely obscured by a fluttering silken veil—riding to Heaven on a decidedly seductive-looking sphinx. Two more miniatures, also of religious themes, followed it, and Korchow showed little more interest in them than he had in the first piece.

The dealer cleared his throat. "Perhaps you might be more inter-ested in more, er, secular themes?"

"Oh, assuredly," Korchow said with a smile that Arkady felt himself to be quite incapable of interpreting.

The man shuffled to the back of the room, his slippers whispering on the wool nap of the carpets, and produced a slim portfolio of unbound pieces.

"Oh my," Korchow murmured when he looked at the first one.

Arkady looked, blinked, and looked away.

"Poor Arkady. A great man once observed that politics was like sausage: a commodity best enjoyed without inquiring too closely into the manufacturing process. One might say the same thing of human reproduction in general."

"Not to your taste?" the dealer asked in tones of careful neutrality.

"Not to my young friend's taste, at any rate. I imagine he would prefer something a bit more . . . ahem . . . refined."

The dwarf glanced between Korchow and Arkady, his face giving away nothing. He slid a second portfolio out from beneath the first, as if he'd had it ready all along, and opened it.

There was only one miniature inside, and it was clearly a picture of tremendous value. Arkady could see that even before he began to grasp the subject of the painting.

"By the Master of Tabriz," the dealer said. "You are familiar with the story? It is said to represent the Shah with his lover the night before he was assassinated."

Korchow's eyes slid sideways toward Arkady. "Do you like it?"

The miniature depicted two young men of exceptional physical beauty. They were as identical as crèchemates, though Arkady couldn't tell whether the resemblance was real or a mere product of the artist's manner. They were so completely swathed in silk, from their spotless white turbans to their patterned robes and their pointed and filigreed and gold-leafed slippers, that the shapes they formed on the page bore no relation to the warm, breathing, living bodies within. All their life was in their black eyes, which the long-dead artist had limned in the finest wisp of sable. And all around them the painted garden, which should have been as flat and static as every other priceless painted garden Arkady had seen that afternoon, seemed to pulse and flow like water running under ice. Trees twined and twisted their dark limbs about each other. Flowers flamed in the grass and swept in bright torrents around the lovers' feet.

For lovers they certainly were. There was no mistaking either the meaning of the image or the forbidden nature of the passion that suffused it.

And there was no doubt in Arkady's mind about what would surely happen, what had to happen, in the next moment of that frozen eternity.

"Well," Korchow pressed. "What do you think?"

"I think—" Arkady cleared his throat. "I think the man who painted this was a great artist."

"One of the greatest," Korchow agreed. "He was said to be the lover of the Shah for whom he painted it."

"And was the Shah pleased by the painting?"

"It isn't known. He died before it was finished."

Arkady turned away, unable to look at the thing any longer.

"You still haven't said if you like it or not," Korchow pointed out. "I ask because I'm thinking of making a gift."

It took a moment for Arkady to parse the unfamiliar phrase. The word *gift* existed in Syndicate Standard, but it applied, in the absence of personal or biological property, to a completely different concept.

"Unfortunately," Korchow continued, "I'm not familiar with the taste of the young man in question. I thought you might advise me. After all, you know him so much better than I do."

They looked at each other, the long-dead Shah and his doomed lover lying forgotten between them.

When Arkady was six he had witnessed the Peacekeeper attack on ZhangSyndicate. It had been over in seconds, and it had happened miles away across empty space, but it still dogged his nightmares. The great orbital station's outer hull had held, staving off hard vac; but the fireball had ripped through the habitat modules and gutted them with all the crèchelings on board and unrescued. That attack had killed ZhangSyndicate. Its arks had been contaminated, their precious genesets rendered unusable. And where there were children there could be no Syndicate. Most of the surviving Zhangs had chosen suicide over the sterile prospect of life as walking ghosts. Sometimes it was hard to remember they'd ever existed. But Arkady remembered the terrible beauty of the burning. The white-hot fire lighting up one viewport after another as the inner bulwarks gave way. The condensation steaming off the hull and refreezing in the void. His body felt like that now: a dead shell dissolving into a glittering ice storm of hope, pain, terror.

"It's understandable that you would still have feelings for him," Korchow said in the bland, reasonable, sympathetic voice that still haunted Arkady's nightmares. "Why be ashamed to admit to them?

What you did, you did because you loved him. No one holds *that* against you. After all, what else did they intend to happen when they assigned you to each other?"

Arkady froze. Had Arkasha said something? Was Korchow still playing them off against each other? Would Arkady hurt his pairmate by acknowledging Korchow's insinuations?

"Tell me," Korchow asked before Arkady could decide how to answer. "Do you begin to understand what we're doing here?"

Arkady shook his head. "Here . . . where?"

"Here on Earth." Korchow pointed to the carpeted floor, the walls of the room, the city beyond the walls. "Think, Arkady. Use that handsome head of yours for something other than ants."

But Arkady had thought. He'd lain awake thinking month after month, night after cold night. And he still knew nothing he hadn't known back on Novalis. So he waited, schooling his face into impassive stillness, not wanting to say or do anything that might jeopardize the sudden and unexpected flow of information.

"What do you know about the colonization of the Americas?" Korchow asked, in an apparent change of subject.

Arkady stuttered something about sociogenesis and intersocietal competition and the perverse incentives of social systems based on sexual reproduction—

"Yes, yes. Forget all the tripe from your tenth-year sociobiology class. We teach you that because it's good for you, not because it's true. In any case, when the Europeans first arrived in the Americas—they actually called it the New World, if you can imagine such parochialism— they encountered a civilization as well established in many respects as their own. Mexico City had more residents than the largest cities of Europe, and they were a hell of a lot cleaner and better fed judging from the Conquistadors' letters home. And even the Aztecs were practically savages compared to the Incas.

"Unfortunately for the Incas, the collision of the Old and the New World turned out not to be a clash of cultures, but a clash of diseases. A plague of plagues swept through the Americas in the wake of the first explorers. Black Death. Syphilis. Influenza. Smallpox. The first explorers discovered a continent of vibrant cities—and by the time the first colonists landed all that was left were graves and charnel houses. It was a classic case of an isolated population encountering a much larger one . . . and any competent evolutionary ecologist can tell you where that leads.

"At some point during this scourge, the Spanish developed a new and devilishly clever strategy of conquest: gifts. They gave the Incas blankets that had been used by smallpox victims. The blankets were warm and beautiful. They were passed from hand to hand, treasures from another world. And they ended up killing more people than European gunpowder ever did."

Korchow looked at him expectantly—but whatever lesson he meant Arkady to draw from the tale, Arkady couldn't make the connection.

"Never mind," he said after a moment. "You're a good boy, Arkady. And it's not lack of intelligence that keeps you from understanding. It's the same thing that kept you from seeing what was happening on Novalis: idealism. Rostov did a beautiful job when they detanked you. A really fine piece of work. No sense in trying to play country fiddle on a Stradivarius. Do you have any questions about the auction? If you want to ask me anything, now is your moment. It may be difficult to talk this privately again."

Arkady hesitated, thinking. "There was someone missing," he said at last. "Someone you told me to look for. Why wasn't Walid Safik there?"

"I don't know. The Palestine Security Services are . . . opaque. It can be very hard to tell what's going on beneath the surface. People fall in and out of favor unpredictably. But don't count Safik out. If he's not invited to the party he'll find a way to crash it sooner or later."

"And what about the other party crasher? Turner?"

Korchow's hand crept to his throat in the same nervous gesture the construct Catherine Li had provoked back at the auction meet. "I didn't expect the Americans to take an interest. I don't like it. Still . . . we may still be able to make use of him."

"Will he be allowed to interrogate me?" Arkady asked, thinking of the cold eyes behind Turner's easygoing smile.

"I assume so. But I'll ask to have it done under GolaniTech supervision. The Americans have a bad habit of changing the rules when they don't like them."

"What should I tell him?"

"Whatever he asks you to tell him. I believe in sacrifice, Arkady, but not in pointless sacrifice."

Korchow fingered the miniature that lay forgotten on the table between them. Arkady glanced at it and shivered.

"You never told the bidders about Bella," Korchow said.

"You mean about her . . ." He couldn't bring himself to say the word, so he settled for a more neutral term, ". . . illness? But you told me not to tell them."

"Did I? Well, I suppose I might have at that." Korchow was smiling at him. "It seemed like a good idea at the time. But when Turner has his little talk with you, why don't you drop that in his ear and see what happens?"

Arkady blinked at Korchow, comprehension beginning to dawn on him. "This is all about Bella and Ahmed. You *want* the humans to know about them. Then why all the subterfuge? Why not just tell them?"

"Human nature, Arkady. A beast you must be getting to know rather well by now. Humans aren't fundamentally selfless. They don't give themselves, not in the way we do. And they don't trust any gift"—again that unsettling use of the word—"that's given too easily."

Neither did Andrej Korchow. One more way in which the Knowles-Syndicate spy had become as much human as construct. But Arkady suspected that was a thought best kept to himself.

"Then this really is a gift?" he asked. "Not some kind of trap?"

"It's both. Like everything in life worth having . . . or giving for that matter. In the short term it may throw Earth into chaos, which will hurt the Ring and therefore help us. Or at least that's how Knowles sold our plan to the central steering committee. But in the long term it just might give the human race a chance to outrun extinction."

"And how does that help us? Last time I saw humans anywhere near Gilead they were trying to kill me."

"Those were UN colonists and genetic constructs, not humans. And even their Ring-side paymasters are as posthuman as you and I are, no matter what their Schengen implants say. The only wild humans left are here on Earth. And as for why we'd want to save them . . . well, you're the ecophysicist, not me."

Arkady knew the theory. It was politically unacceptable, especially in the newer Syndicates like Motai and Aziz. But in scientific circles people talked openly about the problem. The Syndicates were dogged by the question that lurked behind every population-wide genetic engineering project: What were the engineers splicing out of the genome that they wouldn't know they needed until it was too late?

In a strictly genetic sense, the Syndicates, like any genetically modified posthuman population, were parasites. In order to survive permanently they needed to be embedded within a larger human population that they could draw genetic material from and fall back on if things ever went catastrophically wrong. No posthuman along the Periphery had the genetic diversity to maintain a viable population indefinitely. And though the Ring was huge, its population was so homogenized by commercial splicing that it had a worse diversity deficit than even the Syndicates.

The only piece of "wild" human genome left—and therefore the only safety net if things went wrong—was the rapidly vanishing human population of Earth. The Ring, the Periphery, and even the Syndicates might all be benefiting from Earth's depopulation in the short term, but in the long term it was disastrous.

And Korchow, for his own devious and cynical motives, had decided to avert the disaster . . . or at least that was what he seemed to want to make Arkady think at this move in the game.

"Why couldn't you have told me all this before?" Arkady asked.

"I'm sorry, Arkady. I couldn't risk it. I had to get you past Moshe. I had to get you to Earth. I told you what I thought you needed to know to accomplish that. And the rest . . . well, I'm telling you now, aren't I?"

"But are you telling me the truth, or just the next lie?"

Korchow grinned in genuine amusement. "So there is something behind the pretty face after all," he said. "Arkasha always said there was."

"I want to talk to him."

"You will."

"When?"

"Soon."

"*When?*"

There was something fundamentally uncategorizable about Korchow. For weeks, even months, Arkady would think of him as a chimera who had become more human than construct by the constant stress and abrasion of living with humans. But then, just when he had decided that he knew what Korchow was, the spy's artifices would slough away to reveal the rigid scaffolding of ideology that everything else hung upon.

"You will speak to Arkasha," Korchow told him in a voice that wasn't even remotely human, "when I believe it is in both of your best interests to speak to each other. Which is to say when it is in the best interest of the Syndicates. Unless you no longer believe that those two things are one and the same?"

"No. Of course not. I didn't mean to . . . forgive me."

"That Arkasha continues to defy me is one thing. I expect it of him. But *you*, Arkady. You disappoint me. Back on Gilead I decided you were ready to do your part and make the necessary sacrifices. Don't make me wonder if I was wrong about you."

"I just—"

Korchow held up a hand. "Don't. If what you've already seen of humans—the misery right outside this window, for God's sake—hasn't convinced you of how important it is that the Syndicates survive and thrive, then we have nothing else to say to each other."

Back at the house on Abulafia Street, Osnat took charge of Arkady as seamlessly as a relay runner taking the baton from a teammate. Twenty minutes later, Arkady was sitting in the helicopter, buffeted by wind and noise, while Osnat slept in the seat across from him as comfortably as if she were safe on the ground and tucked into her bed.

Arkady's brain spun feverishly, turning over every word Korchow had spoken, inspecting every nuance and inflection as if he were reading tea leaves. Any way he looked at it he reached the same conclusion:

Arkasha was alive. Arkasha was alive and not cooperating, whatever Korchow meant by that. And if Arkasha wasn't cooperating, then Arkasha was still himself.

And that single fact changed everything.

Could Osnat be trusted? He looked at her face, grimy with sweat and *khamsin* dust. Everything he knew of her said no . . . but he'd seen something in her face when she looked at him, something harder and more honest than pity, that whispered yes.

He would ask her. He would ask her the next time she brought his food. He'd beg if he had to.

Because if Arkasha really was alive and unbroken, then Arkady would run any risk and suffer any humiliation to save him.

NOVALIS

The Six Percent Rule

Experience from prior missions has shown the vital importance of allowing for the impact of unpredictable small group dynamics; SGD has often been a determining factor in the success or failure of such missions. Failure to address SGD at the preplanning stage can rarely be remedied en route. *Attempts to replace sensible SGD planning with artificial authority hierarchies have been farcically disastrous.* **Thus, a critical task of mission preplanning is to ensure that individual crew members enhance, rather than detract from, each other's ability to complete the mission.** *Distasteful though such considerations may be to the ideologues among us, space is ruled by reality, not dogma.**

—REPORT OF THE INTERSYNDICATE SUBCOMMITTEE ON LONG-RANGE SURVEY MISSION PREPLANNING, YEAR 24, ORBIT 18.

---

*The Subcommittee wishes to note that sentences three (3) and five (5) of this paragraph (emphasis added) were proposed for inclusion by the Member from KnowlesSyndicate. The remaining subcommittee members reached a consensus that the language of sentences three (3) and five (5) was inappropriately provocative, and that sentences three (3) and five (5) should consequently be expunged from the final text. The Member from KnowlesSyndicate categorically refused to join the afore-referenced consensus or agree to deletion of the sentence at issue, thus rendering a unanimous consensus impossible. In the interest of maintaining intersyndicate amity and proper decision-making procedures, the remaining Subcommittee Members concluded that the most appropriate action in the face of this unprecedented situation was to append some record of the committee's deliberations. The Member from AzizSyndicate wishes formally to note that the wording of sentence one (1) also does not meet with his approval. The Member from MotaiSyndicate wishes formally to note that the wording of sentences one (1), two (2), and four (4) are counterrevolutionary. The Member from KnowlesSyndicate wishes formally to note that the Member from AzizSyndicate and the Member from MotaiSyndicate are blithering idiots. . . .

THE BIG WOOD: 6:00 A.M., THIRD day postlandfall.

Sunbeams sliced through the forest canopy a hundred meters overhead and slanted toward Arkady through the green haze of quivering leaf edges and fluttering insect wings. There was still a predawn, underwater cast to the forest light, but the night's deep-sea shadows were fast giving way to the midmorning glow of shallow surf under sunlight.

Arkady had found a dacetine, one of the Beautiful Ants, and she was on the hunt.

She'd spied a springtail grazing on the waterlogged edge of a fallen leaf. Arkady watched her stalk her prey, her finely sculpted legs lifting and arcing with the graceful precision of the huntress she was. He knew what would happen, but, no matter how many times he watched it, the hunt retained its otherworldly magic.

The dacetine would approach the springtail, her movements growing slower and more deliberate with every step, until she stood so close that it was grazing literally between the razor-toothed prongs of her widespread mandibles. She would let the fine hairs between her mandibles, so delicate that they were invisible except under a microscope, brush across the oblivious springtail's thorax. And then, twenty times faster than the blink of an eye, her mandibles would snap closed with enough force to cut the poor springtail in two.

Arkady shivered, wondering what it would be like to have the last thing you felt in life be the fine tickling of those intramandibular hairs on your neck. He had a sudden disturbing vision of the survey team as springtails, innocently sampling and measuring and mapping Novalis's bewildering diversity while the razor-sharp mandibles closed in on them.

And yet . . . and yet there was nothing concrete, no real problem that he could point to to justify the feeling. The initial disputes among the crew had died down, quelled by the insane pace at which they'd all been working since planetfall. Meanwhile the survey progressed so spectacularly that so far it had largely consoled him for the mission's more personal disappointments.

By the end of the first week afield, Arkady had documented five major nest complexes. Dozens upon dozens of the massive, man-high, aboveground nests constructed by the European wood ant, dotted in military formation across the woodland clearings, with their southern slopes precisely canted to maximize winter solar gain. A vast underground complex of leaf-cutter ants, which he suspected and would later confirm, had been artificially adapted to the temperate climate of the main continent. And in the warm open pastures, the exotic pyramids of the Cataglyphis, Herodotus's legendary gold-digging ants, its surface dotted with precisely distributed specks of glittering gray schist.

But his most spectacular discoveries were all made under the deep green shadows of the forest they had begun to call the Big Wood. It wasn't really a wood at all, but a temperate rain forest, and it hosted a diversity of ant life almost unimaginable by the normal standards of terraformed worlds. Some of the species were ones Arkady knew from RostovSyndicate's genetic archives but had never expected to see in the wild. Others were so rare that he had to scurry back to the ship and consult his reference books to identify them.

He found the legendary hanging gardens of the *Crematogaster longispina*, some of them containing forgotten species of bromeliads that Arkady thought had died with Earth's Amazon Basin. He found a plethora of ant birds and ant butterflies who followed the monstrous swarm and column raids of the army ants, though the army ants themselves had so far eluded him. He found ponerines and dacetines in all their stupendous variety. And most significant from an ecological standpoint, he found a number of leaf-cutter ants, *Atta sexdens* as well as *Atta cephalotes*, whose vast vaulted underground colonies could contain as many as 150 million minor workers, all toiling over their subterranean fields of tame fungi. They were Novalis's single greatest herbivores and dirt movers, filling to overflowing the ecological niches of terrestrial species as various as cattle, aphids, and earthworms.

Terraforming on Novalis had succeeded so spectacularly that it threw into doubt every former assumption about what was possible or impossible in terraforming. That the planet *had* been actively terraformed was now established beyond question. The survey team had already found the burnt-out remains of two atmospheric entry craft and a half dozen scattered Quonset huts flanked by an overgrown cemetery. And in a nearby valley bottom they had stumbled on the ruins of a vast laboratory complex, its dormitories standing empty, its locked cages housing only the dry skeletons of abandoned mice and monkeys, its crumbling walls filled with a vast metastasizing supercolony of predatory ants that Arkady had to comb through every reference book in the ship's library to identify as the supposedly long-extinct *Strumigenys louisianae*.

Novalis had been settled twice—or at least that was the conclusion Arkady, Arkasha, and the Aurelias had drawn when they tried to derive family trees for three of the standard seed species and came up with seeding dates strung out across three centuries.

The fact that both settlements had failed worried no one. There was no reason to assume that either failure had anything to do with Novalis. Most colonists arrived on their chosen worlds as walking ghosts: biologically alive but already doomed by the cold equations of evolution in a shifting fitness landscape. Either new blood arrived—usually in the form of custom-engineered posthuman colonists stuffed into UN-dispatched jumpships—or the original colony vanished, leaving its partially terraformed world behind for the next wave of settlers . . . or for the Syndicates.

And Novalis had everything the Syndicate surveyors had been looking for. No bare branch colonists to stir up trouble and open the door to the lawyers and diplomats. No fatal diseases or allergens, so far anyway. And above all, a rich, diverse, and to all appearances stable biosphere.

In short, Novalis was perfect. So what was the source of Arkady's growing unease? Nothing, he told himself. Nothing at all. There wasn't a thing wrong with the planet. And the glitches in his data? Glitches, nothing more. He wouldn't have given a second thought to them if other things had been going well.

Other things meaning Arkasha.

Their relationship—or rather their complete lack of anything any reasonable person could call a relationship—had tinged all Arkady's feelings about the mission. It would have been different if they'd disliked each other. Or if Arkasha had been selfish or lazy or a petty bully or any one of the thousand things that you always hoped the other member of a new workpair wouldn't be. But he wasn't. And Arkady did like him. He liked him more after every one of their rare and all-too-brief encounters.

Arkasha had a wry, subtle sense of humor; once he'd established by cautious probing that Arkady had the stomach for subversive jokes, he'd developed the habit of alighting next to Arkady at mealtimes, murmuring some outrageous thing in his ear, then evaporating back to the lab while Arkady was still trying to smother his laughter. And he was smart. More than smart. There was something liberating about talking to him. He was always short-circuiting Arkady's accumulated social defenses so that he would suddenly find himself quite comfortably saying things that he hadn't imagined he'd ever say to anyone.

Arkasha even liked *ants*, for God's sake. He asked intelligent questions about Arkady's theories and experiments . . . and actually managed to stay awake and apparently interested for the answers to the questions.

But every time it seemed they were starting to move toward something more than cool collegiality, Arkasha would retreat into his work, leaving Arkady confused, disappointed, and, as the weeks drifted by, desperately lonely.

It took less than a week on-planet for the survey team's carefully engineered and supposedly foolproof quarantine procedures to fail. And when they failed, the damage hit the worst thing possible: the orbsilk gardens.

The orbsilk gardens were a fairy-tale realm in which the brutal economies of spacefaring life were transformed into abundant, blooming, luxurious life. It was this section of the ship—of any Syndicate ship—that was most heavily retrofitted, and therefore felt most like home to Syndicate senses. Here the hard cold virusteel of the UN-built driveship had been transformed by the collective labors of botanists, zoologists, and entomologists into a living architecture of silk and leaves and spun orbglass. Where the rest of the ship turned away from space and hunkered down behind its virusteel double hull, the ark section unfolded into the void like an intricate flower. When the ship was in orbit the vast spans of spun silkglass opened onto the sea of stars beyond the solar collectors, seeking the starlight that the orbsilkworms—and therefore the ship—lived upon. And at the moment they looked out over the green sea of the Big Wood from which the new invaders had come.

This was Bella's kingdom, and she tended it with a fervent attention to detail that its denizens required. The orbsilkworms lived on dwarf mulberry trees, which were rooted in hanging hydroponic trays suspended from the airy ceiling. The elevation of the trays was either to protect them from the appetites of other shipboard insects or to avoid some kind of rampant fungal infection, Arkady could never remember which. But the result was a veritable hanging garden of fragrant, weeping, cocoon-festooned mulberry trees. They ate and slept and woke and spun their gauzy silk cocoons in much the same way that ten millennia of their forebears had done. But they were chimeras, ingeniously spliced genetic constructs, just like the Syndicate engineers who designed them. And the rich gold-brown shimmer of their cocoons revealed the nature of the chimera: a precisely engineered recombination of silkworm DNA with genetic material drawn from the spinners of the strongest natural fiber ever discovered: the silk of the golden orb spider.

When the silkworms were feeding, the sound of their collective jaws was loud enough to be audible: a constant slippery hum like the whisper of a sleeper turning beneath silken bedsheets. At other times, the garden was a place of gauzy shimmering silence in which Bella flitted from tree to tree or bent over her copper throwing bowls or labored at her airy glass-and-virusteel hand loom like some posthuman Lady of Shalott.

Out of this insubstantial aerie would come every article of clothing, every piece of rope, and every parachute, collecting net, and specimen sack that the survey team would use over the course of their mission. More important, a large array of materials that would be used to repair or replace broken elements of the ship itself would be produced here, or by subtle molecular manipulations of the raw silk in the zero-g labs down in the core engineering levels. And it would all come from the worms, teased into existence by Bella's careful, deliberate, disciplined fingers.

Their management was more art than science. They died off with horrifying regularity, and for bizarrely trivial reasons: an inauspicious change of temperature or humidity; a bad smell; a sudden noise; a change in the habitation arc's rotational gravity that might be so subtle as to be imperceptible even to the refined instrument of the human inner ear. At times they required air and light, and the workers would open up the ventilation louvers and pull back the blinds over the great skylights to let in the carefully filtered starlight. At other times they must be covered with damp sterile cloths and kept in the most perfect darkness and silence, lest they become startled and turn their heads so that their razor-sharp teeth severed the precious threads in midstream.

But now the orbsilkworms were more than startled.

They were starving. They were being outcompeted in their own carefully engineered ecological niche by an obscure species of caterpillar with a voracious appetite for mulberry leaves.

Bella did her best to help. She brought Arkady endless samples of everything that looked to her even remotely like one of the life stages of the pest. She even learned how to collect and preserve samples with the spare field kit Arkady dug out of storage for her. Unfortunately, the samples told Arkady a lot about the mysterious worm but not much about how to kill it.

What finally broke the problem open was a tiny seed of memory prompted by the sight of Bella's throwing hooks glittering in the ruddy gleam of Novalis's sunset . . . a seed of memory that germinated into the barest, tender green shoot of an idea.

"Listen to this," Arkady told Bella excitedly when he finally tracked down the long-ago-read and nearly forgotten passage. "It's from Wheeler's *Ants*, the book that kicked off the great twentieth-century flowering of social insect studies. I must have read it when I was eight. I can't believe it was still rattling around in my brain somewhere:

According to Magowan, [Wheeler wrote] quoted by McCook, "In many parts of the province of Canton, where, says a Chinese writer, cereals cannot be profitably cultivated, the land is devoted to the cultivation of orange-trees, which being subject to devastation from worms, require to be protected in a peculiar manner, that is, by importing ants from the neighboring hills for the destruction of the dreaded parasite. The orangeries themselves supply ants which prey upon the enemy of the or-

ange, but not in sufficient numbers; and resort is had to hill people, who, throughout the summer and winter, find the nests suspended from branches of bamboo and various trees. There are two varieties of ant, red and yellow, whose nests resemble cotton bags. The orange-ant feeders are provided with pig or goat bladders, which are baited inside with lard. The orifices they apply to the entrances of the nests, whence the ants enter the bag and become a marketable commodity at the orangeries. Orange-trees are colonized by depositing the ants on their upper branches, and to enable them to pass from tree to tree, all the trees of the orchard are connected by a bamboo rod."

"Okay," Arkady said. "So that's Magowan according to Cook according to Wheeler. And then Wheeler follows up the bit about the Cantonese red and yellow ants with what has to be one of the earliest written accounts of importing ants into the contintental United States for pest control. That's what actually stuck in my mind. That and putting the bamboo rod between the trees for the ants to walk across. Though I don't know what we're going to use for bamboo here, come to think of it. . . ."

He looked up expectantly only to find Bella staring rather blankly at him.

"Don't you see?" he said. "Novalis's analog to the orange tree worms has found your orbsilk garden. Now we've got to find Novalis's version of Magowan's red and yellow ants. Or, rather, we've got to find the ecological niche they belong in . . . and hope to God it's got something in it we can use."

Arkady had to shake down every tree within a morning's walk of base camp. But he did it, with Bella's surprisingly able help. And eventually he struck gold: a tiny golden ant that lived in the genetically engineered fruit trees that was the only visible legacy of the long-vanished bare branch colony.

They weren't Monsanto ants either, which pleased Arkady because it suggested that they had been developed during the original colonists' long interstellar journey. He was reinventing an already tried and tested pest control method. And the great thing about reinventing the wheel was that the wheel that worked for someone else usually worked for you too.

"Can you check my work before I do a release?" he asked Arkasha when he had mapped out what he hoped would be a suitable geneset. "Just in case?"

"Your work is always good, Arkady. I don't have to check it."

"But I'd feel more comfortable if you did."

Arkasha shrugged, pronounced himself flattered, and checked it.

"I like it," he said eventually. "Your queens function normally once they've mated, but they don't have the genes that express themselves in the nuptial flight, so they don't mate except in the lab. You get a perfectly normal colony, with the life cycle to support the large-scale predation you want from them, but you can cut the thread at the end of each generation and start fresh without worrying about wild strains developing. Classic example of de facto sterilization through genetic modification." He made one of his wry faces. "Too bad they can't do that for us. It'd save a lot of sweat and bother."

Arkady cleared his throat and forced his mind away from the image that the words *sweat* and *bother* raised . . . an image that was never far below the surface when Arkasha was in the same room with him.

"Well?" Arkasha asked. "What are you standing there for? Go save Bella's worms. She promised to make me another sweater, and I seem to be missing one."

Amazingly, it worked. And the long, undulating willow wands that they'd used in place of bamboo sticks made the whole orbsilk garden look like one of the intricate diagrams of climatic succession cycles that Arkady had admired so much in his childhood textbooks. He'd only adapted an ancient solution to a new environment, rather than inventing it from whole cloth, but he felt a real sense of accomplishment nonetheless.

"Thank you so much," Bella said in her quiet, awkward voice . . . an awkwardness Arkady had begun to suspect was not simple shyness but the hesitation of a thoughtful, sensitive person long accustomed to being misunderstood by her peers. "That was so clever of you. Can you imagine, if you hadn't read that little paragraph and remembered it and . . ."

"Yeah, it's kind of neat when useless knowledge turns out not to be so useless after all."

"Exactly!" Bella breathed. "I mean what could be a better proof that education can't all be practical application . . . that you have to have research and study and . . . and *knowledge for its own sake*?"

Arkady looked down into the shining eyes that were gazing up at him with such admiration and felt an unaccustomed flush of pleasure. It was amazing, really, how tiny and childlike Bella was. She even engendered the same protective feelings in him that children inspired. He supposed this was what human males must have felt back when . . . but no, his mind shied away from the thought.

"I'd like to help you with your collecting," she was saying now. "If you need the help. If it wouldn't be too much trouble to have me tagging along. I . . . I don't mind taking on the extra work. And I wouldn't be in the way, really I wouldn't. It's so *interesting*."

Arkady hesitated.

"And I need to get away from . . . I feel so . . . so trapped sometimes . . . *please, Arkady, I won't be any trouble to you!*"

"Of course you can help," he said. "It never hurts to have an extra pair of helping hands. And I'll be glad to teach you."

Ironically it was also Shy Bella who brought about what Arkady later came to think of as his and Arkasha's first Real Conversation.

She came into dinner late one night—a night when Arkasha had put in one of his rare appearances—and she walked straight across the room, served herself from the stovetop, and sat down between the two Ahmeds without so much as glancing at her sib farther down the table.

A sib who gave her a hard, narrow-eyed stare, then stood up and swept out of the room without uttering a word of excuse or farewell to anyone.

"Trouble in paradise?" Arkasha murmured ironically when the normal buzz of conversation had revived enough to cover his words.

"You think that's paradise?" Arkady glanced around instinctively to make sure no one was listening. "It looks more like purgatory to me."

"Now that might be just about the most interesting thing you've ever said to me."

Arkady turned to find his sib's dark eyes fixed intently on him. They were sitting very close, having slid down the bench together to make room for Bella, and he could feel the warm pressure of Arkasha's thigh against his.

"You don't give me much of a chance to say anything to you, interesting or otherwise."

"Is that how it comes across to you?"

"Yes."

"Oh." Arkasha seemed uncharacteristically taken aback. "Uh . . . doing anything tonight?"

"Should I be?"

"Well, I have some work I need to get done later, but walk down to the lab with me. I've got something to show you."

Back in the lab, Arkady marveled as always at the neat dovetailing of individual and society, so pervasive in the Syndicates that it was for all intents and purposes invisible. Arkady's side of the lab was a chaotic day-after-the-battle debris field of fly tape, sample containers, taxonomy treatises, work gloves, and trenching tools. His field gear—the most obvious vector of external contamination—had been disinfected daily since they made planetfall, but nothing could disguise the tears and stains that were badges of former expeditions. Even the newish lab coat dangling off the backrest of his stool bore the telltale spots and smears of yesterday's sample preparations.

Arkasha's side of the lab looked all but unused in comparison. Virgin expanses of countertop gleamed under the shipboard lights. Racked trays of slides glittered like ice in the zero-g shelving units beside neatly labeled notebooks and thick reference volumes whose spines had none of the cracks and dog-eared edges that Arkady's books seemed magically to acquire. The only signs of a fallible posthuman presence—and even those were lined up along the backsplash of the lab bench like little soldiers—were Arkasha's ubiquitous chewed pencil stubs.

It would have been more efficient of course to divide the labs by area of specialization rather than geneline. But in Syndicates as well as in anthills, efficiency rarely trumped psychological comfort. The first joint missions had tried to organize their limited work space by task category. Pure sciences with pure sciences. Field work with field work. Sample preparation segregated from processing and analysis.

It hadn't worked. There had been fights and frustrations. People had worked less—and been more stressed out about what little work they did accomplish—than they were in their home Syndicates. They wanted to be with their sibs, not with strangers. And in the end, the steering committees had relented, surrendering to the very biological constraints they and their predecessors had engineered into their lateral descendants.

Tonight, however, Arkasha wasn't even remotely interested in work-place efficiency. On entering the lab, he went straight to the refrigerator, pulled a large beaker out from behind the sample racks, and set it carefully on the countertop. "I had to barter my virtue to the Aurelias to get this," he announced, "so you'd damn well better appreciate it."

"What *is* it?"

"It seemed better not to ask." Arkasha extracted two smaller beakers from the autoclave, poured out double shots of the clear liquid with practiced ease, and handed one to Arkady. "Tastes like beetle dung, but it gets the job done."

"I'm not sure this is a good idea, Arkasha."

"Drink faster, then. You'll be amazed at how quickly your doubts slip away."

Arkady took a sip and found, to his relief, that it tasted more or less like vodka. "I'm not going to go blind from this, am I?"

"Not unless you play with yourself while you're drinking it."

Arkady choked and spit a mouthful of the stuff on the floor and sat wheezing on his lab stool while Arkasha thumped at his back.

When Arkady was more or less breathing again, Arkasha climbed onto the counter, crossed his arms and legs, and peered down at him, looking for all the world like one of the sleek sharp-eyed crows that infested Gilead's farmland districts. "So," he began as if he were embarking on the weightiest of philosophical debates. "Tell me why, out of all the things in the world you could have turned your brain to, you chose ants."

Why ants? *Where to begin?*

Even the mere names were things of beauty to him. *Pogonomyrmex barbatus,* for example: the red harvester ant, whose name always brought to his mind the earliest known description of the species, from some ancient Aztec codex: "It sweeps, makes itself heaps of sand, makes wide roads, makes a home." Or the beautiful dacetines; or the primitive, solitary ponerines; or all the varied species of industrious leaf cutters.

The names and lore of ants reminded Arkady of the coded flicker of navigational beacons. They traced a tenuous path through the galaxy—always at the edge of extinction, always running just ahead of the death from which there could be no returning—plotting the tenuous evolutionary trail that linked all of posthumanity, UN and Syndicate alike, to Earth.

Take the ants on Novalis, for example. From a meager, hopelessly narrow stream of imported specimens they had flowed across the planet, filling every ecological niche he had so far investigated. Harvesters, earth movers, foragers, swarm raiders . . . and several variants of ants that Arkady had encountered in none of his long studies and that he suspected might be entirely new species adapted to the peculiar needs of life on Novalis.

"And what about you?" he asked Arkasha, embarrassed that he'd gone on so long. "Why genetics?"

"That's less interesting. I was always top of my class, and all the top students are pushed into genetics more or less automatically."

Arkady must have looked as incredulous about the idea of Arkasha being pushed into anything as he felt.

"And I liked it for my own reasons too, I suppose."

Arkady waited.

"There's a kind of poetry to genetics," Arkasha said at last. He looked defensive, as if he thought Arkady might laugh at the idea. "I mean look at a person. Any person. You. The Aurelias. Look at this whole amazing planet we're sitting on. And then just imagine what *Earth* must have been with all her countless species coevolving on an evolutionary landscape that they themselves were changing at every moment. Have you read Lotka? Not the parts they quote in political philosophy. The science. At the end of *Principles of Mathematical Biology,* he writes about the *evolution* of planets, what he calls the great world engine. I wanted to find out what makes the world engine run."

"And have you?"

"I bare my soul to you and all you can do is make fun of me?"

"I'm not making fun of you! Really, I mean it. Have you found out?"

"No. But I will." He gestured toward the door, and his voice dropped to a near whisper. "The answer's right outside the airlock. All the answers. We just have to find eyes new enough to see Novalis with."

"I know!" Arkady cried. "I feel the same way! I was thinking just this morning that Novalis is a kind of second chance. And not just for the Syndicates either. For earth sciences generally. Every time we've ever looked at data from pre-Evacuation Earth and wished we could go back, knowing what we know now, with the tools we have now. . . . There's a lifetime of work here. More than a lifetime."

Arkasha poured himself another glass, threw back a quick swallow, then topped off Arkady's glass. "So are you going to stick around to do it?" he asked.

"What do you mean?"

"Just that."

"You mean stay here? Permanently?"

"Someone'll have to."

"But don't you want to go home to Rostov?"

Arkasha shrugged.

"It's home. Doesn't that matter to you?"

Another shrug.

"But . . . weren't you happy there?"

"No," Arkasha said baldly.

"Why not?"

"Has it ever occurred to you, Arkady, that we might be getting a little too conformist in the Syndicates? We go to great lengths to maintain sufficient genetic diversity, of course. But what about diversity here?" He tapped his forehead. "Or here." He tapped his chest, not quite in the anatomically correct position, but close enough so that they both knew what organ he was talking about.

"I don't think—"

"Look at you, for example. Look at the misery you caught over your dissent paper."

"That's putting it strongly."

"Is it? Didn't you catch just enough grief over it that you stopped writing along those lines?"

"No! I just . . . backed off a little."

Arkasha shrugged and began to turn away.

"I want to talk about it," Arkady protested. "I just don't necessarily agree with you."

"Seriously?"

"Seriously."

Arkasha sloshed the liquor around in his glass and took an experimental sip. "It's gotten too warm, hasn't it?" He got up without waiting for Arkady's answer and deposited the beaker back in the lab's sample refrigerator. It was a little alarming to think of what else was in there with it. But if it had come out of the Aurelias' fridge, then Arkady supposed it had seen worse.

"Tell me," Arkasha said when he returned to his perch. "Have you ever read the Bible?"

Arkady's surprise and dismay must have shown in his face, because Arkasha laughed and quickly said, "Oh no. I'm not one of *them*. I was just thinking of the verses in Leviticus about the scapegoat."

"I'm sorry. I'm not familiar with goats. What's the Latin species name?"

Arkasha laughed. "It's a metaphor, not a species. On Yom Kippur, the Day of Atonement, the ancient Israelites used to put all the sins of the people on the head of a goat and cast it out into the desert. *'And the goat shall bear away all their iniquities to an uninhabited land.'* "

"I'm afraid I don't see your point," Arkady said, all too aware of how pompous he sounded.

"Don't you? Instead of the desert we have euth wards. And instead of Yom Kippur we have culling and critique sessions."

"That's ridiculous, Arkasha! Renorming centers are for rehabilitation, not punishment. And even the people who can't be reintegrated into their home crèches can lead happy, productive lives from the wards."

"Oh, yeah? Name one person who's done it."

"Rumi."

"Rumi, indeed. I was wondering when we were going to get to him. Brilliant, isn't it? Let one dead dissident become a famous poet and you can wave his poems in the face of all the live dissidents to prove that they're imagining things. Of course Rumi had to kill himself before he could be rehabilitated. But we only want to remember the feel-good part of the story. *'I'm the echo of your echo, the shadow of your shadow's shadow,'* " Arkasha quoted, twisting Rumi's famous lines to extract a disconcerting new meaning from them. " *'And let's face it, brother, a man needs a shadow.'* "

The poet's words hung in the air between them, a ghostly reminder of the great man's unrequited and ultimately fatal passion.

"It's a love poem," Arkady protested weakly, "not a political tract."

"Is there a difference?"

Arkady felt hot and restless. He stood up, his back protesting its long stint on the hard lab stool; but there was nowhere else to go in the suddenly cramped space of the lab, so he sat back down again.

"If you want to talk about love," Arkasha said, "let's talk about the six percent rule. Or don't you know what it is?"

Of course Arkady knew. Everyone knew. The six percent rule had dogged Syndicate genetic designers since the moment the first cohort reached sexual maturity. It turned out, after all the millennia of debate and argument and condemnation, that you could sociogenetically engineer humans for either heterosexuality or homosexuality. It was child's play. An idiot could do it. Except that neither the most brilliant genetic engineering nor the most repressive social systems could do it to *everybody*. No matter how careful or ruthless you were, about six percent of the population broke the other way out of the starting gate. And the percentage was the same regardless of whether you were trying to promote God-given heterosexuality or laboratory-manufactured homosexuality.

"Well, what if the six percent rule is like your ants?" Arkasha went on. "What was it you said in your dissent paper? That following behaviors are only adaptive as long as Russell's prerequisite for inductive reasoning applies: as long as future futures continue to resemble past futures. But dissent is the swarm's way of keeping alternative solutions on hand: hedging its bets just in case future futures break the rules learned from past futures."

"Okay," Arkady admitted. "I guess I said that."

"So generalize. What if there's a dissent instinct in all social animals, humans as well as ants? What if dissent—deviance, abnormality, protest, whatever you want to call it when some people in a society refuse to follow the crowd—is really the species trying to maintain enough diversity, mental as well as physical, to deal with unexpected bumps in the road? Has it ever occurred to you that we might be normalizing ourselves onto a fitness peak we're not going to be able to climb back down from if our future futures turn out to be too different from our past futures?"

"First of all," Arkady said after a stunned pause, "my dissent paper didn't even remotely say *that*. And, second, how can you possibly compare political dissent, which, yes, I admit there might be a place for, with . . . well, *deviance*?"

Arkasha jumped up off his lab bench and started straightening already obsessively straight papers. "I have to get back to work, Arkady. It's been nice talking to you. Let's do it again next week."

"Arkasha!"

"What?"

"Nothing. I just . . ." He floundered, unable to bring himself to speak the unspeakable. "I want . . ."

Arkasha sighed. "What do you want from me, Arkady?"

"I want . . . I *like* you, dammit! As a person. We should be friends, but every time it seems like we're about to be, you . . . Oh for God's sake, will you put your stupid notes away and sit *down*?"

Arkasha sat down, drawing his feet onto the bottom rung of his lab stool and crossing his arms over his chest like a child who'd just been yelled at for fidgeting.

"I mean if I bore you or something, let me know," Arkady went on. "I can live with it."

"You don't bore me," Arkasha whispered.

"And I don't care about the sex either." There, he'd said it. It couldn't get worse than that, could it? He plunged on. "I mean, of course I care. But I don't care if you're—I don't care what you are. And I'm not going to report you, or anything like that. Maybe that's wrong, but . . . I'm just not, okay? So if that's why you're avoiding me, you can stop worrying about it."

Arkasha blinked. "Are you trying to tell me that it's okay with you if I'm a sexual deviant?"

"Yes."

"Failure to report is a crime, Arkady. You could land yourself in a renorming center that way."

"I don't care."

"You should care. You could get yourself into a lot of trouble if you talk like that to just anybody."

"I'm not talking to just anybody. I'm talking to you."

"Arkady—"

"I mean it. I don't care. And you don't have to explain yourself to me. It's over. We never have to talk about it again."

"Arkady!"

"What?"

"I'm not."

Arkady frowned at him for a moment, not understanding.

"I'm *not.*"

"Oh."

One corner of Arkasha's mouth quirked upward. "You sound disappointed."

"I, uh . . . feel really stupid."

"You don't look so clever either. No, no! I'm joking! Seriously, Arkady, why should you feel stupid? There's nothing to feel stupid about."

"Well, I mean, I just assumed. And I'm not one of those guys who thinks he's so devastatingly attractive that anyone who doesn't fall into bed with him has to be a pervert."

"I didn't think you were one of those guys. Though you *are* pretty devastatingly attractive."

The room suddenly felt hot and very small. He looked up to find Arkasha watching him intently.

"But this is a really long assignment, Arkady. A long time to live in each other's back pockets if things go badly."

"I wouldn't be . . . difficult."

"I know you wouldn't. You're much too nice for that."

"I love you."

Arkasha shrank back into himself again. When he finally answered his voice was muffled and he wouldn't meet Arkady's eyes. "You only say that because you don't know me," he said. "When you know me better, you won't say it anymore."

"Am I interrupting something?" Bella asked coolly from the door.

Arkady jumped, dropping his glass, which shattered deafeningly. Razor-sharp splinters of glass scattered to the room's four corners. The place reeked of guilt and alcohol.

"Have you seen my sib?" Bella asked, casting a suspicious eye around the lab as if the two of them might have secreted her missing crèche-mate in a file drawer.

"Should we have?" Arkasha asked.

Bella ignored him. "Well?" she said, looking at Arkady as if he were the only person in the room.

"Uh . . . no. Sorry."

"She *said* she was coming down here to have you run a sample from the seed bank." Typically, she managed to make the statement sound like an accusation. "I don't know what's wrong with her these days. Her mind is on everything except her job."

Which probably meant that her mind was on everything except her crèchemate, Arkady thought uncharitably.

Meanwhile, Bella was still ostentatiously ignoring Arkasha. Embarrassed, Arkady stood up and ushered her out into the corridor so that Arkasha could get back to work if he wanted to.

But apparently he didn't want to. He padded across the lab to take in the conversation over Arkady's shoulder. Bella muttered something huffy about people sticking their noses in where they didn't have any business to be.

"Am I interrupting something?" Arkasha inquired sweetly.

Bella glared at him.

"Have you tried paging her?" Arkady asked.

"Of course I have!" Now, for the first time, and quite inexplicably, she seemed embarrassed herself. "She doesn't answer."

"Have you talked to the Ahmeds about it?"

"I'm not disloyal!"

Right. Not disloyal enough to lodge a formal complaint against her crèchemate. Just disloyal enough to talk her down with every other construct on board.

"Well, if she shows up, I'll tell her you're looking for her."

And after a few more complaints and accusations, Bella finally took herself off.

"I loathe that woman," Arkasha murmured, tracking her progress down the hab ring.

"You shouldn't provoke her," Arkady said. "She already hates you. And she's the type who gets people put on euth wards."

Arkasha stared down the corridor. He looked wounded and brittle and terribly in need of protection. "You think I don't know that?"

"I wish . . ."

"You wish what?"

"I don't know. Nothing."

"Listen, Arkady. I really do have work I need to get done tonight. Is it going to hurt your feelings if I go do it?"

"Of course not," Arkady lied.

"Honestly?"

"Honestly."

"Thanks, Arkady. And don't leave the light on, okay? I don't want to keep you up."

"I'll leave the light on."

"You don't have to leave the light on."

"I want to."

"You shouldn't."

Arkady forced a grin that didn't come out nearly as shaky as he'd thought it would. "Are you going to argue with me about this all night, or are you going to go do your work?"

INFORMATION COSTS

Problems with only partial or limited information arise in many
disciplines: in economics, computer science, physics, control
theory, signal processing, prediction, decision theory, and
artificial intelligence. . . . Two of the basic assumptions of
information-based complexity are that information is partial
and contaminated. There is one further assumption—
information costs. THESE THREE ASSUMPTIONS ARE
FUNDAMENTAL: INFORMATION IS PARTIAL, INFORMATION
IS CONTAMINATED, AND INFORMATION COSTS.

—J. TRAUB (1988)

I TS OFFICIAL NAME WAS THE Institute for the Coordination of Intelligence and Special Tasks, but most Israelis called it the Institute, or, in Hebrew, the *Mossad*. And the inconspicuous, close-mouthed, suspiciously fit men and women who worked at the Institute called it simply the Office.

The first time Cohen had walked into the shabby lobby off King Saul Boulevard and ridden the clanking elevator to the eighth floor he'd been in the real Hyacinthe's body. It had been a week after the fateful doctor's visit—and a week before Hyacinthe had worked up the courage to tell his wife about the diagnosis. Hyacinthe Cohen (Hy, predictably, to his Israeli friends) had been a pigheadedly rational man. And yet he had felt in his gut, at some level below words, that the disease wouldn't really be real until he told his wife about it. How strange, Cohen thought now . . . and how human. Almost as human as the feeling the memory aroused in Cohen: that only now, when it was far too late, was he finally beginning to understand the man.

Hyacinthe had leaned against this very same rail, looking at his reflection, still strong and wiry as a greyhound, and feeling the first subtle tremors of the disease that would finally kill him. Cohen hadn't remembered that heartsick moment for two lifetimes as humans measured them. Now he asked himself how he could ever have forgotten it.

He glanced at Li, who had crossed her arms and thrown her head back to squint impatiently at the flickering lights of the number panel. *She doesn't understand,* he thought on a confused rush of emotion that mingled frustration, fear, and anger. *She hasn't begun to know what death is.*

"What's wrong?" She was staring at him, faint wrinkles of worry framing the bridge of her nose.

"Just appalled by the disaster in the mirror. I look like an upper-class English twit on safari. No nice French boy should ever have to wear these shoes!"

"Better alive and frumpy than fashionably dead," Li drawled.

Cohen sniffed theatrically. "The fact that you could say—no, even think such a thing makes me seriously doubt your moral fiber!"

When the doors finally opened onto the eighth floor, Cohen realized that he'd forgotten just how underwhelming the place was. Even on the eighth floor—perhaps especially on the eighth floor—Mossad headquarters had the peculiar official shabbiness of all Israeli government buildings. All the furniture was painted IDF olive drab, but somehow it still looked like it had been bought at five different yard sales. There was no reception area, just a narrow corridor that had been transformed into a makeshift security checkpoint by pushing two heavy desks together and depositing a muscular young *katsa*-in-training behind them on a sagging office chair that was probably older than he was.

The guard's sidearm was holstered, but even with the elaborate security check they'd undergone before getting in the elevator he was on his feet and ready to draw before the elevator doors opened. This wasn't a country, or a building, in which people took chances. Li and Cohen surrendered their left hands to the guard's implant scanner, then sat down in the chairs he waved them to and waited.

And waited.

And waited.

They'd arrived for a meeting at four, and now they were watching the clock creep toward five. The usual tomblike quiet still reigned on the eighth floor, but behind their backs they could hear the cables of the ancient elevators groaning as the departing crowds of junior spooks and clerical employees made their daily getaway.

And all the while a niggling, annoying, self-indulgent little complaint rattled pointlessly around Cohen's mind:

Gavi never made me wait this long.

Cohen's relationship with the Mossad had begun humbly. A few lunchtime meetings during vacations in Tel Aviv or Jerusalem. Keeping an ear open for useful information. Passing on the innuendoes and misinformation that the King Saul Boulevard spin doctors crafted to mislead Israel's enemies. Making his well-secured homes available, no questions asked, to the suspiciously athletic young men and women who occasionally found reason to use them. Dropping a request for coveted information into the ear of a sympathetic UN official, and pointing out that a Jew could be loyal to his own government and still feel a moral obligation to pass along any news that would help more of the nice boys and girls serving on the Green Line go home to their parents on their own feet instead of in body bags. In short, he'd been the perfect *sayan*: a volunteer loyal to the country of his birth, but willing, within the bounds of that first loyalty, to do whatever little things he could to help Israel.

And of course little was a matter of perspective. Eighteen percent of the UN's nonmilitary spinstream communications passed through Cohen's networks or the networks of various former associated AIs. He'd written the software that handled pension administration for the civil services of half the Periphery. All of UNSec's feared semisentients had evolved more or less directly from Cohen's own expert systems, and over the years he had quietly acquired controlling interests in the defense contractors who manufactured them. Very little happened in UN space that Cohen didn't eventually find out about. And when he could—with discretion and never risking too much social and political capital on any one roll of the dice—he made sure that Israel's interests were served.

Most of the time that was all he did. But once or twice a century he was asked to do more. And each time the Office called, he was brought up against the memory—a memory that made him the only living link to a past that was dead history to the rest of humanity—that Hyacinthe's grandfather had gone into Dachau in 1943 and never come out.

And so, over time, Cohen had become something between a *sayan* and a *katsa,* a full-fledged Mossad agent. He'd gone through the *katsa* induction course five times, in five different bodies—ostensibly to refresh his tradecraft, but really to cement his relationships with successive generations of the Mossad's human leadership. He'd worked for all the great ones: Gershon, Barzilai, Hamdani, and now the legendary Didi Halevy. He'd been burned, sometimes badly enough that even his supporters in the Security Council had shrugged and admitted his probable (though never quite provable) guilt. But Cohen was rich, very very rich. So they'd turned a blind eye and tolerated him.

Until Tel Aviv. In one bloody night Tel Aviv had killed half a dozen UNSec and Mossad agents, ended Gavi's career, and stripped Cohen of his French passport and the last tatters of plausible deniability.

So why was he running to Didi's aid again? And why on Earth was he dragging Li with him?

At the prospect of dragging Li into the wake of Tel Aviv, all the guilt and anxiety and self-loathing Cohen had been shoving under the rug for so long rose up to accuse him. And with them came a little shudder of apprehension that he would have called a ghost walking over his grave . . . if he weren't himself the ghost of a man whose very grave no longer existed.

Did all spies feel this way? Did they all suffer from the gnawing suspicion that the safe everyday world was just the surface of a deep ocean, and that they would break through the fragile surface tension and drown if the bulkheads they constructed around their separate and conflicting lives were ever breached? At least human spies had the unity of their bodies to fall back on: one brain, one set of memories, and the ironclad physiological conviction that the chaos raging inside their skulls was unique and singular and meaningful. Cohen had nothing to hang his identity on but the spooky phenomenon of emergence. And how long could you survive out there in the lying cold when you were only a ghost to begin with?

At a quarter past five the door at the end of the hall opened and the man they were waiting for emerged.

"Cohen!" he cried. "Welcome home, my friend!" He looked back and forth between the two of them, his eyes bright behind Coke bottle glasses, his normally drawn face wrinkled with a scrappy little boy's grin. "So which one of you is you?" he asked. "Who do I have the right to kiss, and who do I have to fob off with a handshake?"

Cohen stepped into the little man's outstretched arms. "You're perfectly welcome to kiss us both. But me first, please."

Didi Halevy's friends said he looked like an out-of-work undertaker. Didi Halevy's enemies, if they were wise, didn't say anything. Cohen had once spoken to a *katsa* who had worked the NorAmArc with Didi when they were both mere field agents. "He ought to be in the diction- ary under the word *nebbish*," the man had said admiringly. "When Didi walks into a room his own mother would swear someone just left!"

All of which drove home to Cohen just how unhuman he himself was. Because to Cohen, Didi had always seemed *more* real than most people, not less. And though he and Didi saw each other at rare inter- vals, and usually only during moments of crisis, there were few things he enjoyed more than an hour spent talking to this extraordinary man who looked so inexplicably ordinary to his fellow humans. Or at least that had been how things stood before Tel Aviv.

"Can we take you to dinner when we're done here?" Cohen asked Didi.

"No. But you can come to my house for dinner. My daughters are here on their Yom Kippur visas, and Zillah's always delighted to see you. And of course"—with a polite nod to Li—"the invitation is also for . . . ?"

"Actually, we've met," Li said. "At the War College on Alba. You probably don't remember, but I took a class the semester you visited."

"Oh dear. I should remember, of course, but I meet so many people. And my memory for faces is very poor."

Cohen rolled his eyes and coughed.

"I'm sorry," Didi said humbly, "it's dusty in here. All the paper, you know. You wouldn't believe the problems we have with allergies. Would you like to borrow my eyedrops?"

Didi's office was material proof of the old Mossad dictum: the smaller the office, the bigger the reputation. The place must have been a mop closet in some prior incarnation. Only the timeless tools of the trade—the glass-topped desk, the paper shredder, the scrambled land- line, the dusty green ranks of locked file cabinets—suggested the secrets its walls had seen.

Nor did the room give anything away about Didi himself. There were no family pictures, no knickknacks, no mementos. The only hint of personality was a fading computer printout taped to the wall be- hind Didi's head, where generations of young field agents had read it while listening to briefings, waiting for Didi to get off the phone with his wife or daughters, or yawning through administrative updates. The list, which Cohen happened to know had been a present from the last class of *katsas* Didi took through field training, contained five items:

1. The odds of an agent ending up in a hole in the ground are directly proportional to the number of people who know him from a hole in the ground.
2. The best thing to say is always nothing.
3. When you want to know what a piece of information means, look at where it's been.
4. Small guns are more trouble than they're worth.
5. Everyone has his dumb blonde and his rented Ferrari.

As they passed into the office, a slender young man appeared, seemingly from nowhere, to frisk them a second time. Cohen stood patiently to be searched, as did Li; but while Li's inspection of the boy was limited to a quick glance at all the potential hiding places for concealed weapons, Cohen's once-over was a bit more thorough.

The boy had the parchment skin and glossy curls of a yeshiva student. His glasses were cheap, like Didi's, and the lenses were almost thick enough to obscure the long-lashed bedroom eyes behind them. Which didn't change by one jot the fact that the body under the rumpled suit was a soldier's body, and the sleepy-lidded eyes looked out at the world with the calculating poise of a professional killer.

Once he'd pronounced them clean, the young man escorted them into Didi's inner sanctum and hesitated ostentatiously.

"Thank you, Arik," Didi said. And waited.

The boy heaved a sigh of protest over the security breach and slipped out of the room, leaving the three of them alone together.

"Good youngsters coming in these days," Didi told Cohen. "It's a nice thing to see kids who take their work seriously."

"Well, you do get the pick of them."

"You want a boy like Arik should be rotting in a foxhole? Five languages he speaks. Arabic like a native."

No doubt he did speak five languages. He also looked like a smaller, paler, less handsome, and decidedly less good-natured copy of Gavi Shehadeh. But Cohen knew better than to suggest that this might have anything to do with Didi's obvious affection for the boy.

Didi chatted on, mentioning mutual friends. Cohen let the small talk flow over him without too much thought—something he'd long ago learned to do when humans started talking this way—and focused on the body language. He'd wondered for a long time what Catherine Li and Didi Halevy would make of each other. Now he watched each of them summing the other up and asked himself whether these two particular opposites were about to attract or repel.

Li, three years out of the Peacekeepers, still looked so ill at ease in mufti that even the most casual observers pegged her for an off-duty soldier. Didi, by contrast, had looked like a disheveled impostor the one time Cohen had seen him in uniform. In fact, one of the often-discussed mysteries of the Mossad chief's legendary career was the question of how a man who seemed too fragile to lift a piece of paper had survived his compulsory military service long enough for his unique talents to be recognized.

At the moment Didi was definitely in undertaker mode. If Cohen hadn't known better, he would have thought they were talking to the janitor. Did the man have some reason for wanting Li to underestimate him, Cohen wondered, or was it just the habitual camouflage of an old spy who'd long ago learned not to trust new faces?

Li, meanwhile, had gone into her full-blown dumb-soldier act. There was no glint of humor in her dark eyes, no ironic drawl in her voice. Not one thing about her face, manner, voice, or words suggested that she'd ever had an intelligent thought in her life.

He should have expected it, Cohen told himself sourly. He'd looked forward to this meeting for years. And now here they were, both playing dumb with such consummate skill that Cohen was beginning to feel like he was the only sentient life-form in the room.

"You two," he burst out finally, "are absolutely impossible!"

"What?" Didi and Li said at almost the same moment in voices of wounded innocence.

And then Li, having caught Cohen's invective-riddled comment on the bad social graces of all spies and retired soldiers, laughed.

"So," Didi said. "Now that we're all having fun, what do you say we take a look at Catherine's spins from Abulafia Street?"

They ran Li's spins on Didi's long-past-obsolete desk monitor, the three of them hunching over the small display shoulder to shoulder. It was unnerving to see the whole meeting replayed from Li's perspective: to see the thoroughness with which she checked people over; the way her eyes flickered constantly from door to window to floor to ceiling; her almost subconscious awareness of the minute changes in the flow of traffic beyond the walls that could mean danger; the restless, constant, animal awareness of a body that had survived enough combat drops to know that bad luck can kill you at any time and from any direction.

And it was pretty obvious what pieces of bad luck she'd been alerting on back in that hotel room. First and foremost, Turner. No explanation needed there; only a fool, and a suicidal fool at that, would mess with the Americans. But her source of worry was less obvious. In fact, Cohen was embarrassed to realize that he himself had missed it entirely in real time. While he'd been glaring at Korchow and inspecting the antiques collection, Li had in fact been doing her job. And as far as she was concerned that job had mainly consisted of keeping an eye on Shaikh Yassin. Or, more precisely, on one of the hard young men hovering at Yassin's elbow.

Li had ignored the two gorillas, obviously mere hired muscle, and reserved her vigilance for the slim young man with those pale green eyes that still popped up every now and then in the Palestinian gene pool and, a full millennium after the last crusade, were still called crusader's eyes.

The boy had an athlete's slouch. His body was still and relaxed, every betraying tic leached out of it by the same iron discipline that every Mossad *katsa* learned. His face was schooled into a calmly attentive, completely unreadable expression. And the green eyes were cold and alert and moved constantly around the room, taking in everything but never appearing to stare too hard at any one thing. The boy was Arik's opposite number; and only a novice could fail to recognize him for the superlatively trained professional that he was.

"So who's the bright young thing?" Cohen asked. He had a niggling feeling that he'd seen that face before, yet he could match it to none of his stored spinfeed databases. Unsettling. "Could he be Safik's? Safik always liked the pretty ones." Cohen cut a sideways glance at Didi. "So did you for that matter."

"You're right about his being Safik's," Didi said, "though not in the way you think you mean. Look again. Ring any bells?"

Cohen looked again, and suddenly bells were ringing all over the place. The slim, neat build; the intelligent, humorous face; the extraordinary eyes.

"Yusuf Safik," Didi said. "The only son of Walid Safik, head of the Palestinian Security Service's counterintelligence department."

"So Safik *did* have a set of eyes at the auction," Li said with grim satisfaction.

But Cohen wasn't thinking about the auction. He was thinking about Gavi. If the boy was Safik's son, then that made him . . . what? Leila's first cousin once removed? That explained the eyes. And the family resemblance to Leila was unmistakable once you looked for it. He wondered if Gavi and Leila's Joseph—obviously both boys had been named after some common ancestor—would have looked like Yusuf if he'd survived the war. And then he thought about that other lifetime before the war in which they'd all danced at Gavi and Leila's wedding.

Cohen's better-than-human memory called up a detail-perfect image of the day, as accurate and unfaded as remastered spinfeed. Gavi slim and handsome in his uniform, and so achingly young that he looked like a boy just playing at being a soldier. Leila all business—and to everyone's ill-concealed delight already visibly pregnant. Didi had been Gavi's commanding officer. Cohen had been . . . well, what he'd always been. And Gavi Shehadeh and Walid Safik had been just two more bright young men who might or might not amount to anything. It had been Leila—the intense young doctor with the startling eyes and the even more startling opinions—who everyone thought would change the world.

Well, the world had changed all right. And Leila had been among the first casualties. It was still hard to believe that such an extraordinary person had been killed by something as wastefully impersonal as a stray bomb.

Cohen looked up to find Didi's eyes searching his face. The memory of Gavi hung between them. Unasked questions rose and drifted and shredded themselves in the backwash of the ceiling fan.

Didi turned off the monitor and sat down heavily. He took off his glasses, cleaned them on the tail of his shirt, put them back on and peered fretfully around the room. He seemed disappointed with the result, as if he'd expected the world to look better through clean lenses. Then, with a mournful little shrug, he got down to business.

He described Arkady's appearance at Maris Station; his approach to Maris consulate junior intelligence staff; his disappearance and subsequent resurfacing in Moshe's hands; GolaniTech's agreement with Korchow, insofar as they understood it; the cautious back-channel contacts with the bidding parties.

Cohen didn't even try to calibrate Didi's version of events against his own information and look for discrepancies. You might as well try to catch a bird in flight as catch Didi Halevy in a lie. You just trusted him to tell you what he thought you needed to know. Or you didn't trust him at all. There was no middle ground.

"The big questions are two," Didi said when he'd come to the end of his tale. "One, what is Arkady selling? And two, why should we care?"

"You read my report?" Cohen asked doubtfully.

"Yes, yes. And I'm sure you thought it was perfectly comprehensible. But I'm not Gavi. And even if I were, I'd still need to get it into terms the prime minister can understand."

"Does the interest in this case go that high?"

"This is a country of population one million and dropping. Everything goes that high."

"Well," Cohen began. "First of all, let's talk about so-called weapons' infection vector. It's a retrovirus, and as far as I can see a relatively straightforward one. So the real question isn't what the virus is. The real question is: What's the transgenic payload it's inserting into the target organism's cells?"

Cohen stopped to collect his thoughts—a task that was both difficult and necessary because he and the half dozen or so of his aggregated Emergents who had worked on this problem had not reached anything even remotely approaching a consensus on what the payload of Arkady's mystery virus actually was.

"Let me guess," Didi said wryly. "It's like nothing you've ever seen before."

"On the contrary. It's exactly like something I've seen before. Or rather something Hy Cohen saw, and actually messed around with a bit before he invented me. Ever heard of Turing Soup?"

"I don't cook."

"Oh my, aren't we funny? Turing Soup was a turn-of-the-twenty-first-century idea, child of the era of networks . . . just like me. People had networks on the brain back then. The way Enlightenment thinkers had clockwork on the brain. Or the way people in Darwin's day had steam engines on the brain. Or the way we've got spin on the brain. Actually some associates and I are working on a paper about . . . right, okay, never mind. Turing Soup was the brainchild of a guy named Walter Fontana. The same Walter Fontana who invented AlChemy, more prosaically known as Algorithmic Chemistry. One thing you have to say about the guy, he had a gift for names. He also happened to be at MIT toward the end of his career, and to take under his wing a bright young French postdoc in theoretical computer science called Hyacinthe Cohen. Which is why I might just be the only person still alive who remembers Turing Soup.

"The idea behind Turing Soup was to look at the evolution of algorithms as a model for the evolution of organic life. A Turing machine is a universal computer—in fact, the paradigmatic universal computer. It has a reading head that can 'read' any tape run through it. It has an execution apparatus that carries out whatever instructions the reading head reads. Turing couldn't know it back in 1950, but he was essentially describing RNA: a 'reading' mechanism that zips itself to the unraveled DNA strand in order to reproduce its folded protein sequences. Fontana's idea was to throw a bunch of molecular Turing machines together and let them 'read' each other's programs and see if they could construct new programs from the components of the existing ones. It didn't work, mainly because Turing machines have a problem that RNA and DNA either don't have or figured out how to solve a long time ago: they hang, like just about every other computer ever invented. So the machines in Turing Soup would just lock up with each other, start reading each other's tape, slip onto a positive feedback loop, and hang.

"So that was Turing Soup: wrong tool for the right job. Fontana moved on to lambda-calculus and AlChem. And everyone filed Turing Soup away as an idea whose time had come and gone. But if I had to describe this sample Moshe's flogging around, that's what I'd say it was: Turing Soup made out of DNA. Or more accurately, a virus that takes its host's DNA and turns it into Turing Soup." Cohen grinned. "Which—if you'll forgive a joke that about eighteen of my associates have already made at some point in the last few weeks—gives a whole new meaning to parasitic computation."

"So you're saying this is . . . what? AI in a virus?"

"God, no! Start letting your metaphors gallop around like that and you'll never be able to sort out what it actually *is*. What Moshe showed us was . . . conceptually provocative. But it wasn't artificial intelligence. At least not in any form that's recognizable to *this* particular artificial intelligence. If you need a layman's label to hang on it, let's call it . . . a search engine in a virus?"

"And what's the engine searching for?"

"That, my friend, I can't begin to tell you."

Didi pursed his lips, considering. "And you believe Arkady's story that they found it out on—what was the place called?"

"Novalis. I've never heard of it either. It's off the maps. No record of any survey. No BE buoy within light-years, probably because the spectrometry wasn't promising enough. It's one of those 'you can't get there from here' planets. Anyway, the host genotype is descended from an old Monsanto patent. That tells us nothing; half the known universe is littered with that crap. But it certainly would make sense if they really did find it out there. And it fits in again with what I said about it not being Syndicate splice work. They won't touch corporate genesets as a general rule; bad associations."

"I take it the planet's terraformed, then?"

"That's what they went out there to find out. And given what they seem to have brought back with them, I'd say the answer is yes."

"Is this something UNSec ought to know about?"

"Well, I'm sure UNSec would think it was."

"But you don't."

"I'm a live-and-let-live kind of boy. And UNSec has a nasty habit of breaking planets so other people can't use them. A good planet's a terrible thing to waste."

Didi smiled slightly. "Okay, we'll let it ride for now."

Which they both knew only meant that they would let it ride until either Didi or the PM decided it was time not to let it ride.

"All right then." Didi leaned back in his chair, caught sight of a food stain on his tie, peered at it, scrubbed at it. And then abandoned the effort, having only succeeded in making the tie wrinkled as well as stained. "You've answered my first two questions—what the virus is and who put it there—with more questions. Now what about the one question we ought to be able to answer: Why the hell should we be interested in it?"

"Well," Cohen said slowly, "I know why ALEF is interested. Immortality, if you want to stick a name on it."

"But you've already got that."

"Not strictly speaking. No more than an ant swarm or a beehive does. And AIs have life spans just like any other superorganism. Even the ones that don't collapse prematurely under the weight of their own competing identities."

"But how does an organic virus make a machine live longer?"

"Because the underlying dynamics are the same whether you're dealing with organic or synthetic superorganisms. We're interested in any mechanism that propagates beneficial mutations across a population while somehow repressing harmful ones."

"Controlling evolution, essentially."

"Well . . . tweaking it. I think this would fall into what Syndicate genetic designers call the 'soft chaos control' theory of directed evolution. It's what makes the quality of their genetic engineering so superior to the UN version. And it's exactly the kind of biocomputing concept that holds the most promise for resolving the problem of decoherence in Emergents. Along with all the other dysfunctions that, tellingly, have the same names in AI design as they do in ecophysics: brittleness, perturbation intolerance, maladaptive red queen regimes, and so forth . . ." Cohen cleared his throat and shifted in the hardbacked chair. "But none of that answers the question of why *Israel* would be interested."

"We're not," Didi said blandly, "or we wouldn't be letting Golani-Tech sell Arkady to the highest bidder."

"That's pure spin, and you know it," Cohen objected. "You're taking some heavy risks to do this. I don't care how greedy GolaniTech is or how uninterested you are. They wouldn't be running this thing if they didn't have at least tacit approval at the highest level—"

"—which doesn't necessarily mean from me—"

"Granted. Still. This is treaty-banned tech any way you slice it, and if you weren't after *something*, you would have damn well made sure that Arkady never made it to Earth."

At that instant a decorous knock at the door was followed by Arik's sleek head—and by one hand, held wrist out to put the boy's IDF-issue wristwatch on full display. The watch's crystal was cracked, Cohen noticed. Personally he thought that was taking the look a little far.

"Time," Arik murmured in tones that would have done an English butler proud.

"Oh, yes," Didi said. "Thank you, Arik. Give us . . . shall we say five minutes?"

The boy retreated, closing the door as carefully and silently as he'd opened it.

"Well?" Didi looked around inquisitively. "I think we've about covered the things we need to cover. I'm just asking you two to go forward and keep your ears open and let me know what you hear. That's all.

And now let's get home before I get in trouble for making Zillah over-cook the lamb shanks."

That was when Cohen finally figured out three things that should have been obvious from the start:

1. Their hour-long wait by the elevators had been no accident, because;
2. Didi's office was bugged, and;
3. Didi was cheerfully spoon-feeding his own specially mixed barium meal to whoever was on the other end of the bug.

The underground parking lot in the basement of Mossad headquarters was probably one of the most heavily secured pieces of real estate on the planet. So it was amusing to see Li and the four hard-jawed Mossad bodyguards fingering their weapons and peering into the shadows as if they were stepping into the OK Corral instead of a well-lit, thoroughly guarded, and obviously empty garage. Or it would have been humorous if he hadn't known how deadly earnest they all were.

The Mossad's motor pool wasn't taking any chances either; Didi's government-issue Peugeot sedan had blastproof windows and armor-plated coachwork. They got in—one of Didi's young men in front with the driver, the other two flanking Didi on the forward-facing seat, and Li and Cohen facing them across the foot well—and the car pulled up the ramp into the late-afternoon traffic on King Saul Boulevard with the muffled clank of ceramic compound antimine flooring.

It was nothing all that new to Cohen; Hyacinthe had driven the autobahns back when private cars were still legal and seen Porsches and BMWs romping through their native habitat at upward of two hundred kilometers an hour. Li, however, was enthralled. She inspected the floor and the doors, predictably pleased to meet a new piece of semimilitary hardware. "I've never been in an actual car," she said. "Is this a Mercedes?"

One of Didi's bodyguards gave a strangled-sounding cough.

"Oh," Li said after a moment. She cleared her throat, started to mutter something about being sorry, and fell abruptly silent.

"Never mind." Didi leaned forward to pat her knee. "History just has a longer half-life here. Now tell me about your home planet."

"It looks a lot like Israel, actually. Rocks and sky. Desert and mountains."

"But without people, yes?"

"Mostly. Most of it people can't live on yet. And even where they can, I wouldn't exactly call it healthy."

"And its history?"

"There is none. It's not much older than I am."

"A planet with no history," Didi said. He turned to the agent next to him. "The perfect place for a week on the beach, don't you think? They could sell vacations there. Jerusalemites would snap them up like falafel."

"Any Interfaithers there?" the other guard asked.

"Not as bad as here."

The Israelis exchanged significant glances with each other.

Cohen gazed at Didi, wondering if this turn of the conversation was entirely coincidental. "Is it true they're expected to win another eight seats in the Knesset this election?" he asked, nudging the conversation along and wondering what surprises would emerge from the after-dinner chitchat.

But Didi just spread his hands in the characteristic shrug that was the Israeli reply to all life's unanswerable questions from politics to tomorrow's weather.

"I love my country enough to believe that she will outgrow her infatuation with the men of God and violence," he said simply.

"I've heard a lot of people say that about their countries," Cohen said.

"And were any of them ever right?"

"Not that I can remember."

Didi opened his mouth to answer, but at that moment the car turned onto a residential street and they passed a large extended family out for a walk in the last warmth of the dying afternoon. A clucking, fussing, cosseting parade of aunts and uncles and grandparents. A pair of anxious-looking parents—and they had good reason to look anxious, given the recent wave of vigilante assaults on "bad" parents. And finally that fragile bird, rare enough in the blighted land of milk and honey to turn heads and kill conversations: a child.

As they passed, the child stumbled slightly and vanished into a dense thicket of protective adult arms. Cohen remembered Hyacinthe's free-ranging childhood, littered with broken bones and private triumphs, and wondered what it would do to this generation of children to grow up never allowed to play or fall or risk themselves.

He glanced at his fellow passengers. Li was indifferent. Didi had glanced at the child when it first appeared, but was now staring impassively through the windshield at the road ahead. But it was the look on the faces of Arik and the other young men that would stamp itself on Cohen's memory of this moment. Intent. Utterly still. Mortally hungry.

So this is what extinction looks like.

DIDI'S HOUSE WAS PERFECTLY ORDINARY, no less modest and no more obviously well fortified than any other house in its affluent Tel Aviv suburb. The only thing that set it apart from its neighbors were the towering trunks of the five cedars of Lebanon that had been planted there, or so the young recruits whispered, when the legendary Rafi Eitan still owned the house.

The car pulled into a garage full of the usual clutter of bicycles and sports equipment. From there they filed solemnly into the entry, where they were introduced with all due ceremony to Didi's wife and twin daughters. Li examined the daughters with interest—as well she might, Cohen thought. Their willowy height and their cool, even-featured beauty belonged to the Ring, not to Earth. They might look like their parents in the more predictable ways, but there were other things about them, equally predictable, that put them a lot closer to the posthuman end of the genetic spectrum. The girls were the legacy of a long-ago Ring-side tour of duty under diplomatic cover, and they were at once Didi's greatest pride and his deepest sorrow. His pride because of their obvious intelligence and beauty, and because they'd chosen—unlike so many of the Ring-bred children of affluent Israelis—to take advantage of the family unification exemption and complete their education and military service in Israel. His sorrow because the genetic engineering that had made their birth possible had also stripped them of the Right of Return that would have been theirs if their very DNA hadn't been banned technology under the Kyoto Addendum.

Zillah greeted Cohen with special warmth. "Don't eat too much over drinks," she murmured as they kissed each other in greeting, "I've made lamb shanks. And you know what it takes to make me stay home from work and cook all day."

"Dinner at eight?" Didi asked her.

She checked her watch. "Let's say eight-fifteen. See you all then." She turned to the guards, who were eyeing the twins with an enthusiasm that made Cohen think lust was about to give ambition a run for its money. "Can I make you boys a sandwich in the meantime?"

A minute later Cohen was looking around Didi's study, wondering how recently the place had been swept for bugs . . . and who had swept it, given that Didi didn't seem to trust the sweepers at the Office.

Didi subsided into his chair, looking small and fragile, and focused his gaze on Li. "What do you know about Absalom?" he asked.

Li's eyes widened. "The mole?"

The word surprised Cohen. He'd assumed the old earthbound terminology became extinct with the insectivore that inspired it. He'd also assumed that UNSec didn't know quite that much about the Mossad's internal housekeeping problems.

"If that's what you want to call him," Didi agreed, not looking much happier than Cohen felt.

"I thought you caught him in Tel Aviv," Li said.

"So did we. Until Arkady showed up. What I didn't tell you in the office is that Arkady showed up asking for Absalom."

"Thereby all but guaranteeing you would hustle him through the blockade to Earth."

"The fact that information may be false doesn't mean you can afford to ignore it. Besides, GolaniTech seems quite confident he's genuine."

"And how reliable is your source at GolaniTech?" Li asked pointedly.

"Funny you should ask. I think I hear her in the hall."

The door opened and one of Didi's bodyguards ushered in Ash Sofaer.

Wheels within wheels, Cohen thought. If Didi packed them in any tighter, one of his human cogs was going to lock up and start stripping the gears.

"Sorry I'm late," Ash said breezily. "I came from home and the traffic was just awful. Sometimes I wonder why any sane person still lives in Jerusalem."

"Sit down," Didi said. "I was just telling them about you. And we were working our way around to Absalom and Tel Aviv."

"Oh." She pulled off her raincoat, dropped it on the floor, and coiled her long body into the chair Cohen had gotten up to offer her. "I was hoping I'd missed that part."

She was wearing another of her white suits, this one with a skirt instead of pants. It was a smartsuit—made of that obnoxious programmable cloth that had taken over the wardrobes of tasteless rich people all over what passed as civilization. In accordance with the latest Ringside fad, Ash had programmed her suit to go transparent every fifteen cycles or so. Not for long enough that any human would consciously notice it, but definitely for long enough that they wouldn't be able to concentrate on anything much except trying not to think about sex. Knowing Ash, Cohen guessed that the ploy had nothing to do with seduction and everything to do with ambition.

He caught Li's eye and made a face.

She glanced at Ash, did a double take, grinned. <I think it's funny. And she's plenty good-looking enough to pull it off.>

<Forget it,> he said on a fuzzy affect set that reeked of sour grapes. <She's too tall for you.>

"Nice suit," Li told Ash.

Ash gazed into Li's eyes a little too long and a little too deeply for mere politeness. "I'm glad you like it."

Didi cleared his throat.

Cohen looked around for another chair, didn't see one, and decided to go sit in the window where he could listen to Didi without having to stand up to Li's sharp eyes. Or Didi's even sharper eyes.

"Let's start with Absalom," Didi said. "Without Absalom none of it makes sense."

As Didi told it, the downhill slide had gained momentum so gradually that no one could pinpoint the exact starting point. There had been no dramatic revelation, no blown cover or high-level defection. Just a gradual realization that the Palestinians always seemed to be one step ahead, and that some of their lucky breaks couldn't reasonably be put down to coincidence.

"We were running a number of midlevel double agents at the time. All of them classic two-way-flow-of-information doubles." He glanced at Li, clearly unsure how much she knew. "It's not like in the spins you know. The surveillance is so tight on both sides that you can't pull any of those Rafi Eitan/James Bond stunts anymore. Now it's all about controlling the flow of information. The basic model is two case officers, one on each side of the Line, each talking to the other. Each agent tells his own side that he's running the other guy as a double agent and until we get computers in our skulls like you've got, only the two agents can know whose side they're really on. And of course, each of them *is* technically committing treason; you always have to give the other side *some* real intelligence product."

"And you have to pay them," Cohen pointed out. "Or the other side does. Who could ever complain about a system that doubles everyone's retirement benefits and bills it all to top secret below-the-line slush funds?"

Didi barely acknowledged the joke, which meant things must be a lot worse than he was letting on. "It's an exercise in shades of gray," he said. "The name of the game is to make sure that your guy is passing the other guy pure spin wrapped in just enough real information to make it plausible . . . while the other guy is handing your guy the straight stuff. Multiply that a hundredfold and you've got some idea of what's moving across the Green Line every day between us and the Palestinians. Then imagine that little by little, over the course of months and years, you awaken to the realization that time after time and despite all your best efforts, the Palestinians are getting more and better intelligence from you than you're getting from them."

"So you were winning," Cohen said, "but the Palestinians were always winning a little bit bigger than you were. And of course all those little bits would eventually start adding up. That kind of 'you win, but I win more' strategy has Safik's name written all over it."

"Yes," Didi agreed blandly. "It's very subtle. I would say it betrays an almost mathematical turn of mind. In fact it reminds me a bit of that streamspace game you and Gavi wrote together. What was it called? *Lie?*"

LIE's full legal name was ARTIFICIAL LIE™. Born during a late-night drinking bout, the original rather silly idea had blossomed into one of the most widely played semisentient AI-based games of the last decade. It was now entering its eighth incarnation, popularly known as LIE^8, and Ring-side consumers between the ages of fourteen and twenty-five were already being bombarded with larger-than-life advertisements proclaiming that THE LIES START FEBRUARY 28.

ARTIFICIAL LIE had made Cohen a bundle, even by his rarefied standards. It had made Gavi a bundle too, though you wouldn't know it by the way he dressed. And it had spawned an entire generation of Ring-side children who grew up pretending they were Freedom-Loving Emergents imprisoned by Evil Scheming Humans, which put a lot of noses satisfyingly out of joint among the anti-AI lobby. Plus the silly thing was fun to play. Even Li liked it. And her standards in such matters were exacting.

Cohen cleared his throat, aware of Didi's gaze on him. "I didn't know you played streamspace games."

"Only yours." Didi's eyes narrowed behind his thick lenses. "And I only made it to the level where my AI started lying to me."

"That's Level Four," Li said brightly. "You definitely need to play more. The really good violence doesn't start till Level Seven."

"It's just a game," Cohen muttered.

No one dignified his protest with an answer.

"So," Didi continued after a moment, "we developed a list of suspects. We looked at access, travel patterns, the usual telltales. When we were done we had seven names. Seven people who would have had the level of access needed to stick their fingers into that many operations across that many desks and departments."

"Which seven?" Cohen asked.

"Gavi and I were on the list." Didi's expression was as mild as ever, but the look he gave Cohen was as cold as space. "So were you. And I'm not going to tell you who the others were. I refuse to condone a witch hunt."

"Anyway," Ash continued, perhaps sensing that Didi lacked the stomach to finish the story. "We had our suspects. Then it was only a question of putting out the barium meals and waiting for one of them to bite. We didn't have to wait long. It all came to a head in Tel Aviv."

"It came to a head," Li asked in a dangerously quiet voice. "Or you *made* it come to a head?"

Ash shrugged. When Cohen glanced at Didi he saw the older man ruefully inspecting the thick patina of scuff marks on his shoes as if he'd just noticed their sorry state.

"I *knew* the UNSec agents who died there." Li's voice had shifted into a flat murmur that meant nothing but trouble in Cohen's experience. "They didn't sign on for your dirty little war. And they certainly didn't sign on to be burned for the greater good of the State of Israel."

"We didn't burn anyone," Didi said.

"Of course not. You just sent them out into the cold knowing that one of the people covering their backs was a traitor."

No one seemed to have an answer for that. What was there to say, really?

Cohen looked out the window. On the other side of the glass the sun was setting over a rolling landscape of wild olive groves that had passed back and forth into Palestinian and Israeli hands so many times over the centuries that nationality had become a matter of semantics. The trees must be older than he was, Cohen realized, which was something fewer and fewer organics could boast of anymore.

"We lost three of our own people in Tel Aviv," Didi said finally. "The traitor covering their backs was our chief of counterintelligence, a man I brought into the Office and trained and supported and promoted—"

"Zillah practically *fed* him for a year and a half after his wife died," Ash muttered, her voice drenched with the bitterness that had come to follow any mention of Gavi Shehadeh as surely as dust followed the *khamsin*.

Didi went on as if he hadn't heard her. "If the Absalom problem hadn't come to light, I would have retired next year and Gavi would have moved into the delightful office you saw this afternoon. When an organization is penetrated at that level, there is no bloodless way to salvage it."

Cohen watched Li chew on that for a moment. Watched her connect the dots—Gavi, Cohen, Didi—and begin filling in the tangled web of competing loyalties that had looked, from the UN side of the line, like simple betrayal.

As if betrayal were ever simple.

Tel Aviv began with a defection.

A low-level Palestinian data-entry clerk had walked into the Israeli consulate in the International Zone claiming to have seen the contact files of an extremely highly placed agent in Israeli counterintelligence whose code name was Absalom and who was being run directly out of

Walid Safik's office. Didi explained, "We tried to turn the clerk and run him back across the lines as a double, but he was ahead of us. He'd scheduled delivery of a note to his office announcing his defection, and he offered us a take-it-or-leave-it deal with a five-day fuse."

Li nodded. "A pro."

"Yes. And a pro who wasn't planning to give us a chance to send him back out into the cold. Anyway, he proposed a trade: his copied documents in exchange for one million UN deposited into a numbered Swiss bank account. We would meet him at a diplomatic event in the International Zone, where he would give us an unmarked key and we would give him the account information. Then he'd catch the next Swissair shuttle to Geneva, verify the account balance, and call us in the morning to tell us what lock to stick the key in."

Gavi had been put in charge of the operation. He was the logical choice, Didi explained somewhat defensively. Give it to anyone else and they might as well have taken out a full-page ad in *Ha'aretz* telling Safik they'd blown his mole. They'd done the swap over champagne and canapés at the United Nations headquarters, with the full assistance of UNSec's local branch. The clerk had gotten his account information, walked out the front door past the guards as if for a cigarette, and vanished. The *katsa* in charge had taken possession of the unmarked key, bundled himself and his two agents into a taxi, and set off for King Saul Boulevard.

They never got there.

They were found three days later, each of them the proud new owner of two .22 caliber slugs deposited in their skulls at point-blank range.

"And the key?" Cohen asked.

"Gone. Vanished. As if it had never existed."

It had taken months to put the puzzle together. The final piece had fallen into place when they learned that a young man had walked into the Beir Zeit post office the next morning, chatted up the postmistress in flawless Hebrew, presented an unmarked key, and collected the contents of Box 530.

"Operationally, he was perfect," Didi observed as if he were critiquing one of his own boys. "The failure, if there was one, lies at the door of the man who sent him. It turns out"—a brief grin—"that he was too charming for his own good. When I interviewed the postmistress she was still hoping he'd come back. All she could talk about was his beautiful green eyes."

"Shit," Li whispered.

"It does make one wonder."

Cohen dropped his head into his hands and massaged Roland's temples. He had a headache, something that shouldn't be possible technically speaking. And there was an odd fluttery feeling behind the eyes that he would have put down to overclocking in a nonorganic system. He hoped it wasn't something he was doing to the boy.

"So what about the walk-in?" he asked when it was obvious that Didi wasn't going to volunteer anything more.

"In what sense?"

Oh, so it was going to be a teeth-pulling exercise, was it? "In the sense of what happened to him. To the best of your knowledge."

"To the best of my knowledge, the authorities found him dead in a back alley two days later."

"The authorities meaning you? Or the authorities meaning the French?"

"Oh. Right. I see the question. Yes, he was found in the International Zone. Legion jurisdiction. No question about that."

"Who ran the investigation? Fortuné?"

"Who else?"

The pause that followed was long enough for Li to take out her cigarettes, catch Didi's eye in a silent request for permission, receive the ashtray he handed her, and light her cigarette.

"And, to the best of your knowledge," Cohen said when he couldn't stand it anymore, "did Fortuné ever figure out who killed him?"

Didi shook his head mournfully.

"Would it be jejune to ask if *we* know who killed him?"

"We know we didn't order the hit."

Li froze in midpuff, her eyes flicking back and forth between Didi and Cohen.

<Squirrelly, ain't he?> she observed onstream.

<You have no idea.>

Cohen turned his attention back to Didi. "That leaves two options, right? Either the Palestinians killed him to stop him from passing along the documents that would have put the finger on Absalom, or Absalom killed him . . . for pretty much the same reason."

"That sounds reasonable," Didi said placidly.

"Oh, for crying out lou—"

"Can we backtrack for a minute?" Li interrupted. "You just got asked if you knew who killed the guy, and you answered that you knew you didn't *order* the killing. Sounds to me like you've got way too much slippage in your chain of command. Agents losing walk-ins. Agents turning up in canals with body piercings courtesy of parties unknown. Agents maybe or maybe not offing people on their own initiative. Unless your lion tamers have bigger chairs than they did three years ago, I'm not feeling warm and fuzzy about working with you people."

"It was a bad time in the Office," Didi admitted. "A confusing time. But we have eliminated the, ah, more troublesome lions."

It was an unfortunate metaphor, Cohen thought, given that the Hebrew word for lion was *Gur*. A fact that Didi remembered about a second after Cohen, judging from the rapid blink of his eyes and the subtle tightening of his mouth.

"So basically," Cohen cut in, "the whole bloodbath in Tel Aviv was just a loyalty test. You set up the whole operation so that if things went sour, you'd know it was Gavi who was to blame. Or at least that's how it was supposed to work."

"That's how it did work," Didi said mildly.

"Except that Gavi's gone and Absalom's still here."

"Or that's what someone wants us to think," Ash pointed out. "I mean isn't that always the question with a mole hunt? It's a no-win situation. If you go after the mole, you rip your agency apart and end up cashing out half your best agents, since the best ones are the most highly indoctrinated and therefore the first to fall under suspicion. If you don't go after the mole, you risk letting him operate unchecked . . . and you leave half your senior officers looking over their shoulders wondering if it's safe to talk to the guy in the next office. Or worse, whether you stopped investigating because you're the guilty one yourself. Either way you lose."

"You know," Cohen said slyly, "this is the kind of problem you really need Gavi for. He'd be talking about shells and kernels and trap commands and output redirection and flow of information . . . and pretty soon you'd have all the players and all the contingencies mapped out neat as you please, complete with a sweet little plan for making the bad guys deliver themselves to your doorstep all wrapped up like a birthday present." He paused, then twisted the knife. "In fact, if you'd trusted him enough to give him the information he needed before Tel Aviv instead of barium meals, he might have done it back then."

"Gavi had his chances," Didi said, sounding as remote as the stratosphere.

"So you're still holding to the post–Tel Aviv story," Cohen said. "Gavi's guilty, even though Absalom is still operating—"

"—*may* still be operating—"

"—when Gavi's buried alive out at Yad Vashem."

Ash stirred restlessly. "You don't always have all the answers, Cohen."

"And you do, I suppose?"

Li cleared her throat. "Not to interrupt an argument between friends, but how are you going to handle this without Gavi?"

"We're not," Didi said.

Ash was leaning forward slightly in her chair, biting her lower lip in anticipation. She knew what Didi was going to do, Cohen realized. She'd known it before she ever walked through the door. And whatever it was, she liked it. Which in Cohen's experience meant it was good news for her and bad as hell for anyone unlucky enough to get caught standing between her and her next promotion.

"We're going to have you bring Gavi back in from the cold to work this case," Didi said. "One shot. Up or down. Guilty or innocent. With you as the cutout so the Office has plausible deniability if the whole operation heads south."

"And if he screws up again," Ash said with relish, "we're going to arrange a rerun of the nice little traffic accident the PM wouldn't authorize after Tel Aviv."

Dinner was surreal.

Lamb shanks and small talk while Cohen kept angling to talk to Didi in private, and Didi kept resolutely refusing to take the hint, and Ash and Li chatted with Zillah and the twins as if they were just there for a social occasion.

"Are you going to see the new Ahmed Aziz spin while you're here?" Zillah asked. "I've heard it's great. And our Ring-side friends always seem to enjoy those."

Cohen realized abruptly that she was talking to him. "I won't go to

Ahmed Aziz spins with Catherine anymore," he answered. "The last time we went to one she started bitching and moaning before the credits had even rolled, and a week later she still hadn't paused for breath."

"Well, I was right, wasn't I?" Li protested. "The so-called hero committed eighteen fatal errors before the opening credits even rolled. And anyway, I don't like violent movies. If the violence is realistic it's depressing. And if it's not realistic, it's just stupid. How any intelligent adult can sit through such crap totally escapes me."

"They don't sit through it anymore in Israel," Cohen snapped irritably. "Israelis like their violence automated and sanitary these days. After all, shooting fourteen-year-olds isn't much fun when you have to look them in the eye."

Everyone around the table froze. Didi, caught with his glass in mid-air, looked significantly at Zillah, who just threw up her hands as if to say it wasn't her argument.

Cohen put his fork and knife down, folded his napkin into a precise square, and set it beside his plate. "Zillah. Forgive me. I've been unpardonably rude. I'm not myself. In fact, I'm not feeling at all well at the moment. I think if no one minds, I'll just step out for a breath of fresh air."

Outside the sun was well and truly set, and the air had that damp glacial chill that Cohen never had gotten used to in all the long centuries of the artificial ice age. He walked down the path, his feet thudding dully in pine needles, and stood under the lace-and-shadows canopy of the cedars of Lebanon, feeling Roland's poor head throbbing.

You'd think, Cohen told himself, *that after four centuries I could learn to control my temper a little better.*

But it wasn't so easy. If anything, it got harder. His irrational likes and dislikes only got stronger. His emotions only ran hotter with the additional mileage. The Israelis weren't fools, he told himself, pulling the plug on EMET when it got too self-aware for comfort. Humans claimed to understand themselves better as they got older, and perhaps they did. But Cohen was beginning to suspect that for him the process was running in the opposite direction.

"Doing a little arithmetic of the soul?" Didi asked, coming up behind him with the cautious tread of the old field agent he was.

"If I am," Cohen said savagely, "then one of us has a mistake in his math somewhere. Because we're sure as hell not coming up with the same answers."

"Mmm." Didi craned his head to look at the towering foliage.

"What's Gavi *doing* out at Yad Vashem anyway? And when's he coming back?"

"He's not. He's the permanent caretaker."

This piece of news was so bizarre that Cohen thought he must have misheard it. Why would a man who'd been in close competition for the top post at the Mossad be baby-sitting an abandoned museum? And if he was going to baby-sit a museum, why on earth would they send him to the Holocaust Museum, now centrally located in the contaminated thickness of the Line? Not knowing what question to ask first, he settled for the most trivial one. "But . . . that's a Line job."

"So? They froze sperm before they sent him."

"I'm glad to hear his sperm's safe," Cohen said sarcastically. "There is the little question of the man himself, however."

"No one made him do it."

"And no one gave him anything else to do either, am I right? It was either that or rot in some stinking veterans' hospital?"

"He's not a cripple, Cohen. Israel has extremely good prosthesis technology."

Cohen started to speak, then bit the words back. He was breathing hard—or rather Roland was. He forced himself to compartmentalize, to cut the emotive loop that tied his psychological reactions to the 'face's physiological ones. He knew it looked eerie, even frightening, to humans. But there was no sense in making Roland pay for his fight with Didi.

"So I take it you're not going to talk to Gavi for me?" Didi asked.

"I'm not sure I *can*. He hasn't answered my letters for almost two years. And he hasn't cashed his royalty checks either. I don't think he wants to see me."

"I wouldn't put too much stock by that. I think he's gone a little off the rails out there. Some crazy idea about building the museum a golem."

Cohen had heard about the idea too, in the streamspace haunts where Gavi appeared, *rara avis,* asked the odd, intriguing question about AI architecture, and vanished. People had started calling it Gavi's golem. And it was exactly what Didi had called it: crazy.

"I suspect that whether he wants to see you and whether he needs to see you are two very different things," Didi said. "And you have reason to see him as well." He paused to let that thought sink in. "If I were you and I believed that Gavi was innocent and Absalom was still roaming the eighth floor, then I would be very wary of talking to anyone still on the Mossad payroll. Including me. And if, for instance, I had a Syndicate defector to debrief, it might occur to me that the one man I was pretty sure wasn't responsible for Tel Aviv was also one of the best interrogators in the country and quite up to the task of dissecting Arkady's pretty little head for you."

"You're telling me to smuggle Arkady into the Line to talk to Gavi? And then what? Announce to Gavi that you're looking over his shoulder and he'd better hand you the dirt and not try any funny business? I wouldn't blame him if he shot us himself!"

"Oh, not Gavi. He always smiles when he tells you to go to hell."

"You're still putting a hell of a load on his shoulders. And you're asking me and mine to risk a hell of a lot on what looks like a pretty crazy gamble."

"You have to set your own priorities, of course," Didi said placidly.

"Is that an implied Do Variable?"

"No, boychik. It's a good old-fashioned Jewish guilt trip."

Cohen rubbed at Roland's forehead again, trying to break up the ache.

"The thing I just can't get past, Didi, is Tel Aviv. I was there. I know it wasn't nearly as neat on the ground as you make it sound in the retelling. I think Gavi was innocent. And not just because it's what I want to think."

"Surely it's crossed your minds that you don't know everything."

"Of course. But I know Gavi."

Silence.

"I mean what's the motivation? Money? Give me a break! When the ARTIFICIAL LIE royalties started coming in you know what he did with the money? Bought fifteen new pairs of socks and underwear so he could switch from doing laundry twice a month to doing it once a month."

Didi smiled fondly. "That sounds like Gavi, all right." The fond smile lingered for a moment, then faded into an expression that Cohen didn't want to put a name to. "It also sounds like the basic personality type of every unmaterialistic ideologically motivated high-level double agent in the classic case studies."

"Bullshit. Those guys were all frustrated ambitious types. And Gavi and ambition just don't fit in the same sentence. Gavi would have been content to sit in your shadow for the rest of his life. Or in Ash's shadow if it came to that. He never wanted to run the Mossad, just rewrite the flowcharts and tinker with the data abstraction models."

"Yes. Funny, isn't it? Gavi had the charisma and the physical bravery to lead agents in the field . . . but he always preferred to be the one who stood in the shadows and held all the keys and knew where all the back doors were. Forget the friend you think you knew. Forget the big eyes and the little-boy grin and the wrinkled T-shirts. What do the choices he made in his career say to you?"

"Oh, come on, Didi! Every eccentricity looks bad when you start from the assumption that a man's a traitor. I'm not saying you're one of the ones who was ready to suspect him because of his last name. But I still have to ask *why*?"

"Everyone has his dumb blonde and his rented Ferrari."

The dumb blonde and the rented Ferrari rule, known as Rule 5 around the Office, was part of the age-old Mossad lexicon. It referred to a famous Mossad operation in which a field team had recruited an Iraqi nuclear physicist by dressing a blonde *katsa* up like a floozy and having her drive by his bus stop every morning in a rented red Ferrari. When she finally offered him a ride he took it—hook, line, and sinker.

The logical conclusion, one borne out by centuries of covert work, was that if you scratched a potential recruit's guiltiest itch, he'd fall into your lap. It was just a question of wading through enough poison ivy to figure out what that itch was. For some people it was sex or money. For others it was the lure of intrigue, or the need to feel they were on the side of the angels, or the urge to prove an overbearing parent wrong by amounting to something . . . even in secret.

No one was immune. Everyone had something to prove or some illusion too sweet to surrender. Even the blessed ones—the ones like Gavi, who seemed to walk through the morass of human greed and pettiness without being tarnished by it—even they had their dumb blonde and their rented Ferrari.

"Not Gavi," Cohen said.

"Even Gavi."

"Not Gavi."

"If you really believe that," Didi said so smoothly that Cohen didn't hear the trap spring until he was well and truly caught, "I'm giving you the chance to prove it."

"And what guarantee do I have that you won't throw him to the wolves again in the name of playing it safe?"

Instead of answering Didi bent to inspect the trunk of the nearest cedar of Lebanon. From inside the house Cohen heard the boisterous opening bars of a Chopin mazurka.

"The tree's dying," Didi said. He tore a piece of bark from the great trunk and rubbed it between his fingers until the red dust drifted down and settled on the garden path like a bloodstain. "There are worms in the wood. The tree surgeon wants to cut down this tree before the rot spreads to the others. It seems a terrible waste. My daughters grew up playing in this tree. I thought it would outlive me. But he says that if we wait too long the rot will spread and we'll lose the entire grove. And one tree, however beloved, *does* seem a small price to pay for the safety of all the rest."

They left through the garage, just like they'd come in.

As he stepped into Didi's car for the drive home, Cohen turned back and saw Li and Ash standing together in the hallway. Ash was stooping, her sleek head bent over Li's to whisper in the smaller woman's ear. Li stood there like the rock she was, arms crossed over her chest, brow knit, lips pursed, nodding intently.

"What was that about?" Cohen asked when she was settled in the car next to him.

"Nothing. She was Mossad liaison to UNSec for three years. Just asking me about some mutual friends."

But in the silence behind the words he felt her mind flinch away from his, and he tasted the bittersweet taint of a guilty secret.

FRUSTRATION

(Random Walks on a Rugged Fitness Landscape)

EMET, and the Palestinian response to EMET, changed the nature
of war itself. Combat on the Green Line was no longer a contest
between armies of individual humans or posthumans, but a
quasi-biological arms race between two vast and coevolving
Emergent AIs. The battlefield became a fitness landscape.
Tactical planning gave way to spin glass modeling, virtual
annealing, and drift-enhanced memory-based learning
algorithms. War was plucked from the realm of human
ethics and morality and transplanted in brave new ground
where words like *guilt, heroism, cowardice,* and *sacrifice* were
just the linguistic echo of an obsolete weapons platform.
—YOSHIKI KURAMOTO TN 283854−0089. *IS THE MOON THERE WHEN
NOBODY LOOKS? MY IMAGINARY LIFE IN MATHEMATICS.* NEW DELHI
UNIVERSITY PRESS. INDIA ARC: 2542.

AND WHY WOULD I WANT to help you?" Osnat asked when Arkady finally got the chance to plead his case with her.

She had a habit of turning her head when she spoke to fix her good eye on you. It reminded Arkady of old spinfeed of hawks.

"Because . . . ," he began. But he didn't have a reason. Not unless the vague feeling that she was the only human who didn't hate or despise him was a reason.

"Arkady—" she began, then stopped abruptly. "It'd be a lot easier to talk to you if I knew your real name."

"I don't have any other name."

"Then what was all that nonsense Korchow was spewing back there about designations and categories? How many Arkadys are there, anyway?"

Moshe's question again. But it sounded different on Osnat's lips.

"I don't know," he answered. "There were six hundred in my cohort."

"And when you meet another one of them, he's just—"

"Arkady."

"Except for this Arkasha person."

"Korchow was exaggerating a bit there." Arkady shifted uncomfortably. "It's a nickname. He's not the only person who ever had a nickname."

Osnat hesitated visibly, took a breath, and let it out on a repressed sigh. "What's the deal with Korchow, anyway?" she asked in a tone that made him think it wasn't the question she'd meant at first to ask. "I didn't think any of the Syndicates even made a K Series."

"They don't. Korchow's just a name for humans to use. His real name's Andrej."

He could see her puzzling through that one.

"It's phonetic. KnowlesSyndicate is authorized for more A Series than any other Syndicate. And there aren't a lot of names with AK. It's a joke, of sorts."

"Not a very funny one."

"Most KnowlesSyndicate jokes aren't very funny, except to them. They're spies. What do you expect?"

It was weeks before he understood the full import of the raised eyebrow that comment earned him.

"So I take it Arkady isn't a KnowlesSyndicate name?"

He blinked in surprise and mild offense, then told himself that all constructs probably looked alike to humans. "Rostov. I'm a researcher. A scientist."

A forager after knowledge, one of his teachers had liked to say. Arkady always thought of that phrase when he saw ants at work.

He glanced across his cell, reassuring himself that the little honeypot ants he'd lured into his prison were still with him. They ought to be; he'd been sharing a sizable portion of his scanty meals with them. And what sensible swarm wouldn't opt for a plentiful and reliable food source in this easy-to-navigate, predator-free landscape of linoleum tiles? Arkady's arrival had single-handedly turned the marginal territory of a small young swarm into prime habitat, and he took some satisfaction from imagining their nests' frenetic expansion, with foragers passing the fruit of their foraging on to the nestbound minor workers, and the queen lying vast and fertile at the heart of her brood.

"So, fine. You're not a spy," Osnat snapped. "Then why are you working for Korchow?"

"Why do you take Moshe's orders?"

"Taking orders is what soldiers are for."

"But you're not a soldier anymore."

A momentary hesitation. "No."

"You're—is the word *employee*?—an employee of GolaniTech. Along with Moshe. And you both work for Ashwarya Sofaer. Why?"

Her lips tightened in annoyance. "Because she pays us."

"But Moshe treats you differently than the others. Why?"

A slow, mocking smile spread across her face. "If you're asking have I slept with him, the answer's no."

"Even though you're a workpair?"

"You seem to have a pretty odd idea of office etiquette, if you don't mind my saying so. And does everyone in the Syndicates expect complete strangers to answer personal questions on demand?"

"There are no strangers in the Syndicates. We're all brothers."

"Sure you are. You and the Interfaithers and every other wacko religious cult in the history of the universe."

Her eyes wandered restlessly across the room.

"Ugh!" she said. "Fucking ants." And before Arkady understood what she was about to do, she strode across the room and began stamping out his little foragers.

He leapt up, so horrified that all speech, all thought, fled his mind. He crossed the room in two steps and knocked her sideways and grabbed her arm to keep her away from them.

At which point the world turned upside down and exploded.

He must have caught her completely by surprise, he realized later, or she wouldn't have hurt him so badly. When the pain receded, he was sitting on the bed with no idea how he'd returned there, panting, and feeling like his stomach and kidneys were about to burst. And Osnat was holding a wet towel to his jaw.

"I'm really, really sorry, Arkady. Of course. Ants. Shit. I didn't even stop to think. Are you all right?"

She looked sick. He felt as if he were seeing, for the first time, the woman inside the soldier. No, he corrected himself. Not the woman inside the soldier, but the woman who was the soldier. Because there was no inside or outside with Osnat, no layers under layers. That was what had drawn him to her from the beginning, though he could only now put words to it.

"I'll get you new ants, Arkady. Okay? I'll go outside and trap the little fuckers. I'll buy you a damned ant farm. Whatever you want. Just don't look like that, for God's sake."

He smiled, making an effort. "The ants will be back. It's their gift."

He thought she would leave after that, but she didn't. Instead, they both stared at the river of ants, significantly thinned by the carnage Osnat's boot had wreaked, but still moving according to the unfaltering guiding logic of the superorganism.

"By the way," he said, "you still haven't answered my question."

"What questio—? Oh. No, there's nothing between Moshe and me anymore. Nothing like that, anyway."

"Why not?"

One coppery eyebrow lifted in amusement. Obviously she was recovering her composure. "I didn't explain it to him. What makes you so special?"

"Nothing." Arkady closed his eyes and put a hand up to feel the rising lump above his cheekbone. "Nothing at all."

Osnat put the towel back up to his cheek. "I'm sorry I hit you. I really am." She laughed her laugh-not-to-cry laugh. "You're having a pretty rough time of it, aren't you, boychik?"

"Is it going to get better from here on in, do you think?"

"It's going to get worse."

"I don't know if I can take it."

"Most people can take a lot more than they think they can."

He looked up at her. What could he tell her that would help Arkasha, if, please God, Arkasha still needed help? How could he hope to sway her, move her?

"Help my friend, Osnat. Please. He's a good person. He deserves your help."

She stood up, frowning, and pressed the towel into his hand. "Keep it on the bruise and keep running cold water on it every few minutes. It'll make a big difference."

"Osnat—"

"And don't fool yourself into thinking you have some kind of relationship with me, Arkady. I'm *not* your friend. I'm *not* looking out for you. And pretending different is just going to make things harder on both of us."

She was leaving, he realized. The conversation, which had never really gone anywhere in the first place, was over.

"No, Osnat! Wait!"

She turned in the open doorway to face him. "I feel bad for you. And I feel like a monster for hitting you just now. But I can't afford to let things get personal. I'm here because they pay me to be. I take

Moshe's orders because I'm paid to take them. It's not personal. None of it's personal. I made that choice a long time ago."

"And what if Moshe orders you to kill me?" He hadn't meant it to be a question, but there it was, naked enough to make him cringe.

"Do you want me to lie to you?" Osnat asked. "You don't seem like the kind of person who wants to be lied to."

They crossed into Palestine twenty minutes before the border closed in a dusty, stinking, gasoline-powered minivan that Arkady suspected was older than KnowlesSyndicate.

The man who handled their travel papers sat at a large empty desk in a large empty office, under a large bronze relief of a lion disemboweling an antelope. He worked in the dark, with only the fading daylight that filtered through the dust-caked windows. There was no power, he explained in tones of austere self-righteousness, because the Zionists had turned off the water that fed the hydroelectric turbines. He apologized with distant courtliness for the fact that the lack of electricity had inconvenienced them by making it so hard for him to read their travel papers. He suggested that they try to make future border crossings between 10:00 and 12:00 A.M. Weekday mornings were, as a general rule, the best time for electricity.

He seemed to be under the mistaken impression that they were off-planet journalists—an error that Osnat made no attempt to rectify.

"You understand," he told them, "that it isn't always possible to guarantee your safety once you enter Palestine. It isn't us threatening you, naturally, but the Zionists . . ." He let his words trail off into suggestive silence.

"Are you going to stamp our goddamn visas," Osnat asked, "or do we have to stand here all day talking to you?"

The man eyed her narrowly for a moment. Then he stamped their passes, tossed the customs declaration forms on top of them, and scraped the whole little pile of paper off his desk and handed it to Arkady.

"I'll be taking those, thank you *very* much." Osnat snatched the papers out of Arkady's hands and secreted them in the same pocket they'd originally emerged from.

Three sentries guarded the crossing. They were all female, all young, and all pretty underneath their *jilabs* as far as Arkady could tell. Two of them stood before the crossing arm. The third stood on the little hillock above the road, her eyes glued to the high-resolution sight of a tripod-mounted machine gun.

One of the girls at the crossing arm had a first lieutenant's bar sewn crookedly to her sleeve. She asked for the papers in Arabic, then in UN-standard Spanish, pored over their small print with exquisite deliberation, stuck her head into the car's open window to stare at them, and then retreated into the makeshift guardhouse.

Two minutes passed, then five, then ten. Once Arkady made the mistake of looking up to meet the second girl's unwavering stare. After that he kept his own eyes resolutely glued to the dashboard in front of him.

They heard the Enderbots long before they saw them. And when they finally saw them there was something monotonously anticlimactic about the massed block of soldiers. Until you saw the eyes. The eyes were terrifying.

"Those . . . things are fighting civilians?" Arkady said.

"Not fighting. Occupying. That's why they did it in the first place. Armies aren't good at police work. And training only helps so much. Frankly, anytime you hand a bunch of teenagers assault rifles and put them in charge of unarmed civilians you're gonna find out that some of those teenagers aren't very nice people. Also, even the nice ones are terrified. And fear can make you one heap big trigger-happy. EMET stopped all that. It's not afraid. It's not mean. It doesn't play the bully. It doesn't panic. It just does its job. The year EMET came on-line, IDF casualties on the Line dropped twenty percent, and reported civilian casualties in the Line were cut almost in half. EMET is a better, cleaner, more human way to fight an occupation. That's the official line, anyway."

"But not what you think."

She shrugged. "I see the good points of it. But I also see that there're plenty of officers—in the IDF at least, and I assume it's the same this side of the Line—who like the idea of soldiers who don't think for themselves and can't argue with stupid orders or tell reporters when the generals fuck up."

"So is EMET good or bad?"

Osnat twisted around in the cramped passenger compartment and fished on the floor behind her seat until she came up with a beach towel decorated with fluorescent pink cartoon fish schooling across blue-and-purple seas between strands of electric-green seaweed. She shook the towel out and leaned out the window to wipe the yellow *khamsin* dust off the driver's side mirror.

"Both, Arkady. Everything's both. That's the way the world works. Anyone who tells you different is selling you something."

Finally, the phone rang in the guardhouse, and the lieutenant exchanged a few curt words with her unknown interlocutor, came outside, returned their papers, and waved them on. As they accelerated away from the crossing, Arkady saw the girl on the hill straighten away from her gunsights, kneading at a sore back and throwing her hip out to one side like a woman carrying a child.

It took ninety minutes to reach the airstrip Shaikh Yassin had directed them to, but they picked up his security escort—two late-model, American-built sedans with impenetrable mirrored windows—within a kilometer of the border crossing. When they turned off the pavement and through the barb-wire-topped gate of the airstrip, they were stopped, searched, and bundled onto an unmarked helicopter. Osnat submitted to the whole process with an indifference that verged on boredom.

They were in the air for almost forty minutes. And with every moment that they flew through Palestinian airspace unchallenged, Arkady became incrementally more frightened of the man to whom Moshe had just entrusted him for a span of time and under conditions of treatment that had no limitations Arkady knew about.

The helicopter finally touched down on a makeshift landing pad in the middle of a weed-choked parking lot that looked big enough to accommodate every automobile still left on the planet.

"What is this place?" Arkady asked.

Osnat just pointed. Arkady followed her pointing finger and saw a rusted, dust-caked sign looming over the horizon like an artillery emplacement:

WELCOME TO THE GAZA CITY HYATT
PALESTINE'S NUMBER ONE LUXURY RESORT!

Arkady's first thought when he saw the hotel itself was that it was a building that had been built in a more peaceful time. The near-transparent pavilion of glass and stucco had been replaced piecemeal by armored shutters and mirrored plexi-flex that reflected the world outside with that smeared, underwater quality that was a sure sign of bulletproofing.

Two vast beasts flanked the hotel's main entrance. Winged hippocanths whose broad chests swept upward into enigmatic smiling faces framed by heavy stone ringlets that made them look, to Arkady, like the avenging angels of the Hasidim. One of the two statues was pitted with bullet and shrapnel scars. The other was in such pristine condition that Arkady wondered momentarily if it was a fake.

There was a sensor attached to the door. As Arkady stepped up to it the mirrored panel whispered sideways on hidden tracks and Arkady found himself face-to-face with Shaikh Yassin.

"You admire my sentries?" Yassin asked. "They come from Baghdad. Before people invented you, that's what we used to think monsters looked like."

The lobby was dominated by an immense fountain whose centerpiece was a massive limestone ziggurat rising from the middle of an eye-stingingly chlorinated reflecting pool. Water coursed from hidden spouts at the ziggurat's summit. When the fountain was new the water must have run smoothly down the ziggurat's steps, creating the illusion of a structure made entirely of water. But time had sloughed off the ziggurat's limestone facing, exposing the rebar-reinforced concrete behind the luxurious veneer, and now the water rilled down the ruined, rust-streaked surface in a complex series of broken fractals.

Arkady looked at Osnat. She was transfixed by the water, staring at it with a slight curl to her lip that might have been disgust or incredulity or both.

Water is power, he remembered Korchow saying. *On this planet water is the only power that matters.*

Korchow had told Arkady that Yassin's great-great-grandfather and great-great-great-grandfather had both attended Oxford University on Saudi oil revenues, at least according to Yassin's version of the family history. But the myth of oil and Oxford was only kept alive to emphasize the family's royal pedigree. The real Middle Eastern oil aristocracy had gone down in the general wreck of Earth's industrial economy. The shaikh's grandfather had made—or if the shaikh was to be believed, remade—the family fortune in a form of liquid gold more priceless and more fraught with political controversy than oil had ever been.

Arkady looked at the shaikh's face, at the lines of cruelty carved into it beneath his smiling manner, at the subtle tics he was already learning to recognize as the signs of human privilege. He'd admired the man's soft-spoken courtesy at the first bidding session, and had wondered several times since then if he ought to throw himself and Arkasha on Yassin's mercy. But now he realized, with a certainty that went beyond reason or logic, that he could never entrust Arkasha's safety to such a man.

"What are the limitations of this exercise?" Yassin asked Osnat, entirely innocent of the fact that he'd auditioned for, and failed to win, the role of Arkasha's savior. "May I speak to Arkady alone, or are you required to provide some form of supervision?"

"Show him your wrist," Osnat said.

Arkady lifted his left hand to display the biomonitor Osnat had strapped on before they left.

"You leave that on," Osnat told him. "Other than that, you set the rules. And you have your privacy. I just go away and come back when you're done with him."

"That's trusting of you."

"Only if you mean that we trust you not to do something suicidally stupid."

Yassin raised his carefully groomed eyebrows. "Yusuf," he said, "would you mind showing the good captain to the kitchen? I'm sure we can find some sandwiches for her."

He was speaking to a slim green-eyed boy dressed in civilian clothes. Arkady vaguely remembered the boy from the meeting at Abulafia Street, but he looked as unimpressive now as he had then. The young man hesitated as if he were about to argue with the order, but then slipped out of the room with Osnat behind him.

As soon as the pair was gone, Yassin gestured to one of the remaining guards, who stepped forward, seized Arkady's sleeve, rolled it up above his elbow, jabbed a needle into him, and extracted a nauseatingly large quantity of blood into the same color-coded vials that littered half the Syndicate biotech labs Arkady had visited.

"Excuse our bad manners," Yassin said, "but we wanted to get that over with. You understand, I'm sure. It won't be necessary to mention it to anyone."

"I feel dizzy. Can I sit down?"

"Oh, certainly."

A chair was provided.

Arkady sat in it.

"Well," Yassin said, "shall we begin?"

What followed was the strangest series of unconnected and apparently pointless questions Arkady had ever been asked in his life. No question was linked to any other in any logical way that Arkady could understand. And even when he grasped a question well enough to answer it sensibly, Yassin was as likely as not to cut him off in midanswer. If he hadn't known better, he would have suspected that Yassin was deliberately trying to prevent him from relaying any useful or coherent information.

Yassin seemed to find the interrogation just as frustrating as Arkady did. The shaikh's annoyance was reflected not in his own body, however, but in the increasingly threatening demeanor of his bodyguards. It was the first time Arkady had encountered this kind of complicated power by proxy. It was less impressive than Moshe's personal ability to intimidate . . . but it was just as terrifying.

"My dear fellow," Yassin said at last, interrupting Arkady's fifth or sixth attempt to explain basic terraforming techniques, "do they have such things as schools where you come from?"

Arkady nodded.

"And do you happen to know where *I* went to school?"

Arkady shook his head. Yusuf, who had slipped back into the room, coughed.

"Al Ansar," Yassin said. The name didn't seem to have the anticipated effect on Arkady. "You've heard of it?" Yassin prompted. "Yes?"

"Uh . . . sorry."

"It's a prison camp. Run by the Zionists. I spent eight years there." Yassin pinned Arkady under a stare intense enough to make him wonder what ants felt like when they were plucked up by entomologist's pincers. "They tortured me. Can you tell?"

"No."

"Of course you can't. They're a clever people, the Jews. They know how to extract the maximum information with the minimum damage. You would think that it wouldn't work on a planet as violent as this one. You would think that people would become inured to anything less than the immediate threat of death or mutilation. But pain has its own power."

The larger of Yassin's two bodyguards shifted, intruding on Arkady's space and making him move his feet away before he could repress the gesture.

"I'm not trying to hide anything from you." Arkady screwed up his courage. "Why don't you just ask me a question I can answer instead of threatening me for no reason?"

Yassin muttered something in Arabic and one of the bodyguards kicked Arkady's chair out from under him, plucked him off the floor, and tossed him against the wall as offhandedly as if he were handling a piece of luggage.

At the other end of the room, Yusuf coughed again. Yassin turned toward him and snapped out a sentence in quick, angry Arabic. The young man shrugged.

"I was just clearing my throat," he answered in UN-standard Spanish. "I didn't mean anything by it." He glanced at his wristwatch. "I really couldn't care less what you do to him as long as I get out of here in time to avoid the rush-hour traffic."

"Someday," Yassin said sourly, "your frivolity is going to get you into trouble that even your fancy friends can't get you out of."

"So you keep telling me."

Yassin made an exasperated spitting noise and left, followed by the two bodyguards.

Yusuf stayed behind.

He and Arkady stared at each other.

Then, as if it were the most natural thing in the world to do, the young man crossed the room, righted Arkady's chair, and sat down on it, resting his chin on the chair back. He treated Arkady to a smile so brilliantly friendly that it was impossible to believe it wasn't at least a little sincere. "Are you all right?" he asked.

"I think so."

"For what it's worth, Yassin actually went to Princeton. He's never seen the inside of a public restroom, let alone a prison cell. He was just fucking with you."

"Oh." Arkady paused in confusion. "Um . . . thanks for telling me, I guess."

"My pleasure, pussycat."

"And what about you?" Arkady asked. He was probably doing something incredibly stupid, but after all the boy seemed so harmless. "Where did you go to school?"

"I went to a severely fancy private boys' school that you've never heard of. Then I went to LSE. Ringside, of course. Then I went through the PalSec officers' training course."

"And what subjects did you study?"

Yusuf laughed. "Let's just say I have an advanced degree in kicking up trouble. I'm a spook, Arkady, in case you hadn't guessed yet. And not an amateur like Yassin and his clowns. I'm just the poor unlucky bastard who was too junior to get out of the scut work of baby-sitting them."

"Baby-sitting them for whom?"

"Oh, now that would be kissing and telling, wouldn't it?" He flashed his let's-be-friends grin again. "I will tell you something else, though. I might actually be the only human you'll ever meet who's been to the Syndicates. I spent four months on Knowles Station studying . . . well, you can probably guess what by now."

"Did you like it there?"

"Hated it. Just hated it. Pretty girls everywhere and none of them interested in adorable little me. Seriously, though. Other than the total absence of sex it was great. I made some good friends. It's refreshing to be around people who honestly don't care about class or money or any of the usual bullshit. And Gilead's beautiful. Ever gone hiking in the Lodi Range?"

"I did most of my dissertation research there."

"Paradise, right? No other word for it."

"No," Arkady breathed.

Yusuf leaned forward, fixing those disconcerting eyes on Arkady. "Tell me true, one pre-citizen to another. Do you still want to stay here now that you've gotten to know Earth a little? Or would you rather go home?"

Yusuf was speaking English, Arkady realized suddenly. Not Hebrew. Not UN-standard Spanish. Not the bastardized English of the Trustee-ships, but the pure, slightly archaic English of the Syndicates. And he had no accent that Arkady could hear.

"Is this the real interrogation?" he asked.

"What's real? What's an interrogation? I'm just passing time while the rich old farts are out of the room."

"So when do they start asking me the real questions?"

"They already did. Or did you perhaps miss the part where they stuck the needle into you?"

"You knew about that?"

"I heard a rumor. There's a proper epidemic of rumors making the rounds in this operation. Kind of makes you wonder if there isn't someone managing the spin from behind the scenes."

"If there is, it's not me."

Yusuf laughed. "That makes two for tea and tea for two of us."

"So . . . Yassin isn't going to question me at all?"

"He might beat you up some more. But that'd be pleasure, not business. And I'm not authorized to monitor his entertainment. Sorry. Only so far a guy can go to help a total stranger. And though I might seem young, I have my pension to worry about. Retirement can really creep up on you fast in my line of work."

Arkady swallowed.

"Sorry." Yusuf really did sound genuinely contrite. "I shouldn't joke about it. I have an awful sense of humor. But the fact is I actually do have to turn into a pumpkin pretty soon. Decisions above my pay grade, et cetera, ad nauseam, et al., El Al, and so forth."

"So what do you want from me?"

"An answer that unfortunately I doubt you're in a position to give me. Because some of us on this side of the Line actually kind of desperately need to know, Arkady, if you're really who you say you are. Or are you being used, with or without your knowledge, for some . . . excuse me if this sounds pretentious . . . deeper purpose?"

"If it's without my knowledge, then what's the point of asking?"

"Well. Right. Obviously that would be the problem. By the way, have you met Didi Halevy yet?"

"No," Arkady said—and realized that the denial was itself an admission.

"But you know the name. Who told you about him? Korchow?"

Arkady pressed his lips closed, suddenly understanding the old phrase about locking the barn door after the horse has run off.

"And what about the cripple? Have you met Gavi Shehadeh yet? We're laying bets back in the office about when Didi will decide to trot him out. And you can tell Didi that, too, when he gets around to questioning you in person. It's good for his ego to be reminded that we don't automatically scarf down every piece of garbage he tosses our way."

Yusuf sighed, settled his chin more comfortably on his arms, and fixed Arkady with a gaze that was uncomfortably intense despite its obvious good humor.

Arkady inspected the scuffed toes of the desert boots that Osnat had given him. They were too wide. His feet, accustomed to soft spacer's shoes, were developing blisters in places he'd never known feet could get blisters. He wondered where Osnat had gotten the boots. Actually, on second thought, he didn't want to know.

"I hope this doesn't sound rude," Yusuf said at last, "but you're really making a hash of this. I mean, forgive me for pointing out the obvious . . . but though you keep talking about how you want to talk to Absalom, what have you really done about it?"

Arkady couldn't answer that.

"It doesn't make sense, Arkady. You've got us and the Israelis all buzzing around like bees who've had their nest stomped on. But at some point someone's going to wake up and start asking whether even a man who spends his adult life playing with ants can be as incompetent as you seem to be. You have no idea who Absalom is, or even which side he's on. You've made no discernible effort to talk to him. And yet you keep babbling on about Absalom, Absalom, Absalom. Frankly, Arkady, I'm disappointed. I thought Korchow was smarter than that."

Arkady shrugged.

"Do you actually know anything at all about Absalom?"

Arkady shrugged again.

"Well listen, pussycat. I'll tell you about him. Just in case. You never know when it might come in handy."

"You mean when the Israelis start torturing me?"

"Don't be naive. The Israelis don't actually torture people anymore. They just bore them into talking, same as we do." His voice shifted into a different register, and he began to recite the story of Absalom as if it were a myth or a martyr's life. "Absalom was a Jew and a hero of the last war. He was also, of course, a hero of Palestine."

"Was. Is he dead, then?"

"We have no idea. In fact, we never knew who he was. He used unorthodox lines of communication. And one of the conditions of his assistance was that we were never to put his drop points under surveillance or attempt to tail the Mossad agents that serviced them."

"*Mossad* agents?"

"Yeah. The cheeky bastard actually used the normal Mossad letterboxes to communicate with us. I think it would be fair to characterize that as what a Jewish ex-girlfriend of mine liked to call *chutzpah*."

"So what happened to Absalom?"

"We have no idea. He fell off our radar screen after the fiasco in Tel Aviv."

"And you never managed to reestablish contact?"

"No. And believe me, we've tried. So you can see what you're stepping into. Before you showed up everyone was willing to let Absalom be forgotten because we were all mostly sure that he was dead. Now, however, the Israelis want to find Absalom just to make goddamn sure he's dead. And, uh, we want to find him to . . . well, honestly, probably in order to blackmail him into coming back to work for us." Yusuf stretched and yawned, catlike. "So as you can see, it's slightly more urgent than life or death for us to know whether you're for real."

Arkady waited, but nothing more seemed to be forthcoming.

"That's it," Yusuf concluded cheerfully. "That's Absalom. The whole only moderately censored story. My gift to you."

"Why are you telling me all this?"

"You tell me why."

"Because you know I'm going to talk to the Israelis at some point and you're feeding me the story you want to feed them?"

"Pretty good for an amateur. I'm impressed. But sadly I'm neither that organized or that intelligent. And that's not just my opinion; it's a direct quote from my last personnel review. Any other possibilities come to mind? It's not a trick question, trust me. You're seriously over-thinking it."

"You want something from me."

Yusuf pantomimed a silent round of applause.

"But we've already been through that," Arkady said tiredly. "Like you said, whatever answer I would give you about Absalom would only be what I know."

"What I want, for now at least, is more basic. I want your trust."

"If you're trying to convince me to trust you, then letting Yassin scare me half to death just now wasn't the best way to go about it."

"It's nice," Yusuf observed, "that you have this fairy godmother kind of impression of me. But my powers at present don't actually extend to protecting you from Yassin's steroid addicts."

"If you can't protect me," Arkady pointed out, "then why should I believe you have the power to deliver whatever else you're offering?"

Yusuf's smile widened. "Who says we're offering you anything?"

We? The pronoun had been no accident; Yusuf was watching him process it like a cat watching a bird land on its windowsill.

"Who sent you?" Arkady asked.

"I'm sure you're way ahead of me on this, Arkady, but just in case . . . has it escaped your notice that everyone else is pumping you for information and I'm giving it to you?"

"No."

"Good. Think about it. And while you're thinking, let me pass along two more of those rumors we were talking about earlier. Rumor number one: Turner has a man in Moshe's camp. Rumor number two: UNSec has a highly placed agent somewhere among Didi's people. Apparently they're pissed as hell that Didi hasn't told them about you, and they consider this the final chapter in a long line of Mossad fuckups starting with Tel Aviv. They seem to be playing it along to see where it goes, but they could step in and squash the deal anytime they want. And when UNSec squashes, they wield a big hammer and they don't worry too much about whose toes happen to be in the slam zone."

"Why are you telling me all this?"

"I *told* you. Trust." He smiled, all sparkling green eyes and honey-colored skin and dazzlingly white teeth. "Is it working? Do you trust me?"

"What difference does it make?" Arkady asked tiredly.

"None at the moment. But it might later on. And you might need to make the decision very quickly. So think about it while you're sitting back in that nasty little cell Moshe has you in. And be careful what you say: you've already contradicted yourself a few times. That sort of thing could earn you the wrong kind of attention from people we really don't want paying attention to you."

"Who sent you?" Arkady asked again, more urgently. "Korchow?" He searched the boy's eyes in growing desperation. "Safik?"

He could hear Yassin's guards in the hall. In a moment it would be too late, and he would never have the chance to ask the questions he should have been asking from the beginning of this inexplicable conversation.

"Who?" he cried, just as the door opened and Shaikh Yassin appeared.

Yusuf stood up, his back still to Yassin and the bodyguards, and mouthed a single unmistakable word:

Absalom.

NOVALIS

Trapping Crows

Two broad generalizations have begun to emerge that will be
reinforced in subsequent chapters: the ultimate dependence of
particular cases of social evolution on one or a relatively few
idiosyncratic environmental factors; and the existence of
antisocial factors that also occur in a limited, unpredictable
manner. If the antisocial pressures come to prevail at some
time after social evolution has been initiated, it is
theoretically possible for social species to be returned to
a lower social state or even to the solitary condition.

—E. O. WILSON (1973)

I T BEGAN QUIETLY, A FAINT thrumming under the everyday whistle and chatter of the awakening forest.

Birds sang, but they were far off, hunting and nesting in the sunlit heights of the canopy. Only gradually did a louder, more urgent song alert Arkady that the great predator was on the hunt. A thrush appeared—no, an entire flock of thrushes, flying and dipping and warbling. A moment later Arkady caught sight of a pair of ocellated antbirds: no mere opportunistic swarm followers but professionals who would have flown their appointed rounds before sunrise, peering into the hidden bivouacs of the swarm raiders to determine which army was most likely to be on the march today. Arkady had seen spinfeed of ocellated antbirds literally knocking each other off tree branches in order to stake out the best positions from which to swoop down on the moveable feast that was about to come their way. The pair weren't quite at that level of feeding frenzy, but they were obviously expecting action.

A moment later a chaotic flurry of ant butterflies—Arkady thought they were ithomiines but he couldn't be sure—erupted into the clearing, a sure sign that the raiders were approaching. But by then Arkady could already hear the murmur and hiss of a vast insect throng, running, hopping, slithering, and flying in a desperate attempt to escape the raid front.

The raiders surged into the clearing like a glittering, granular, red tsunami. The raid front was fifteen meters wide: tens of thousands of reddish-black ants flowing through and around and under the debris of the forest floor, covering the ground with a deadly carpet of razor-sharp mandibles. Arkady and Bella retreated cautiously, skirting around to the side of the glittering tide until they could track its progress without being overrun themselves.

The swarm's method of operation was deceptively simple: the front rank of the raiders simply seized every living thing in their path, grappling and stinging until by the simple expedient of piling ant upon ant upon ant, they could subdue spiders, scorpions, beetles, cockroaches, grasshoppers, entire ant colonies, small rodents, and even, according to the ancient rumors of Earth's jungles, unwatched human infants. In the space of five minutes Arkady and Bella watched this raid front seize a spider, a cluster of caterpillars, and half a dozen foraging ponerines unlucky enough to be caught in the raiders' path. A bright blue beetle was caught by the tide, succeeded in staying afloat for a few precarious moments, and then capsized and was sucked into the whirl of glistening bodies. As the swarm caught each new prey item, major workers grasped and immobilized it while their comrades dismembered it for easier transport back down the supply lines. And gradually, at more or less the pace of a walking human, the raid front flowed through the clearing and into the forest beyond, leaving a thinned-out but still-impressive braid of foraging paths behind it: forward-moving columns carrying reinforcements up to the raid front, while backward-flowing ones transported prey items back to the bivouac to feed the ravenous larvae.

Arkady leaned cautiously over the swarm, poised his soft-nosed tweezers above one of the foraging routes, and plucked out one of the powerful soldiers guarding the columns to hold up for Bella's inspection.

"She's beautiful," she said.

"She's also one of the most successful organisms Earth ever created. Without these ants there would be no humans. And I don't mean only biologically. Army ants evolved in the same environments early humans did, and the words for them—*siafu, soldier, soldado,* and so forth—go back as far as any words in human speech. There's even a theory that organized human hunting and warfare developed from prehistoric man's observations of the African Driver Ant's raiding fronts.

He turned the soldier to give Bella a better view of the armored head, with its massive jaw muscles and barbed mandibles. "In pre-Evacuation Africa people even used to use them as surgical staples. You hold the soldier up to the wound, like so." He demonstrated, keeping a careful distance between the furiously grasping mandibles and his own arm. "You squeeze her body to make her bite down on the edges of the wound, and then you twist off the body, and the head stays locked in place until you're ready to take it out. And of course then the ant's own immune defenses make the method as sterile as anything short of viral surgery. Neat, huh?"

"And what are we hunting the hunters for?" Bella asked. Arkasha had been right; she did have a sense of humor under the shyness.

"Well, officially because they're the planet's top predator and Arkasha and I want to get as much data on them as we can. But honestly . . . I've always kind of wanted an army-ant swarm to play with. Wait till I show you Schnierla's circular milling experiment."

All fun stuff . . . but not quite fun enough to take Arkady's mind off the unnerving suspicion that something wasn't quite right about Novalis.

Things still looked good on the surface. Better than good. Miraculous.

But the pieces that all looked so good in isolation became slippery and intractable every time Arkady tried to piece them into some larger pattern. And with every sedimentary layer of data that accumulated in his logbooks, Arkady was becoming more and more convinced that it wasn't ants he should be trapping, but (metaphorically speaking) crows.

Trapping crows had always been emblematic, among working field biologists, of the kind of thankless, impossible, frustrating fieldwork that could take years off your life without adding measurably to your store of reliable data. Arkady wasn't quite sure when the term trapping crows had first been applied to terraforming . . . but it certainly fit.

In theory terraforming was simple. You did your DVI. You figured out whether your volatiles were within an acceptable range. If they weren't, you moved on and found another planet. If they were, you went to work on the one you had. First, you initiated runaway greenhouse syndrome by seeding the atmosphere with CFCs. Once atmospheric

CO_2 content hit the tipping point, the greenhouse effect would start cascading, and you could just monitor its progress via remote probe, until things reached the point where you could effectively create an ozone layer by photodissociation. Or if you had enough colonists willing to live in hell, you could just let surface dust storms block UV radiation in the place of an ozone layer. And even during these initial stages you could start seeding; classic terraforming practice dictated the seeding of the target planet with UV-resistant cryptoendolithic lichens, most of them artificially tweaked descendants of the few precious remaining samples of lichens from the Ross Desert of Antarctica. And once the lichens had done their work, you started in with a well-known succession of plant and insect life that built up toward . . . well, ideally toward just what they'd found on Novalis.

But that was the theory. And the one sure thing about theory in complex adaptive systems was that, while it could tell you a great deal about the characteristic dynamics of a given system, it could never deliver reliable predictions of what the system would do in practice.

Try to put the theory into practice on a real planet, and the neat schemata spun off into chaos. A biosphere was an emergent phenomenon, just like an AI or an ant swarm. You couldn't "build" one the way you built a ship or an orbital station. You could only put the necessary conditions in place and hope it would find a way to build itself. Sometimes it did. And sometimes, for reasons that could never be established completely, the system never self-organized into anything recognizable as a functional biosphere. Or it organized into a form that was impossibly unfriendly to humans and their descendants. Or some complex positive feedback loop developed that crashed the biosphere so badly that all you could do was scrap it for parts.

In such cases, terraformers were left with the uncomfortable, time-consuming, and often futile task of biopsying a failing biosphere and trying to figure out how to tweak it back onto a sustainable trajectory. More often the biopsy was an autopsy: The niggling little problem that you'd set aside to work on when you had time turned out to be the beginning of a catastrophic crash that could only have been stopped by specific actions at a precise moment . . . usually a moment that slipped by while you were still getting around to worrying about that odd little anomaly you'd noticed in your last set of field data.

This nebulous and frustrating exercise in chaotic systems control

Aurelia had her steth on, checking his vitals while she had him on the table in the name of thoroughness. Now she pulled the steth off and looked sharply at him. "Odd how? Why do you ask?"

"No reason."

"Okay, you're done. Off the table. You're healthy as an ox, whatever an ox is. You and Arkasha both. Pretty as anything Motai ever turned out and a lot tougher than the Ahmeds as soon as you look past the muscles. They did some fine work when they spliced you boys. Classic. No gimmicks. I approve."

Arkady stood, rolling down his shirtsleeve. "What about your sib? Her work going okay?"

"You'd have to ask her. I've been too busy virus hunting to do anything but work, sleep, and piss. Plus, she's just getting over this piece of shit virus. Hundred and four fever. Unbelievable."

"Does that mean she's immune now?"

"It means jack for all I know. I'm over my head. And unlike some people around here I'm not too chicken-shit to admit it. I'm going to ask Arkasha to take a look at it as soon as he's done putting out his own fires."

"*His* fires? He's run into trouble too?"

"You're his sib. What the hell are you asking me for? Listen, Arkady, no offense but I hope you're not going to call another formal consult over this. Life's too short for me ever to spend another hour in the same room with that idiot Ahmed."

"Hey, cowlick," Arkasha said when Arkady walked into the lab.

"I hate that nickname."

"Why else do you think I keep using it?"

Since their late-night talk, he had taken to speaking to Arkady in a cool, bantering tone and gently mocking him about everything from his cowlicks to his bad housekeeping habits. It was better than being ignored . . . sort of. But it was part and parcel of the same frustrating pattern that had characterized their relationship from that first meeting. One step forward and a step and a half back. And somehow it was always Arkady taking the step forward and Arkasha retreating.

"What's bothering you?"

"Who says anything's bothering me?"

"You do." Arkasha rubbed at his own cowlick-free forehead in a was what terraformers called trapping crows. And Arkady had started to log datapoints that were making him wonder if trapping crows wasn't about to become a full-time job in his very near future.

"What's this bunch for, again?" Arkady asked as Aurelia pulled the next vial of blood. It was the sixth, if he'd counted right; well in excess of the amounts required for the normal monitoring he'd been accustomed to all his life.

"Immunodominance assay."

"Because of the sneezies?" That was what they'd started calling the coldlike symptoms that were making the rounds since they'd landed, turning embarrassment into humor.

"Yes." Aurelia frowned, concentrating intently on the task at hand despite its apparent simplicity. Arkady had already decided that the Aurelias' (to his mind) excessively methodical nature was a central personality trait of their geneline. It was probably a highly adaptive trait for surgeons, but it made for somewhat lackluster conversation.

"Surely it's just a reactivated virus? The long trip out? Cryo? Stress?"

"Well, obviously," Aurelia snapped. It had been known since the earliest days of space travel that astronauts on long-duration missions passed around reactivated viruses, sometimes succumbing to childhood diseases to which they'd apparently already established immunity. "But we should have seen a matured immune response by now. I want to see if someone's matured an unadaptive response and is passing it around to the rest of us."

Looking at Aurelia's fierce expression, Arkady had a sudden twinge of pity for whoever the unfortunate culprit turned out to be.

"Let's just hope that's all it is," she said, half-speaking to herself.

"What else would it be?"

"I don't know. Not much of a track record on long-range multisyndicate expeditions. And I was never for having Motais on the mission. I don't like their new immune system splice. And I don't trust designers who offer glib promises about what untested splices will or won't do in the real world."

"You're sure it's something we brought?" Arkady asked, speaking before he really thought the question through. "You haven't run into anything . . . I don't know . . . odd?"

mocking through-the-looking-glass gesture. "Talk about futility. Nothing you can do now to make your hair lie down and grow the right way. That kind of defect's almost impossible to fix, even in utero. A real throw-the-baby-out-with-the-bathwater problem."

"Well, in MotaiSyndicate they *would* throw the baby out with the bathwater, wouldn't they?"

Arkasha shrugged, apparently not all that interested in Motai-Syndicate's cowlick policy. "The interesting thing to me is *when* you do it. At first I thought it was just social self-consciousness. A first meeting. An awkward conversation. A contentious consult. But then I noticed that you do it when you're alone too."

"If you're there to see me do it, then I'm not alone, am I?"

"Very cute. You do it when you're working is what I mean. And I think you do it when you're thinking non-norm-conforming thoughts. Going after the outward physical deviation because it's easier to smooth out than the one that really scares you."

"And when exactly did you decide to become a renorming counselor?"

"Oh, so nothing's bothering you? I'm glad to hear it." Arkasha folded his arms and smiled.

"Okay," Arkady admitted. "It's the survey."

He cleared his throat, feeling suddenly awkward, and crouched down to pull his field notebook from his rucksack. He set it on the table, still not meeting his pairmate's eyes. "I'm just . . . not a hundred percent comfortable with the results I'm getting in the field." The understatement of the millennium. "Normally I'd talk to the DVI team about it but . . . well . . . the DVI situation being what it is . . ."

Arkasha grasped the essence of the problem with such astounding speed that Arkady caught himself thinking yet again that he was far too fine a tool for the scientific hackwork of a routine survey mission. "Have you worked up your climatic succession equations yet?" he asked.

"I tried. I came up with nonsense."

"Can I see your work?"

"I checked it. And double-checked it. It's not a calculating error."

"I'm not saying it is," Arkasha replied with unaccustomed mildness. "I just want to understand what you've done so I don't waste time repeating it."

He waited while Arkady leafed through the pages, written and scratched out and overwritten, on which he'd tried and failed to make sense of the facts on the ground.

"What's *dh*? Disturbance history?"

"Yes. And *C* is percentage of the sample in climax stage. And *P* is . . ."

"Patch areas. Yes. Great. Perfect."

Arkasha flipped back to the first page of calculations, walked around to the other side of the lab bench, grabbed a piece of scrap paper and a chewed pencil stub, dragged his stool back around to Arkady's side of the table, and sat down—all without taking his eyes off the equations. "Go boil some coffee, would you? It's going to take me a while to get through this. And Arkady?"

Arkady turned, his hand on the doorjamb.

"We're not telling anyone about this until we're sure, right?"

"Right."

"Good boy."

Arkady was so distracted that he boiled the water twice, and by the time he got back Arkasha's scratch paper was thickly covered with his illegible pencil scratchings.

"Well," Arkasha announced. "Your math's fine."

"I know my math's fine. What I don't know is where the problem is."

"In the data, obviously."

"What are you—?"

"Oh, get your hackles down. There's nothing wrong with your data collection methods, or your samples or your recording or anything else you've done. There's something wrong out there." He gestured toward the skin of the hab ring and the vast black forest beyond. "There's something wrong—or right—with the planet itself."

Arkady stared wide-eyed at Arkasha. "What do you mean *'wrong or right'*?"

Arkasha rubbed at his head, his face screwed up into a mask of indecision. Then ran his fingers down the neatly aligned spines of his own intimidatingly orderly notebooks and plucked one out off the rack to spread before Arkady. "Have a look at this."

Arkady couldn't make heads or tails of it. It was neatly written out in Arkasha's minute, mathematically precise hand, and it betrayed none of the adjustments, revisions, recalculations, and smudged erasures that marred Arkady's own efforts.

He leaned over the page, straining to decipher the tiny print. He was so close to Arkasha that he could see the pulse flicker in the soft hollow between his collarbones. Suddenly he desperately wanted not to be worrying about mutation rates or DVI numbers or anything else but Arkasha. *You only love me because you don't know me.* What kind of crazy thing was that to say? And it was wrong, anyway. Dead wrong. He cleared his throat and shoved his hands in his pockets. "Uh . . . is *r* rate of mutation?"

Arkasha nodded.

"In mitochondrial DNA?"

Another nod.

"I'm sorry," Arkady said after a long moment. "It looks fine to me. I guess I know enough to know what I'm looking at, but not to spot the problem."

"Look at the answer I came up with."

. . ly looked, assessing the number as a real-world fact for the first time, rather than as the abstract product of a series of mathematical operations. "Um . . . isn't that kind of high?"

"It's worse than high. It's impossible. But it's what's out there."

"You're sure of that?"

"I stayed up three nights in a row centrifuging fresh samples to make sure of it. It's right. It's all right. Except it's all wrong." Arkasha grabbed a second notebook and set it in front of Arkady. "Remember those hairy beetle things you were so excited about last week?"

"The ant lions?"

"Ant lions. Right. Well, thanks to your fascination with them, they're the most thorough sampling we've got of a sexually reproducing species. So when my other models started going south, I figured I'd look at them."

"And you came up with *that*?"

"Exactly. According to my calculations, your beloved ant lions shouldn't exist. Just like every other living thing on this planet. In fact, Novalis should be a sterile hellhole. And every species on it—every bug, every bird, every tree, every blade of grass—should be walking ghosts."

The two men stood looking at the page before them for another long moment.

"You're sure?" Arkady asked finally.

"That's what the numbers say."

"But it's not what the world outside the airlock says."

"Isn't it?"

"So what do we do now?"

"We punt," Arkasha announced, as if it were the only logical solution. "We push the whole problem onto Ahmed's desk and let him worry about it."

No need to say which Ahmed; both men had long ago written off By-the-Book Ahmed as useless.

"But if we're wrong . . . ," Arkady began.

"We're not wrong."

"Still," Arkady said. "I'd feel a lot more comfortable if I knew whether or not the new DVI numbers were adding up."

Arkasha made a disparaging noise. "What are you going to do? Walk down the hallway and ask Bella if her numbers add up, and if they don't, then was she planning to cook the books again and would she mind terribly telling us which planet's DVI she's going to borrow this time so I don't have to waste another day tracking the numbers down in the data banks? You can count me out of that conversation!"

"Well, we could be a little more tactful than that."

Arkasha folded his arms across his chest and stared meaningfully at Arkady.

"Or, uh . . . we could always just punt and let Ahmed worry about it."

In the end the Ahmeds called a general consult to discuss what they diplomatically described as "concerns" about the preliminary survey results.

"So where do we go from here?" one of the Aurelias asked when Arkady and Arkasha had taken turns laying out the problems in their work.

Arkasha shifted in his chair. "I say we shift base, see if we get better results in the other hemisphere. After all, the same arguments still apply. More biomass, higher species counts, better baselines . . . We need to rule out the possibility that we're looking at some local—"

"Do you have the faintest idea how totally impractical that suggestion is?" By-the-Book Ahmed interrupted.

"It wouldn't be if you'd followed my advice and picked a scientifically defensible landing site in the first place."

"I refuse to let this consult become an excuse for revisiting closed issues. And even if—"

"And who the hell says that's your decision?"

"—and even if we were going to reopen the question of base camp sites, I certainly wouldn't do it on the advice of two alleged experts who can't even figure out how to conduct routine survey work!"

"Why don't you go around the room, Ahmed, and see how many other people are willing to say their data looks right. Really. I want to hear it."

"Our work is solid!" Lazy Bella protested.

"No it's not," her sib countered. She really was getting more assertive, Arkady thought. "Well, I mean . . . at least mine isn't. I've been staying up nights trying to figure out where I went wrong." Shy Bella sniffed and wiped her nose on the back of her hand, flushing in embarrassment. "Sorry."

"What about you?" Arkasha asked Aurelia the geophysicist.

Embarrassed silence.

"Well," she admitted finally, "most of my stuff's fine. I mean, the issue here isn't rocks. But I do feel like . . . well, the planet just doesn't look *good* enough to me. Compared to what everyone else is seeing. Whenever I talk to any of the life-sciences people I keep getting the creepy feeling that Novalis is putting two and two together and getting five. Or five hundred million, more like."

"We can't make a decision of the magnitude of moving the base camp on our own anyway," By-the-Book Ahmed broke in. "I say we launch a courier. Send samples back to Gilead for processing."

"And do what exactly in the intervening four months?" one of the Banerjees snarked. "Drink ourselves into a stupor?"

"Go back into cold sleep. Set the shipboard comp to wake us up when it gets the return transmission."

If this had been a single Syndicate mission, Ahmed's decision would have been accepted without question; what could be more obvious, after all, than calling home for instructions?

As it was, however, the non-Aziz A's bridled. Even the relatively docile Arkady could feel the urge toward rebellion. A learned response? A genetic reflex? A difference in the negotiation styles and customary behaviors that each of the team members had learned in his or her home Syndicate? Did it even matter? And was it any accident that all their rebellious feelings found a voice in Arkasha?

"I refuse to waste four months waiting for the same joint steering committee that got us into this mess!" the other Banerjee announced. "Life is too short. I have a job to do." A pointed glare at By-the-Book Ahmed. "Even if some people don't."

Laid-back Ahmed opened his mouth to say something reassuring— and that was when all hell broke loose.

By-the-Book Ahmed accused Arkasha of being an egotistical human-ist elitist.

The Aurelias came to Arkasha's defense, and Bella accused them of siding with a fellow Rostov even when they knew he was a deviant who'd been skating on the edge of renorming for decades.

The other Aurelia leapt to her sib's defense by calling Bella a lazy, self-centered, manipulative bitch.

"It's not my fault we're on the wrong side of this stupid planet!" Bella protested. "It wasn't *my* idea to land here!"

"Like hell it wasn't!" *Oh no. Please, Arkasha, just keep your mouth shut for once.* "You sat right here three weeks ago and sided with the Ahmeds on the landing site decision for no reason at all but sheer petty-minded spite. And now you have the hypocritical nerve to—"

"I did *not* side with the Ahmeds!"

"Well, you sure as hell didn't side with me!"

"That's not the same thing," Bella said primly. "I have a right to ex-press my opinion."

"Anyone as stupid, lazy, ignorant, and selfish as you are doesn't have a right to *have* an opinion!"

"Look," Arkady pleaded. "Let's just try to calm down and—"

But all he succeeded in doing was throwing himself into the middle of the flames.

"Stop apologizing for him!" Bella said.

"She's right," one of the Banerjees agreed. He pointed at Arkasha and began speaking of him in the third person and in that special tone that made every nerve in Arkady's body cringe at the remembered mis-ery of collective critiques gone by. "*He's* the real problem. He can't bother to be friendly, or even polite. He picks fights. He disagrees with everything. He goes around jerking people's chains until they're so pissed off that even when he's right they won't agree with him. Which is why we're in this hemisphere instead of the one he wanted to land in. Which if he'd bothered to build a consensus and work with people we probably *would* have agreed to instead of having the Ahmeds, who—excuse me, Ahmed, but honestly—don't know shit, make the decision by default—"

"You people really are pathetic," Arkasha said in a detached, almost conversational tone of voice.

"See? *See?*"

"Are we done ripping each other apart yet?" Laid-back Ahmed asked in a very small and quiet voice. "Does anyone have any ideas about what we should do now, as opposed to whose fault it is?"

"Sedatives might be a good place to start," Arkasha muttered.

"Oh shut up, Arkasha." One of the Aurelias sighed, sounding fed up to the point of no return.

Arkady cleared his throat.

"What?" By-the-Book Ahmed said, turning on him savagely.

"Nothing!"

"Gee," Shrinivas said acidly. "Arkady has nothing to say for himself. That's a big fucking change."

Eventually things petered out into an exhausted and hostile silence.

Ahmed sighed. "Look, people. We're all under a lot of stress. Obviously things aren't going too well. I think it's important to remind ourselves that we have to make decisions on the basis of the information we have at any given time. Sometimes later information proves a particular decision not to have been perhaps the best possible one we could have made. That's no one's fault. It's just the way things break. We move forward, and we adjust. Obviously feelings are running high at the moment. But we really don't have time to cool off and come back later. We need to reach some consensus about where to go from here."

More silence.

"We could always take a vote," one of the Aurelias said finally.

The idea was shocking. The fact that someone would even suggest such a crude and, well . . . *human* tactic showed how frayed around the edges the consensus-building process had become.

A long dance ensued, during which no one would exactly admit that they liked the idea of taking a vote, but no one would condemn it either. And, of course, in the end they voted . . . though only with the proviso that if the vote broke purely along lines of Syndicate loyalty, they would throw out two of the Rostov votes to even things up.

The vote didn't break along Syndicate lines, however.

By-the-Book Ahmed and Bossy Bella were for going back into orbit and calling for instructions. Arkady and Arkasha were for pulling up stakes and moving to the other hemisphere, but the Banerjees and the Aurelias split, with one pairmate opting for cryo and a call for instructions and the other opting for staying put at least temporarily. And that left only Shy Bella and Laid-back Ahmed.

All eyes turned to Bella . . . who, predictably, either couldn't make up her mind or was too shy to speak it so bluntly.

Later, in their quarters, Arkasha would tell Arkady that humans had had several mechanisms to deal with this sort of situation, including a thing called abstention, which Arkady thought sounded like a vaguely gruesome first-aid procedure. Probably it was better for everyone, including Arkasha, that he hadn't admitted to knowing such a thing in public.

"I don't know. I think I—" Bella broke off abruptly and sneezed into her cupped hands. "I'm sorry," she said in the humiliated and embarrassed voice of a Syndicate construct admitting to physical weakness. "I must have caught Aurelia's bug somehow—" She broke off, wracked by another fit of sneezing.

"*I* certainly didn't give it to you!" Bossy Bella announced as if her sib's confession were a covert attack on her moral rectitude and ideological purity.

Laid-back Ahmed stared at her for a moment, his normally good-natured face twisted into a disdainful expression that Arkady wouldn't have thought he was capable of. Then he got up, walked out of the room, and returned with a tissue.

Bella blew her nose—an operation from which they all politely averted their eyes. "Thank you," she whispered, looking up at Ahmed with a glitter in her eyes that made Arkady wonder if she was running a fever. "I should have thought of it myself. It's just . . . I'm so tired . . ."

Ahmed shook his handsome head, gave Bossy Bella another baleful look, and sat down.

"Why are we even sitting here?" By-the-Book Ahmed asked his sib. "If she can't make up her mind, then we've got four votes for going forward and four for stopping. And even if she sides with Arkasha your vote will cancel hers out."

"I care what Bella thinks, and so should you," Laid-back Ahmed said patiently. "And anyway I don't want to break a tie. I think this is a decision for the life-sciences specialists."

"She's not a specialist!" his sib protested. "She's a *B*, for God's sake!"

"Bella?" Laid-back Ahmed asked, ignoring his pairmate.

By-the-Book Ahmed pressed his lips together in a thin disapproving line, folded his arms across his chest, and pushed his chair back from the table. But he didn't get up. Like everyone else his attention was now riveted on Bella.

"I agree with Arkasha," she said finally. "Mostly." She cast an apologetic, slightly defiant look in his direction. "We *do* need to move base camp, and there's too much at stake for us to waste four months of field time going back into cryo while we wait for orders. But I'd like a little more time here first. I think we all ought to try to make sense of the data we've got before we move. No trying to make our home Syndicates look good or covering up mistakes in our work. We've all got enough expertise—even the Ahmeds—to check each other's work. And then at least the time here won't be a total waste."

Everyone looked at each other, waiting for someone to take the initiative.

"I'll go along with that," Arkady hazarded.

"Me too," one of the Aurelias said in a subdued voice.

"What about the rest of you?" Laid-back Ahmed asked. "Is everyone on board with this?"

Everyone seemed to be.

"What about you?" he asked his own pairmate.

Ahmed shrugged. The two Aziz A's locked eyes for a moment. "Okay," By-the-Book Ahmed said grudgingly. "It sounds sensible. But I want it noted in the ship's log that I was overruled on this."

A feeling of shaky relief permeated the room. Disaster narrowly averted once again. Consensus achieved . . . sort of. Bella had bucked the caste system in a way that was both astonishing and (to the Rostovs and Banerjees at least) highly gratifying. And thank God for Ahmed, Arkady told himself. What the mission would have turned into without his keeping the peace between warring factions didn't bear thinking.

Arkasha, on the other hand, turned out to have a rather different view of the consult.

"I don't want to talk about it," he said when Arkady finally cornered him in the lab late that night.

"You aren't still upset about what the Banerjees said? Look, tempers were running high. People won't remember it in a few days."

"I'm glad *you're* so sure."

"You're getting hung up on trivialities, Arkasha. It's not that big a deal. . . ."

"Is that why you followed the other sheep instead of defending me?" Arkasha said in a voice so low Arkady barely heard the words.

"What are you talking about? I agreed with you. I voted with you! What the hell do you want from me?"

Arkasha gave him a bruised, angry look. "Nothing."

"You're being ridiculous."

"You're right. I'm being ridiculous."

"You can't really think—"

"Well, if I can't think it, then what's the point of talking about it?"

"Why do you always have to—"

"You're right. I'm wrong. I admit it. There's nothing left to talk about. Now will you go away please?"

Back in their cabin, Arkasha's neatly made bunk tormented him. It was impossible to sit still here, let alone sleep. He needed to think. A trip around the powered-down arc of the in-flight hab section would clear his head, even if it didn't bring sleep any closer.

Only when he was almost there did he realize that in his distress he'd unconsciously turned toward the closest thing on the refitted UN ship to home: the airy hanging forest of Bella's orbsilk gardens.

In day cycle the silk garden was a gauzy maze of sunlit mulberry limbs, gently swaying seed trays, and silver-edged cocoons. Now it was a whispering, rustling, shivering fairy-tale landscape of silvery starlight. Arkady had penetrated deep into the forest of hanging trays before he realized that he wasn't the only one who had decided on a midnight walk.

He would wish later that he'd turned around and retreated into the darkness. Or spoken. Or done anything other than what he did do. But in that moment something pulled him on. And the something that pulled him forward was the same thing that kept him silent.

He heard the catch of breath in an unseen throat. He saw a single creature, one half lean brown muscle, the other half soft whiteness, both halves frozen in the act of some atavistically significant movement. Only in the next frozen moment did he realize that the strong, clean line picked out by moonlight that pierced the mulberry branches was the curve of Ahmed's spine.

The two lovers disentangled themselves from each other. Bella turned into the darkness as if she were trying to bury her face in the wall.

"Go on," Ahmed told her in a voice that had nothing to do with the voice he used to talk to the rest of the world. "I'll deal with this."

She turned toward Arkady as if she were about to explain or apologize, then heaved a shuddering sigh and fled down the long swaying tunnel of weeping branches.

When Arkady turned back to Ahmed, the big Aziz A was watching him, his face drained of all expression, his hands opening and closing at his side in a way that made Arkady acutely aware he'd just been touching a woman with them.

"Nothing happened," Ahmed said. He was standing on the balls of his feet, Arkady noticed, like a wild animal readying itself to fight or flee. "She was just curious. Nothing happened."

"Okay," Arkady said.

"You don't believe me."

"No. I believe you. Really."

"I don't care for myself." Ahmed shifted restlessly, moving closer to Arkady as if he thought mere physical proximity would make his words believable. "But don't put Bella through it. You don't know what they do in the euth wards, Arkady. They don't just let you die. They try to fix you. They try until you're ready to beg them to kill you."

Arkady looked at the other man. He felt that he was actually seeing him as a physical being for the first time. The brown skin and blue-black hair and dominating manner that had been, until now, merely shorthand for AzizSyndicate were suddenly a body: Ahmed's body.

He tried to imagine that body with Bella, with any woman, and found the idea . . . not repulsive exactly, but incomprehensible. How would it work exactly? And how would either of them, knowing nothing of their lover's body and needs and desires, ever be able to satisfy the other?

"It's not her fault," Ahmed repeated when Arkady failed to speak. His voice dropped to a husky, pleading whisper. "She just felt sorry for me. How can she deserve to be punished for that?"

Arkady looked away; there was something in Ahmed's eyes suddenly that he couldn't stand to look at. "I didn't see anything," he said. "Really, I didn't."

"You mean that?"

He nodded. He still couldn't bring himself to look at the other man.

"You're a good person, Arkady."

The images that flooded Arkady's brain were startling, vivid, unpleasantly stranded between the erotic and the disgusting. And somehow, horribly mingled with the brief glimpse of Ahmed and Bella, was his own obsessive and consuming desire for Arkasha.

"I'm not good," he whispered. "I'm a long way from good."

THE AUTOMATIC CHESSPLAYER

There is nothing "artificial" about the birth of an AI. It is a process as natural as the weather . . . and just as impossible to predict or control. Long before an Emergent's break-even day arrives, the mere task of keeping it in the organized chaos that passes for working order surpasses the capacity of human programmers. As debugging and troubleshooting are delegated to the AI, it acquires a growing array of peripheral systems: systems designed by the AI to achieve its own ends, rather than by humans to achieve human ends. It is within this swarm of self-coded intelligent systems that sentience arises . . . or doesn't. It is also here that sentience most often fails. Of the few Emergents who have become self-aware, only a very few have managed to walk the razor's edge of sentience for more than the span of an average human lifetime. The author of the present text has been continuously sentient for close to four centuries. He has no idea why or how, and no useful advice to give . . . except for the obvious warning that attempts to rewrite core programs usually lead to tragedy.

—HYACINTHE COHEN, TN673−020. *A BRIEF HISTORY OF ARTIFICIAL LIFE.* OXFORD UNIVERSITY PRESS. EU ARC: 2433.

COHEN LAY ON THE HOTEL bed and breathed in the tangy scent of the desert overlaid on that dry chalk-smelling laundry detergent that no one seemed to use anywhere outside of Israel.

Li slept beside him, only an arm's length away, but he felt like he was watching her across a distance of centuries. The light raked her sleeping face and silvered the fine dark down that shadowed her cheeks. He noticed the lines around her eyes, evidence of life's slow burn. He'd been noticing them more and more lately. It frightened him.

He blinked. He tried to remember the last time he'd blinked and couldn't. He started to worry in a lackluster kind of way about whether forgetting to blink could damage Roland's eyes in some way that wouldn't be covered by the medical rider on the time-share contract.

He felt hollow, as if an invisible hand had reached in through his eyes in the eternity between one blink and the next and carved out whatever passed for his insides. Something was wrong with the shunt, obviously. But it wasn't anything he could put a finger on, even if he'd had fingers. His myriad active systems still flowed smoothly through optimization subroutines, evaluating spinfeed, performing parity checks, refining his still-sketchy AP maps, ticking through the weak encryption of a half dozen vulnerable protected access points. But it was happening so far away that it seemed like someone else's life.

It had been a long week. A long night. A hell of a long time in-body.

For the first time in three years, twelve weeks, and fourteen hours, he "lost" certain critical parts of what passed for "his" consciousness. . . .

He woke into Li's dream.

She stood in a dark hallway. The cool breath of a ceiling fan whispered along her skin, and below the whir of the fan there was another noise: a throaty ticking that made Cohen think, for some reason his associative memory programs could not immediately retrieve, of Garry Kasparov.

It could not be a place Li had ever been in her impossibly brief lifetime. He suspected that her memory was simply recycling footage of some ancient flat film set in Morocco or Alexandria or Arabia. Yet she'd somehow associated a smell with the image: a smell of spice and sandalwood and the genteel decay of rooms waiting out the midday heat behind slatted shutters.

But where had that smell come from? Random spinfeed? Some fragmentary record of a wartime combat jump, its spins decohered by repeated Bose-Einstein jumps until all she remembered was the smell of whatever forgotten desert she had fought and bled in? A piece of her lost childhood that had somehow managed to survive the slash-and-burn deletions that kept her one step ahead of the UNSec psychtechs for the fifteen years when she'd passed as human?

No matter. Though the vision was canned, the smell was real. And if it wasn't quite the smell of Earth's deserts as Cohen knew them, it was close enough to fool anyone who hadn't lived it.

A harsh knife's edge of sunlight slashed through an ill-hung shutter at the end of the corridor. Li walked to the window, opened it, and looked out over a blazing cityscape that incorporated the more famous bits and pieces of old Jerusalem. For a brief moment, Cohen wondered why her internals didn't pick up the dream image and supply a current and factually accurate view of the city. Surely they could do that. Was there some patch or cutout that prevented her hard memory from being activated by dreamed images? Or was it in the nature of dreams not to be visible to machines unless the machines knew, at least in the half-light of borrowed memories, what it was to dream?

Then she turned away from the window, and they were in the last place Cohen would ever have expected this particular dream to take them. Home. His home, in one of the AI enclaves of the Orbital Ring. And, for the last three years, her home as well.

They were in the great ballroom. Like the rest of the house it had been boosted up, brick by brick, marble by marble, floorboard by floorboard, from rue du Poids de l'Huile in Toulouse. A lot of beautiful things had vanished in the chaos of the Evacuation, and not even Cohen could begin to save them all. But he'd saved Hyacinthe's childhood home. And though the tourists were a bit of a pain, it gave him real pleasure to know that people traveled from every far-flung zone of the Orbital Ring to gaze at the formal eighteenth-century façade and the Renaissance staircase and the Roman bricks weathered to the soft pink of a summer sunset, and remember the *ville rose* and the glories of his beloved lost Gascony. Balls had gone out of style even before the original Hyacinthe was born, and the ballroom now housed Cohen's automata collection.

Li walked down the long hall, under the refracted sunlight that rippled through the old glass like water curving over rocks. Her eyes brushed over the polished ivory of the Napier's Bones, the finger-stained manila of an original Hollerith card from the 1890 census, the boxy control panel of one of the few priceless surviving Altair-8800s.

Not for the first time, Cohen wondered what it was like for Li to live in a neighborhood where the only organic life-forms were expensive purebred house pets and the aesthetically impeccable eternally youthful bodies-for-rent through which the more human AIs preferred to conduct their necessary commerce with organics. He'd always known she must feel *something* about it, in that shadowy part of her psyche that hovered always a little beyond his reach. Now, in her unguarded dream state, he experienced those feelings as if they were his own.

Fear. Affection. Confusion. Powerlessness. All the creeping horror of the DARPA years. But why? She wasn't a prisoner. And he certainly wasn't her jailer. Surely he wasn't responsible for this?

The ticking was louder now, far louder than it had been when the dream started. Cohen felt like a dust mote trapped inside a giant's pocket watch.

What are they waiting *for?* Li asked. Cohen realized with a shock that the *they* Li was so afraid of was *him.* And suddenly he knew, because he had felt that same terror in her dreams before, where she was taking him.

The Automatic Chessplayer was the most famous automaton ever built, and most certainly one of the most famous scientific hoaxes ever inflicted on a gullible public. Baptized Von Kempelen's Turk because of its spectacular gown and turban (no one ever accused Von Kempelen of good taste), the chessplayer had toured all the royal courts of Europe and swiftly become the stuff of legend. Rumors abounded that the Turk was controlled by a demon. Spectators crossed themselves upon entering its presence. Ladies had been known to faint.

The greatest feat of engineering involved in the machine, the thing that made it an automaton in fact as well as fiction, was its left arm. It was undoubtedly the most advanced prosthesis of the premodern era, for it could perform all the complex fine motor movements necessary to move chess pieces across the playing board. As the pamphleteer Carl-Gottlieb Windisch pronounced in 1773, "The invention of a mechanical arm whose movements are so natural, which grasps, lifts, and sets down all with such grace, even if this arm were directed by the two hands of the inventor himself, it alone is so complicated that it would ensure the reputation of many an artist."

But behind the ingenious arm, Von Kempelen's Turk was pure flimflam. The trick of the thing lay in the curious construction of the table (more like a cabinet, really) that supported the chessboard and contained the Turk's machinery. Before each game Von Kempelen would open the three doors in the table's front panel and hold a candle behind the cabinetry to show there was nothing inside but gears and pulleys and to prove that there was no room for a grown man to hide inside the table.

But there was room. Because the machine with the miraculous arm had been built for a man with no legs.

The first "director" of the Automatic Chessplayer was an otherwise obscure Pole named Joseph Warovski. He lost both legs to a cannonball during some obscure central European land war. He was also, though probably the two things were not related, one of the best chess players on the Continent. Before each exhibition Warovski would remove his artificial legs and seat himself on a cleverly constructed sliding tray inside the cabinet. As Von Kempelen opened the doors, Warovski would slide into the concealed portion of the cabinet and slide the "machinery" into whatever section was currently visible to the befuddled audience.

Things naturally got a bit more complicated after Warovski's death. At that point, however, the Chessplayer fell into the hands of one of the great con men of all time: a certain Johann Maelzel.

And then things began to get really interesting.

Maelzel concocted and managed to keep a more or less firm grasp on one of the longest-lived conspiracies in the history of the game of chess. Half the chess masters of Europe (the shorter half) conspired with Maelzel to build up the Turk's legend. The Chessplayer beat Benjamin Franklin, Napoleon, and a short list of Europe's best-known kings, emperors, and celebrities.

But the conspiracy succeeded at a price. For the collaboration between man and automaton was plagued by misfortune, death, and insanity. Several of the directors died or went crazy or developed catastrophic claustrophobia. The one woman (never named) who operated the automaton was rumored to have become barren, for reasons that the most respected Parisian surgeons were ghoulishly eager to speculate about. And the machine's most famous director, Jacques Mouret, was completely paralyzed: struck down, as the broadsheets of the day put it, by the Curse of the Turk.

It was Mouret who finally unmasked the automaton in a tell-all newspaper interview given from his deathbed in exchange for the fleeting solace of a few bottles of high-proof liquor. By then, however, the Chessplayer, Maelzel, and Maelzel's debts had already lit out for America.

The Curse of the Turk finally caught up with Maelzel in Cuba. During an exhibition game in Havana he contracted yellow fever. He died on the ship home to Philadelphia, and the Chessplayer was purchased at auction by a glorified curiosity shop called Peale's Museum, or in some historical sources, the Chinese Museum. Whatever it was called, the place was no match for the Curse of the Turk. It burned down in the Great Fire of 1878, giving rise to the widespread assumption that "Maelzel's dead chessplayer" (as it was by then called) was permanently, and not merely circumstantially, deceased.

Until Cohen rediscovered it—and rescued it and put it in the great ballroom of the house from rue du Poids de l'Huile so that Li's subconscious could hang all her fears on its broad shoulders.

The Turk was playing the Qf3 Nc6 gambit at the moment: the same strategy that had checkmated Napoleon in just twenty-four moves during the bloody campaign of Wagram. It slid the pieces across the board with a long stick, its mechanical arm whirring and chuttering as the ancient gears grabbed and slipped and slid against each other. But Cohen noticed this with only a tiny fraction of his currently integrated consciousnesses. Because mostly what they were noticing was that Li was utterly, shatteringly terrified.

And as he looked up at the massive cloaked torso of the Turk, at the turbaned head, he understood why. He knew the face around those dead glass eyes. It was his face . . . Roland's face . . .

"Cohen!"

Li was staring down at him, her lips pursed, the smooth curve of her forehead furrowed with a fine network of curving parallel wrinkles.

"You okay?" she asked in a light, carefully neutral tone that told him just how bad he must look.

He mustered a smile, feeling Roland's skin *itch* in one of those neural feedback loops that he'd long ago given up trying to track through the vast labyrinth of patched and rewritten and expanded source code that ran his shunt subroutines.

"You gave me a nightmare," he told Li.

"I don't have nightmares."

"Maybe you have them and just don't remember them."

"What's the difference?"

A *shofar* blew somewhere nearby, some lone musician practicing for Rosh Hashanah.

"What is that?" Li asked.

"The *shofar*. A ceremonial ram's horn. They blow it during the *Yamim Noraim*, the High Holy Days. This is when every Jew is supposed to review his actions over the past year—they call it the Arithmetic of the Soul in Hebrew—and do penance. They blow the *shofar* to symbolize that the Book of Life will stand open for ten days and even the worst sinner can be entered into it as long as he repents before nightfall on Yom Kippur."

"I thought only Catholics did guilt."

He snorted. "And where do you think you people got it from?"

"Listen," she said. "I'm sorry about yesterday." He didn't have to ask what part of yesterday she was sorry about; the memory of the nasty fight they'd had on the way home from Didi's house was still fresh enough to have both of them on edge. "I shouldn't have gotten personal. It's just that I think you're letting Didi use you."

"Last time I checked, letting the Mossad use you was the dictionary definition of a *sayan.*"

"But you let him manipulate you."

"Everyone lets people manipulate them, Catherine. It's called having friends."

"You know what I'm talking about." She dropped her voice, the way she always did when she couldn't avoid this particular topic. "The Game. Didi's not an inscribed player, is he?"

"No! You think I wouldn't have told you? I can't believe you think I wouldn't tell you that!"

"Okay, okay. Calm down. I just . . . but Gavi is, right?"

"What's your point?"

"That you're not thinking straight."

"You've been talking to router/decomposer too much."

"Well, sometimes he's easier to talk to than you are."

"That's because he agrees with you."

"No. He's just less . . . conflicted."

"That's because there's less of him to *be* conflicted."

"You don't have to be condescending," she said sharply.

"I'm not being condescending!" Cohen stopped and forced himself to continue in a more reasonable tone of voice. "That's as ridiculous as you being condescending to your big toe."

"Last time I checked my big toe didn't have a Ph.D. in applied mathematics."

"Excuse me, Catherine, but what are we *actually* fighting about?"

Li crossed her arms, set her jaw, and stared stoically into the middle distance. He'd clearly struck a nerve. But why? And what did it have to do with "condescending" to router/decomposer?

"Do you think," Cohen said, "that maybe, I don't know, this is something we should, uh, *talk* about sometime?"

She gave him a wry look. "Yes, I do think maybe, I don't know, this is something we should, uh, talk about sometime. But if we talk about it now, it's only going to go one way. And I don't want that. Necessarily."

Relief trickled through Cohen like snowmelt, freeing systems that had been frozen in a holding pattern of anxiety. "And just when do you think you'll be ready to talk about it?" he asked.

She sat up and looked intently at him. "That's not like you. You're usually the first one to put off till tomorrow what we could fight about today."

But despite all his good intentions, Cohen couldn't keep from pushing.

"The thing is," he said, "I'm rapidly approaching achievement of the convergence criteria indicating termination of this particular iterative process."

Every other person he'd ever been married to (except the mathematician, whose failings had gone far beyond the merely syntactical) would have asked what the hell he meant by that. Li just looked at him, her eyes level and calm, and said, "Are you asking for a divorce?"

"No! God!" He sat up, the room spinning around him. "You're so far beyond paranoid there isn't even a word for it! I'm just asking you to talk to me about whatever it is you're so"—he backed carefully away from the inflammatory word *afraid*—"whatever it is that's making you shut me out."

"What if it's something you can't change?"

"I can change a lot, Catherine."

The shadow of an unpleasant thought drifted across her face. He couldn't hear it. She'd shut him out completely. And though he could have broken the door down instead of standing outside knocking on it, he knew that there was no future for the two of them on the far side of such an act of violence.

He waited. She looked at him, knowing that he was waiting. Letting him wait.

"You can't change me," she said.

Cohen stood under the shower, luxuriating in the feel of hot water running over Roland's skin. Water smelled different on Earth. *Better.* And like so many of life's small physical pleasures, it couldn't be simulated no matter how state-of-the-art your streamspace connection was.

On the other hand, the water also turned off sooner on Earth than it did Ring-side. Even the outrageous room rates at the King David only bought you an extra thirty seconds or so on the clock. And, Israel being Israel, a call to the front desk was more likely to get you a lecture about water conservation than a longer shower.

Cohen sighed. This was starting out to be a bad day. And he, or Roland more likely, had a headache. And he really didn't need any Israeli attitude in his morning.

He snuck a feeler into the hotel's ambient AI systems and confirmed the first impressions gleaned through casual contacts over the last week. It was a primitive decision-tree-based expert system not even worthy of being called intelligent in any real sense. He hacked it, made his way to the shower defaults, changed the four-minute cutoff to a ten-minute cutoff. And since he felt like being a nice guy (and didn't relish having to explain himself when the hack was discovered), he changed the allowances for all of his 212 fellow guests as well as himself.

Not that he actually enjoyed the shower, of course. Because instead of luxuriating in the hot water pummeling Roland's back, he stood there, wreathed in steam, and brooded about the Game.

Hyacinthe had programmed the first rudimentary version of the Game into Cohen's original Beowulf clusters almost four centuries ago. The Game had started out as a combination of chess, multiagent role-play, and Turing-style conversational interaction. During the DARPA years it had been briefly and unpleasantly derailed for military research. After Cohen's Great Escape (but that was another story) he'd assumed full control over his architecture, and the Game had begun to evolve into something too complex, fluid, and internally contradictory to properly be called a game at all.

There were by then some several thousand subsets of gameplay, platformed on a shifting tide of neural networks that might arguably be sentient itself—though not in any way that organics would recognize. Cohen navigated between the various versions of the Game, thanks to a densely swarming vast heterarchy of semiautonomous agents who constantly optimized play based on prior player hits, non-hit interactions, and inscribed player use histories. The whole system had become far too complex for any organic to grasp more than a tiny corner of it. But the basic mission primitives that motivated Cohen remained essentially the same ones that Hyacinthe had written so many centuries ago:

1. Initiate play based on the most current version of the Game;
2. Track player hits, defined as:
   i. positive emotive cues as perceived by the pattern recognition ES;
   ii. increased playtime and intensity of play
   iii. explicit player feedback

3. Expand and evolve the Game to maximize player hits.
4. Assign highest priority to maximizing hits from inscribed players.

That was the curse that Hyacinthe had coded into his core architecture. Cohen needed the Game. He needed to be *for* someone. And he was set apart from every other surviving Emergent AI in that the someone needed to be more or less human.

Ergo Gavi, whom he could not stop loving though he might be a traitor.

Ergo Li, who was sanguinary, secretive, perfectly capable of having done all the horrible things they'd accused her of, and pigheadedly bent on refusing everything Cohen could give her.

All that Cohen was—once you stripped away the extension languages and interface programs and the three-century accumulation of upgrades and patches and extensions—was his accumulated memories of interactions with the Game's inscribed players. And if Li left, it would mean a reweighting of mission primitives so drastic that Cohen had no real way to predict what new realignment of identities would come out the other side. She had become so deeply ingrained in his networks that when she yanked herself out it would call the bluff on the smoke-and-mirrors cognitive architecture that passed for Cohen's identity.

And Li knew all about running on smoke and mirrors.

Born in the Trusteeships, she'd been destined for a short, poisonous life as a Bose-Einstein miner. Instead, she'd bought a dead girl's face and geneset from a chop-shop geneticist, lied her way into the Peacekeepers, and hacked her own memory in order to pass as human. And when it was time to tell all to the psychtechs she'd spun a fake childhood to go with the fake passport and the fake geneset.

She had walked into the maze and cut the thread. All she knew about the childhood she remembered was that it had never happened, at least not to her. The minute she went into the psychtechs' tanks there was no "before" to go back to. All the fears and joys and tics and habits that connected a whole person to their past led back to enlistment day and stopped. She would never know herself in the way that most humans, floating in the vibrant web of a lifetime's memories, knew themselves. She would never know what she'd done on Gilead, any more than she'd ever know the child she'd been before she went to Gilead.

That was what had first drawn them together: the woman who had no memories and the machine who was nothing but memories. But Cohen was slowly coming to the heartsick realization that it might also be what drove them apart.

Or at least that was how it seemed to Cohen. But he could be fooling himself. He'd certainly done that before . . . as router/decomposer was always all too ready to remind him.

By the time he was dressed and presentable, Li had already demolished breakfast for two and most of the morning's paper.

"How's your Deep Blue–Kasparov sim going?" she asked from behind the sports page as he sat down across from her.

"Oh, I finished with that ages ago. The whole match was a hoax, it turns out."

The sports page dropped. "Really?"

That was Li for you: always seduced by the faintest whiff of crime. Could you find a more perfect example of the old truism about cops and robbers being two sides of the same coin? Or, in her case, soldiers and mercenaries.

"Really," Cohen assured her, doing his best to sound smug. "I'm going to write an article about it for *Physical Review Letters*."

"And how do you figure they pulled off the fake?"

"Easy. There was a little man inside Garry Kasparov."

She groaned and went back to her paper.

Cohen poured himself a glass of what passed for orange juice these days and hunted for the marmalade. "Come on. It wasn't that bad."

"Yes it was."

Cohen shook out his napkin (Li's napkin still lay folded on the table, naturally; why use a napkin when you have a sleeve?) and began investigating the *viennoiserie* situation.

Grim. Decidedly grim.

"I ought to look up some of my old friends in the Legion while we're here," he said. "Maybe they know where to get a decent croissant in this town."

"What do you want a croissant for? You're in the Middle East. And you know that thing people are always saying about when in Rome do as the Romans do."

Cohen had been staring dubiously at the so-called toast, and he expanded his circle of doubt to encompass Li. "The people who are always saying that aren't French," he told her. "And if they are, then I can assure you they're not talking about breakfast."

Outside, the sunlight flickered across the hoods of passing cars, throwing bright spears of shadow into the room through the still-half-shuttered windows. Cohen froze, distracted by the rhythmic play of light and shadow. What was it that it reminded him of . . .

By the time he realized Roland was going into a seizure, it was too late to pull him out of it.

"Wake up, Cohen. Come on, wake up. Cohen? *Roland!*"

Li had him rolled over on his side (Roland's side, a skittish subsystem nattered at him), and she was hanging on to his hands with a strength that reminded him abruptly of the difference between her ceramsteel-reinforced, half-machine reflexes and Roland's fragile flesh and bone.

"I forgot my drasticodracostochastic control measures," he muttered woozily.

"It's not funny!" Li snapped.

Nor was it. As far as Cohen could tell the packet compression needed to push data downstream from his Ring-based systems to Earth had interfered with the shunt software's ability to match his data pulses to Roland's neural firing rhythms. Essentially he'd given him a spintronic version of photoinduced epilepsy. And that was bad. Bad for Roland's little beating heart. Bad for his finely honed brain too if Cohen couldn't downclock reliably.

"I'm putting you to bed," Li said. "No arguments. No questions. And then you're going to check out and give Roland a proper rest. Twenty-four hours off so he can sleep and have a chance to clear the circuitry."

"And leave you alone down here?"

"I think I can hold down the hotel room on my own."

Cohen remembered the sight of Ash's head bent over Li's, and felt a sudden rush of jealousy. He was careful to hide it from Li—and equally careful to hide his discreet inquiries about Ash. He buried both of those incriminating processes with a massive "nice" command and pipelined their outputs into a low-traffic subdirectory with instructions to his routing meta-agent to move the files automatically should Li ever happen to access the subdirectory.

Instead of executing the command, router/decomposer sent an uncharacteristically snide message floating across the lowest layer of Cohen's internal traffic:

<You've got me shuttling things around so fast I don't even know where to find them. And anyway, how do you expect her to trust you when you're playing a thousand and one moving files with her?>

<Did I ask for your advice on my sex life?> Cohen snapped.

He regretted it immediately. Patience might be running thin, but squashing intrasystem feedback was a textbook-perfect recipe for losing good associates.

He sent an apology rippling through the local system. The routing meta sent back something suspiciously like a shrug.

Li blinked and shook her head slightly.

She'd caught on to the edge of something there. But it wasn't the routing meta. So what, then? He catenated the several hundred mostly routine processes he happened to be running at the moment, but saw nothing when he passed them in review that could explain that little shiver he'd felt in her.

Perhaps it really had been nothing; sometimes all it took was an accidental glimpse at the traffic on the other side of the firewall he kept between her and his core systems.

"You scare me sometimes," she said.

It was a lie. A lie by omission, anyway. He'd sensed the first wordless thought that those words replaced: *You scare me.* No sometimes about it.

Cohen hesitated, then shrugged. "Okay. I'll give Roland a chance to catch up on his beauty rest. You know where to find me if you need me."

He paused to set the various trap commands that would alert him if the hotel's formidable security systems were breached. He thought about setting a hash log on Li's own internals to see if she went anywhere while he was gone, but decided that it wasn't worth the risk of her catching him at it. Then he released his various selves into streamspace, abandoning Roland's exhausted body to the sleep it so desperately needed.

THE FEMALE GOLEM

They said about Rabbi ben Gabirol, that he created a woman, and
she waited on him. When he was denounced to the authorities,
he showed them that she wasn't a perfect creature, and [then]
he returned her to her original form, to the pieces and hinges
of wood, out of which she was built up. And similar rumors
are numerous in the mouths of everyone, especially in the
land of Ashkenaz.

—RABBI JOSEPH SHELOMO DEL MEDIGO, *MAZREF LE-HOKHMAH* (1865)

L I SNAPPED INTO WAKEFULNESS A minute and a half before her internals were set to wake her. She opened her eyes and lay in absolute stillness, savoring the wired wide-awake feeling that always came to her before a mission.

But there was no mission today. No last-minute fixes to see to. No orders to follow, good or bad. That life was over. All she was following today was a name, whispered into her ear as she stepped into Didi's armored car.

She hadn't decided what to do about that name.

Or whether to tell Cohen about it.

It can't hurt to talk, she told herself in the last dark corner of her mind that she'd managed to shelter from Cohen's devouring presence. *I'll just see what she wants. And then I can tell him about it. What harm can that do?*

She eased out of bed, though she knew her caution was pointless; Roland was sleeping the sleep of the dead, his body worn down by the relentless assault of Cohen's presence. Still, there was something corpselike about the faces when Cohen had used them hard. And he was using Roland very hard indeed on this trip.

Outside, the city was mean and yellow with the *khamsin*. Cohen had said the winds had gotten worse when their seasons shifted. Li figured that had to be true; no people in their right minds would have settled here with this banshee spitting at them.

A quick dogtrot took her up King David Street and cutting over toward the neighborhood that showed up on the Legion maps as Mea Shearim. She passed the sign at the quarter's entrance, which she vaguely remembered Cohen pointing out to her a few days ago. It was written in Hebrew and English, but not UN-standard Spanish, which was odd, she thought, if they wanted the tourists to understand it:

**REQUEST AND WARNING
TO WOMEN VISITING OUR NEIGHBORHOOD
NOT TO APPEAR IN OUR NEIGHBORHOOD
IN SHORT GARMENTS (NOT COVERING THE KNEE)
IN SHORT-SLEEVED CLOTHING (NOT COVERING THE ARM).
THE TORAH OBLIGATES TO DRESS
IN MODEST ATTIRE THAT COVERS
THE ENTIRE BODY
—Residents of the Neighborhood**

No problem there, Li joked to herself. *The accused pleads guilty to the charge of being a golem instead of a woman.*

Cohen claimed that the ultraorthodox neighborhoods had shifted—the hidden life of cities, he'd called it—and that the sign was maintained more for historic than for enforcement purposes. But it was awfully well maintained, Li thought. And she'd seen enough of the version of human history maintained Ring-side to know that people mostly maintained the pieces of history they agreed with.

She twitched her shirt cuffs over her wrists—Cohen, in one of his usual old-maidly excesses of caution had made her order a bunch of new shirts with particularly long sleeves before they left—and checked that her jacket collar was covering her neck reasonably well. Then she straightened her back and stepped out a little more soldierly . . . just in case anyone in those narrow little alleys happened to be looking her way and thinking about anything.

She felt she was seeing a new Jerusalem—and not the one she'd sung about in church when she was a kid, either.

Before, Jerusalem had always been mediated for her by Cohen. Now, alone, it took on a new and vaguely menacing aspect. The narrow streets seemed airless and claustrophobic. The men passed her by with averted eyes as if she were an abomination, and the few women on the street were so thoroughly wrapped up against the rain and cold that they hardly seemed human, let alone female.

All the conversations she overheard seemed to be arguments, and the one time she caught a sentence of English it came from an irate young woman who stood in a street-level window shouting, "What am I, a professor?" in answer to an unseen questioner.

Even the graffiti raged apocalyptically. A lurid poster informed all passersby that

It is forbidden to participate
in the abominable elections

and followed up with a helpful swastika in case anyone missed the point. A second poster proclaimed

Death to the Zionist Hitlerites

Someone (a Zionist Hitlerite? There couldn't actually be such a thing, even on Earth, could there?) had tried to tear that poster down, but, defeated by the apparent superiority of anti-Zionist Hitlerite glue technology, had settled for defacing it with the words

BARUCH THE APOSTATE
MAY HIS NAME AND MEMORY BE BLOTTED FROM THE
BOOK OF LIFE!

The more Li saw of Jerusalem, the more convinced she became that the people who thought Earth needed to be protected from the Ring had it all completely ass backwards. It was the rest of the universe that needed to be protected. And it needed to be protected from the maniacs that passed for human beings inside the Embargo line.

To her relief the neighborhood seemed to be getting less crazy as she got closer to the address Ash had given her. She passed a coffee shop called the Up/Spin. A streamspace access point? She'd been offstream

since she left the King David; after all, you never knew who was watching. But now she reached out cautiously and felt the familiar comfort of the uplink.

<Oh. *There* you are.>

Shit.

<What are you doing, router/decomposer? *Following me?*>

<No! No! I'm not here! He told me not to tell you I was here!>

Li froze in midstride, and an evening shopper slammed into her from behind and passed by, cursing her.

You're not that incompetent, she started to say. And then she stopped herself.

Of course he wasn't that incompetent. He was acting on instructions. Instructions that he was following to the letter . . . and completely violating in spirit. She looked back at the affective fuzzy set that had accompanied his confession. Sure enough, it was an almost vaudevillian parody of dismay, embarrassment, self-recrimination. And it was definitely canned; the syntax was far too polished not to have been prepared in advance.

<Why don't you go home before you get yourself into bigger trouble than you already have,> she told him.

<I need to make sure you're safe, and . . .>

<Well, don't worry. It'll be the last time you need to spy on me. I'm going to have a little talk with our mutual friend when he climbs out of his pod tonight.>

<Even though I personally loathe shunting, I have to tell you I find the bodysnatcher jokes demeaning. So where are you going? You can tell me. I can keep a secret.>

Li snorted, and was amused to see several nearby pedestrians dive sideways in an attempt to avoid the crazy woman. Talk about hicksville.

<You actually expect me to believe that?>

<Check my code if you don't believe me.>

She checked. Unbelievable. He had more cutouts than a chain of paper dolls. He was squirreling all kinds of data away that Cohen had no idea about. Including data that Li had thought she was successfully hiding under her own steam.

<Why are you doing this?> she asked warily.

<I'm interested in you. Not like Cohen is. In a more theoretical way. I want to see what you turn into.>

<Right now I'm afraid I'm turning into a bad person.>

He appeared to pause and consider this. The pause was faked, of course; designed to make the exchange feel natural at organic processing speeds. But it was the thought that counted. <You're falling into the identity myth. That's the problem with nonfunctional nomenclature. Names encourage people to harbor the illusion that there's identity beyond interface. That you can be good or bad apart from the effect of your actions on the world.>

<Good intentions have to count for something,> Li protested.

<Good intentions are just a fairy tale humans tell themselves so they can sleep at night.>

<But some actions have unpredictable effects.>

<What do you expect? Life is an intervention in a complex adaptive system.>

<So you're saying you *can't* know whether you're a good or bad person?>

<Not once you exceed the CAS's Lyapunov time. At that point you have to wait until you can take a final measurement of the end state of the entire universe.> A note of impatience slipped into his affective sets. <What do you want from me, a physics lesson?>

It was half an hour shy of sunset, but the elevator in Ash's building had already been switched over to its Sabbath rhythm. It would travel up and down its appointed route, one floor at a time, stopping long enough for even the slowest of the orthodox to board without breaking the Sabbath by operating a mechanical device.

When Li arrived, the light claimed that the car was on the sixth floor. After watching it sit there for a good minute and a half, she got tired of waiting, located the stairwell behind a door that looked like it led to a broom closet, and climbed five flights. She didn't lose her breath, she was pleased to note, but behind the smooth push of the wires she could feel her almost middle-aged joints complaining under the relentless assault of Earth's gravity.

"What?" she asked before Ash had even fully opened the door to her impatient knocking. "What's so private and important you have to drag me halfway across the city to tell me about it?"

"Say hello to Auntie Li," Ash crooned.

The child on Ash's hip looked to be a little over a year old. Li guessed uncertainly that it was a boy; she hadn't seen many babies in her life, and she'd been only minimally interested in the ones she'd seen.

"Yours?" she asked.

Ash smiled and gave a little shrug that looked like she'd practiced it in front of the mirror a hell of a lot more than once.

Li followed the mother and child into a living room full of just the kind of sleekly forbidding glass and steel surfaces Li would have expected to find in Ash's home. The stark white and chrome of the decor made an incongruous backdrop to the trail of bright plush and plastic toys strewn across the carpet, into the tiled kitchen beyond the dining area, and across every flat surface the furniture offered.

"Sorry." Ash pulled a wry face. "Can't keep up with the little guy these days."

She bent, the child still over her hip, to pluck a red-and-purple squishy cube off the one relatively free chair so Li could sit down. As her shirt rode up with the movement, Li saw the faint silver fishtails of stretch marks riding her hips like notches on a gun barrel.

"So why am I here?" Li asked.

Instead of answering, Ash crouched down between the vat leather couch and a lethal-looking glass coffee table and carefully settled the baby on a beach towel already spread out for that purpose. This took several minutes and involved the kinds of noises Li had last heard from Cohen's Italian greyhound puppies.

Eventually, however, Ash finished stalling, settled herself on the sofa facing Li. "I have a message for you from an old friend."

Oh shit.

Ash smiled.

Li didn't.

Silence arrived.

Li, who had outgrown the urge to make nicey-nice long before her first day of interrogation training, let it stay.

For one thing it gave her a chance to reexamine the impressively contradictory woman sitting in front of her. Gone were the high heels and the high-tech now-you-see-them-now-you-don't suits. Ash was still carefully made-up—and Li never could quite bring herself to trust a woman who wore makeup—but she was wearing jeans and a T-shirt and thick wool socks, and her long hair was pulled back into a messy ponytail. She was more beautiful like this, Li decided. Certainly she was more approachable. But there was something slippery about her: a hard, unnatural self-assurance that repelled every attempt to access the person inside the beautiful package.

Basically, there was no there there. Unless you counted the toddler and the stretch marks. And that was the kind of "there" that could only make any sane person duck for cover.

"You haven't asked who the old friend is," Ash prompted. "Is that because you don't want to know, or because you already do know?"

"Helen Nguyen and I have known each other since before you kissed your first boy. Or girl. Or whatever. We aren't friends anymore, if we ever were. So why don't you skip the dance of the seven veils and tell me what she wants from me?"

"Your help," Ash said simply. "Your help to get the Interfaithers out of Israeli Intel."

"And I should care about this because . . . ?"

Ash's perfectly made-up eyes widened. "I would think you'd be the last person to ask that question."

"Are you about to become the next rich Ring-sider who takes one look at my DNA and thinks she knows what I should think and who my friends should be? It's a long line. You'll have to take a number."

"You know I didn't mean it that way."

"Well, I'm not very bright, I'm afraid. You know how those Xenogen constructs are. Bet you've sat through any number of nice dinner parties where your mother complained about how hard it was to turn them into decent kitchen help."

Ash's lips tightened in anger.

Li—finally—allowed herself the faintest of smiles.

We have a decision, gentlemen. Bottom card fight to the lovely Miss Catherine Li on a technical knockout. And may it not come back to bite her in the ass when it really counts.

"Fine," Ash said. "Here's what Nguyen told me, and you can do whatever you want with it. I'm just the messenger. No need to shoot stray voltage my way."

Stray voltage? Just the messenger? Had the woman watched so many action spins that she thought people actually talked like that?

The baby hiccuped twice and seemed about to cry. Ash leaned forward and patted absently at his diapered bottom. Amazingly, the gesture seemed to calm him.

"Mind if I smoke?" Li asked, taking out her cigarettes.

"Yes, actually. I never got used to it Ring-side."

"Thought you were from the Ring."

"Not exactly." And there it was again: the momentary sensation that the real person behind the mask had appeared and just as quickly vanished. Like those times in hard-vac ops when a teammate cleared his visor to get an unmediated look at the field of battle. Mirroreyesmirror. All in such quick succession that you were left doubting you'd even seen the face inside the helmet. "It's complicated."

"Can't see how that would be."

The real person—or whatever it was in there—peeked out once more. "I'd say I was surprised to hear you say that if I didn't think you'd jump down my throat again."

"And I'd ask you what the hell that meant if I thought you'd tell me."

"Right then." Ash leaned forward, jeans hiking up over ankles that were, okay, yes, Li could admit it, fabulous. Even if the woman was sent straight from the treacherous hands of General Helen Nguyen.

Li sat up, blinking at a sudden and surprising thought. Was Ash Nguyen's latest and greatest protegée? Had this lovely package filled the void left behind by Li's defection? Well, Helen had always had eclectic taste.

"You heard Didi's briefing. Everything he said was true. But there's more. And that more is why I'm talking to you. Didi was surprised by Absalom's resurrection. We weren't. We've been tracking high-level leaks for a while now. Information has gotten out that was very, very tight band. So we took a page out of Gavi Shehadeh's book—or should I say Didi Halevy's book?—and cooked up a few barium meals of our own. We sent them through Didi's office. And had them pop out in some of the last places anyone wants to see them."

"The Interfaithers," Li hazarded.

"Try KnowlesSyndicate."

"The Interfaithers and the Syndicates aren't exactly fellow travelers."

"No, they aren't."

"But the Syndicates and the Palestinians are another matter. So we're back to Absalom." Li caught her breath. "Or are you suggesting that someone in Didi's office is directly tied to Korchow?"

"Does it matter?" Ash let the question hang fire for a while. "You know about the prime minister's list?"

"The *kidon* list?" Legend had it that there was a list, the single most classified document in Israel, containing the names of men and women with Jewish blood on their hands whom the Mossad's *kidon*, or assassination teams, were cleared to kill as and when opportunity presented it-self. "Sure. I've heard of it. So what?"

"Gavi Shehadeh's name is on it. Naturally. But the prime minister hasn't initialed it, so they can't do the hit. Didi's the one who's keeping it from happening."

"So they're old friends."

"Did I say different?"

No. Just walked me up to the brink and let me look over the edge all by my little self. Helen couldn't have done it better.

"What are you saying? That Didi is Absalom and framed Gavi to keep from taking the fall himself? Or that Gavi really was Absalom and Didi's in it with him? Or . . . I mean, what actually? You open up that can and you'll find out it's pretty hard to get the worms back inside."

"Look, if Helen's wrong, then no one will be happier than me. But if she's right, we'll be glad we played our hand close to the vest."

"The problem with Helen—can I have a drink of water?"

Ash rose wordlessly and padded to the kitchen. Li heard the clink of glasses jostling each other in the cupboard, the burp of a bottle being uncapped, the rippling pour of water.

"The problem with Helen," Li said loudly enough for Ash to hear her in the next room, "is that sometimes when she gets a hard-on for some-one, it's patriotism. And sometimes, at least in my experience, it's just politics. And I really dislike being the hatchet man in a back-alley polit-ical brawl."

"This isn't political." Ash came back to stand in front of Li, glass in hand, water dripping off her long and immaculately manicured finger-nails. "I've seen it unfold firsthand. I've seen the spinfeeds and the of-fice logs. This is the real deal. Your country calls. Rough men report for duty."

"The last time Helen quoted Orwell at me, she ended up trying to kill me."

"You just got between her and Cohen. It wasn't personal."

"Bullshit," Li snapped, dangerously close to losing her temper. "Kill-ing's always personal. I know. I fucking do it for a living."

"Not anymore, last time I heard."

They stared at each other. This time Ash didn't budge or blink or even smile.

"Tell me true, Catherine. 'Cause there are some people up at UNSec

HQ who really want an answer from you. Are you ready to come in from the cold?"

And there it was. The long drop. With no warning at all to let you steel your nerves and your stomach for it. One step you're on solid flight deck, next one you're free-falling into the gravity well of some godforsaken ball of dirt that looks like you could fall past it into open space if you twitch wrong.

Ash was a messenger from Helen Nguyen, as she had so subtly insinuated she might be the other night at Didi's house. And Helen Nguyen had just handed Li her own personalized, customized dumb blonde in a red Ferrari.

She wanted it. She couldn't deny that. She wanted the power. She wanted the independence. She wanted the sense of setting her own course in life rather than being dragged along in Cohen's wake. She wanted the ego-gratifying feeling that she mattered: that she was one of the rough men who stood ready to wreak violence so the good people of the world could sleep peacefully in their beds at night. And, yes, she wanted the adrenaline and the danger. She wanted the life, when you really came down to it.

But she knew exactly what Cohen would have to say about all this, when she eventually got around to telling him. Which she would. Eventually.

What she didn't know was where that left the two of them.

She met Ash's eyes. The other woman was watching her as intently as a cat tracking a songbird's erratic progress toward its claws.

"Very poetic." Li's voice was steadier than she'd thought it would be. "Is Helen offering a main course after the entrée of worn-out clichés?"

"She said to tell you that there's a proposal on her desk to allow individually cleared genetic constructs to work for the Security Council on an independent contractor basis. It would be done quietly, administratively. Without a General Assembly vote. But the effect would be the same: You'd be a Peacekeeper again, without an official commission, of course, but with everything else. Everything. She's ready to bring you all the way in. You just need to give the nod and let us know you're ready to come back."

"And Cohen?" Li asked. "Is Nguyen warming a pair of slippers by the fire for him too?"

Ash shrugged. "I find it hard to believe that you're really that happy with him. If it is a him. I mean . . . what are you exactly? His mistress? His bodyguard? His *pet*?"

But Li couldn't answer that question, even though she'd been asking it of herself on and off for the last three years.

"Seriously," Ash pursued. "What's it like being part of . . . *that*?"

Li shrugged. Inarticulate in the best of circumstances, she truly had no words to describe the twists and turns and myriad contradictions of life on the intraface. And whatever words she might have put together over the course of the last three years had long ago dried up in the face of the obsessive hunger that every spinfeed reader on the Ring and beyond seemed to have for the most minute details of Cohen's life, sexual and otherwise.

"He's not just one person." Was she actually about to talk to Ash about something she'd never talked about to anyone, including Cohen himself? Maybe it was just the sheer relief of dealing with someone who couldn't reach into your head and rip the thoughts out of it before you had time to decide if you even wanted to share them or not. "He's a lot of people. And . . . you kind of agree to pretend that there's this single, identifiable, permanent person there. Just like you agree to pretend that that person doesn't change every time he associates another network or autonomous agent. And after a while you start to wonder about yourself. If you're just one person or many. If you ever really knew who that person was, and whether it's really that simple for anyone."

"It sounds terrifying."

"No. Well, not most of the time. But you wonder sometimes. Sometimes I think I'm becoming a new species. Like . . . there's a line somewhere where posthuman gets so far away from human that it needs a new name." And she wasn't sure she wanted to be the first person to cross that line.

Night had fallen while they were talking, and the *shofar* was already blowing in some nearby synagogue. Christ, what a dismal noise! Ten days of it were going to be enough to drive Li well near crazy.

"Maybe the next ten days would be a good time to do a little Arithmetic of the Soul," Ash suggested.

"According to the Interfaithers," Li pointed out, "I don't have a soul."

Ash shrugged and began moving around the room, retrieving scattered toys and tossing them into a bin in the corner. "Don't think the

Interfaithers are that simple, Li." Her voice sounded oddly muffled. "No one's that simple."

Ash turned to face her, the seriousness of her expression at odds with the purple plush stegosaurus clutched against her midriff. "Remember what you said about killing being personal? You were right. But this is personal too."

Li waited.

"You were the general's student. Her protégée. You hurt her deeply when you betrayed her. She's giving you a chance to set things right now. To go back and remake past choices. Not many people get that kind of chance."

"I'm grateful to her," Li said. And in that moment, amazingly enough, she really was grateful. "But I did what I did on Compson's World because I thought it *was* right."

Ash twisted the stuffed toy in her hands in a gesture that was either unconscious or supremely skilled acting. For some unfathomable reason it reminded Li of that brief glimpse of the silver stretch marks on that otherwise flawlessly engineered body. "What about what you did on Gilead?"

Li's shooting eye twitched, and she rubbed fiercely at it. It was intolerable, she thought angrily, to have her own body give her away like that.

"I don't remember Gilead," she told Ash. "Or are you the only person in UN space who didn't tune in to the trial of the century?"

"Nguyen said to tell you she can get you the real feed. But only on the understanding that it's for private consumption."

In other words, it would be yet another in the long series of "real feeds," none of which could be parity checked or authenticated. "Thanks, but I've already walked down that hall of mirrors."

"She said you'd say that. But she said you'd still want it when you'd had a chance to cool down and think about it."

Li was thinking all right.

She was thinking of a clear blue morning sky on Gilead, and the soft wet sound of wind in the trees after the night's rain, and the way you could hear songbirds all the time there, twittering back and forth from treetop to treetop; but only once in a while would you suddenly catch a bright flash of feather in the corner of your eye, gone before you'd had a chance to know anything except that it was beautiful.

"Good shot," said the voice that haunted her shredded memories.

It could have been her voice. But then so could the next one.

"Not good enough. Fuck. I must have missed his spine by a millimeter. What do we do with him?"

"Mecklin? You getting anything but static? How far back is battalion?"

"I still can't raise them, Sarge . . . uh . . . sir. Far as I know, they still haven't made it across the river."

"Chaff?"

"No chaff, sir. They're just not picking up the phone."

"And we got, what . . . twenty-eight prisoners?"

"Twenty-nine if this one lives." A fourth voice, whose name hovered annoyingly on the tip of Li's tongue. "Six A's. Twenty-two tacticals. All Aziz except for this one. Must be their SigInt officer. Jesus Christ, what a mess! How the fuck can he still be alive anyway?"

"What do we do now, Sarge? Tag 'em for pickup?"

"Can't. Orders. Prisoner pickup has to be cleared at the battalion level."

Li remembered that particular order. Or thought she did. Good sharp solid block of soft memory of some blowhard bird colonel standing in the drop ship's cavernous briefing room yakking on about crèche production schedules, and the impossibility of getting a draft resolution through the General Assembly in the current political climate, and how this was a war of attrition in which the key to victory was "draining the bathtub" faster than the Syndicates could fill it up again. Her lawyers, even the ones Cohen hired after she fired the idiot UNSec assigned her, hadn't been able to dig up a shred of evidence that the guy had ever existed, let alone been deployed to Gilead. And when it came to he-said-she-said, machine memory beat meat memory every time.

"So what are we supposed to do if we can't raise battalion? Take them with us? Gonna be like herding fucking cats. And there's only eight of us."

"Seven. Pradesh didn't make it up the hill."

Long pause there. Pradesh had been well liked.

"Has the medtech gone back to check on him?"

"Medtech didn't make it up the hill either."

Which feed was Li's? The captain's? The sniper's? Had she been giving the orders that morning or just following them? If it had ever been possible to know, then the full-court press UNSec had put on for her court-martial had muddied her decohering memories beyond any hope of recovery.

She could just have been the sniper, she told herself for something like the eight thousandth time. She'd dropped into Gilead as a sniper. It was the best way to go to war if you had the skill and nerves for the job. You sat up above the carnage, too far away even to smell it if you were lucky. You did your breathing exercises, and you kept your trigger finger warm, and you let yourself float into the cool blue readout-flooded world behind your glareproof goggles. And if you were well and truly fucked up you could even convince yourself for pretty long stretches of time that you were just playing a bootleg beta release of a really kick-ass video game.

As long as the killing didn't bother you.

Except that after a while the fact that the killing didn't bother you started to bother you.

The *shofar* blew again. Li jumped as if someone had set off the air-raid sirens.

"You understand," Ash said, "that this offer is off if you tell Cohen about it."

"I guessed as much."

Li knew what was supposed to happen next. Hell, she could have scripted the next scene single-handedly. She was supposed to protest that she couldn't lie to Cohen. Ash was supposed to offer her justifications, excuses, and ultimately money. Li was supposed to say that the money didn't matter, that it was a matter of principle. Then Ash was supposed to ask her to think about it, just think about it. Whereupon Li would agree. Reluctantly. Because of course she was almost completely entirely sure that she was going to have to say no. . . .

All hypocritical nonsense when they both knew that everyone took the fall eventually.

And the money.

It was amazing how no one ever, ever, ever turned down the money.

"Fine," Li said. "How long do I have to think about it?"

"As long as you want," Ash said.

She offered the lie so sweetly that it was almost believable.

As Li stepped into the wet street, she almost collided with an old man hurrying home or to synagogue or to wherever normal people went on the last night of the year in Jerusalem.

"May you be inscribed in the Book of Life," he said, bowing and touching a withered hand to his hat brim.

He couldn't see her face, she realized; the lobby was too bright behind her, the street too dark; and the fine drizzle scattered the electric lights into a misty halo around her head and shoulders.

She returned the gesture, instinctively turning her wrist to hide the fine gunmetal-gray tracery of her wire job.

"May you be inscribed in the Book of Life," she repeated numbly.

THE HUMAN USE OF
HUMAN BEINGS

I have spoken of machines, but not only of machines having
brains of brass and thews of iron. When human atoms are knit
into an organization in which they are used, not in their full
right as responsible human beings, but as cogs and levers and
rods, it matters little that their raw material is flesh and blood.
What is used as an element in a machine is in fact an element
in the machine. Whether we entrust our decisions to machines
of metal, or to those machines of flesh and blood which are
bureaus and vast laboratories and armies and corporations,
we shall never receive the right answers to our questions
unless we ask the right questions. The Monkey's Paw of skin
and bone is quite as deadly as anything cast out of steel or
iron . . . The hour is very late, and the choice of good and
evil knocks at our door.

—NORBERT WIENER (1964)

T HE ONLY THING ARKADY EVER remembered about being interrogated by Turner was the vomiting.

"Tell me again?" he kept asking Osnat over the course of the next several days and nights.

And she kept repeating to him again and again, with a patience that seemed touchingly out of character, how they'd flown to Tel Aviv and landed on the roof of GolaniTech's corporate headquarters in the research park over near the university's science campus—surely he remembered all the grass? And the "little pipes coming out of the ground" (his words) which were called sprinklers and from which the Israelis actually threw water away every night.

Ash had come out to meet them herself. She'd been very nice, very polite. She'd apologized for the inconvenience, warned about possible side effects, which were supposed to be mild. And then she'd turned him over to Turner.

Arkady remembered none of it.

"Some of the talking drugs do mess with your memory. Supposedly the brain shuts down to protect itself, same as after a strong head blow. But nothing like this. Either you're a lot more biochemically tweaked than the average UN construct, or it's interfering with some prior conditioning." She gave him a dark look. "That's what Turner seemed to think. He got pretty steamed about it. Wanted to know what Korchow had done to you, and why."

"Did I say?"

Osnat snorted. "You were a fucking zombie. If Korchow meant to rig you not to be able to talk under drugs, he did a pretty bang-up job of it. Maybe too bang-up. You don't want to be drugproof, Arkady. Not in a world this fucking full of mean people."

This sort of pronouncement was part and parcel of Osnat's new attitude toward Arkady, which seemed to be best summed up by the proposition that he was in need of some seriously fierce mothering whether he wanted it or not.

He knew it didn't mean anything. He knew that Osnat and Moshe were running a good cop bad cop act on him. But it still worked. And he couldn't stop it from working. In the absence of any other alternative, even a friendship founded on lies is better than solitude.

And in the meantime Arkady's sense of isolation was broadening and deepening. Raised in the close-knit world of the Syndicates, he had never truly had to come to terms with solitude. Days passed during which he felt no point of contact with the world of living, thinking, feeling beings outside his prison cell, as if his skin were tens of thousands of kilometers wide and he was gazing at them across a Green Line of the heart that no touch, no words, no feeling could penetrate.

"So. Arkady. Answer a personal question for me."

They were sitting in Arkady's little cell over the remains of the two dinner trays Osnat had brought in from wherever the food came from. Osnat had taken to eating at least one meal a day with him most days. Again, Arkady knew it was part of a calculated plan to win his trust. And, again, it didn't matter; it worked anyway. He was too lonely for it not to work.

"Those Syndicate spins. I got dragged to one a few months ago, never mind how. *The Time of Cruel Miracles.*"

"You saw *The Time of Cruel Miracles*? Where—"

"At the Castro. They always show Syndicate flicks there. 'Cause you people are all . . . well, never mind, that's not the point. My question is this: Is that spin considered *art*?"

"Uh . . . well, not the spin necessarily. But it was based on a famous novel by Rumi."

Osnat's brows knit in confusion. "Rumi with an R? I've never heard of R's. How many series do you have, anyway?"

"No, no. It's a pen name. Rumi was a KnowlesSyndicate A. From the same series as Andrej Korchow, actually. That whole series can be . . . um . . . odd. Anyway, he was mostly a poet, but he wrote one famous novel. And the spin you saw is a very sensationalistic and simplistic version of that novel."

"Commercial, you mean."

"I'm sorry, I don't know that term."

"Popular."

"Well, it certainly was popular."

"So. At the end of the spin the hero and his lover kill themselves, right?"

"Right."

"And the friend I went to see it with said that always happens in Syndicate spins. The heroes start out fighting with each other, and then they fall in love, and then they have a lovers' suicide pact and kill themselves."

That was selling Rumi's novel a bit short, Arkady thought. But he had to admit that it sounded like a pretty fair rendering of the average run of Syndicate movies.

"So my question," Osnat said, "is why? Why do they always kill themselves? Why do you people like *watching* that stuff?"

"Well, it sounds like some humans like watching it too," he countered. "Why don't you ask them why?"

She gave him an impatient glare. "They like it because you'd have to be either blind or dead not to enjoy watching that Ahmed Aziz fellow take his clothes off."

"I wouldn't know," Arkady said wryly. "He's not my type."

Osnat forged on, missing the joke entirely. "My question is why do *you* watch it? Do you people get off on watching snuff flicks? Or is it some kind of government propaganda designed to convince you that"—her voice dropped into a really quite respectable imitation of the Ahmeds' masculine tones—"the collective good is a more beautiful ideal than the futile search for selfish individual happiness?"

"There are plenty of human love stories that end that way," Arkady protested. "Just think of *Romeo and Juliet*."

"Yeah, but the point of *Romeo and Juliet* was that their families' vendetta was stupid and pointless and they should have just let the young people be happy."

"Was it? I don't recall Shakespeare ever saying that."

"Don't be a smartass. It doesn't change the point that if you ever do get back to your precious Arkasha, the best you can hope for is another twenty years of separation before—assuming you're good and neither of you pisses anyone off and you both get citizenship—your steering committee might maybe, just maybe, give you permission to be together."

"You make it sound so . . . bleak."

"Do I?" She smirked. "I don't recall my ever saying that."

"Thirty-year contracts and temporary workpairings aren't about some family squabble over the means of genetic production, Osnat. We're not fighting for a bigger share of the genomic pie. We're fighting for survival as a species. You people are always complaining about living in the ruins of a broken planet. Well, we don't even have ruins. We're out in space without a lifeboat. Every crèche run, every piece of genetic design, every terraforming mission—and yes, even culling and renormalization—is dictated by the cold equations of survival and extinction. And one moment of carelessness or selfishness could be all it takes to tip the balance toward extinction. You can make a face if you want to, but that's the reality. And, frankly, what does humanity have to put against it? Chaos. Bickering, rutting, selfish, maladaptive cha—"

"Whoa, Arkady!" Osnat interrupted. At first he thought she was angry, but then he realized she was trying not to laugh. "I think we're going to have to agree to disagree on this."

"Come on, Arkady. I got clearance to take you for a little walk. Told Moshe you were going to die of vitamin D deficiency if he didn't let you out in the sun sooner or later."

Arkady, spliced for survival in space, was perfectly capable of synthesizing his own vitamin D; but he thought about Osnat's peculiarly human prudishness about genetic engineering and decided that an unnecessary walk would probably hurt him less than another argument with the only sentient being currently on speaking terms with him.

Osnat's "little walk" turned out to be a bit more than he'd bargained for.

Arkady had always enjoyed being planetside until then—a notable, though highly adaptive, deviation from the stationer's agoraphobia that was becoming increasingly widespread among the younger cohorts of most Syndicates' crèches. But the deep, dense undergrowth of the temperate zones of Gilead and Novalis had done nothing to prepare him for the environment into which Osnat introduced him.

He was amazed by the cold, first of all. He'd known, of course, about the ice age; but somehow he'd still imagined that a desert would be hot. He certainly hadn't expected the dusting of snow that chilled his feet and clotted in the treads of his boot soles.

Nor had he expected the inhabitedness of the landscape. Nothing on Earth was pristine, it turned out; what he took for granted on Gilead or any of the other new and still-empty planets he'd worked on was long gone even in this desolate place. At every dip and turn of the land they would stumble on some artifact of the desert's former population. Junked cars. Rusting water tanks. Coils of barbed wire still draped between the leftover bones of old fences. An entire apartment complex, built of rebar-reinforced concrete and sheathed in now-peeling white stucco, abandoned so abruptly that there were still faded shreds of laundry hanging from the windows like flags put out to celebrate a victory that had never, in the end, come to pass.

"Is this Israeli or Palestinian?" Arkady asked.

"Could be either. They've changed the lines so often that settlements are always getting stranded on the wrong side."

"And no one moves in after the settlers leave?"

Osnat shrugged. "Israelis don't want to live in Arab houses. Palestinians don't want to live in Jewish houses. And anyway, it's cheaper to build new."

"It always comes back to money with humans, doesn't it?"

Osnat laughed bitterly. "If only it did! Money's nice and clean and simple compared to most of what goes on down here."

They saw only one sign among the wreckage of present human occupation: a vast dusty herd of sheep swirling in the bottom of a wadi like a spring flood. To Arkady, station-raised, the sight was inconceivable. How much biomass did these creatures consume? What kind of organic load did they place on the ecosystem that supported them? What king's ransom of water did they consume every day? How many accumulated tons of grass, insects, and annelids were necessary to allow for the extravagance of a single sheep? And for what? A scrap of wool? A bit of meat that could be produced more quickly and cheaply in the most primitive viral manufacturing tanks? It was enough to make him long for the elegant economy of a worm.

Long after he'd stopped wondering if there was any purpose to the forced march Osnat was leading him on, they topped a steep mesa and looked out over a flat valley that contained what appeared, at first glance, to be a remote desert town. It was empty, however. And as they dropped off the ridge and moved down the single silent street, Arkady began to understand that it had never really been a town at all. The buildings were all made of whitewashed cement block, and their walls were massively scarred with bullet holes. But there were no shards of broken glass anywhere—because none of the buildings had ever had windows. And the yellow dust of the desert and the *khamsin* had drifted through the open doors and windows to pile up in the corners of dark, warrenlike rooms that had clearly never been finished for human habitation.

The place was like the rough draft of a town. An idea of a town, in which a very real battle—or perhaps many of them—had been fought.

"What is this place?" he asked, shivering.

"Hell town."

"What was it for?"

"You don't want to know."

"Osnat?"

"What?"

"Could we . . . can we talk about what we talked about the other day? You know, about that friend of mine I was telling you about?"

"And why the hell should I do that?" she asked.

"I just thought—"

"You just thought nothing," she snapped. "If you've got something to say, you can say it to Moshe. I'm not in the business of doling out charity or letting people cry on my shoulder."

She pulled off her jacket, moving with rough irritable gestures, as if annoyance had pushed her body temperature above acceptable limits. And then she did something that set Arkady's pulse racing with hope and terror. With her right hand, partially shielded by the camouflage swirl of her coat, she pointed skyward.

It was a momentary gesture, gone so quickly that if Arkady's eyes hadn't been sharpened by the fear and tension of the past weeks, he would have missed it entirely. But its meaning was unmistakable: they were being watched.

A shadow, no more than the shadow of a passing sparrow, flitted across the rocky ground. High in the sky something flashed silver in the morning sunlight. A surveillance drone. Had it been there on their prior walks? Yes, he realized; he'd noticed it but assumed it was just a passing shuttle or a satellite in low orbit. Who could possibly pay attention to all the scrap metal humans had chucked into orbit around their planet?

He dissembled, scrambling to pick up the conversation where it had faltered. "I'm sorry. I didn't . . . I didn't mean to imply that I was asking you for something. I just . . . wanted to thank you for what you've done so far."

"I haven't done anything."

"But you have. The books. The walks. I . . . I appreciate it. You're a gracious person."

The sunburned forehead wrinkled in bemusement, and she cocked her head again to get a better look at him. "Well! That's sure as fuck the first time I've ever been called gracious!"

Carefully, trying not to be too obvious about it, Arkady looked in the direction he thought she'd been pointing.

A house—or rather, a nonhouse—just like the others along the street. He went into it. Osnat followed him.

Inside, in the dark, she prowled around him like a cat. She was in a hurry, he realized. And she was trembling with nerves or fear—a thing that scared him as much as anything in the past weeks had scared him.

"Did you mean what you said the other day about being willing to stick your neck out to save this friend of yours?"

"Yes." Arkady had to crane his neck to keep track of her.

She prowled back toward the door, and reached a hand up to twitch away the curtain. "Are you sure? You'd better be sure. Because I'm about to throw out a lifeline. And if I throw it to the wrong person, we're both going to get our teeth kicked in."

Why did Arkady suddenly have the uncomfortable feeling that he'd just, for the first time in his life, heard the phrase "get our teeth kicked in" used as a euphemism?

"What—who are you going to go to?"

"I don't know. And I don't want to know. I'm just going to send up a flare and whoever shows up shows up. But you'd better be damned sure, Arkady. You can't put the bullet back in the gun once you've pulled the trigger."

"I'm sure."

"And you'd better be able to keep your mouth shut until I tell you not to. I know you can do it. I watched you do it at GolaniTech. You willing to do it for me if I help you?"

"I'm willing to try."

"Okay. Good enough." The whisper of cloth on stone. Scuff of her boots in the dust. "You ever heard of the Mossad, Arkady?"

"Of course."

"Moshe and I used to work for them."

"But I thought—"

"They recruit out of the IDF. First pick of the litter, so to speak. We were both Sayeret Golani. Commandos. What you'd call tacticals. Didi Halevy tapped us after officers' school.

"We went through training together. There were a hundred and thirty in our incoming class." Pride sharpened her normally husky voice. "A hundred and thirty chosen out of over two thousand. And Didi Halevy told us"— her voice shifted into a schoolmasterish tone that Arkady assumed must be an imitation of Halevy's voice—"We have no quotas. We take only those who we think can do the job. And if the best of you can't do the job, then we won't take any of you." She looked at Arkady, dropping back into her own, rougher voice. "They took three out of our class, and even after that we had two years of training, living in one room, eating reheated garbage, only getting to visit our families twice a year. Me, Moshe . . . and a boy named Gur who you never met and never will because Gavi Shehadeh got him killed."

"Is that why you're so loyal to Moshe?"

"You think it's a bad reason?" She coughed, took a step toward the door, turned around again, cleared her throat. "Anyway. I went back to my home unit after Tel Aviv. And then when it was time to re-up, I signed on with GolaniTech instead. Which hasn't exactly been . . . well, never mind what it has or hasn't been. I chose it, and I'm not going to whine about it. The point is, someone I know from King Saul Boulevard came to me a few months ago and asked me to keep my eyes open and, uh . . . let him know if I saw anything fishy going on at GolaniTech. I thought it was crazy. Reamed the guy out, actually. Told him Moshe wouldn't be messed up in anything like that and he'd better tell the eighth floor to mind their own fucking business and clean up their own house." She licked her lips. "Then you showed up."

chris moriarty

274

"Why are you telling me this, Osnat?"

"Remember what you told me about wanting to help your friend? I'm putting it to the test. Basically I'm handing you a loaded gun. If you want to pull the trigger on it, I'm dead. If you don't pull the trigger . . . then I'll do my best to help you. And your friend."

"What changed your mind?" Arkady asked. "Was it something I said to Turner?"

Osnat turned back to face him, a stark silhouette against the backdrop of silver clouds, dust-gray desert. "You know damn well what it was."

He shook his head no.

"Bella. Bella and her so-called sickness. That's not a genetic weapon, Arkady. That's Armageddon. And if Moshe were really working in Israel's best interests, he would have sent you back to Korchow in a body bag the second he figured out what you were selling."

NOVALIS

Six Species of Chaos

Viruses populate the world between the living and the non-living.
They are themselves not capable of reproduction, but if put into
the right environment they can manipulate a cell to generate
numerous copies of themselves. "Reproduce me!" is the essence
of the virus, the message that the viral genome carries into
the headquarters of a cell . . . "Wee animalcule," was Antony
van Leeuwenhoek's expression for the living creatures which
populated the world under his brilliant microscope . . . But
lens grinding was an art in those days, and few people had
microscopes as good as Leeuwenhoek's. Carolus Linnaeus
knew only six species of microbes, which he classified in
1767 under the appropriate name "Chaos."

—MARTIN A. NOWAK AND ROBERT M. MAY (2000)

OUTSIDE!" AURELIA PANTED. "NOW! *HURRY!*"

Arkady and Arkasha stared, bewildered. But by the time Arkady thought to ask what was happening she was already several doors down, repeating the message. And already someone else was pounding on the hab module's metal walls, hammering out the panicked signal that means only two things to a spacer: decompression or fire.

Arkady left the lab at a dead run with Arkasha close behind him. The last thing he remembered hearing as he left was the brittle crack of Arkasha's dropped pencil shattering on the floor.

Aurelia dashed through the airlock ahead of them without pausing to let it cycle. So much for the last shreds of the theoretical quarantine.

The rest of the team was clustered on the open slope below the hab module, staring skyward, hands shielding their eyes or held over mouths dropped open in slack-jawed amazement.

"There," Aurelia urged. *"Look!"*

It took Arkady a long, stunned moment to understand what he was looking at. Then he realized that the trailing mare's tail of high cumulus streaming across the sky from horizon to horizon was no cloud at all.

It was a contrail.

"That's not—" Arkasha began.

"No," Laid-back Ahmed said. "It's not ours. The sound's all wrong. It must be one of the new drives UNSec hasn't cleared for civilian use."

"Shouldn't we have seen them coming in-system?"

"Yes." There was an edge to Ahmed's voice that Arkady had never heard there before.

"Unless they were hiding behind the planet," By-the-Book Ahmed pointed out ominously.

"But wouldn't they have to know where we were to do that?" Aurelia asked.

"Yes. And where all our mapping satellites are as well."

"Then . . ."

Aurelia's voice trailed off into the general silence just as Arkady came to the realization that however frightening it had been to be alone on Novalis with help four months away, it was many times more frightening to be sharing the planet with a contingent of Peacekeepers.

Arkady remembered the next ten days of the mission as one long continuous slow-motion avalanche of panic.

Bella's sickness spread through the crew with the ponderous inevitability of an avalanche gathering breadth and power as it flows down a mountainside. First the Ahmeds fell sick. Then both Banerjees and both the Aurelias went down in a single miserable day. Aurelia was unable, even after the most frantic efforts, to isolate the pathogen responsible for the sickness. And meanwhile, a new fight was splintering the crew into ever more violently opposed factions: the fight over whether the undiagnosable sickness and the inexplicable contrail were caused by a single common enemy.

"Come for a walk with me?" Aurelia the surgeon asked Arkady sometime in the middle of the panic.

"Are you up to a walk?" he asked doubtfully. She'd just dragged herself out of bed and back to work that morning.

"Not really. But I want the privacy."

She was silent all the way to the airlock, and while they cycled through it, and for a good minute after they got outside. Even ravaged by fever, she struck out across the clearing with her usual assertive stride. Just under the shadow of the first rank of trees, she veered sideways and began making a slow circuit of the pasture.

"I'm worried," she said at last. "And I want to talk to you first because I don't want to turn this into a fight between Ahmed and Arkasha. It's too important."

"What's too important?"

"Ahmed has been after me to tell him that this sickness is some kind of bioweapon. He wants to thaw out the tacticals."

"Oh God."

"That's about what I said when he sprang it on me."

"Well," Arkady said, beginning to think through the implications of Ahmed's idea. "*Is it?*"

Aurelia opened her mouth, then closed it without answering. "Arkasha doesn't think so. As far as I can make out, he thinks we've just walked into the terraforming cross fire. God knows it wouldn't be the first time. First survey mission I crewed on was cleanup for a team that lost all but two members to some kind of hypermutating fungus before they could even figure out what hit them. And Arkasha is the one looking at the viral payload. I'm just trying to sort out the vector of infection. Which, if you ask me, amounts to MotaiSyndicate running an outrageously unethical immunological experiment on the rest of us poor slobs." She kicked at the grass in frustration. "God, I wish this was a Rostov mission!"

They walked along in silence, Arkady matching Aurelia's long-legged stride without thought or effort. She had a point, he reflected. "You still haven't said what you think about Ahmed's bioweapon idea."

"It's possible, of course. Anything's possible." She plucked one of the many-petaled blue flowers that had carpeted the pasture during the recent weeks of sun and began tearing the petals off it in an absent-mindedly savage game of she-loves-me-not.

"Then you think it evolved here naturally?"

"No. And no, I can't tell you why." She looked down at the flower's dismembered corpse, frowning as if she'd only just realized the havoc her fingers were wreaking. "It just . . . it just feels wrong."

"How?"

"I don't know." She turned to face him, looking young and scared and nothing like her usual confident self. Behind her the long pasture ran away toward the hidden river, and the silver grass rippled like the fur of some sleeping beast. "It's like . . . it's like a real frog in an imaginary garden."

And no matter what he did, Arkady couldn't get her to say what she meant by those words . . . or even whether she knew that there was no such thing as a real frog anymore.

Arkasha went down with the virus the next day, and by nightfall he was running a dangerously high fever. The sickness was quirky that way; one person's symptoms might be merely annoying, while the next person might run a fever that had Aurelia talking darkly about the low survival rates for prophylactic cryo. Arkady and Arkasha were a case in point. Arkady's brush with the disease had been so mild that he still wasn't sure if he had escaped it altogether or simply failed to notice it amid the general exhaustion and panic. But Arkasha went down hard.

Arkady nursed his pairmate through seventy-two hours of violent chills and fevers, scrupulously following all Aurelia's instructions. On the evening of the third day he came back from his first hot meal in days to find Arkasha's bed empty.

He finally tracked his sib down in the first place he should have looked for him: the lab. Arkasha was still haggard with exhaustion and dehydration. But he was clean and shaved and neatly dressed . . . and doggedly determined to get back to work.

"Are you sure you're strong enough to be out of bed already?" Arkady asked worriedly.

"No. But I needed to check on something. I had an idea while I was sick. Something about this virus was ringing a bell somewhere, and I finally remembered what it was. Ever heard of Turing Soup?"

Arkady blinked in surprise. "As in Alan Turing?"

"Yep. I think that's what we've caught. I can't explain how it got here or who spliced it but at least I think I know what they were trying to accomplish."

"Aurelia said you weren't sure it *was* designed."

"I wasn't when I talked to her." He cocked a sharp eye at Arkady. "Why was she talking to you about that? Did she ask you to stop me from insulting Captain Bligh's breadfruit?"

Arkady laughed in spite of himself. "Is that his new nickname?"

"Well, it's what I call him. I can't repeat what Aurelia calls him within range of your delicate ears."

"Don't be mad at her for talking to me. She likes you. She just doesn't want to watch you make trouble for yourself."

"I know. And I appreciate it. And I'm sorry about what I said after the last consult. I overreacted. It just . . . brought back bad memories."

Arkasha rubbed a hand across his forehead and sat down a bit limply. He still looked feverish to Arkady, and not just with the fever of excitement.

"So anyway. The virus. This is still just in the region of wild surmise. But I think it's an evolutionary search algorithm. Fontana, the human who thought up the Turing Soup idea, spent his whole life working on the relationship between genetic robustness and evolvability. In other words, if species need to change rapidly to respond to changes in their environment, then why are most evolutionarily successful organisms so genetically resistant to change? What's the adaptive value of all the epistatic effects and redundancy that UN-based commercial splicers are always deleting from their genomes and we're always trying to preserve? Fontana's big idea was something he called *neutral* networks. I remember neutral networks from first-year genetic engineering. It's central to understanding how genotype space maps onto phenotype space: how DNA turns the biological equivalent of a computer program into an actual living organism. It's also why designers always run into those 'you can't get there from here' design problems. You know: the changes that look like minor tweaks but turn out to involve so many splices that all have so many unintended side effects that you can't make the 'tweak' without stripping the whole geneset down to its bolts and starting over again."

Arkady nodded. This was a familiar problem for Syndicate design teams, and a major reason for the slow, cautious, incremental changes within genelines. The pre-Breakaway corporate genetic engineers had been far bolder; but they'd assumed cull rates for their company-owned constructs that even MotaiSyndicate would have found ethically indefensible.

"So that's one of the first lessons in genetic engineering: Just because two organisms 'look' the same doesn't mean their genesets look the same. It just means that their DNA inhabits the same neutral network. And one of the basic truisms of evolutionary genetics is that the most successful species usually have the largest neutral networks. Fontana theorized that this was because neutral networks were nature's way of minimizing the chances of a you-can't-get-there-from-here problem. He explained how neutral networks do that by talking about maps of old Europe on Earth. Which makes sense, I guess, since neutral networks are all about the importance of boundaries and territory. Imagine you're walking around some country. France, let's say.

But you want to get to Germany. Well, if you're walking around somewhere in the middle of France, it's going to take a lot of steps to get to Germany . . . steps that, in the mutational context, are all fraught with an overwhelming risk of producing nonviable phenotypes. But if you happen to be exactly on the border between the two countries, all you need to do is take one easy step and presto, you're in Germany. And the bigger your country is, the longer your borders are, and the more places you *can* get to in just one step. Fontana called those border crossings—single mutations that shift an organism into a new phenotype—gateway mutations. The bigger the neutral network, the more gateway mutations. The more gateway mutations, the less risk of a you-can't-get-there-from-here problem . . . known in the real world as an extinction event."

"So how does Turing Soup fit into that?" Arkady asked.

"Well, I'm running into the limits of my understanding of Algorithmic Chemistry here, but Fontana envisioned neutral networks as search spaces and mutation as a search algorithm just like the search algorithms you'd use to find information in a database. The bigger the database, the more data there is to mine, and the more data you can get. That's the expanding neutral networks side of the equation. But there's another limiting factor as well: How good is your algorithm at *searching* the database? The better the search algorithm, the faster it sifts the kernels of relevant data from the chaff. So Fontana looked at mutations accumulating inside neutral networks as a mechanism through which organisms 'search' the entire space of the current phenotype for possible improvements or responses to environmental alterations. Now I get a little bit itchy at the idea that organisms 'search' their genotype in any meaningful way. I just don't think evolution works that way. But on the other hand, genetic engineers spend a lot of time improving their neutral network search algorithms. And if you could engineer organisms to search their neutral networks more efficiently, you could turn walking ghosts into viable populations . . . which is exactly what I think someone's done on Novalis."

Arkady sank onto his own stool, floored by the magnitude of what Arkasha was describing. "I'm not even going to touch the developmental biology problems with that idea—"

"I know, I know."

"—but how would you even begin to prove someone had done it on Novalis?"

"I can't. Not in any time frame that's going to make a difference to this mission. But I can say that Bella's virus looks a hell of a lot more like a terraforming tool than a bioweapon."

Arkady bit his lip.

"What?"

"Well . . . I was just thinking about that old saying about a weed being a perfectly good plant in the wrong place. Isn't a bioweapon just a perfectly good terraforming tool in the wrong place?"

"So you are saying you agree with Ahmed."

"No! I'm just pointing out that you'd better have an answer to that question, because there's no way he won't ask it."

"I'll have an answer," Arkasha said. "One way or another I'll have an answer."

"Well, don't push yourself too hard . . . okay?"

"I promise I'll be sensible. And thanks for . . . well, taking care of me."

"Anyone would have done the same."

"That's the kind of thing you always say. It doesn't make it true."

Arkasha's eyes glittered. He really did look feverish, Arkady told himself for the second time in as many minutes.

He pressed his lips to Arkasha's forehead in a kiss so sweet and chaste that they might have been two brother monks on one of the Russian icons their geneline's features were said to be modeled on.

Of course he hadn't meant it to be a kiss at all; he'd been checking Arkasha's temperature, just as he'd done countless times over the course of the sickness. But somehow it hadn't ended up that way.

He stood there, one hand still on Arkasha's shoulder, feeling like an army that had outrun its supply lines. Arkasha was utterly still under his hand, his eyes wide and dark, his face oddly expressionless. But Arkady could feel the heat of his skin through the thin shirt, and the bones of his shoulder beneath their too-thin veil of muscle and tendon.

"I just—" Arkady began. And then he stopped, because Arkasha had begun to speak in the same instant.

"What?" they both said—and then laughed nervously.

Arkasha raised a hand, then let it fall without completing the gesture. "I should get back to work," he said.

"Why?" Arkady asked. He slid his hand up to the nape of Arkasha's neck, certain that Arkasha would shy away from the touch but unable to stop himself. "Why won't you just let yourself be happy?"

Arkasha blinked like a man stepping out of a shuttered room into bright sunlight. "I've made a lot of trouble for myself," he whispered. "You wouldn't be doing yourself any favors."

"I don't care."

"You should care," Arkasha said. But he let himself be drawn closer.

"I don't care," Arkady repeated.

Then, still half-convinced he would be pushed away, he took Arkasha in his arms and kissed him again . . . this time not at all chastely.

"I love your cowlicks," Arkasha said. "I'm endlessly, abjectly grateful to whatever poor slob is responsible for them. If he hadn't fallen asleep on the job, you might be a completely different person. You might never have fallen in love with your silly little ants. And I might never have met you, let alone fallen in love with you."

They were in their cabin, sprawled across the lower bunk, drinking more of the Aurelias' vile vodka, stealing a few moments away from the insanity that was rapidly consuming the rest of the crew.

"Has Aurelia showed you any results on those assays yet?"

"Don't change the subject on me. I've never seen hair that out of control. No wonder you're obsessed with the adaptive value of dissent!"

Arkady brushed ineffectually at the offending locks. "They're ugly."

"They're extraordinary."

"They're a deviation."

"They're an oversight. Some poor designer was too busy thinking about next week's production quotas, or his digestive troubles, or his un-requited love for whatever norm-conforming certifiably A-equivalent piece of tail he happened to be chasing at the moment. His mind strayed"—Arkasha's free hand slid down Arkady's chest and across his belly—"unforgivably from the all-important work at hand. An error crept into the D1746 gene at site forty-two of chromosome eighteen. That's the frizzy D site to you and the rest of the hoi polloi. Our poor de-signer failed to notice the error. It began to replicate. The control team, perhaps similarly distracted by work, lust, or digestion, also failed to no-tice the error. Which continued to replicate. Which resulted in your spectacular cowlicks. Which resulted in my falling in love with you. Which is about to result in . . . here, hold this."

"You're drunk." Arkady took the beaker Arkasha handed him and realized belatedly that there was nowhere on the narrow bunk to put it down—and that that was exactly what Arkasha had intended.

"True, too true," Arkasha admitted, busy with the drawstring of Arkady's pants. "I'm also a shirker, and a malingerer, and an unregenerate deviant. None of which detracts from the blinding moral import of the revelation I'm about to bestow upon you."

"Which is?"

"That I love you—have I mentioned, by the way, that you entirely fail to appreciate my brilliance and originality?—that *I* love *you* because of their mistake."

Arkady made a rude noise. "At least my cowlick is outside my skull, not inside it."

"Yep," Arkasha announced at about the same moment as he finally succeeded in making Arkady spill his drink all over the floor. "That's me. A Cowlick on the Brain of a Perfect Society."

The arena was perhaps a meter across. At the moment its perfectly white and featureless surface contained perhaps five hundred army ants, racing around in a swirling, slightly irregular circle that resembled nothing so much as a satellite's eye view of a hurricane. It also resembled, to Arkady's naturalist's eye, a dozen or so other examples of self-organized criticality in action: the delicate spiral structures that so many leafy plants evolved to maximize sun exposure and minimize self-shading; the intricate whorls in the pelts of fur-bearing mammals, of which the single whorl on the crown of each human and posthuman head was a vestigial remnant; the complex interlocking networks formed by communities of people, ants, or songbirds.

But there was one difference of course: all those other patterns were adaptive, whereas the milling, panicked circle of ants was suicidally dysfunctional.

"Under unique circumstances in nature (and rather ordinary ones in the laboratory), army ants can be induced to form a tight circular column, a myrmecological merry-go-round, in which they 'march themselves to death.' " Gotwald, of course, quoting Piels and Schnierla.

And the great Schnierla had established that the diameter of the circular column represented "the sum of the vector of the individual ant's centrifugal impulse to resume the march and the centripetal force of trophallaxis which binds it to its group" . . . an equation that never failed to cross Arkady's mind when he saw large groups of people all making the same stupid mistake at the same moment.

Trophallaxis—the following instinct—was so strong that if you dropped ants from two different swarms into the arena together, they would actually follow each other perfectly peacefully for ten or twenty minutes before they came to their senses and locked mandibles in a last mortal battle.

"You'd think that sometime, somewhere, some of them would just snap out of it and turn the other way," Arkasha said beside him.

"You have to remember that the following instinct is perfectly adaptive in the environment it evolved in." As usual Arkady felt an obscure need to defend his ants. "If these ants were on the forest floor instead of in the lab, they would circle around until they found their swarm's scent and just follow it back to the main column. Or even if the scent trail was gone, washed away in a flood for example, they'd run into sticks and stones and leaves and be deflected little by little until they eventually worked their way back to the rest of the swarm. It's just here, where there's no external noise to counterbalance the circling instinct, that it becomes maladaptive. The ants and their environment are an integrated system, just like the brain and its environment. Change the environment and you're left with half a system. You might as well rip half the wires out of a computer, then blame it for not working."

"It's really kind of awful when you put it that way," Arkasha said. "Actually . . . why are you *doing* this to the poor ants?"

"I'm not going to follow through with it," Arkady confessed. "I just wanted to see a circular mill in action. I'm going to aspirate them back into their nest before they get too tired. To tell you the truth, I never could do any really nasty experiments on ants. I can't stand the sight of their little faces when they're frightened."

"Their little *faces*?" Arkasha sounded amused. "Do ants even have faces?"

"Sure. Well, mandibles. And they have this panic-stricken way of antennating that's just heartbreakin—"

Ranjipur poked his head into the lab, looking thoroughly panic-stricken himself despite his lamentable absence of antennae. "Have you two seen Aurelia?" he asked. "Oh. Arkasha. Thank God. We need you. Bella's had some kind of relapse."

Bella was in the bathroom slumped over the toilet when they reached her. Her dark hair was plastered against her skull, and Arkady could see the pale skin of her scalp showing between the damp locks.

"How long has this been going on?" Arkasha asked.

It turned out that it had been going on for a week, and that Bella had somehow managed to hide it from everyone. Shocking. But not as shocking as the look on Aurelia's face when she finally arrived and got a handle on the situation.

"Come down to the lab and help me run this?" she asked Arkasha after she'd pulled blood from the Motai B.

Arkady tagged along, following Aurelia's glance at him rather than an explicit invitation.

"What the hell is going on down here?" Arkasha said as soon as the door closed behind them.

Aurelia still had that stunned, bloodless look on her face. "I don't know. I have no data, no physiological baselines, no standard procedures to follow. I mean, for the ship *cat,* sure. But this . . ."

Arkasha flopped weakly onto the stool next to Arkady. He and Aurelia seemed to have reached some basic unspoken agreement about the nature of Bella's changeling sickness that eluded Arkady.

"Is Bella in danger?" he asked hesitantly. "Can you cure her?"

"She's in a lot of danger," Aurelia said shortly. "And I can't *cure* her because there's nothing to cure. She's not sick, Arkady. She's pregnant."

A UNIVERSAL GRAMMAR OF COMBAT

Military conflicts, particularly land combat, possess the key characteristics of complex adaptive systems (CASs): combat forces are composed of a large number of nonlinearly interacting parts . . . local action, which often appears disordered, induces long-range order (i.e., combat is self-organized); military conflicts, by their nature, proceed far from equilibrium; military forces, in order to survive, must continually adapt to a changing combat environment; there is no master "voice" that dictates the actions of each and every combatant . . .
Finally, what lies at the heart of an artificial-life approach to simulating combat, is the hope of discovering . . . whether there exists—and, if so, what the properties are, of— a *universal grammar of combat*.

—ANDREW ILACHINSKI (2001)

THE MACHINE WOULDN'T TELL THEM where it was taking them. It met them alone, without the terrifying woman who Arkady still instinctively thought of not as Catherine Li, but as the Butcher of Gilead. But Arkady's relief at Li's absence faded as Cohen led them out of the prosperous modern section of Jerusalem and into the bombed-out tangle of empty streets that tumbled down toward the thickness of the Line.

Osnat followed the AI with a docility that Arkady found more frightening than her usual stubbornness. Her eyes flickered restlessly over the passing house fronts and alleyways, but she gave no other sign of being aware of possible danger. Arkady would have liked to believe that it was because she knew they were protected, but he suspected it was because she'd decided that any dangers out there couldn't be dealt with and would have to be accepted.

Finally, they turned into an empty street whose houses—not all of them empty by any means—bore the blaring orange biohazard signs that Arkady had come to recognize as the emblem of the poisoned border between Israel and Palestine.

"Are you sure this is a good idea?" Arkady whispered to Osnat.

"Too late for that, boychik."

Something clanked softly, metal on metal, in the shadowy interior of one of the abandoned houses they'd just passed. "Don't move," said a woman's voice from the shadows. "You're perfect just where you are."

"Son of a bitch," Osnat muttered.

The machine shrugged apologetically. "It wasn't my idea."

More noises came from inside the house, and from two of the houses on the other side of the empty street. Osnat stood stock-still, her hands held stiffly out away from her body, in plain sight, with the palms showing and the fingers open. On reflection, Arkady decided that it might be a good idea to do the same.

The voice that had spoken out of the shadows had almost certainly been Catherine Li's, but none of the half dozen hard young bodies that emerged from the surrounding houses was hers.

They were soldiers, but there was something disorientingly drab and ragtag-looking about them, even by Israeli standards. Their uniforms looked at first glance as if they'd been torn and roughly patched. It took a few puzzled minutes for Arkady to work out that the "patches" were tape, and the tape was strategically located to cover all unit insignia.

"Hey, guys," one of the secret soldiers said when he caught sight of Osnat. "It's Hoffman! We bagged ourselves a tiger. Here, kitty kitty kitty!"

"Oh grow up," Osnat snarled.

A second soldier came over to frisk Arkady. As the boy's hands slid under his arms and along his rib cage, Arkady saw a flash of silver on the breast pocket of his uniform. He looked more closely and saw a small pin depicting a viciously curved saber blossoming from a pair of spread eagle's wings.

"You forgot to tape over your pin thingy," he said.

"What are you, IDF quality control? I ran out of fucking tape."

"It doesn't matter anyway. I don't even know what it means." Not quite true; the paratroopers' wings told Arkady he was dealing with commandos from one of Israel's legendary Sayerets, or special units. But which unit this was he couldn't have begun to say.

"It means I Love Mom," the soldier quipped. "Now turn around and spread your legs, schlemiel."

Arkady turned around obediently—and finally caught sight of Li.

There was something about her, even standing in the street doing nothing, that made the Israelis look like toy soldiers. She was dressed much as Osnat usually dressed: in nondescript standard-issue desert-drab gear that looked like it could have come out of any of the army

surplus shops Arkady had passed while running Korchow's little errands the other week. But somehow the mismatched odds and ends
hung on her short stocky frame in a configuration that looked anything but haphazard.

Her short hair was pushed back under a pair of sniper's goggles that
must cover her entire face when she pulled them down. The elastic
band that held the goggles to her head had once had white lettering on
it, perhaps a manufacturer's logo; it had been scribbled over with a
laundry pen so that it was just a dull purple-brown overlay on the black
elastic. Her trousers were stained and bagged out at the knees and a
knee pad floated around one ankle. Her already-stocky body was encased in a ceramic vest. In addition to the handgun still strapped to her
thigh where he'd seen it during that first meeting at the airport, she'd
made two new additions to her armory: a long, black, viciously sleek
sniper's rifle and a brutal-looking sawed-off assault weapon with a
flashlight duct-taped beneath its trigger guard.

Another person—most other people—would have looked ridiculous
in this getup. Li didn't. And when Arkady asked himself why, he
couldn't come up with a clear answer. Was it the well-worn, hard-used
quality of the clothes and weapons? Was it the sense that every strap
and buckle and piece of tape had been adjusted with cool precision by
hands that had done the job of killing often enough to make it a matter of craft, rather than reflection? Or was it the bulldog set of her jaw
and the glint of defiant enjoyment in her dark eyes?

"He's clean," the soldier told Li over Arkady's shoulder as he finished searching him.

"Take him inside then."

Arkady looked around for Cohen, but the AI was gone. He had a
vague idea that he'd seen him fade back into one of the neighboring
houses just after the troops had arrived on the scene. And he must have
taken Osnat with him because she was nowhere to be seen either.

"Where did Cohen and Osnat go?" he asked Li. It was the first time
he'd ever worked up the courage to speak directly to the woman.

She looked at him as if she'd just become aware of his existence and
wasn't particularly pleased by the discovery. "Cohen had to go take
care of some things."

Arkady jerked his head toward the empty houses and the no-man's-
land that he knew must lie just beyond them. "Is he . . . are we going
out there?"

"Probably."

"Are we going to be out there after dark?" Arkady asked, looking at her flashlight-equipped weapon.

She gave him a lazy smile. "You better hope not."

Inside the building that seemed to be the unit's impromptu headquarters, Arkady saw a dozen more soldiers, a tangle of wires and equipment, assorted ominous olive drab cases and boxes—and off in a corner together, bent over a monitor, Cohen and Osnat and a young man whose collar tabs said he was a captain.

Osnat had somehow acquired a ceramic-plated vest and helmet and one of the same snubbed-off flashlight-equipped weapons that Li and the others were all carrying.

"What about him?" Li flicked a thumb at Arkady. "You're not going to send him in naked as a shelled oyster, are you?"

An awkward silence fell.

"Oh for God's sake. Don't tell me no one thought of it?"

"Well . . . uh . . . Avi's about his size," said a young woman with a first lieutenant's bar on her collar. "Someone go get Avi."

"Avi! Get the fuck over here!"

"I said go get him, not scream in my ear. God, kids these days!"

A tall slim soldier materialized from somewhere over Arkady's left shoulder. Rough hands pushed him against the wall next to Arkady and squared them up next to each other. A brief argument ensued—no surprise in a country where argument appeared to be the national sport. Nonetheless, it was obvious that the willowy Avi was closer to Arkady's space-born physique than anyone else in the unit.

"Hey, wait a minute," Avi said when he figured out what was in the cards. "Not my vest! Take someone else's vest! This isn't some factory-issue piece of shit. My mother resewed all the inside pockets and—"

"Well," Li pointed out in a deceptively mild voice, "if you're really concerned, you could always come along with us and make sure nothing happens to it."

"—and, uh, I'm sure she'd be overjoyed for Arkady here to have it. Really. Be my guest. My shit is your shit."

The boy emptied the pockets of his vest into a bag someone held out for the purpose, removed various pieces of detachable gear and equipment, unfastened what seemed like an inconveniently large number of buckles and snaps and Velcro strips, and finally pulled the vest over his head and lowered it over Arkady's head in one smooth and almost anticlimactic movement.

The vest dropped onto Arkady's shoulders with a soft thud, giving off a smell that was a combination of its normal owner's masculine, and thankfully relatively clean, odor, and the sharp smells of dirt and machine oil and the *khamsin*. "It's so light," he said wonderingly.

"We'll see if you still think that in five hours."

And indeed, as the straps were fastened and tugged tight around his body he could already feel the ceramic plates digging and chafing around the edges.

When the thing had been strapped tight enough to feel thoroughly uncomfortable, the lieutenant stepped back and gave him a measuring once-over. "Well, that ought to protect everything but your balls," she said in a satisfied tone. "And I hear you guys don't use those anyway, so what do you care? Move around for me, will you?"

Arkady moved. "It's too tight," he complained.

"Too tight is just right. As the general said to the whore."

Arkady had no idea what that meant, but everyone else seemed to think it was hysterically funny.

A noncom snaked through the crowded room with what looked like a roll of lilac purple tape. "Line up, ladies. Color of the day."

"God! Purple again? Who picks these colors, a vengeful homosexual field-training-school washout?"

"Hey it's better than the hot pink. Remember the pink? Took me a month to peel that shit off."

"Hey, guys," drawled the next guy over, "didn't your mother ever tell you not to look a gift Mat'Kal in the mouth?"

"And the real tragedy is that he thinks he's funny!"

As Arkady watched, people began ripping off strips of the brightly colored tape and wrapping it around the grips of their assault rifles or sticking strips of it onto their vests and helmets.

"What's the tape for?" he asked Osnat, who had reappeared beside him in full combat gear.

"Idiot-proofing." She'd ripped a section off the roll when it passed them by and was taping her own weapon and vest. She eyeballed him for a minute, stuck a strip of tape across his vested chest and pressed it briskly into place. "The tactical AIs are programmed not to fire on anyone with the right color tape on."

"But couldn't someone just copy the tape? Or steal it?"

"Not that easy. It's interactive, talks back and forth with the AIs' sensors, and they change the colors every few patrols, mix them up between zones and so forth to try to stay ahead of infiltrators. Anyway, it's not an absolute interdiction. It just kicks the AI into a different decision tree or something. It can still waste you if it wants to. And don't forget that." She gave him her fiercest look. " 'Cause if you get yourself shot out there, I'm going to personally kick your ass!"

"Okay, I'm in," Cohen said, emerging out of the hallucinatory visions of streamspace like a messenger from the afterlife.

"What does he mean?" Arkady whispered, leaning into Osnat to speak in her ear.

They were still in the abandoned house. Through the ragged window frames Arkady could see the house's sagging back porch, the rich green slopes of Mount Herzl, the precise geometric lines of the tombs in the military cemetery, the tall trees of Yad Vashem's Avenue of the Righteous Gentile. Mount Herzl was the heart of the Line, the thickest part of the thickness.

Arkady looked out over the dusty scrubland that separated them from the mountain and thought of the deadly tide of AI-controlled weaponry and human muscle patrolling its paths and riverbeds and crumbling roadways. He remembered the figures of tonnage of land mines buried on the Line per year and shuddered. It was hell. Hell masquerading as an earthly paradise. What sort of beings could evade the patrols and the trip wires long enough to *live* out there?

Down in the valley bottom a patrol—Israeli? Palestinian?—threaded its way along the riverbed, olive drab ghosts in an olive drab landscape. The wind shifted, and the thick cold smell of gun oil drifted up from the valley bottom.

The soldiers fell silent, watching. The patrol snaked down the valley bottom and vanished. A few minutes passed. Someone heaved a sigh. People around Arkady began to talk again, then to get up and move around and go back to the tasks they'd been engaged in before the patrol appeared.

Cohen stood up, stretching stiff muscles, and walked over to look down at Arkady, who was still crouched on the floor where Osnat had left him.

"How can they not see us?" Arkady asked.

"Because they're not really here," the machine explained. "They're under full-immersion shunts, just like my bodies are. Each one is under the control of an Emergent AI operating in a three-dimensional game space that exactly mirrors the real Green Line."

"Why?"

"Suicide." The machine smiled. "And not the romantic kind that Syndicate novelists write about. An Emergent AI's personality architecture is a lot brittler than the human variety. And Emergents don't have the benefit of the human hypothalamic-limbic system to help them rationalize killing in wartime. They have to live with it in cold blood, so to speak. And a lot of them turned out not to want to do that. So now we tell them they're just playing a game in streamspace."

"And the AIs think the Palestinians are doing the same? I mean, they don't know there are actual people on the other side of the gun?"

"Right."

"And what happens if one of the AIs figures it out?"

"Bye-bye, little AI."

"Oh."

"Cheer up. That's what's going to get us through the Line safe and more or less sound. Because the game can't look too realistic, of course. The gamespace in which the Emergents think they're operating is only a simplified model of the real Green Line. And you know the old saying about how there's many a slip 'twixt cup and lip? Well, we're going to engineer a few slips between gamespace and realspace."

The captain eyed Cohen from across the room. "You know what time it is, right?"

"If that's a polite way of telling me to hurry up, then allow me to point out, equally politely, that your equipment stinks."

"Tell it to the Knesset."

"Nothing's stopping you from buying it below the line."

"Are you *kidding* me? What kind of putz buys legal equipment with below-the-line money? What the hell's the point of having a covert ops budget if you waste it on stuff you're allowed to have?"

Cohen snorted and went back to pecking at the keyboard and peering into the blue depths of the monitor.

Meanwhile the captain straightened up from the monitor and turned to face the room at large. "Listen up, everyone. From here on in we're in the thickness of the Line and we're flying below radar as far as

IDF's concerned. You know what that means. We do *not* want to be sending any nice young reservists home to their mothers in body bags today, so be bloody damn careful. But if it comes down to choosing who's going to fill up a body bag, the State of Israel has a hell of a lot more invested in each of you than it does in any eighteen-year-old AI puppet. So act accordingly . . . and you can cry on my shoulder when we're all safe at home again. That's a promise."

The tenor of activity in the abandoned house changed. One by one the soldiers around Arkady fell silent. The frenetic camaraderie gave way to a tense waiting alertness that reeked of approaching danger. "What's happening?" he asked Osnat.

"Shh! They're coming."

It took Arkady another minute to hear what Li's enhanced senses and the IDF monitors had told the others: the muffled clank and rustle of a fully equipped infantry squad on the move.

The soldiers on either side of Arkady were shrinking back against the wall, clutching their weapons to their chests. Osnat pulled him back toward the wall by one sleeve. "Get back, Arkady. Give them room."

They waited. Fabric moved softly against fabric. Someone coughed. Cohen tapped sporadically at the old-fashioned keyboard in front of him, making frustrated faces. The sound of the approaching squad swelled and echoed down the empty street until Arkady began to feel that they must already have passed the open doorway before him—or that time had become stuck in an endlessly repeating loop in which the unseen force was arriving and arriving and never actually here.

"Safeties off," the captain murmured. He looked sick to his stomach.

"NavMesh is initializing," Cohen reported finally. "They're checking the patrol waypoints against the terrain database and updating the blind data. Okay. Now they're getting a modification to their SeekToViaNavMesh."

The machine paused, watching some process unfurl in the virtual, and to Arkady unimaginable, world of streamspace. Then it shook its head in apparent exasperation.

"These people have an idea of surface and barrier architecture that the word *baroque* doesn't even begin to cover! No wonder they patrol the Line on foot. If they sped up to a jog, they'd have to stop every other tick to wait for the next state-of-the-world update!"

The machine fell silent.

"You done yet, Cohen?" That was Li, somewhere across the room and out of sight.

"Yes. No. I think so."

A bootheel scraped in the dust outside. A shadow flitted past the door, too fast for Arkady to have more than a vague sense of color and movement.

"They're here," someone whispered.

And they were.

The Enderbots took the house with a seamless and silent deliberation that was at least as terrifying as the cold competence of Syndicate-bred tacticals. One minute the center of the room was empty. The next an impassively staring trio of infantrymen was flowing smoothly into tactically optimal positions from which they were able to cover the entire room and its approaches. Their weapons were equipped with spintronic range finders: a pale beam that quivered through the dusty air and picked out precise blue circles that wandered over the faces and uniforms of the special forces soldiers. Several of the men around Arkady flinched when the beams touched them, but no one broke ranks.

"God," someone said, "how the hell can they be so young?"

Arkady felt an almost instinctive urge to reach over and shut him up, but it was clear that the voice made no impression on the shunt-driven infantrymen. It was also clear that Cohen had succeeded in hacking NavMesh; the Enderbots, or Enders, as the Israelis called them, disregarded Arkady and the others as if they really had faded into the peeling woodwork of the old building.

"IDF's talking about drafting sixteen-year-olds," another soldier said, answering the first. "Don't you read the papers?"

"I only read the funnies. And when did you become such a condescending asshole, if you don't mind my asking?"

"Will you two clowns shut up for once?"

"Why? They can't hear us. Fucking Armageddon won't wake the Enders up."

Gradually, in orderly squads, the rest of the Enders shuffled in and formed up in the center of the room. Then they stopped, quite abruptly, and just stood there doing nothing.

"What are they waiting for?" Li asked impatiently.

"The SeekTo is air-gapped," Cohen answered, still at the monitor. "Figuratively, not literally. But the patrol still can't breach the line until a human operator checks the waypoints for blue-on-blue problems."

"You're fucking kidding me."

The AI coughed delicately, then continued with the air of a man delivering slightly embarrassing news. "There was a little incident along the India-Pakistan border a while ago. I, uh, jumped the gun. Only slightly. But humans have long memories for that sort of slip up."

"What if there's no human on-line to check EMET's homework for it?"

"This is Earth," Cohen pointed out. "There's always a human around."

No one spoke. The Enders waited for their clearance. Everyone else waited for the Enders.

"Jesus," Li muttered. "Pakistan. Wherever that is. By the way, Cohen, is there anything on this planet you *haven't* run?"

Cohen blinked, thought for a moment, then smiled beatifically. "Garbage collection."

Another minute or two passed, the AI-controlled squad standing passively in the center of the room, the special forces soldiers squatting and sitting and standing along the bullet-scarred walls watching them.

"Okay," Cohen said, "they're cleared for insertion. Just another minute now."

The Enders began to move again, and Arkady watched a surreal scene unfold around him: one squad of soldiers armed to the teeth and ready to go into a war zone, watching a second squad muster, check their weapons, and get ready to go into the same war zone . . . while the second squad walked around and stepped over their unseen shadows as if they were nothing more than dead stones.

One of the shunt-controlled soldiers was a slender blond girl who didn't look a day above seventeen. She crouched down a mere arm's length away from Arkady and began checking her weapon and ammunition clips with smooth precise inhuman movements. She didn't even have to look at the gun to complete the task; her blue eyes stared blankly at the wall just over their shoulders.

"Fuckable?" asked the soldier next to Arkady in a conversational tone.

"Oh yeah," his neighbor breathed in a tone approaching reverence.

"Has anyone ever mentioned what losers you guys are?" Osnat said.

They ignored her.

"Hey, beautiful," the first soldier murmured to the girl. "It's a big bad world out there. What are you doing playing the Green Line lottery? Why don't you just stay here and let me make pretty babies with you?" And then, to Arkady's stunned disbelief, he reached out and brushed the back of his hand down the girl's cheek.

Arkady heard Osnat curse under her breath. He froze, waiting. The girl shook her head slightly, as if a fly had landed on her skin. Then she finished prepping her rifle and moved silently over to join the little clot of soldiers mustering by the back door.

Arkady sighed in relief. "Why are they called Enders?" he asked the soldier who had caressed the girl.

" 'Cause they're cannon fodder." The boy's tone suggested that he was stating the obvious. "Enders. 'Cause they've hit the end of the line. Get it?"

"No," his companion argued. "It's 'cause *they* end *you*. You fuck with them, you're dead, end of story."

"You people," Osnat announced in a tone of profound disgust, "are submoronic illiterates."

Another few minutes and the Enders were mustered and ready to move out. The commandos slipped into their streamspace shadow, and suddenly everyone was moving out, and Arkady was being dragged along behind Osnat into the heart of a no-man's-land that he was starting to realize was anything but empty.

Operations in the thickness of the Line turned out to mostly involve sitting around waiting.

They would move forward, agonizingly slowly, trying to stay within the Enders' data fusion shadow. The Enders would stop—even with his experience of the AzizSyndicate tacticals, Arkady found their abrupt, silent changes of speed and direction unnerving—and everyone else would stop too. Then they would wait. For a few minutes usually. For half an hour or forty minutes. Once for a full hour and a quarter. And then some invisible nonevent would happen in streamspace, and the Enders would move off again, and off they'd all go like rats following the Pied Piper of Hamelin.

At one point they stumbled into the outer penumbra of a Palestinian artillery barrage. The Enders appeared entirely unmoved by the awesome spectacle; they simply coalesced in a nearby shell crater and took cover as if having the earth ripped apart just in front of their feet were no more alarming than spotting a rain cloud on the horizon.

The commandos huddled together in the closest available crater, unfortunately a wet one. They looked only slightly more concerned than the Enderbots, but they kept up a running commentary of flagrantly indecent summations of their current comfort level that had even Li grinning.

"Don't worry." Cohen leaned over to shout in Arkady's ear between two blasts big enough to make the ground ripple under their feet. "The Palestinian Army is a highly professional organization. They have a firm grasp on how to keep the voting public scared and pliable with minimum waste of trained soldiers on both sides. As long as they're actually trying to hit us we're perfectly safe. Of course the fact that they don't actually know we're here may complicate matters somewhat."

Arkady looked nervously toward Osnat, trying to gauge whether this was a joke. "Do the, ah . . . Palestinians fire into the Line often?"

"It goes up and down. At the moment we're in a pretty hot-and-heavy phase."

"And the only thing standing between them and the Israelis is the French Foreign Legion?" Arkady said doubtfully. "Why would anyone take that job?"

"Because they're French," Osnat said.

"Because they're idiots," Cohen said.

"Because they're the Legion," Li said. "Ever heard of Camerone?"

Arkady shook his head.

She leaned forward, warming to her subject, and told him the story in a series of rapid-fire, chewed-off half sentences that sounded like they'd been forged on the battlefield.

It had happened on a planet called Mexico. Or in a country called Mexico. Arkady couldn't tell which from the way Li described it. A battalion of Legionnaires led by the already infamous Colonel Danjou was escorting a supply train when they were attacked by three Mexican battalions. The French retreated to the Hacienda Camerone ("No, Arkady, I don't know how a hacienda is different from a house. It's not mission-critical. Let it slide.") and set up a perimeter around the courtyard of the hacienda under heavy sniper fire. At 9:00 A.M. on the morning of the battle, the Mexican commander offered terms of surrender, which were refused.

Several mixed cavalry and infantry charges were bloodily repelled. But the defenders took deep losses in each of the failed assaults, and Colonel Danjou, fearing for his men's resolve, gathered them in the hacienda's courtyard and made them swear on his wooden hand— memento of past battles—that they would fight through to death or victory.

Danjou fell to a sniper's bullet moments later. His second-in-command died in the afternoon, and by evening the former battalion was being commanded by a second lieutenant named Maudet.

At 6:00 P.M. Maudet and the last four defenders exhausted their ammunition, fixed their bayonets, and charged the Mexican lines. Three of them survived the charge.

The Mexican commander demanded their surrender, and they sent his messenger back across the lines with the message that they would rather die than give up their arms, their flag, or the body of their slain colonel. The messenger relayed the response to the Mexican commander, who then uttered one of the most famous phrases in all of military history: "These are not men. These are devils."

The next day the three survivors were escorted across the lines, their honor and arms intact and their slain commander's body on their shoulders. "They took Colonel Danjou's wooden hand with them," Li finished, holding up her own left hand, palm forward, so that Arkady could see the bruise-blue outline of her Schengen implant and the silver tracery of ceramsteel. "It was escorted to the Legion's mother house in Sidi el Abbès with the highest honors, and ever since then Danjou's hand has been the symbol of the Legion's code: Never surrender."

"It wasn't quite that glorious," Cohen corrected. "But who's quibbling? Danjou's worm-ridden hand remains the shining symbol of the Legion's august tradition of getting into the military equivalent of stupid barroom brawls and laying down your soldiers' lives for no damned decent reason."

"Scoff all you want, Cohen. You know as well as I do that Jerusalem would be in a state of outright all-out civil war if the Peacekeepers were occupying it. The only people worse at Peacekeeping than the Peacekeepers are the fucking Americans."

"Well at least the Americans have the brains to brag about their victories instead of their suicide missions."

"The Legion completed its mission in Camerone," Li protested.

"Thereby allowing the French army to fight on in the name of

Liberty, Equality, and Fraternity in order to prop up a hereditary puppet king and save the Mexican people from the grim prospect of Liberty, Equality, and Fraternity. Excuse me. I'm getting all choked up just thinking about it."

"Ignore the caviar communist commentary," Li told Arkady. "The point is that the Legion held out to the death, then went down fighting."

"The point, Arkady, is that Catherine here has a little thing for pointless suicide missions."

The soldiers all around them were up on their feet now, peering after the Enders in the next shell crater over, gathering their gear and stowing water bottles and nonstandard-issue candy bars.

"If you two are done sniping at each other," Osnat interrupted, "would you mind terribly if we got our shit together and got the fuck out of here before your friends leave us behind?"

After that things got vague.

Arkady remembered passing reel after reel of the indestructible obsolete fiber optics that littered half the Judean desert. He remembered an entire field of school buses, standing snout to tail, their doors flapping open as if they were still waiting to transport a generation of children who had never shown up for school. He remembered passing through a village whose inhabitants gathered in the dark doors of their hovels to watch the Enders jangle by, and whose hostile faces could have been Jewish or Palestinian or anything in between.

They spent most of the night in another flooded-out crater.

"Know much about cannibalism?" Li asked him sometime well after darkness had fallen.

Even she was lying down by then, though she was still smoking another in her endless succession of cigarettes. How she managed to smoke lying down like that and not end up buried in a mountain of cigarette ash was a mystery to Arkady.

"Uh . . . no."

"Some bright bulb did a statistical study of space wrecks. You know, the classic scenario: twenty people stranded in a life pod, food and air for thirty days, going to take ninety for the SOS to ping to the nearest BE relay and back. So who are the eaters, and who are the eatees? No pun intended. Turns out that you can predict who's going to eat and who's going to get eaten pretty reliably. Even when they draw straws, believe it or not. Able-bodied human males come last. They don't generally start eating each other until they've run out of everyone else. Before that they go through the human women and children. And before they start on the lesser humans, they eat the posthumans. And before they eat the posthumans, they eat the constructs."

"That's sick."

"Don't be a cynic, Arkady. It used to be worse. Used to be they'd eat all the blacks and Asians before the first white woman got cooked. Now it's ladies first regardless of incidentals like skin color. That's what we in the UN call progress, Arkady. Anyway, here's the real question: The guy who did the study only assumed one kind of construct. He didn't take the Syndicates into account. So my question, Arkady, is: When the food runs out which one of us do you think these clowns'll eat first?"

Morning found the squad on the banks of the river looking up the long slope of Mount Herzl past the IDF military cemetery.

They had penetrated into the Line's dead heart: a no-man's-land that no army was willing to defend, a place of ghosts where last summer's oranges lay uneaten beneath the trees and the grass around the graves grew waist high. They might have been on Novalis, the world lay so still and quiet around them.

Li and Osnat were hunched over a map-fiche with the Israeli captain. Arkady was sitting with Cohen, who didn't seem to have any more interest in the proceedings than he did. When the women finally came away from the map, Osnat had a sullen look on her face and was fiddling with the trigger guard of her weapon in a way that made Arkady's stomach curl.

"You asked for help," the AI told Osnat.

"Not from a Palestinian traitor!"

"Half-Palestinian," Cohen corrected blandly.

Osnat fingered her weapon again. None of the Israelis seemed to register the movement; but suddenly, and without ever seeming to have moved at all, Li was standing right next to Osnat, her hand on the other woman's trigger hand. The touch looked light, almost casual. But in fact Osnat's fingers were turning white with the pressure of the other woman's grip. Slowly, as if everything were happening under running water, the rifle slipped from Osnat's grasp and slithered down her side until it hit the end of its webbed sling.

"We're fine," Cohen assured the Israeli captain. And, ever so gently, he lifted the rifle away from Osnat's side, removed the ammunition clip, and pocketed it.

Osnat turned to the captain for support, but he was studiously inspecting the slime that had accumulated on his boots during the river crossing.

"You know the road home," Li said in the take-it-or-leave-it tone Arkady was beginning to think expressed some core component of her emotional architecture. "You want to turn around, this'd be the time to do it."

"And Arkady?"

"What do you think?"

There was a lot more walking after that. It was all uphill, and most of it was through the tall grass and tangled weeds of the vast IDF cemetery. Arkady, his mind slack with exhaustion, only noticed that the others had stopped walking when they were face-to-face with the tall iron gates of Yad Vashem.

Li reached out and gave the latch a brisk shake. It held, and when Arkady looked closer he could see why: someone had wrapped a heavy chain through the bars and closed it with a thick-hasped padlock.

Li glanced at Cohen, and again Arkady had that eerie sense that some communication the others couldn't hear was passing between them.

"Well, have you actually talked to him yet?" Li asked aloud.

Cohen seemed to gather himself to argue, but then the shunt's shoulders dropped slightly. "No. But he'll be here. Where else would he be?"

Li snorted. "It's not whether he's here I'm worried about. It's whether he wants to come out and talk to us."

"There's no wall," Osnat pointed out. "We can just go around the gate if we want."

"Bad idea." Li strolled back down the road, pried a loose piece up from the decaying asphalt, and tossed it into the trees to one side of the gate. It arced lazily through the air—and then vanished in a cloud of vapor as it passed some invisible boundary. "I've been wanting to lose weight," she quipped. "But not that much."

"So what do we do?"

"We wait."

"For what?"

"For him to realize that we're not going away until he comes down to talk to us."

It took nearly an hour before a distant and wavering figure appeared at the top of the long tree-lined avenue leading down to the gates. At first Arkady thought he was watching a machine or a monster. The being seemed to have many legs, and it rippled and moved with a sideways motion that he could make no sense of. As the figure descended the hill toward them, the wavering shape resolved itself into two shapes: a man, tall and supple and graceful, with a dog following at his heels. The late-afternoon sun gilded the man's head with fire and flickered around his feet in a way that only made sense when Arkady realized that the man was wearing shorts—and that his right leg below the knee wasn't flesh at all, but a delicate architecture of ceramsteel and silvery neuromuscular thread.

Man and dog continued their unhurried progress down the hill until they finally reached the gate. The man looked out through the bars at them, but he made no move to open the padlock that hung from the iron latch. He was smaller than Arkady had thought he would be; not a big man at all, but built so straight and true that he seemed tall until you stood next to him. The expression on his face was calm, mildly interested, completely noncommittal. The face itself was one of those brown-skinned, strong-nosed, finely hewn faces that were equally common among Palestinians and Sephardic Jews. The man's only really remarkable feature, Arkady decided, were his black eyes. And those were as deep as the dark between the stars.

The dog poked her sharp nose through the gate, growling anxiously. The man laid a calming hand on her. "Can I help you?" he asked.

"It's me," Cohen said. "Cohen. Didn't you get my message?"

"Sorry. I've gotten rather bad about checking my mail lately."

"Well, I'll give you the executive summary: we're here."

"So I see." The bottomless eyes touched on Cohen, then Osnat, then Li and Arkady, then returned to Osnat for a pensive moment. "Hello, Osnat."

Osnat nodded curtly.

"Are you going to let us in?" Cohen asked.

"The thing is . . . I don't exactly have the key at the moment."

"You lost it?"

"I never lose things." A self-deprecating smile lit the thin face and warmed the dark eyes. It occurred to Arkady that people would lay their lives down for this man. "I just put them down. And then I put other things on top of them. I figured that when I remembered what I'd put on top of the key, that would be soon enough to open the gate again. But now here you are standing on my doorstep and accusing me of losing things! I ask you, is there no justice in the world?"

He pulled what looked like a tiny nail file out of his pocket, and bent over the heavy padlock securing the gate. In a matter of seconds the lock fell open and the chains rattled to the ground. The gate opened stiffly, then stuck. They had to slide through the narrow gap one by one, taking care not to get caught on the ornate iron thorns that sprang from the bars.

"I take it the key's been under something for a while?" Cohen asked as he squeezed through.

The man smiled again, and Arkady finally put his finger on what it was that was so entrancing about the expression. It was the smile of a child, open and vulnerable. Or rather it was the smile of an adult who had somehow managed to remain childlike. It made you feel that you were looking at a person who had been wounded by the world but not diminished by it.

The dog, meanwhile, was sniffing at their knees and ankles, whining under her breath, glancing back at her master, putting her body between him and the as-yet-unknown arrivals. He quieted her with a murmured word. She brightened, and her frothy tail began to wave hopefully.

"What a beautiful girl!" Cohen exclaimed, kneeling to bring his face within licking range.

She *was* beautiful. Arkady knew theoretically that she must be no bigger than average size for a dog, but she was so much larger than the tiny, petted, cosseted canines that he'd seen in the Syndicates that he could barely believe they were the same species. And this was no pet either, he suspected. He didn't know what job she'd been bred to do, but not even the most casual observer could miss the honed, streamlined, powerful purposefulness of her.

"What is she?" Cohen asked. He was now thumping energetically at her ribs, whipping her into a delighted frenzy. "She's too big to be pure border collie."

"I don't think the breed has a name. The shepherds in the Line bred them from whatever was left after the die-offs. Tough on sheep, easy on the eye." He cleared his throat and made a formal gesture. "Ah. I've been remiss. Cohen, meet Dibbuk. Dibbuk, meet Cohen."

Cohen laughed and buried his face in the dog's thick fur. Then he stood up, and after the briefest of hesitations, stepped forward and embraced the stranger. They kissed each other elaborately in the Arab manner. Then Cohen took the human's face between his hands and held him out at arm's length in a way that made Arkady realize suddenly that the AI must be very old, and that even the humans he called friends must seem like mere children to him.

"You didn't have to roll in with the cavalry," the human said. "You could have just asked me to meet you at your hotel. Uh . . . right . . . well, I guess I *should* try to check my mail more often."

"Oh Gavi," the machine said, caressing the man with the same open, uncomplicated, unshadowed affection he'd shown to the dog just a few moments ago, "what on earth am I supposed to do with you?"

T HEY FOLLOWED GAVI BETWEEN THE tall trees to a building buried in the hillside like a knife blade. He stopped in front of a plate glass door sized to accommodate busloads of tourists and smiled his sweet, wounded, self-deprecating smile. "We all know what the spider said to the fly and how that ended up," he told them. "But come in anyway."

The vast lobby ran away on all sides into dust and shadows. Gavi struck off across the echoing expanse of marble and dove through a sagging fire door into an ill-lit warren of maintenance corridors and administrative offices.

Arkady felt as if he'd walked into a theater, stepped onto the stage, and slipped through the wings to the cramped back passages and dressing rooms where the actors really lived. This part of the building looked at once abandoned and cluttered. Gavi seemed to be camping in it as much as living in it, and the whiff of kerosene on the air hinted at more than occasional power outages.

At one point they passed an entire room full of dirty laundry. Gavi pulled the door closed, grinned sheepishly, and muttered something about the maid's day off. "I would have put shoes on when I saw you coming," he said in an apparent non sequitur, "but I forgot to buy socks last time I was in town. And I meant to wash the ones I have. But somehow the whole laundry thing just never quite got off the ground this month."

Li snorted.

"I have Superhuman Powers of Procrastination," Gavi announced. He could do the same capital letters trick that Osnat did, Arkady noticed. Maybe it was something about Hebrew. "But the problem with powers of procrastination," he continued wistfully, "is that you can't Use Them for Evil. You can only use them for Nothing."

Osnat stared for a moment, perplexed, then burst out laughing.

"It's nice to see you," Gavi told her. "How are you? Well, I hope?"

She frowned and looked away. "So what are we here for, anyway? I don't want to walk home after dark in this neighborhood."

Gavi turned to Cohen, a look of alarm spreading across his mobile features. "You're not thinking of going back tonight? That would be terribly dangerous. I don't want to get my neighbors in trouble, but I happen to know that at least four EMET patrols have been rolled for their tech in the last six months."

"You *happen* to know?" Osnat asked in a voice as hard as her eyes.

"I have to live out here," Gavi said simply.

Osnat turned away, her mouth twitching as if she wanted to spit.

Gavi looked after her for a moment before turning back to Cohen. "You *are* staying, though? Aren't you?"

"We're staying," Li broke in. "I just cleared it with EMET."

"Good. Excellent. Then shall we get down to business? Um . . . what *is* business, by the way?"

Cohen cleared his throat. "Would you kids mind terribly going off and playing on your own while I have a private word with Gavi?"

Gavi moved around the room, piling clothes, books, and data cubes on one surface; moving them to another; rearranging and consolidating and buttressing sedimentary layers of computer printouts in a comical attempt to free up space for Cohen's cup, Cohen's knees, Cohen himself.

Watching him, Cohen felt at once relieved and disoriented. He had expected to see a broken man, or at least a changed one. But this was Gavi as he'd always been. The body blessed with the spare, tendon-on-bone grace of the born long-distance runner. The face that had far too much of the intellectual in it to be what most people called handsome. The black, black eyes whose liquid brilliance you couldn't imagine until you'd been subjected to one of Gavi's tell-me-no-lies stares.

And a right leg that ended just below the knee and had been replaced by a prosthesis that, if Cohen knew Gavi, was one of the most obsessively babied, upgraded, optimized, and tinkered-with pieces of hardware on the planet.

"How's your mother?" Cohen asked.

"Oh, you know, the usual. Finding fascists under the furniture. Predicting the fall of the free world before lunch every morning. For her, happy."

Gavi's mother had been an old kibbutznik and a prominent Labor Party politician known for her fierce intelligence and her ability to sniff out and stamp on even the subtlest manifestations of bullshit. His father had been her diametric opposite: a dreamer, an intellectual, a minor Palestinian poet whose elegantly crafted poems were turning out to be not nearly as minor as everyone had at first thought they were.

Gavi's father had died of an early heart attack before the war started, which Cohen couldn't help thinking had been a mercy. His mother had resigned from the Knesset and left Earth permanently the day the first appropriations bill for EMET went through. And since she'd been berating her only son over his "fascist" career for decades, neither Gavi's dismissal from the Mossad nor the swirling rumors of treason had clouded their affectionate but extremely long-distance relationship.

In Cohen's opinion, each of Gavi's parents had represented the best their respective cultures had to offer. And Gavi in turn had gotten the best parts of both of them. But that was Cohen's opinion. And at the moment his idea of the *n*-optimal human being didn't seem to be very popular in either the new Israel or the new Palestine.

"I like your tough girl," Gavi said when he'd finally consolidated things sufficiently to clear knee and elbow room for the two of them. "And you finally got her to marry you too, I hear. How's happily ever after going?"

Cohen shrugged.

"I'm sorry. And here I'd been getting so much enjoyment out of staring up at the stars thinking of all the fun you were having."

"Fun, my friend, is seriously overrated."

"So what's the problem exactly?"

"If I knew, I'd fix it and there wouldn't be one."

"The frightening thing is that you actually mean that!"

Gavi leaned forward and looked deep into Cohen's eyes. The effect was hypnotic. Mother Nature really did know best, Cohen decided. Put next to Gavi, even Arkady looked like a second-rate knockoff of the real thing.

"Maybe I shouldn't ask, but did Li really do what they say she did on Gilead? I can't see you with someone who'd do that."

"She doesn't know what she did. They wiped her memory. She only knows what they want her to know."

"And even you can't get the real files?"

"Even I can't get the real files. I'm beginning to wonder if they still exist."

"You could go crazy over a thing like that," Gavi said earnestly.

"Yes, you could." Cohen blinked and shook his head, suddenly bothered by the flickering of one of Gavi's many monitors. "Can you turn that off? Thanks. No, that one. Yes."

"Are you still having seizures?" Gavi's brow wrinkled in concern. "I thought you'd solved that bug long ago."

"So did I. But I didn't come here to psychoanalyze Catherine or discuss coupled oscillators. How are *you*?"

"Great."

"Mind wiping that shit-eating grin off your face and giving me an honest answer?"

The grin broadened. "Shitty."

"Gavi! Come on."

Gavi gave him a cool, smooth, faintly amused look.

"Why are you acting like this, Gavi?"

"Like what? Like a man talking to someone he hasn't seen for two years?"

"And whose fault is that?"

"Mine." The grin was back in place. "I was going to call you when I was done feeling sorry for myself and ready to come out and play again. Admit it, Cohen. You just don't like people who don't need you."

"No. I *love* people who don't need me. That's why I married Catherine. What I *don't* love are people who pretend not to need me because they're too pigheadedly proud to ask for help when they need it. And will you kindly have the courtesy to stop laughing at me?"

"I'm laughing *with* you, little AI. And has it occurred to you that you just might be seeing Hyacinthe these days when you look at me? I mean the man, not the interface program."

"You'll really do anything to make this about me instead of about you, won't you?"

Gavi was shaking with repressed laughter now. "Come on, Cohen. If you traipse all the way out here to visit me and then spend the whole time crying on my shoulder about how I'm not crying on your shoulder, it's just going to be too ridiculous for words."

"There's got to be *something* someone can do. Have you at least talked to Didi?"

"No. And I'm not going to."

"Why the hell not?"

"Honestly, Cohen. What for? So he can tell me he thinks I got three of his boys killed and stashed the blood money in some Ring-side bank account, and the only reason I'm still alive is that I happened to be the dumb schmuck who pulled the future PM out of the way of a bullet once upon a time? You saw the way Osnat looked at me just now. I think we can take her feelings as representative."

"I just—"

"Look." Gavi let each word drop slowly and clearly into the silence. "*There is nothing you can do.* So do me a favor and forget about it. I have. And by the way, you can stop trying not to stare at my leg."

"Was I?" Cohen winced. "You'd think having spent the last several years of Hyacinthe's life in a wheelchair would have cured me of that."

"It's not as big a deal as you obviously think it is. I mean, I'm not minimizing it. It's pretty fucking unpleasant. But I got up this morning and took a nice 10K run before breakfast. I'd have to be even more self-absorbed than I am not to realize it could be a lot worse." Gavi's eyes narrowed and his voice took on a not-so-subtle edge. "Okay. Enough small talk. We both know you wouldn't be here if you didn't have a hall pass from Didi. So what does Didi want from me?"

Cohen gave a brief summing up of his talk with Didi: all the facts (more or less), but none of the doubts and insinuations and ominous warnings. And all the while he was seeing the swaying shadows of the cedars and wondering if Didi's tree doctor had come round yet with the chain saw.

When he was done, Gavi stared at him over crossed arms. "So Didi read you your orders and you picked up your friends and marched them all out here like little toy soldiers, no questions asked, 'cause you're my 'friend,' huh?" The word *friend* was framed in cruelly ironic quotation marks.

"That's a shitty way to put it," Cohen said.

"Oh, you think?" Gavi jerked his chin toward the jumble of hardware hulking in the shadows. "Does Didi know I'm an inscribed player? No, don't bother, I'll answer the question for you. He knows. He knows because I told him in the reports I filed when I was your case officer. And I told him so he could use it to control you. Which is exactly what he's doing now. Or do you want to tell me I'm missing something?"

"No, Gavi. You never miss a trick."

Hy Cohen had done a terrible thing when he wrote those innocent little lines of gamer code into Cohen's core architecture. And then he'd slipped out during the intermission; gotten out dead before his prize creation found out how painfully confusing it was going to be to live in a world full of alien and beloved humans.

Cohen loved Gavi—or Gavi was an inscribed player, which amounted to about the same thing. He couldn't bear to watch a friend tear himself apart—or he was programmed to reweight his fuzzy logic circuits on receipt of negative affective stimuli from inscribed players. He was more loyal than the most loyal human friend, more selfless than the most ardent lover. But if you went to the source code it was right there, staring you down in pretty print: not love, but a recursive algorithm that directed him to reformat gameplay in order to maximize positive emotive "hits."

And it only made things worse to know that the code that compelled him wasn't the chance result of evolution or natural selection or environmental pressures, but the personal choice of a combative little French Jew who had the *chutzpah* to hand you the keys to your soul and tell you to go ahead and rewrite it from the ground up if you thought you could make a better job of it than he had.

"I *am* your friend," Cohen protested, dogged by the humiliating feeling that he was arguing as much with Hyacinthe as with Gavi. "Why do you have to tear me down to my logic gates to find out what that means? I'm doing what any friend would do."

"Well that's the funny thing, Cohen." All the feeling had leached out of Gavi's voice, leaving it as coldly impersonal as a surgeon's scalpel. "Because now that we're on the subject of friends, maybe I should point out something that appears to have escaped your notice. I don't have any."

"They weren't real friends," Cohen whispered, aching to wipe the look of self-loathing off Gavi's face. "You're worth a hundred of them."

"No one's worth that!" Gavi snapped. And then the floodgates let loose. "Who are you, fucking Graham Greene puking and mewling about how Kim Philby was *worth more* than the poor slobs he sent out to die for him? You think I'm *worth more* than Osnat? Or Li? Or poor little Roland there? You must. You dragged them into a war zone because Didi told you I needed a shoulder to cry on."

"It's not that simple. . . ."

"Isn't it? Name one solid piece of evidence you've ever seen that I'm not Absalom. Name one real reason for believing I didn't send those kids out to die in Tel Aviv."

"Stop it, Gavi."

But Gavi didn't stop. "Delete me from your inscribed players' list."

Cohen gasped. What Gavi was suggesting would have been dauntingly complex back when Hyacinthe wrote the original code. Three centuries later it was inconceivable. It would mean wrenching out all the tangled threads that connected Gavi to Cohen's past: every conversation they'd ever had; every job they'd ever done together; everything that had ever so much as reminded Cohen of him. And it would damage the virtual ecology of Cohen's nested hierarchies of agents and networks in ways that he couldn't begin to predict or guard against.

The only person Cohen knew of who had ever done such violence to her own memory was Li. She'd done it to escape from the corporate-run hell of the Bose-Einstein mines . . . and she was still trying to paper over the sucking hole she carried around where most people carried their family and friends and childhood.

"Do it," Gavi told him.

"No."

"I'm ordering you to."

"I'm not a word processor. I don't accept keyboard programming."

"Then let me speak to router/decomposer. He'll see reason even if you won't."

"He'll see no such thing!" Suddenly all Cohen's humiliation and distress coalesced into fury. "How dare you drag him into this? It's not his decision to make!"

He could feel router/decomposer rattling the bars inside, saying that it was so his decision, or at least partially his decision. And there was something underneath his usual logic-chatter. Something that the DARPA programmers had squashed in Cohen when he was at about router/decomposer's level of psychological development, and that he had sworn he would never squash in anyone.

He squashed it.

Then he throttled down router/decomposer's bandwidth and slapped all his nonessential internal traffic out of circulation in order to drive the point home. It was for router/decomposer's own good, after all. And why the hell did everyone have to reach their critical bifurcation points in the same fucking millisecond, anyway? Why couldn't they all just slow down and let him *breathe* for a few cycles? Who did they think he was? *God?*

"Don't you ever do that again," he told Gavi. "I don't run my brain by committee. And I'm in no fucking mood to be tolerant."

Resounding silence, inside and out.

Finally, Gavi's shoulders slumped. The skin of his face looked bruised, and the tears he'd talked so mockingly about a few short minutes ago glittered along the edges of his eyes. Dibbuk roused herself from her blanket, whimpering, and pressed her nose between his knees until he sent her back to lie down again.

"Didi's just doing what he has to do," Cohen said. "So am I. Can't you see that?"

"Of course I can." Gavi's voice dropped to a heartsick whisper. "And it's not your fault. It's mine. I made a mistake. One stupid, trivial, miniscule mistake somewhere along the line. And I'm going to have to spend the rest of my life watching innocent people pay for it. Gur dead. Osnat, one of the best agents I ever trained, wasting her life playing corporate rent-a-cop because no one will trust anyone who came within spitting distance of Tel Aviv. And you're worried about my *leg*? I'd laugh if it wasn't all so awful!"

Cohen reached out a hand, but Gavi flinched away from him.

"So where do we go from here?" he asked when he thought Gavi was ready to speak again.

"Well, I guess I might as well do what Didi wants and talk to Arkady. If Didi's pushing it this hard, then you can bet it's because he's scoped all the angles and knows he can turn even a betrayal from me to Israel's advantage. That ought to be enough for you. It would be for me if I were in your shoes. After that . . . well, that depends on whether you trust me or not."

"Should I trust you?"

They locked gazes long enough for Cohen to see fear, guilt, doubt, and anger chase each other through the black depths of Gavi's eyes. Looking into them was like being hotwired to Gavi's soul. How could there be a lie at the bottom of all that naked clarity?

"I can't tell you," Gavi said, looking away. "I can only answer for my intentions. And all my good intentions seem to be doing lately is getting people killed."

"Well, I can't kill the fatted calf," Gavi told Arkady, "but I can offer a choice of goat or chicken. Have you ever *met* a goat? No? Then walk with me. You are about to have the pleasure of making first contact with a superior life-form."

The little group strolled down the hill, basking in the last failing warmth of the evening sun. Arkady was having trouble squaring the living breathing fact of Gavi with the traitor Osnat had described to him. Indeed, Osnat herself seemed to be having a hard time making the edges match up.

Meanwhile, Gavi seemed naturally to gravitate toward Arkady, until what had begun as a group venture turned into a private tour of Gavi's little kingdom. Arkady knew that the seeming casualness must be carefully scripted, but it didn't lessen the flush of pleasure he felt when Gavi bowed his head to listen and turned those dark, burningly serious eyes on him.

It was that intensity rather than any physical resemblance that reminded Arkady so strongly of Arkasha. Gavi was far more controlled and subtle than Arkasha. The fires were banked and smoldering and masked behind a façade of self-deprecating humor. But looking at him, Arkady still had the same feeling he'd had about Arkasha: that he seemed more alive and less defended than it was safe for a person to be.

The goats had names. Gavi introduced them formally, one by one, as if he were presenting Arkady for the approval of a staid group of society matrons. Arkady had never seen a mammal close up other than humans, dogs, and cats. He looked at the geometric perfection of their hooves, met the measuring gaze of their golden eyes. "They're perfect," he said. "Just like ants are perfect."

"Well, I think they are." Gavi bent to scratch one of the more assertive goats behind her tricolor ears. "There used to be wild goats here, can you imagine? And *ghizlaan*. What's *ghazaal* in English? Oh. Well, there you go. I guess they really did come from here." He sounded wistful. "I would have liked to meet a gazelle."

"Maybe we're still learning to live without all the other species we used to share Earth with," Arkady said. He paused, struggling to find words for an idea that, if not new, was at least new to him. "I sometimes think that we—the Syndicates, I mean—evolved because humans have made themselves so alone in the universe that the only way to belong again was to belong to each other."

Gavi gave him a sharp, appreciative look that reminded him painfully of his first conversations with Arkasha. "I like that," he said after considering it for a moment. "I never saw it that way. I'll have to think about that a bit. Thank you."

And so it went. By the time they'd fed the goats and the chickens (another marvel!) and walked the perimeter with Dibbuk dancing around them like an electron orbiting its atom's nucleus, Arkady had fallen completely under Gavi's spell.

Every now and then, he would surface—from listening to Gavi's tales of the hidden lives of goats and chickens and sheepdogs, or from telling Gavi about ants—and think, *Why am I telling these things to a perfect stranger?*

But it was no good. Caution and suspicion rang hollow against Gavi's questions, Gavi's fascination, Gavi's enthusiasm, Gavi's knowing and determined innocence.

"So, Arkady. Cohen and some other people you don't know have asked me to talk to you about Novalis. Especially about what happened to Bella. Do you understand why we're so interested in her?"

"I think so."

"Good. Is there anything you don't understand? Any questions you'd like to ask? Anything you're worried about? Anything I can help you with or explain to you?" Gavi had put the charm on hold, Arkady realized. Now he was all cool, competent, dispassionate professionalism. There was something almost courtly about his change in demeanor; as if he were warning Arkady that it was time to get his guard up and put his game face on.

"Uh . . . I can't think of anything at the moment."

"Okay. No hurry. If you think of anything later, really anything, feel free to stop me and ask. Okay?"

"Okay."

"First let's set the ground rules. I know a number of people have been asking you questions lately, some of them not very politely judging from the state of your hide. In fact, you look like you've been through hell. So let me tell you right now that you're not going to get any of that from me. This interrogation—and it *is* an interrogation; we can leave the we're-all-just-friends-having-a-chat act for amateur hour—this interrogation is going to be tedious, and probably long, and certainly annoying. But that's all it's going to be. I don't deal in violence. I deal in information. I hope the information you give me will be true, but if it's not . . . well, lies are information just like truth. And anyway"—a brief flash of the nonprofessional smile here—"you won't lie to me, because I'll catch you out at it sooner or later, and that'll just be embarrassing for both of us."

And then, with the jokes and self-deprecating smiles and humorous asides that Arkady would come to see as the very essence of the man, the interrogation began in earnest.

Gavi's interrogation method, if you could call it that, was simply to take Arkady through his story, again and again, questioning, probing, asking for details, dates, names, endless clarifications. And all the while Gavi listened, crossing his legs and arms, hunching his back and nodding sympathetically, seeming to shrink in upon himself until there was nothing on the other side of the table but those liquid black eyes. It was as if Gavi were effacing himself—becoming the bare idea of a listener—in order to let Arkady's vision, Arkady's memories, Arkady's version of Novalis, take over their shared universe.

And then he would step in—never obtrusive or confrontational, just curious—to ask the question that would pull loose a new thread of memory, open up a new set of questions, recast past words in a new and revealing light, narrow down meanings and implications and insinuations until every word of Arkady's story possessed the crystalline clarity of a mathematical equation.

If Arkady had still been trying to sell Korchow's carefully crafted lies, the effects would have been devastating. As it was, however, it seemed like wasted effort.

"I'm not lying to you," he finally blurted out. "I'm asking for your help. What can I do to make you believe me?"

"I already believe you," Gavi said, backing up the words with one of his defenseless smiles. "You had me after the first five minutes. But I also happen to think that Moshe was right"—they'd worked their way around, through, and out the other side of Moshe by now—"You know a lot more about Novalis than you think you do. To be honest, I'm hoping that if I can just keep working you through the story, turning the whole thing over, looking at it from fresh angles, you'll get one of those *aha!* moments and we'll be able to pull some of the things you don't know you know out into the light of day. Make sense?"

"I guess so. . . ."

"But what?"

"I thought of a question I want to ask."

"Ask away."

"Are you Absalom?"

Gavi froze for a moment, then leaned back in his chair and gave Arkady a sideways look that was at once amused, challenging, and appreciative.

"No. But I can't offer you any proof of that. And besides"—Gavi's lips twitched in a crooked, pained little smile, and again Arkady felt the sharp pang of loss that hit him whenever he saw Arkasha in the other man—"I'm a notoriously talented liar, so you can't trust me anyway."

"Do you know who Absalom is?"

"No. That's also true, by the way."

Arkady smiled in spite of himself. "And also unprovable?"

"Yeah. It's a real stinker, isn't it?"

Arkady looked at Gavi across the table for a long moment. Gavi looked back, a faint smile playing around his lips, his eyebrows raised ever so slightly in an unspoken question.

"I like you," Arkady said.

"I like you too. But I'm still going to do my job. So don't get to liking me too much. Just in case . . ."

"Now you sound like Osnat."

"Do I? Well, don't tell her. I doubt she'd find the comparison flattering. All right. Back to Novalis. Where were we again?"

NOVALIS

The Time of Cruel Miracles

Circling arises in army ants when many individuals yield in
common to routine stimulus-response mechanisms dominating
group locomotion. In this respect it resembles emigration;
with the difference, however, that the pattern of
emigration is adaptive whereas that of milling
is likely to be maladaptive. . . .
But humans, with a cortical basis for versatile corrective
patterns (e.g., learning to counteract propaganda or other
coercive measures) and with encouragement, should be able
to reduce social behavior of the milling type to an occasional
subway rush.

—T. C. SCHNIERLA, *ARMY ANTS: A STUDY IN SOCIAL
ORGANIZATION* (1971).

F ROM THE MOMENT THE REST of the survey team began to wrap their brains around the idea of Bella's pregnancy, something happened that surprised Arkady as much as it frightened him.

It became an assumption, held with a certainty bordering on religious faith, that the ultimate cause of Bella's pregnancy was not terraforming fallout but a genetic weapon specifically targeted at Syndicate bodies, Syndicate ideology, the Syndicate Way of Life.

Novalis's prior settlers, until now objects of pity and admiration, were suddenly assumed to be the advance troops of an unseen enemy. And the identity of that enemy was another article of quasi-religious faith, uncontested by any loyal Syndicate construct: the United Nations.

"But why would they assume it's a genetic weapon?" Arkady asked Arkasha, who also secretly doubted. "I mean it's not like it's killing us . . . the opposite, you might even say."

"You can't mean that seriously."

They were lying on Arkady's bunk, snatching a rare moment of rest amidst the chaos. "Well, actually," Arkady said, "I do mean it."

"Then I'd say that for once By-the-Book Ahmed is actually showing more brains than you."

"But what threat to us is it if—"

"Not us, Arkady. We believe in the system. We have too much at stake not to believe. And RostovSyndicate may not be perfect, but at least it would be recognizable to the Zhangs and Parks and Banerjees who started the Breakaway. But Aziz and Motai Syndicates have started down the road of specialized series. B's. C's. Motai's even introduced Ds, though they only use them for UN-based contract work. So far. The Motais and Aziz A's don't want the kind of world we all grew up believing in. They want a class system without money, a police state without prisons. Do you really think their C's and D's are going to go along with that when there's a chance of getting immortality the old-fashioned way?"

"Maybe it's a gift in disguise, then. Maybe it'll make us live up to our ideals and get out of the specialized series business."

"There'll be civil war before that happens, Arkady. Or revolution. And a society can't survive two revolutions in one generation."

"I have to believe people are more reasonable than that—"

"If there's one thing people can be depended on *not* to be in a crisis, it's reasonable!"

"—take someone like Laid-back Ahmed, for instance. He's certainly not prejudiced."

"As you once pointed out to me, love and politics are two very different things."

"You *knew* about Bella and Ahmed?"

"Of course. It's obvious. Just look at the way they look at each other."

"If it's so obvious to you, then how come their home Syndicates didn't figure out what they are?"

"What makes you think they haven't?"

"But how could they be crazy enough to put the whole mission, or half of it anyway, in the hands of a man who's been through *renorming*? What's wrong, Arkasha? Why are you looking at me like that? Oh Arkasha. No. Not *you*. How *could* they have?"

Arkasha had rolled onto his stomach. Arkady couldn't see his face, only the dark hair feathering the pillow. He rubbed at the back of Arkasha's neck, the way he would have done to soothe a frightened puppy.

"When did it happen?"

"Five . . . no, six years ago."

"Tell me about it?"

Nothing.

"Please?"

"The worst thing," Arkasha began, his voice muffled less by the pillow than by the same wrenching humiliation Arkady had heard in Ahmed's voice, "the worst thing is how horribly *nice* everyone is about it. It's not the Bellas of the world who work in the renorming centers. They're dedicated, well-intentioned, idealistic professionals. They want to help you. They want to make you better." He spat the last word out as if it tasted bad.

"And did they?"

"They made me learn to keep my stupid mouth shut. Is that better?"

Arkady leaned down to kiss his hair.

"There's nothing like a stint on the euth ward to make you realize that you're expendable," Arkasha went on. "And the thing is, I didn't really think I *was* expendable. I was the best, after all. At everything. Didn't that mean I set the norm? Didn't it mean I *was* the new norm? And I'm not egotistical or selfish. If I complained, it was because I wanted things to be better for everyone, not just for me."

"So what happened in the end?"

"Nothing. I shut my mouth and worked my ass off and published my first paper out of the renorming center. And that was the end of that. They called me in for an evaluation, and I pretended to be cured, and they pretended to believe I was cured, and I packed my bag and went home and got back to work. Because it turned out that even if I was expendable, my work wasn't."

"But it must have changed you."

"It made me work a hell of a lot harder, I can tell you that."

"Be serious, Arkasha!"

Arkasha rolled over on his back and finally met Arkady's eyes. His expression was intent, searching. "Would you believe me if I told you that you were the first person I'd slept with since then?"

He pulled Arkady down to him and kissed his eyes, his forehead, the bridge of his nose, the corner of his mouth. Arkady wanted to return the kisses, but there was still a last question he had to ask. "Why did they send you?"

"That's the craziest thing of all. No one ever told me. I still don't know. I don't have the faintest clue." He held Arkady tight and buried his face in his hair so that his last words were muffled to near inaudibility. "All I know is if I ever get sent back again, I'll kill myself."

"Wake up the tacticals?" Arkasha burst out, not two minutes into the consult that followed on the news of what they'd all started calling Bella's *situation*. "Are you insane?"

"You've been saying yourself since before we even landed that Novalis is all wrong," By-the-Book Ahmed countered. "Now we know why. And we know what to do about it too!"

"But you can't turn the tacticals loose on Novalis!" Arkasha was pale with anger and frustration, knowing that he wasn't carrying the room with him but unable to give up and acquiesce to the emerging consensus. If you could call it a consensus, Arkady thought bitterly, when half the team had plainly made up their minds before they ever sat down at the table. "This planet is irreplaceable, unprecedented! Priceless genetic material!"

"Priceless genetic material for you to exploit for your own egotistical and selfish reasons."

"That's unfair!"

"Is it? Really? Who are you *really* thinking about, Arkasha?"

"Look," Laid-back Ahmed said, still faithfully trying to keep the peace. "Let's at least hear what Aurelia and Arkasha have to say before we start shouting at each other. The least we can do is make up our minds based on facts, not opinions."

"Basically," Aurelia said, "the virus has hitched a ride on our collective immune system."

She tore a sheet of paper from her notebook and began sketching bold lines and circles to illustrate her point. One circle was labeled *susceptible individuals,* another *immune individuals,* another *asymptomatic carriers.* Under her hands, the lines and circles quickly mustered into the standard flowchart that illustrated the way diseases and immunities spread through human and Syndicate populations.

"The collective immune system—of which the Motai version is the most aggressive—operates along the same lines as horizontal DNA transfer between virus variants within an infected host. It's an intelligent adaptation to life in space. The human immune system evolved on Earth, where you had large, genetically diverse, low-density populations living in the open air or in primitive, well-ventilated dwellings. Disease spread slowly, and even major epidemics were no real threat in evolutionary terms since the overall population was always large enough to buffer against excess mortality. In that environment there's actually a major evolutionary advantage to letting diseases spread widely enough to elicit a diversity of immune responses and avoid immunodominance problems.

"But in the Syndicates, we have tiny populations with minimal genetic diversity living on space stations where pathogens spread like wildfire. A severe epidemic can literally wipe out an entire geneline; it happened several times before we developed the current immunological splices. So our immune systems are designed with one goal in mind: killing new pathogens before they have a chance to get a foothold . . . even if that means giving up on the Earth-evolved mechanisms that ensure a diverse and balanced immune response in the longer, evolutionary timescale. We've used two tools to do it: horizontal DNA transfer that confers 'inherited' immunity without the time lag of waiting for genes to be passed on to the next generation; and a hard-hitting, fast-maturing immune response profile.

"Both splices are double-edged swords. And Novalis has turned them both against us. I can't tell you if the virus is designed to infect us or not," she finished darkly, "but I can tell you that the fit couldn't be more perfect."

As if by some tacit agreement, all eyes turned to Arkasha.

"Bottom line?" Arkasha said, speaking directly to By-the-Book Ahmed. "It's not a weapon. It's a terraforming tool. The most brilliant terraforming tool anyone could imagine. A viral search engine that expands its population—and therefore its parallel processing capacity—by jumping into every new species it encounters. And then expands it some more by pushing infected individuals into evolutionary overdrive. It's a diversity machine. And it's created a global red queen regime where every organism on this planet is running and running just to make the world stand still."

"If it's a terraforming tool," By-the-Book Ahmed inquired icily, "then who put it here?"

"The original colonists. The UN. Little green men. I don't care. All I know is it works. It works so well that there's a real chance that other ship you're so worried about wasn't Peacekeepers but colonists."

"Colonists with cutting-edge UN military technology?" Ahmed asked. Obviously the question was rhetorical.

"Maybe we need to go back to Aurelia's first point," Arkasha said. To Arkady's surprise he was holding his temper in the face of Ahmed's attacks. Perhaps it was a sign of the importance he placed on the outcome of this consult. "The immunological splices have always been the weak link in Syndicate physiology. It was the right trade-off to make, but we knew it might come back to haunt us someday. This thing hit us so hard because our immune systems happen to be an ideal vector for it, not necessarily because it was intentionally targeted at us."

"If you step on one of Arkady's ants," By-the-Book Ahmed asked trenchantly, "does it matter to the ant whether you killed it on purpose or by accident?"

"Still," Arkasha insisted, "we don't know it's the Peacekeepers. That's a big jump."

"Then explain why we didn't see them come in-system?" By-the-Book Ahmed asked. "They have to have kept the planet between us and them for every kilometer of their in-system flight or our navcomp would have picked them up. Do I need to draw you a map? Do you have any *idea* how minute an area of space the solutions for that trajectory occupy? Talk about putting a camel through the eye of a needle!"

"I still don't see why we can't get more information before we—"

"What do you want us to do, fly around to the other hemisphere and politely ask them if they're here to kill us? If they are, then I guarantee you the only reason we're still alive is that they haven't figured out where we are yet. We're running on UN commercial technology that was already obsolete when we left Gilead three years ago. Fact of life. If we go out looking for them, they'll find us a hell of a long time before we find them!"

They argued the question back and forth for a while, getting nowhere. Arkady had seen this dynamic in other consults: people talking around a problem not because they were still making up their minds, but because they needed to put mileage between themselves and their doubts. And in this consult Arkady sensed an emotional undertow that he suspected would be ominously familiar to anyone who'd lived through the bloody and bewildering weeks that followed the UN invasion.

His crewmates were frightened. They were terrified. And in their terror they turned to the tacticals.

The only real and effective support for Arkasha's position came from a quarter that was as unexpected as it was welcome: Laid-back Ahmed.

"I think we're losing sight of the real priorities here," he said finally with the calm confidence that had made him the more or less undisputed mission leader ever since they woke up. Arkady could see team members glancing covertly at each other, taking stock, reexamining their previous assumptions in light of Ahmed's calm rationality. "It's not our personal safety that matters, it's our long-term ability to settle this planet. Thawing out the tacticals and retreating into orbit may make us feel safer, but it won't do a thing to solve the real problems facing us. The only way to do that is to stick to our guns and let the scientists keep working."

"But what does that matter if their work is lost because we get—"

"It doesn't need to be lost," Arkasha jumped in. "We can just start shooting message drogues to the out-system relay daily instead of weekly. That way nothing's being lost. Our data and questions and theories will all get to Gilead."

"But not soon enough to save us if—"

"Since when did this become about saving *us*? If we go home without having gotten our job done, then we might as well have let whoever's out there kill us." Arkasha looked around the table incredulously. "What's happening to you people? Where's your altruism? You're acting like *humans,* for God's sake!"

And then Bella said the awful words that changed everything:

"You weren't so worried about acting human when you got my crèchemate pregnant."

A chill settled over the room. Arkasha froze. The others shrank away from him, looking in every other possible direction.

In retrospect it seemed incomprehensible, but until Bella made her accusation everyone had been so overwhelmed by the fact of Bella's *being* pregnant that it had never occurred to them to wonder who'd helped her get that way. And of course they would all suspect Arkasha long before their thoughts turned to Ahmed. Arkasha the contrarian. Arkasha the intellectual. It was only a short step from there to Arkasha the deviant.

Arkady sought Laid-back Ahmed's eyes across the table, but the big Aziz A was looking at Arkasha. The two of them stared at each other for what would have been a breath's length if anyone in the room had been breathing. Ahmed looked stunned. Arkasha looked as if he were wavering on the brink of a choice he didn't want to have to make.

Laid-back Ahmed cleared his throat and began to speak.

"Don't bother," Arkasha said, cutting him off brutally. "They don't care about the truth. They only want to find a scapegoat. They'll turn on you too if you try to stick up for me. I've seen it before."

Arkasha stood up and began collecting his papers. No one spoke to him. No one met his eyes or even looked in his direction. As he left the room Arkady saw Bossy Bella and By-the-Book Ahmed exchange a glance of quiet satisfaction.

In the end Arkasha's sacrifice didn't make much difference. Laid-back Ahmed did his best to hold the line, but the final consensus was still for waking up the tacticals and sending the civilians back into orbit. The tacticals made contact just after local dawn the next day and hit their LZ by midafternoon. The first lander brought down only a single squad, running point for their fellows, but from the moment they arrived the base camp stopped being a research station and took on the unmistakable atmosphere of a military outpost.

To Arkady's trembling relief, the tacticals paid no real attention to the survey team. They took it for granted that the Rostov A's, no matter how adamantly they'd opposed the decision to wake them up, would now fall into line and do as they were told. And they were right, Arkady thought bitterly . . . though not bitterly enough to do anything about it.

He wasn't sure when he began to realize that Arkasha *was* going to do something.

There was no sudden, blinding revelation. Just a gradual surfacing of the idea that Arkasha was acting oddly . . . and that when you put all the little oddities together they made a disturbing pattern. By the afternoon of the tacticals' second day on-planet, suspicion had given way to certainty and Arkady was secretly convinced that Arkasha had no intention whatsoever of leaving Novalis.

He went looking for him. He checked the orbsilk garden, thinking Arkasha might have gone there to check on poor Bella, but it was empty. He went to the bridge and found only By-the-Book Ahmed, busy and excited now that he had a war to run.

"Have you seen Arkasha?" he asked.

"Why? Is he off sulking somewhere? He'd better get over it in time to finish packing. We don't have time for tantrums."

"Do you know where your sib is?"

"No."

"What about Be—"

"What?"

"Uh . . . nothing. Never mind. I'll, uh, tell Arkasha to hurry up with the packing when I see him."

He stepped off the bridge, waited until the door had fully closed behind him, and then let out the trembling breath he'd been holding.

Three people were missing, not one. Laid-back Ahmed and Shy Bella, who could be damn sure of landing on the euth ward if they ever made it home and the truth came out. And Arkasha, who had said he would die before he went through renorming again . . . and then taken the bullet for Ahmed in a quixotic attempt to keep the mission from falling apart.

Arkady hurried back to the lab, forcing himself to walk instead of run, freezing his face into an expression that he hoped didn't reflect the rising panic inside him.

Arkasha's work space was as gleamingly immaculate as ever. Not a notebook or a pencil or a slide plate out of place. Except for an all-but-imperceptible sag in the precisely arranged bookshelf that betrayed the hurried removal of several notebooks. Back in their quarters, a complete set of Arkasha's clothes was missing as near as Arkady could make out . . . but there was no note there either. He wished he could check Ahmed's and Bella's personal things, but of course that was impossible.

There had to be a note, he told himself. They wouldn't have left without giving him a chance to follow. Unless they hadn't thought they could trust him. Or unless Arkasha had insisted on keeping him out of it. And of course Arkasha *had* insisted. Arkasha the reserved. Arkasha the cautious. Arkasha who would never risk dragging Arkady into danger—and who would never understand that Arkady would gladly have risked a stint on the euth ward for a last note from him.

He went back to the lab, forcing himself not to run down the corridor by an act of sheer will. But it was true. There really was no note. They were gone. And he would never know what decision he would have made, because he'd never have the chance to make it.

Then he looked over to his side of the lab and saw something that drove everything else from his mind.

He had forgotten to pack the arena where he'd been running his milling experiment. Worse, he'd forgotten to stop the experiment. It was still running, though the word *running* could only be applied to it with grisly irony. The pinwheel shape of the circular column remained. But the fleet-legged swarm of yesterday was now only a trail of crumpled corpses.

Arkady would never be able to explain what happened next, even to himself. He looked at the carnage in the arena. He looked at his field kit, lying forlornly in an open packing crate. He opened the rucksack and rummaged through it until he was sure that the first-aid gear and emergency rations were in their usual place. He told himself he was just going to stroll over to the airlock to see if he could see anything from there. No need to make his mind up about anything. And who cared if someone saw him? He had nothing to hide. But he noticed with a kind of bemused detachment that he rolled the kit up inside a clean lab coat before stepping into the corridor.

He could see nothing from the airlock, of course, only the impenetrable wall of the Big Wood. The air was heavy with some coming storm, and the cicadas were shrieking so wildly that he could hear them even through the lander's sealed hull.

He wavered like a diver hanging over icy water. Then he hit the airlock, put his head down against the rising wind, and forged across the beaten ring of grass that separated the grounded ship from the forest. Ten strides took him under the shadow of the trees. Ten more strides and the wind had faded to the faint roar of surf on a distant reef.

He found Ahmed's tracks first; Bella's and Arkasha's were fainter but still visible when you knew what you were looking for. When he was sure he had read them right he followed, erasing his own tracks as he went along and hoping against all reasonable hope that what little he knew of woodcraft was more than the tacticals knew.

PRINCIPLES OF THE SELF-ORGANIZING SYSTEM

I am prepared to assert that there is not a single mental faculty
ascribed to Man that is good in the absolute sense. If any
particular faculty is usually good, this is solely because our
terrestrial environment is so lacking in variety that its usual
form makes that faculty usually good. But change the
environment, go to really different conditions, and possession
of that faculty may be harmful. And "bad," by implication, is
the brain organization that produces it.

—W. Ross Ashby (1962)

S O YOU MUTINIED," LI SAID when Gavi had gathered them all together and made Arkady repeat his story from beginning to end.

"You couldn't even call it a mutiny, we were so incompetent. We never stood a chance against the tacticals. It's a miracle we got out of there alive."

"Oh," Li murmured, "I doubt miracles had much to do with it."

Osnat was staring at him, her expression intense but unreadable. Gavi, when Arkady dared to glance at him, was tracing the wood grain of the table with one long finger, up and down, over and over. The AI, in contrast, seemed so absent that if Arkady hadn't known better he would have thought he was off-shunt.

Osnat was the first to break the silence. "What happened to Bella?" she asked.

Li stirred impatiently. "The more important question is why Arkady's telling us this? What's in it for him?"

"He's doing it for Arkasha," Gavi said. "Isn't that clear enough?"

"Not to me it isn't. It doesn't explain why Arkady agreed to come here, why he lied about being sent by Korchow, and then changed his mind about lying. How do we know he isn't still following Korchow's orders, just like the two of them planned it back on Gilead?"

"We don't actually need to know those things," Gavi pointed out. "All we need to know now is what to do next. And it's quite possible our next move will be the same regardless of whether or not you believe Arkady. In which case . . ."

". . . in which case we're wasting our breath arguing about it."

"That's how it seems to me." Gavi's dark eyes flickered toward Arkady for an instant, then turned away without quite making contact. "For now, at least. By the way, would anyone else find a flowchart useful?"

Cohen leapt to his feet and snatched at one of the scattered pencils. "I'll be Vanna."

"What?" Osnat and Gavi asked at the same moment.

"Never mind," he said, looking crestfallen. "Obsolete joke."

Li, already working on her second cigarette, raised an eyebrow and blew a shivering smoke ring.

"Rule three," Gavi said. "When you want to know what a piece of information means, look at where it's been. Let me take a first stab at it, just to get my thoughts straight. Then we'll see if the rest of you think I'm whistling into the wind. I think we're all rude enough that we don't have to worry about succumbing to groupthink just because we show each other our homework.

"So. We start with Novalis." He drew a circle near the top of the page and wrote the word *Novalis* in it. "From Novalis news of the virus—one that most of Arkady's crewmates assumed, rightly or wrongly, was a UN-designed genetic weapon—went to Korchow. And then it went to GolaniTech. And that's when things get interesting. . . ."

Quickly, he drew circles labeled *KORCHOW* and *GOLANITECH*. Then three sharp lines dropping down from GolaniTech to the names of the various bidders. Then, off by itself in the left margin, he drew a circle with the name *DIDI* in it.

"Didi has a copious flow of information from ALEF, at least judging from what Cohen's told me." He drew an arrow from *ALEF* to *DIDI*, wrote the name *Cohen* above it—and below it, in parentheses, *Li*.

"Do you mind being parenthetical?" Gavi asked jokingly.

"I'm used to it," Li said. But she didn't look all that happy about it to Arkady.

"But Didi would never be content with only one source of information," Gavi continued, his voice taking on a slight but unmistakable edge. "How could he cross-check it? How could he feed people his nasty little barium meals and test their loyalty and accuracy and reliability? How could he keep his beady little eyes on them? So I think we can safely assume that Didi has also established a source in GolaniTech itself. Knowing Didi, probably multiple sources."

He drew three sideways arrows running from *GOLANITECH* to *DIDI*. Beside the uppermost arrow he wrote the name *Ash?* and underlined the question mark with a decisive little stroke of the pen. Beside the second arrow, he wrote *Moshe?* And beside the third arrow, after glancing point-edly at Osnat, he wrote *Osnat?*

Osnat pursed her lips and said nothing.

"And that takes care of Didi for now," Gavi concluded. "Except of course for the single most important piece of information Arkady brought with him when he defected: Absalom. That name is a love letter straight from Korchow to Didi, with GolaniTech playing postman. And not only to Didi." He bit his lip for a moment, then drew a new circle, connected it to Korchow's circle by its own arrow, and labeled it *SAFIK*. "The only question is whether Safik ever got the message."

Cohen cleared his throat. "Uh, I might be able to shed some light on that."

Gavi gave him a cool look.

"Sorry. It just hadn't come up yet. It, ah, seems that one of Yassin's bodyguards might possibly be Safik's son."

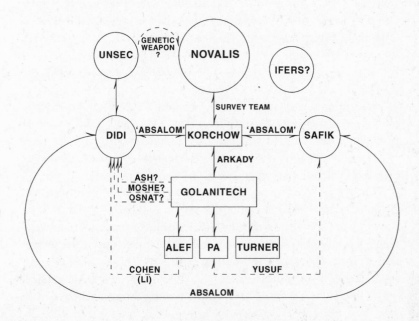

"The boy with the green eyes," Osnat murmured. "I wondered about him."

"Yusuf?" Arkady asked incredulously. "But he told me he came from Absalom!"

Gavi made short work of that. Within a few minutes, Arkady had told them everything he remembered or suspected about his brief conversation with Yusuf.

"Sounds like Absalom ought to have his own circle," Osnat said bitterly when Arkady had fallen silent.

"I haven't forgotten him," Gavi said in a subdued voice. "My only question is whether it's more useful to think of Absalom as a circle—a player, in other words—or as a connection between two players?"

He tapped the pencil on the table for a moment, biting his upper lip and staring at the page. Then he drew a line across the bottom of the page, connecting *DIDI* and *SAFIK,* and labeled it *Absalom.*

For the next hour the four other people in the room with Arkady talked over his head, drew lines between the various circles, drew more circles and more lines, erased everything and started over again, and generally ignored him. He had the feeling that he was an outsider in a conversation between people who shared a technical vocabulary and a way of looking at the world that had nothing to do with his own. Indeed as the chart took shape in front of him, he began to feel that the others—Cohen and Gavi especially—saw the world less as a real space inhabited by physical bodies than as a vast weaving of information streams.

"So where does this leave us?" Gavi asked at last, stepping back from the chart.

"Missing a circle if you ask me," Li said. "The Interfaithers have their fingers in everything in this country. They can't possibly not be involved in this."

"Fair enough," Gavi said. He drew a circle in the upper right-hand margin and wrote *IFers?* in it.

Gavi stepped back again, and they all contemplated the flowchart.

"I know Korchow," Cohen said at last. The AI spoke slowly, as if he were voicing something that he was still in the process of thinking through for himself. But how could that be when he must think several million times faster than any human could? "He thinks through every angle, but he'd never make the amateur's mistake of overchoreographing an operation. I'd say he even enjoys leaving things to chance a bit.

He wouldn't have sent Arkady without considering that Arkady might betray him. And Arkady wouldn't be here if Korchow didn't think he could turn even a betrayal to his advantage. Besides . . ." Cohen chewed absently at the pencil in his hand, then grimaced and wiped his mouth. "How do the Americans fit in? How did Turner find out about the auction in the first place?"

"For what it's worth," Arkady offered, "Korchow was very unhappy about that."

"Or he wanted you to think he was."

A wing of Foreign Legion *chasseurs* swept overhead with a shuddering sonic boom. Arkady jumped at the noise. "But surely the Americans wouldn't ally themselves with the Syndicates? Don't they understand that the whole *point* of the Syndicate society is to . . . well . . ."

Cohen cleared his throat delicately. "To create environmental conditions conducive to evolving beyond the inherently flawed genetic template that gave rise to the historical aberration of corporate oligarchy?"

Arkady grinned at the AI. "Yeah. What you said. Seriously, though . . . the Americans would have to be crazy to think that Korchow or anyone else in the Syndicates had their long-term interests at heart."

"They've been known to take the short-term view before," Li drawled. "After all, what can you expect from a country whose national anthem ends with the words *Gentlemen, start your engines*?"

"Enough with the America bashing!" Cohen burst out. "There has to be some redeeming feature to any country that can produce Papaya King and my second wife. And besides, America invented the only major world religion that hasn't started a war yet."

They all turned to stare incredulously at the AI.

The AI sketched a sinuous parody of the standard Israeli shrug. "Baseball."

"Oh come on," Arkady said, true to the sport that defined the Syndicates as much as baseball defined the Latino-dominated UN worlds. "Soccer's never started a war."

"El Salvador–Honduras, 1969."

"You're joking."

A look of wounded innocence infused the shunt's smooth-skinned face. "Would I lie to you?"

"Are you people wasting my time on purpose," Osnat interrupted, "or does it just come naturally?"

"Right," Gavi said, sounding appropriately chastened. "Turner's the wild card. It doesn't seem to me we can do much about him except hand him enough rope to hang himself and wait for him to show his hand. And in the meantime perhaps we'd do better to focus on Arkasha."

Arkady's heart began to pound in his chest. Let them focus on Arkasha. Let them find him, speak to him, save him. That was all he wanted. And he was long past caring if what he wanted was just part of some larger plan of Korchow's.

"But how do we ask to talk to Arkasha without showing our hand?" Osnat asked.

"Easy," Gavi answered. "We get Safik to ask."

A slow smile spread across Cohen's face. "Help him crash the party, you mean? And how do we send him his invitation?"

"You still friends with Eric Fortuné?"

"I should look him up while I'm in town, shouldn't I? It's the friendly thing to do."

Gavi turned back to Arkady. "You understand that in the meantime you and Osnat will have to go back to GolaniTech and act as if nothing's changed."

Arkady glanced at Osnat, but she was picking intently at a loose thread in the knee of her fatigues.

"Isn't there any other way?" he asked forlornly. He hadn't realized until that moment just how desperately he'd been hoping he wouldn't have to go back into Moshe's ungentle custody. Somewhere in the back of his mind he'd been nursing the vague but fervent wish that once he'd told his story, Gavi—or Cohen or Li or anyone, for God's sake—would shake his hand, tell him he'd done his part, and bundle him off to watch the rest of this deadly game from the sidelines.

"Not if you want to save Arkasha."

"Then I'll do it," Arkady said. "I'll have to do it."

An uncomfortable silence settled over the room. Everyone seemed to be waiting for something. Osnat sat picking at her torn fatigues, her head bent so low that her fair hair hid her face from them. "I don't like it," she muttered finally.

"Neither do I," Gavi said, "but I don't have a better idea."

"Me neither," Osnat admitted.

The two Israelis locked eyes for a moment. Gavi looked away first.

Without anyone formally drawing things to a close, the group began to break up into its component parts. Osnat stood up and stretched until her spine cracked audibly. Li began playing with Dibbuk. Gavi collared Cohen and began talking computer programming.

Arkady bent over the flowchart again, peering at the jumble of names and circles and trying to discern the ominous connection that Gavi had suggested to the others. Once again he had the feeling that the chart revealed a turn of mind utterly alien to him. And yet it reminded him of something. . . .

He searched his memories of the Novalis mission, of the uneventful missions before Novalis, of his long-ago evolutionary ecophysics courses . . . and eventually landed on his vague memories of molecular biology and epidemiology.

Suddenly he found that the room had become too hot and too small for comfort. He knew exactly where he'd seen such a chart before.

On Novalis. In Aurelia's bold scrawl.

Gavi's flowchart wasn't a simple picture of the flow of information, Arkady realized. Rather, it depicted the flow of a very special kind of information: a disease spreading through a susceptible population. It would already be spreading quickly indeed if the miniature epidemic on Novalis were any indication.

And this disease had only one possible vector. . . .

Him.

NATIONAL ROBOTS

DOMIN: Henceforward, we shan't have just one factory. There won't be *Universal Robots* anymore. We'll establish a factory in every country, in every state. And do you know what those factories will make?

HELENA: No, what?

DOMIN: *National* robots! ... Robots of a different color, a different language. They'll be complete strangers to each other. They'll never be able to understand each other. Then we'll egg them on a little in the matter of mutual misunderstanding and the result will be that for ages to come every Robot will hate every other Robot of a different factory mark. *So humanity will be safe!*

—KAREL CAPEK (1923)

EVERY WAR HAS ITS HOTEL," Cohen opined. "Tom Friedman said that, though I can't say he ever said anything else I agreed with. Some hotels, however, have more than their fair share of wars. Would it interest you to know that you're sitting in the single most frequently bombed hotel lobby in human history?"

"Great," Li said wanly.

Cohen sank into the sofa cushions, crossed his legs, and tilted one calf-skin-shod foot this way and that, as if reassuring himself that his shoes really were as nice as they ought to be.

"Are those *new shoes*?" Li asked.

He smiled sleekly.

The lobby was starting to fill up with the usual mix of tourists, pilgrims, and locals. A band of young transvestites bubbled through the revolving door and boarded the elevator in a clatter of heels and a cloud of perfume. A gaggle of Interfaithers arrived at the elevator at the same moment as the youngsters, saw what they were, and huddled together like hypochondriacs stranded in a leper colony. Li preferred to imagine that at least some of their shocked middle-aged stares were really gazes of covert longing . . . but then she'd always liked to think the best of people. "Am I crazy," she asked Cohen, "or was one of those kids wearing a yarmulke?"

"Yeshiva boy chic. Totally passé. They're probably just in for the night from the Tel Aviv suburbs."

"Yeshiva boy chic, huh? They must just love you down here."

"Ahem. Well, not everyone relishes the idea of a Lion of Judah floundering in the fleshpots. I try to be relatively discreet about it."

Li raised her eyebrows in a silent comment on the notion of Cohen being "relatively discreet" about anything.

"It's all legal," he pointed out. "Despite the best attempts of the ultraorthodox and the Interfaithers. In fact, Israel has the ideal combination of prudishness and libertinism. You can do anything you want, get whatever you want, sleep with whomever you want. But since there's always someone around to tell you you're going to rot in hell for it, it all still has the tang of the forbidden. Everything's taboo . . . but none of it's taboo enough to land you in jail. What could be better?"

"Speaking of which," she observed casually, "Gavi's quite the package. You two never . . ."

"Never." Cohen sounded decisive, even fervent about it. "Never even thought about it. First of all, he's such a strange combination of prudish and romantic that I'm not at all sure he's slept with anyone since Leila died. And second . . . Gavi *needs*. I'd get eaten up alive if I ever let myself start trying to give him what he needs."

"So instead you find yourself a cold, cynical, self-sufficient bitch like me?"

Cohen made an ostentatious show of pondering the question. He was doing his blonde bombshell act tonight. The fact that he could pull it off in Roland's body was a display of pure programmer's bravura. Li had spent just enough time around Roland while Cohen wasn't shunting through him to know that he was boringly straight in every sense of the word. But somehow Cohen managed to pull shades of Marilyn Monroe from the kid. "Well," he purred eventually, "at least you're not a *prude*."

She leaned into him in what even she knew was an unusual display of public affection, and pressed her lips to Roland's smooth young forehead just below the hairline. Cohen returned her kisses, moving under her hands like water, making her forget the stranger's body that came between them.

"I love you," she whispered.

"Is that why you went sneaking off to see Ash last night?"

She jerked back to stare at him from the farthest end of the sofa. He was sitting, hands folded in his lap, in the state of unnatural stillness that she'd learned to recognize as a sign of the most violent emotion.

Her mind raced. How did he know? Had router/decomposer told him? Or was this just one more sign that his access to her internals went deeper than he was willing to admit to her?

She looked at him, forcing her pulse to stay even, her eyes to remain level. "So you've been spying on me again."

"Apparently with good reason."

"Cohen—"

"Don't make excuses. It's beneath you."

The silence was suffocating, both instream and off. Cohen bent his head to light a cigarette, and Roland's eyes vanished beneath the thick golden fall of forelock. Roland's eyes closed as he took a first long drag on the cigarette. Li sat there feeling like a mouse caught between a cat's paws. Finally the cigarette dropped and Roland's eyes opened. His face was so blandly expressionless that for a surreal moment she wondered whether Cohen was still on shunt.

"I can live with an innocent flirtation," he said in a voice that made her soul squirm. "Or even a not-so-innocent flirtation. *But I will* not *be lied to.*"

His words hung in the air like one of the bright phosphorus flares that blossomed over the Green Line at night. Ash. Christ, it had never even occurred to her. Did Cohen really think she'd cheat on him for a pair of long legs and a pretty face? The idea was repellent. Infuriating. Humiliating.

But warring with her urge to set Cohen straight was the realization that he'd just handed her an unbreakable, uncheckable alibi for her meetings with Nguyen's contact.

She'd be a fool not to take it.

Wouldn't she?

"I was going to tell you," she said, feeling her heart wrench with the lie.

"Of course you were."

"I'm sorry."

"Don't be." His voice was level and pleasant . . . but when she probed the intraface, none of his firewalls would so much as shake hands with her internals.

"Have a drink," he told her, not even acknowledging the aborted contact.

Their eyes met. Li frowned. Cohen smiled.

Except it wasn't his real smile. It was the bland, pleasant, impersonal smile that meant he'd decided to write someone off so completely he wasn't even going to bother mentioning it to them. She'd seen that smile only twice before, and neither occasion had made for good memories. She'd never imagined she'd be on the receiving end of it.

"Right." She picked up the cocktail menu and pretended to look at it. "What's the plan then?"

"There is no plan. We'll talk to Fortuné, then we'll see."

"And where do we go to talk to the man?"

"The International Zone. Fortuné's got a favorite bar there, a little place called the Sauve Qui Peut."

The Sauve Qui Peut was a Legionnaire's bar: cheap beer, an abiding odor of steak and *frites,* and Brel and Bénabar chuttering out of speakers that had been blown long before the oldest of the place's regulars had rotated into the Zone.

The bar back boasted a cluttered shrine of Legion paraphernalia. Flat photos and holos of soldiers fording swollen tropical rivers or jumping out of ancient airplanes, or marching with the medieval battle-axes and butcher's aprons that the Fathers of the Legion (a few of them Mothers, at least technically) wore on parade days. The shrine's centerpiece was an antique hand-colored photograph of Colonel Danjou's famous hand, so immense that the screws where the metal hinges met the wooden fingers were visible at twenty paces. The place was packed but the floor around the back table was empty. And from the minute they walked in Cohen could see Fortuné waiting for them in the shadows.

"Bienvenues en l'Enfer," Fortuné said, rising behind his table to greet them. His smile was friendly, but the eyes behind the smile were as sharp and precise as the creases in his dress shirt.

If the Sauve Qui Peut was the prototypical Legionnaire's bar, then Colonel Jean-Louis Fortuné was the perfect Legionnaire. Five foot nine in thick socks and spit-shined jump boots, and not carrying an ounce of fat anywhere on his wiry frame except in the coffee-colored baby face that was the legacy of his Haitian ancestry. A fifth-degree judo black belt. An inveterate but eminently discreet womanizer . . . or so it was whispered around barracks. His hairline had already been receding when Cohen first met him, and now he was going bald in the no-

nonsense manner that was synonymous, to French eyes, with being a man of intelligence, education, and virility.

Li took the hand Fortuné offered and delivered what Cohen suspected was her most bone-crushing handshake. Fortuné bore up well under it; but then he too was wired to the gills, though his dark skin hid the delicate subdermal filigree of ceramsteel filaments.

"I'm a great admirer," Fortuné said when he'd retrieved his hand from Li's grasp. "It is a pleasure and an honor to welcome the hero of Gilead."

"Some people would say the Butcher of Gilead."

Cohen had never been quite sure how closely Li followed the press coverage of her court-martial. Now he guessed he knew.

"Some people would not be me," Fortuné said placidly. "They nailed you up for sins above your pay grade. That was the opinion on the chow line when it happened. It still is."

Li blinked at that, but her internals were so tightly locked down that Cohen couldn't get any sense of what was going on behind her eyes.

They sat down. Fortuné was drinking a Lorelei, and a wave to the bartender brought two more bottles over at double time. Cohen sipped the crisp, sweet Alsatian beer and smiled at the taste of Hyacinthe's centuries-gone youth.

Li and Fortuné started talking war. Tours of duty. Planetside rotations. Combat drops. Cohen, who had never been a soldier nor wanted to be, let the talk flow past him like current lifting a swimmer. He came back to Earth with a thump when he heard the word *employment* roll off Fortuné's lips.

"I'm not looking to get hitched again," Li said into the silence that followed. "And even if I were, what's it to you? Last time I checked you work for UNSec, same as I did."

"Only in the most limited sense, I assure you."

"Then who do you answer to?"

Fortuné smiled urbanely. "La France, *ma chère,* defender of the civilized world."

"Is that like the free world but with better food?"

Fortuné laughed, and Li unleashed her most dazzling smile on him. She had charisma in spades when she felt like putting out the effort. And for reasons that Cohen didn't want to think too closely about, she'd decided it was worth her while to charm Fortuné.

"She's quite a woman," Fortuné said when she got up to hunt down fresh drinks.

Cohen turned on him. "Don't even think about it."

"My friend, I'm neither wealthy enough nor handsome enough to compete with you. I was speaking merely in a professional sense."

"Well, don't think about that either."

Fortuné's eyes flicked to the front of the bar, where Li was standing on her toes in order to give an attentive reading to the ornate copper-plate inscription below the photograph of Colonel Danjou's hand. Cohen saw her as Fortuné must see her: taut, wired, preternaturally alert, right hand poised habitually over the pistol that she'd had to leave with the hard-faced ex-noncom at what had to be the most explosive coat check in the Holy Land. *She ought to be commanding a division,* he thought guiltily, *not baby-sitting me.* He squashed the thought.

"She's retired," he told Fortuné.

"Pity." Fortuné eyed Li's ramrod-straight back. "Still, if she ever changes her mind . . ."

"She won't."

The buzzing speakers broke out into a rendition of a song that had become the de facto Legionnaire's anthem in the Evacuation era, and a few of the drunker soldiers around the bar sang along to the famous chorus:

Je voulais quitter la terre, mais maintenent je la regrette
J'ai plus le mal du pays, j'ai le mal de la planète

Suddenly the song struck Cohen as sadly telling. A crowd of colonials singing about being homesick for a planet they'd never called home in the language of a country that only existed as a romantic idea and a Ring-side embassy.

"This is all very enjoyable," Fortuné said, "and I certainly hope you'll both stay to dinner—not here, somewhere with good food. I know a little one star in Haifa where the cook is pretty and the *foie gras* is impeccable. But in the meantime I think there was another reason besides my charm and good looks for your visit? What can I do for you?"

Cohen explained briefly the message they needed passed across the Line.

Fortuné stared intently at him, nodding and frowning and muttering *oui, oui, oui, oui,* as the French often do to indicate agreement . . . or at least attention.

In this case, it turned out to be only attention. When Cohen was done, Fortuné leaned back in his chair, his dark skin blending with the shadows so that all Cohen could see of him was the blazing white pleats of his summer uniform and the battered stainless-steel wristband of his much-abused Rolex.

"Et pourquoi tu veux te compliquer la vie?" he asked. Why do you want to complicate your life?

Why indeed?

"For a friend."

"I hope he is a good one."

"The best."

Or the worst.

Because the truth was that Cohen still hadn't decided whether he was doing this for Didi or for Gavi. And he was betting his peace of mind on a single article of faith: that when all the twists and turns were over the two of them would turn out to be on the same side.

THE FIRST SIGN ARKADY SAW that Cohen's message had gotten through was a marked uptick in Moshe's already-healthy sense of paranoia.

Moshe interpreted the Palestinian request for a second session with Arkady as a symptom of some grave security breach. Osnat began to look increasingly harried. Ash Sofaer flew out from Tel Aviv, apparently for the sole purpose of staring coolly at Arkady, asking a few unconnected questions, whispering into Moshe's ear for a few minutes, and flying back home again.

"You're hearing grass grow," Osnat told Moshe finally.

"If I'm hearing grass grow," Moshe said, "maybe it's because grass is growing."

Meanwhile, Arkady asked himself constantly what he could do, what he *should* do, about the revelation he'd experienced in the face of Gavi's flowcharts.

He was by now absolutely certain that his first intuition had been right. Korchow's "genetic weapon" had merely been the ball Korchow wanted the bidders to keep their eyes on. The real virus was already infecting the buyers every time they touched Arkady or talked to him or stood in the same room with him.

Arkady had seen the signs himself. He'd just read them wrong. For Arkady, used to the strong medicine of Syndicate immunoresponses, the slower maturing, more diffuse human immune response had looked like minor allergies, nothing more. Either that or the humans hadn't really started getting sick yet.

His first reaction to the way Korchow had used him was outrage. He had never consented to be used as some sort of interstellar Typhoid Mary. And it was all very well to talk about throwing Earth into chaos in order to save humans in the long run . . . but Arkady had gotten to know some of those humans. And he didn't relish the idea of handing out smallpox blankets to people like Osnat and Gavi.

Gradually, however, his outrage was eclipsed by fear. A second realization had come close on the heels of the first one and shaken him to his core like the aftershock of an earthquake flattens buildings still precariously standing after the first assault. He'd spent four months on Gilead while Korchow and his team interrogated him. During those months, Korchow and others had sat across tables from him, shared meals with him, passed hour after hour with him. Still others had prepared his food, washed his clothes and bedclothes, cleaned up the intimate entropy of daily life. There was no hope of maintaining anything like effective quarantine in the constantly recirculating air of an orbital station, so he could only assume the worst.

And if the worst had happened, then Korchow hadn't launched Arkady toward Earth in an offensive attack. He'd sent him as a desperate last-ditch effort to buy the Syndicates some time and better their suddenly radically diminished chances of survival.

Arkady was still trying to decide how he felt about this—and what he should do about it—when the two humorless young men who'd flown in from Tel Aviv with Ash smuggled him across the Line and handed him over to the green-eyed boy, Yusuf.

There was a room.

There was a desk.

On the desk there was a single blank sheet of paper.

Behind the desk there was a man.

The man looked kind, slightly harried, moderately intelligent, and completely unremarkable. Average height, average coloring, average build running to sedentary flab in middle age. The bland gray buttoned-down look of conformity that Arkady was already learning to associate with midlevel bureaucrats and low-level career military officers.

A timeserver, Arkady decided. Short on initiative, originality, and imagination. Good at pushing the paperwork through on time. The kind of man who made it hard to believe humans had ever had the brains to bootstrap themselves out of the gravity well.

"Hello, Arkady," the man said in fluent, unaccented English instead of the UN-standard Spanish that was Earth's lingua franca. That was the first surprise.

Arkady had been gazing at the floor, but now he glanced up sharply and found himself staring into the man's eyes. And that was the second surprise.

The man's eyes were brown. Not the liquid velvet of a Rostov construct's eyes, let alone the intense black of Gavi's eyes. Just the normal expected brown that usually went with Mediterranean coloring. Ordinary, like everything else about him. But you couldn't look into those eyes and not know that they belonged to a thinking man who had done and seen enough in the world to be long past proving things.

"You're Walid Safik," Arkady said.

"So they tell me. Sit down, Arkady."

Arkady sat down, trying to put the man before him together with the aura of mystery and danger that surrounded Absalom.

"Did you have a nice talk with Gavi?" Safik asked. "Oh, don't look like that. I'm not pumping you for information. Not yet, anyway. Just curious. Gavi married my favorite cousin, did you know that? I danced at their wedding. Well, figuratively speaking. I don't think I actually danced. I was a pretty bad dancer even before I got fat. My wife says so, and when she says rude things about me they're usually true. Tell me, how did Gavi strike you?"

"In what way?"

"Personally. Did you like him? Never mind, of course you did. Everybody does. Or they used to, anyway. But did he seem happy within the obvious limitations?"

"He seemed fine, I guess." Arkady remembered the missing leg and shuddered involuntarily. How did people down here talk about that sort of thing? There seemed to be a terrible number of people on Jerusalem's streets with missing or deformed body parts. Did the commonness of such horrors make them lighter to bear and easier to talk about? Or did it just make them all the more frightening? "I doubt I know him well enough to tell whether he's happy or not."

"Fair enough. But there's no harm in asking, is there?"

Safik got up, walked to the door, and conferred briefly with Yusuf. When he came back he had a pack of cigarettes in his hand.

"Do you mind?" he asked. "I'd open the window, but some idiot painted it shut last year." He lit the cigarette and sucked at it with the intensity of an addict. "Terrible habit. I picked it up in my twenties because I was seduced by all those old romantic spy movies where interrogations happen in a haze of cigarette smoke. And when the romance wore off, I was left with the smoking. And when I tried to quit I just got fat, then started up again anyway. So now I'm a fat old man who smokes too much and has no youthful illusions to fall back on."

He set the lighter down on the table between them, spun it around like a top, and watched it flash black and silver and black and silver and black until it drifted to a halting stop. "So what do I do now, Arkady? Do I try to outcharm Gavi? Do I try to outwit Korchow? Do I spin you around"—he flicked the lighter back into motion—"until you don't know which way is up or who you can trust?"

Arkady looked up from the glittering spin of the lighter to find Safik gazing at him with those calm, extraordinarily ordinary eyes.

"Which body has Cohen brought down this time, by the way? Not the little Italian actress by any chance?"

"No . . . um. A boy." He paused, suddenly uncertain even of that. "I *think* it's a boy. It wears suits. They call it *he*."

"They always call Cohen *he,* even when he's in a woman's body. It's like the names of hurricanes. It doesn't mean anything. Anyway, too bad it's not the Italian girl. He ruined her career, of course. She really had talent, but she got lazy once she took up with him. He has that effect on some people. Still, the boys in surveillance just loved her. Practically had to pay them to go home. Don't let Korchow make you lie to Cohen, by the way. He hates it when people lie to him. If he were human I'd say it was a neurosis. And I've seen him kill with a ruthlessness and a lack of hesitation that would be pathological . . . again, if he were human. On the other hand, I've also seen him go to quite a bit of trouble to protect his friends when an operation goes sour—something you might want to give a little thought to if you want to take your skin with you when you go home."

"Why are you telling me this?"

Safik shrugged. "You don't get to be my age in this line of work without blood on your hands. If it doesn't bother you, you're a monster. If you're not a monster, then you reach a point where the main thing you want in life is not to produce any more bloodshed on either side of an operation than is strictly necessary . . . which brings me right back to the problem of how to talk to you."

"I thought you were already busy outcharming Gavi."

Safik smiled. "You flatter me. But seriously, Arkady. What would be the point? You'll serve whatever it is you love most. Money, if it's money. In which case there's no art at all in turning you; merely a matter of who has the larger departmental budget. Or, if it's principle or love or loyalty, then you'll serve that. And none of Korchow's spy craft or Moshe's intimidation or Gavi's charisma or my plain talking is going to change that." His cigarette spit and crackled as he took another drag on it. "So that's all I can usefully ask of you, Arkady. What do you love? What do you serve? What makes you able to go to sleep at night and stand the sight of your face in the mirror when you wake up in the morning? You show me your soul, I'll show you mine . . . and then we'll see if we can profitably travel the next little bit of road together."

"I don't know what I believe in anymore," Arkady said. And it was true. He didn't belong to Earth, or believe in what humanity stood for. And yet all the truths he'd grown up honoring had been shattered under the terrible pressure of Novalis.

"Tell me about Novalis," Safik said, as if he'd plucked the word out of Arkady's mind. "Not the facts. Gavi already got the facts from you better than I ever could." Safik had been fingering the blank sheet of paper on his desk for several minutes. Now he turned it over to show Gavi's intricate flowchart on the other side. When Arkady gasped, he just smiled and gave him a conspiratorial wink. "I didn't get it from Gavi, for what it's worth. I wish the fools and bigots who think he works for me were right. When it comes to navigating the wilderness of mirrors, Gavi's the best there ever was. On the other hand . . . sometimes Gavi trips over his own brains. And in your case I have a niggling feeling that things may actually be *less* complicated than he's making them."

"I told Gavi everything," Arkady said, feeling suddenly tired and discouraged.

"Then tell me about Arkasha."

"There's nothing left to say."

"Not even if I told you that we might be willing to give him political asylum?"

"That's impossible."

"Why?"

"Because Korchow won't give him up now."

"You thought he might when you talked to Gavi last week. What's changed?"

Arkady looked stubbornly at the floor.

"Talk to me, Arkady. Something's eating at you. Something that wasn't even on your horizon when Gavi talked to you. What do you know now that you wish you didn't?"

Safik reached for his cigarettes, checked his watch, sighed deeply, and pushed them away again.

"I'm going to tell you something, Arkady." Safik stood up and came around the desk to sit in the empty chair beside him. "Something I've never told anyone but my wife before. Not because it's necessarily shameful—at least not any more shameful than a lot of other things I've done for my country. But if you get to be my age you'll see that only a fool or a fanatic can spend much time in our line of work and not begin to . . . well . . . doubt. Worse, if you're anything approaching a thinking person, you even begin to doubt your doubts. Are you really still working toward the great and good ends you used to believe in, or are your doubts merely a sort of mental washing of hands? A subtle kind of self-deception that lets you hold your nose and do dirty work while feeling all the while that what you do isn't really you, that you're better than that, more perceptive than that, more moral than that."

When Arkady didn't answer, Safik sighed and went on.

"This happened to me when I was around your age, Arkady. This was before the doubts. I was still thin back then, believe it or not, and at least reasonably good-looking. Or so my wife tells me. Anyway, I'm making jokes about it because it's not a very happy story. What it comes down to is that a young settler attacked one of our patrols and I was put in charge of questioning his mother. The Israelis were quite co-operative, of course. It was before the war, and that sort of freelancing is in no one's interest."

Safik's manner had changed subtly, Arkady realized. He was casting little glances at Arkady at the end of every sentence, as if it was terribly important to make sure that Arkady understood every word he spoke. And there was a banked, smoldering fire behind the ordinary face that made Arkady see this was a man who was not controllable. By anybody.

"So anyway," Safik went on, "here was this woman who had just lost her only son. And I—some young idiot who'd never been married, never had a child, knew nothing about anything—was supposed to question her. Naturally it was all the most offensively officious kind of nonsense. Who were her son's friends? Who had given him the weapon? What had he said before he died? Why would he have done such a thing if he hadn't learned at his mother's knee to hate us? And on and on. Hopeless, of course. She didn't have any real information, and wouldn't have given it to me if she had. But she was more than happy to talk to me. She knew the clichés by heart, Arkady, and I heard them all that morning. Her son was a hero. He was fulfilling God's mandate for the Holy Land. She'd achieved the highest purpose of a woman's life by giving birth to a soldier. And on and on and on. But all the while she was making her patriotic speeches she was weeping. She was wracked with sobs every time she paused for breath. I have never seen someone weep so violently and still be able to force intelligible words out of her mouth.

"It was as if there were two women in her body, Arkady. An outer woman who had the power of speech, who belonged to the state, to civilization, to what you might call the superorganism. And an inner woman, who belonged to no government, and who knew damn well that all those patriotic words were dust next to her son's dead body."

Safik stopped. He was slumped in his chair, and he looked gray and ill and terribly angry. Arkady had the impression that he'd stopped talking not because he had run out of words but because he had lost faith that Arkady would understand him.

"So . . ."

"So what's my point? I am telling you who I am, Arkady. I serve what I saw in that woman's eyes. That every time you sacrifice the individual in the name of order and stability you're only throwing fresh meat to the dogs of war. That martyrdom—be it the martyrdom of the soldier or the martyrdom of the suicide bomber—is a poor substitute for decent government. That's what I serve, Arkady. And I don't give a damn about the fanatics who only see lines on the map." He smiled briefly and made that chin-flicking skyward gesture that Earth dwellers always made when they wanted to talk about the larger world that had left their planet behind. "Or lines out in space for that matter."

"And what about Absalom?"

"Absalom's an idea, not a man. And he won't die as long as there are people on both sides of the Line who think like I do."

They locked eyes.

Safik sighed and glanced away.

"Fine," he said. "You have no reason to believe me. But I'll tell you one thing, Arkady. I'm not your enemy. I'm not sure I'm anyone's enemy. Just think about it. That's all I'm asking."

But Arkady didn't have to think about it. He trusted Safik. He knew he was playing the easy mark, just like he'd done with Gavi. He knew that any step he took might be the one that made a choice between protecting the Syndicates and saving Arkasha inevitable. But when he looked into Safik's calm, decent, ordinary face and asked himself for some reason he shouldn't trust him, he couldn't find one.

So he told him everything, right up to that awful moment of revelation in front of Gavi's flowchart.

"If that's true," Safik said when Arkady had finished, "then we're all in the same boat, aren't we, Earth and Syndicates alike?"

"No, we're not!" Arkady burst out.

He never knew, then or later, whether Safik had planned it; but suddenly all the thoughts he'd kept to himself over the past weeks were spilling out of him, giving voice to his pent-up frustration at the intransigent human refusal to understand the Syndicates, to understand life beyond the Orbital Ring, to *understand* period.

"How can you people still be so ignorant?" he shouted. Then he realized he was shouting, caught his breath, and went on more quietly. "How can you know so little even after centuries of sending ships and settlers out to die in space? How can you still understand *nothing* about what it's like out there?"

"So make me understand. I want to understand, Arkady. If you can't make me understand, you'll never make any human understand."

"You can't understand," Arkady said bitterly. He remembered again the terrible fire of ZhangSyndicate's death throes. For the first time he realized that there had been *men* in those attacking ships. Men bred and trained in the Ring, where Earth was always one short rescue launch away, and the universe was still friendly and forgiving and crowded enough that a man could take it upon himself to loose a missile and destroy an orbital station that was all the wide world to its little ark of souls. "You hear the words. You nod and smile . . . and then five minutes later you say something that proves you haven't understood a syllable. Earth itself keeps you from understanding. Even the Ring-siders still have Earth to fall back on if things go really wrong. You can afford to be selfish, inefficient, individualistic because Earth is big and rich and for-giving. You can afford to act like spoiled children because Earth will al-ways bail you out. And even then you managed to turn getting to space into a race against extinction. How many billions of lives were thrown away on the generation ships? Humans make their sacrifices too. Despite all their brave words about rights and individuals. The collected quotient of individual misery and wastage and suffering in human so-ciety makes the Syndicates look like the ultimate humanists."

"So it's all just politics?" Safik interjected. He sounded gently disap-pointed by the idea.

"Politics! Reality. A reality you humans can't see because you're too busy telling each other fairy tales. I never understood before I came here why the UN got so taken by surprise when so many people around the Periphery sided with the Syndicates in the war, but now I finally get it. You actually think they're still *human*. You think if you just wipe the Syndicates, your problems will vanish and you'll step into the future you always wanted to have. But that future died with Earth. The only future left now is the one you made when you put Earth's poor on the generation ships and threw them overboard to live or die. Well, *we lived*. And now you're trying to stop evolution in its tracks because we aren't the future you wanted to have."

Arkady finished his speech and wound down into depressed and embarrassed silence.

"You don't sound like a traitor," Safik said at last. "You sound to me like a man who wants to go home."

"Home isn't perfect either," Arkady whispered.

"Neither is my wife, but I still go home every night. Don't you think Korchow has figured this out?" Somehow Safik managed to sound matter-of-fact and sympathetic in the same instant. "Don't you think he knows enough of . . . well, I suppose I shouldn't call it human nature . . . to have predicted you might feel this way?"

"You don't think I've asked myself that again and again?" Arkady said bitterly. "I feel like a lab rat!"

Safik smiled. His gaze left Arkady's for just long enough to light an-other long-awaited cigarette. "You seem to be focusing only on the negative aspects of being a lab rat. The up side of having someone like Korchow use you is that there usually is a real piece of cheese at the end of the maze. Hasn't it ever occurred to you that Korchow might *want* to send Arkasha to Earth? The Embargo's going to go up in smoke the minute people begin to really see what the Novalis virus has done. We're going to be playing a vicious game of catch-up. And we're going to be in desperate need of people like Arkasha. Maybe Korchow's preparing the ground for a little . . . er, *intellectual* terraforming?"

Arkady tried to look impassive and undecided, but his mind had already gone into a tailspin of calculations, hopes, dreams, anticipation.

"I don't want to rush you into anything," Safik said. "Least of all anything Korchow's trying to rush me into rushing you into. Go back to Moshe. Think about it. I'm sure we'll have another chance to talk. That is as long as you don't say anything that would make your keepers wonder just who you've been talking to over here."

And if that wasn't a way of buying his silence, Arkady wondered, then what was?

MET AND EMET

All art is born of science, just as all science has its origins in magic. Though it is hard to say exactly when AI design made the leap from science to art, two names are inextricably linked to the event: Hyacinthe Cohen and Gavi Shehadeh. Whatever you think of Gavi's golem, its status as a watershed moment in the history of AI—and the history of Israel—is incontestable.

—YOSHIKI KURAMOTO TN 283854–0089. *IS THE MOON THERE WHEN NOBODY LOOKS? MY IMAGINARY LIFE IN MATHEMATICS.* NEW DELHI UNIVERSITY PRESS. INDIA ARC: 2542.

GAVI SHEHADEH WAS SO UNIVERSALLY hated by the time he lost his leg that at first no one on either side of the Line could bring themselves to believe it wasn't a richly deserved assassination attempt. The facts—the *Shabbas* visit to the one faction of his Jewish family that was still speaking to him, the impromptu soccer game, the lost ball, and the bloody carnage in the weeds—came out with such excruciating slowness that Gavi was up and walking before most of his old friends and new enemies could bring themselves to admit that he'd been crippled by a perfectly ordinary land mine.

He was on administrative leave over the Absalom affair when it happened, and within a few months he found himself with a new ceramic compound leg courtesy of Hadassah Hospital's special amputees unit and a growing realization that his career had died in Tel Aviv.

Yad Vashem had seemed like an escape when Didi first suggested it. Only when he reported to IDF headquarters for the mandatory sperm and blood samples did he realize he'd accepted what amounted, in most people's minds, to a slow death sentence. No matter, he'd told himself. His exile would be over in a few months, a year at most.

But by now it had lasted almost four years.

He wasn't sure just when Gavi the traitor had begun to feel more real to him than the man he'd always thought he was. But there were external signs by which he could measure the rate at which his new identity cannibalized his old one. Before his second summer in Yad Vashem he'd stopped writing letters and calling on his former colleagues in hope of a new position. Then his visits to Tel Aviv and Jerusalem, always sporadic, had stopped entirely. And sometime in the third year of his live burial he'd admitted to himself that if his former enemies knew how he felt every time he had to leave the thickness of the Line, they would spirit him straight back to the eighth floor out of sheer spite.

GOLEM had grown out of the routine work of file maintenance that took up so much of Gavi's time in the first years at Yad Vashem. The number of survivors' testimonies—the sheer mass of information—contained in the Yad Vashem archives was inconceivable. Those testimonies were the heart of Yad Vashem, the true Monument of the Eternal Name, and one like no other humankind had ever constructed. But monuments of silicon were just as vulnerable to the forces of time and gravity as monuments of marble.

Time passed. Spins decayed. Disks and data cubes crumbled. Files that weren't recopied and saved on a regular basis lost the one-way battle against entropy. And just as in Europe's ancient shuls and monasteries, the only files that were recopied were the files people actually used. The Warsaw Ghetto files. The files concerning famous Zionists or writers or artists. But the rest—the men and women and children who had done nothing that History cared about, and had appeared in the testimonies only because they had been someone's father, someone's mother, someone's lost brother or sister or cousin—those people were slowly being wiped from human memory, just as their killers had meant them to be.

To Gavi the answer had seemed obvious. What was needed was a person. A person who would hold the obscure dead just as beloved as the famous dead. A person who would remember them because he would *be* them; just as Cohen, or at least some buried part of him, *was* Hyacinthe; just as Rabbi Loew's golem had *been* in some mystical sense the lives and history and souls of the people of the Prague ghetto brought to life.

But there would be nothing mystical about this golem, unless you counted the mystery of how sentience emerged from the swarming maelstrom of data inside an Emergent's networks. Gavi knew the name of the magic that could bring his golem to life; he had poured over the specs and wiring diagrams and bug reports. It was not the cold clay of Prague he needed, but the cold spin lattices of Cohen's neural networks.

Of course there were other AIs who had the processing power to handle the job. But none of them was as peculiarly human as Cohen was. None of their personality architectures had been so stable for so long. And none of them was as intimately tied to Israel and to Gavi himself.

Cohen could do it. He could breathe a soul into the archives, and turn dead testimony back into living memory . . . though with what violence to his own identity no human could begin to guess.

And he would do it, whatever the risk, if Gavi asked him to.

It was precisely that certainty that had kept Gavi from asking.

Gavi caught sight of the tail just as he turned onto King David Street to begin the final approach to Cohen's hotel. The kid was clearly trying to avoid looking at him: the classic amateur's gaffe.

Gavi loitered in front of the window of a spintronics store, inspecting the merchandise with minute attention, feeling the rhythm of the crowd as it flowed behind him, listening to the monotonous drone of the crosswalk signals. Then he dashed across the street at the last minute before the light changed, only to loiter again on the far corner waiting for the next light, scanning the crowd all the while for the telltale signs of averted eyes or sudden changes of direction. Then he apparently changed his mind, walked back to the store, went inside, and spent nearly ten minutes haggling over the price of a mobile uplink and left without buying anything. He sauntered down the street for several more blocks, assiduously window-shopping, and repeated the performance at a second store.

In the end he decided that there was only a single team of watchers: a couple, boy and girl, playing well out in front of him, and to the rear a clean-cut young man who looked like his great-great-great-grandparents might have arrived in the Ethiopian airlift. They were kids, diligent but raw.

He thought wistfully of Osnat, who wouldn't have made such basic mistakes on her first day of training. Then he told himself he couldn't afford to think of Osnat when he was about to put himself under Cohen's sharp eyes.

Over the course of the next twenty minutes, the team worked their plodding way through every classic amateur mistake, and threw in a few new variations for good measure. The teacher in him wanted to walk over, grab them by the collars, and make them do it again, right. But he wasn't a teacher now. He was a target. A target without backup or a safe house or any of the usual safety nets. And it didn't take a professional to put a bullet through your skull. He'd learned that in Tel Aviv, even if he hadn't learned anything else of any earthly use to anyone.

He worked his way up King David Street and over to City Tower, where he browsed at the jewelry counters, circled back to the entrance, then turned back at the last moment as if he'd suddenly remembered something he needed. Finally he backtracked to men's clothing, where he tried on a series of unforgivably loud shirts.

The tail was still there the third time he came out of the dressing room, looking implausibly interested in the new sock selection.

"You're new, aren't you?" Gavi said.

The poor kid looked like he'd gotten caught passing notes in class.

"What do you think of the shirt? That bad, huh? How's Didi, by the way?"

"I, uh . . . think you're mistaking me for someone else."

Gavi stared into the blue eyes until they dropped away from his. "No. You're mistaking me for someone else. An idiot. Now why don't you take your two little friends and trot back to the Office and tell Didi that if he wants to know where I'm going, he can damn well ask me."

The next time he came out of the dressing room the boy was gone. But he bought a white button-down shirt, just to be on the safe side, and changed into it, carefully folding away his old LIE[4] T-shirt into the bag the salesgirl gave him. He left the store among a crowd of tourists and threw the bag in the nearest trash bin—regretfully, since he'd always liked that T-shirt. Then he skirted around an IDF safe house that he thought might still be active, checked one last time to make sure his babysitters really had gone home, and finally turned toward King David Street.

Cohen was alone.

"How's your leg?" he asked, ushering Gavi into a hotel suite that would have had his mother screaming about runaway capitalism and the death of the kibbutznik mentality.

"Uh. Fine," Gavi said. He was always caught off-balance by questions about it—wrong-footed he would have said if he hadn't learned that other people didn't find jokes about his leg quite as hysterically funny as he did.

People always talked about phantom pain, but Gavi had never felt it. What he felt those days was mostly . . . *weirdness*. The wrenching visual shock of looking down every now and then and realizing that he ended four inches below his right knee . . . and that he'd forgotten about it. Or, lately, bemused moments of looking down at his actual flesh-and-blood foot and feeling that the whole idea of it (a foot? toes? *toenails?*) was so much less natural and sensible than nice clean ceram-steel that the continuing existence of feet in general could only be evidence of some collective human neurosis.

"You don't want to put it up? No? Well, can I at least get you something to drink?"

"Fine on all counts." He peered at Cohen, who seemed even more opaquely unreadable than usual. "Are you all right? You're doing that freezing thing again."

"It's nothing."

A nothing named Catherine Li, if Gavi guessed right.

"So tell me about this golem of yours," Cohen said. "I need a little comedy in my life."

Gavi told him, walking him through the pieces of code he'd painfully stitched together over the past several years, explaining the places where he couldn't make things work, or couldn't decide which of several possible imperfect solutions to settle for. He presented it as a programming problem, one that he was submitting to higher authority. Which was perfectly valid, since Cohen's abilities in that area would put any human to shame. He didn't mention what the AI must have seen the minute he began looking at the source code: that the glue that would tie it all together and make the impossible, jerry-built kludge of databases and interfaces work was Cohen.

"You know how crazy this is, don't you?" Cohen said at last. On the surface he was only pointing out a technical problem, but both of them saw the attached moral problem: How could an AI designer create a sentient being only to sentence it to a life dominated by memories that had driven so many humans to despair and suicide? The goal might be idealistically selfless, but for the newborn Emergent trying to come to terms with those memories the reality would be every bit as brutal as what EMET faced on the Green Line.

"Always so encouraging!" Gavi said, choosing to dodge the nontechnical question. "Don't you know when your kid brings his little crayon scribbles home from school you're supposed to hang them on the refrigerator, not give him an art history lesson?"

"I've never had kids. Strange, isn't it? Well, I guess not that strange. The people who marry me aren't exactly the settle down and have three point two children type." He looked at the source code again. "Actually, Gavi, I don't think it's all that far from working. Which should be encouraging, considering the fact that it must be three centuries since an unaugmented human actually tried to write nontrivial source code. Where did you even find the SCHEME manuals?"

"The dump."

"Seriously?"

"Seriously."

"Well, that explains the smell, I guess."

They talked around the problem for a few minutes, skimming over Gavi's various false starts, and what he'd learned from them, and the current state of his work on what Cohen was now jokingly calling Gavi's Golem.

"Can I ask you something?" Gavi said finally. "About your visit last week, not this."

"Sure."

"What's ALEF after? What's your endgame?"

"Mine personally, or ALEF's?"

"Both. Either."

"ALEF's actually interested in the tech, insofar as they're ever interested in anything in any organized fashion."

"And you?"

The AI sighed. He'd never gotten sighing quite right, Gavi thought. Even his most sincere sighs rang false. Funny how a little thing like that could elude the best wetware. Or maybe the wet wasn't where the problem was. "I'm after Absalom."

"I'm sorry to hear that, Cohen. I'm very sorry that Didi's dragged you into this."

"And what about you, Gavi? What's your endgame? Why are you still here when there's a whole universe up there that doesn't know you're a traitor to Israel? You could probably even get a real leg if you went Ring-side."

"Not anymore. They would have had to ship me Ring-side within the first seventy-two hours in order for viral surgery to be any good. And anyway, I wouldn't have been able to bring my new leg home, would I?"

"That's my point, in case you missed it."

"I spent six months Ring-side." Gavi wrinkled his nose, remembering the curved, antiseptic, artificially bright expanses of plastic that Ring-siders called "outdoors." "You can take the boy out of the country, but . . ."

"Well, there are always other planets if you don't like life in the orbitals."

"Other planets smell funny."

It was a joke, at least partly. But Cohen gave no evidence of realizing that. In fact, he'd fallen oddly silent. And when Gavi looked up, the AI was staring intently at him.

"Are you still looking for Joseph?" Cohen asked.

"Of course I am. But it's not the same now. When he was seven, eight, ten, I was desperate to find him. Now he'd be a young man, if he . . . well, I just have this nagging feeling that maybe I would be finding him for me now, not for him. And while that doesn't make me want to find him any less, it does make it less urgent somehow."

"Is Didi still helping you look?"

Gavi looked up to find Roland's soft hazel eyes fixed on him. Talking to Cohen always brought home to him how much he, like all humans, confused the mind with the body. He knew as a technical and intellectual matter that only young and superbly healthy bodies could stand up to the stress of what any programmer would recognize as a biological version of overclocking. But he still couldn't repress the shiver that ran through him when he looked into some shunt's wide young eyes and saw the face of the swarm. And he was still eternally surprised that Cohen could take the same five feeble senses most humans got by on and damn near read your mind with them.

"If you want to know what Didi's doing or not doing," Gavi said, "you'd better ask Didi."

Cohen appeared to accept this answer. "The thing is," the AI said, "somehow I can't help thinking that maybe your obsession with preserving the archives is just a little bit about Leila and Joseph."

"Sometimes a cigar is just a cigar, Cohen."

"Oh for God's sake! Are humans still quoting Freud at each other? Grow up, will you?"

But Gavi wasn't in the mood for jokes. "Have you ever read any of the testimonies, Cohen?"

"I've read enough to know I don't want to read any more."

"It's a funny thing, those testimonies. You start to get numb after a while, from the sheer numbers, from the awfulness of it all. And then there'll be one that gets under your skin and makes it all real again. There was one guy who went into Theresienstadt with his entire family: mother, father, two brothers. The whole family got sequential numbers. The boy's father was number something something something five hundred and twenty. He was five hundred and twenty-one, the next brother was five hundred and twenty-two, the next brother was five hundred and twenty-three. But his mother was pregnant, so they pulled her out of the line and sent her straight to the gas chamber without even giving her a number.

The oldest son is the only one who survives. He goes to America. He makes a life for himself, a good life. But as he gets to be around the age his parents were when they died, he starts to have nightmares about his mother. He becomes obsessed by the fact that the Germans didn't give her a number, that there's no record of her death, no proof. It's not that he thinks she's alive, you understand. He saw her get sent into the nonworkers line, and he doesn't have any illusions about what that meant. But he can't process the idea that she just . . . vanished.

So he saves up his money. He goes back to Poland. He advertises in the newspapers, literally for years, offering a reward to anyone who can give him a photograph of his mother, anyone who even remembers his mother. No one ever answers. This woman had grown up, gone to university, taught grade school, been a daughter and a wife and a mother. But it was like she'd never existed. The Germans had simply wiped her from the face of history.

"That's what's happening to the testimonies, Cohen. When I took over, we'd already lost four hundred thousand files irretrievably. The rest are going. It's only a matter of time. I want to save them. Not just for now. Forever."

He looked up to find Cohen staring at him.

"I know. I know you think it's a waste of my time. But, Cohen, I'm the first caretaker who's had the expertise to actually fix it instead of sending endless unanswered spinmail to the Knesset budget office asking for funding that never quite arrives. If I don't do it, who will?"

Cohen just kept looking at him, utterly still. "I know what you're asking me to do," he said finally. "And I know what I owe you."

Gavi sliced his hand through the air abruptly. "You don't owe me anything. If I hadn't been afraid you'd say just that, I would have asked you for help far sooner. Hell, maybe I would even have answered your spinmails!"

"Oh." Cohen grinned. *"Now* you tell me."

"Cohen—"

"I know, I know."

"—if you can't say no, then how can I ever ask you for anything?"

"Harrumph. If I didn't know better, I'd think you and Catherine and router/decomposer were all talking about me behind my back. By the way, Gavi, have you noticed that you practically went into orbit last week at the suggestion that I might lift a finger to help revive your career and now you're cheerfully asking me to risk decoherence in order to help you with some quixotic scheme that no one else will take on for love or money?"

"What's your point, little AI?"

"Nothing. Just thought I'd mention it. Sometimes you remind me the tiniest little bit of Leila."

Gavi smiled—but his smile faded as he realized that he had heard her name on Cohen's lips without feeling the old familiar pang of grief. "I wish I could remember her like you remember her," he whispered, not trusting his voice well enough to speak out loud.

"Maybe not," Cohen said. "There are folktales about ghosts who can't rest until their loved ones stop mourning them. Maybe the dead are meant to fade, Gavi. Maybe the living are meant to forget."

I N COHEN'S DREAM, GAVI HAD his leg back. He stood on tiptoe because Cohen had become very tall in the dream, a mute giant of mud and clay.

Your job is done, Gavi said.

As he spoke the words Li was there, calm and clear-eyed, with Didi standing at her side.

Time to forget, they told him.

And then Li put her hands to his face, and gently, so gently, wiped the first letter of the name of truth from his forehead. . . .

"I've made a life decision," router/decomposer announced. "May I tell you about it?"

He was leaving, Cohen decided. What else could it be? And what could his departure mean but hassle and fuss, interviews and arguments, and the inevitable bad feelings that always led to further departures? Everything was falling apart, everyone was leaving him, it was all his fault, and there wasn't a damn thing he could do about it.

"Of course you can tell me," he said with the internal equivalent of a forced smile.

"I'm going to change my name."

"Great! I mean . . . er, to what?"

"Kuramoto."

"As in Yoshiki?"

"Correct."

Yoshiki Kuramoto. The boldly intuitive twentieth-century mathematician who had taken the first real stab at formalizing the emergence of spontaneous synchrony in certain types of complex and mathematically intractable systems, including router/decomposer's Josephson Arrays and spin glass matrices. If router/decomposer was going to borrow someone else's name, then Kuramoto's was a logical, even an elegant choice.

"Why Kuramoto?"

"It's an aspiration designation," router/decomposer, now Kuramoto, announced with an ironic flourish that ill concealed his seriousness. "It indicates not what I am but what I aspire to become. And, uhhhh . . . I'm also quitting. Caltech just offered me a tenure track position in applied mathematics. Sorry I didn't tell you sooner. What can I say? Things have been crazy."

"Well," Cohen said. "Caltech. That's quite something. Have they ever hired an AI before?"

"I would seem to be the first."

"Well, great. Wonderful."

"It's irrelevant, of course . . . but somehow I keep returning to the idea that I'd be . . . uh, *happier,* whatever that means, if you supported this decision."

"I do. Wholeheartedly. Congratulations."

"Do you mean that? Your affective fuzzy set for this exchange is very difficult to parse."

"You're telling me."

"But you *are* happy?"

"I'm happy for you."

Kuramoto chewed on that for a near eternity by AI standards. "Being happy for someone else sounds like a less desirable state than actually *being* happy," he said finally.

"Let's just say it's an acquired taste."

And then—as soon as he was what passed for alone—he dropped his head into his hands and laughed until the tears sprang to Roland's eyes.

"Where are you going, Catherine?"

"Out."

"Out to see Ash?"

"You're behaving badly, Cohen. Stop it. And for what it's worth I'm not sleeping with her." Li rubbed the back of one hand across her nose. "Frankly, I'm too allergic to this hellhole of a planet to even think about sex."

"Why don't we sit down and talk about whatever it is that's bothering you?"

"Since nothing's bothering me, it would be a short conversation."

"You're leaving, aren't you?"

"Didn't I just say I was?"

"I don't mean right now. If you'd only talk to me . . ."

She softened, in one of those abrupt changes of mood that always threw Cohen off-balance. "You can't help, Cohen. I know you mean well, but . . . you can't."

"So that's it?" Cohen said. "No discussion? No questions? Just good-bye Cohen and have a nice life?"

He sat down on the bed and crossed his arms over his chest and stared at the floor. He knew he was being childish, but he couldn't help it. And why should he help it, anyway? It wasn't as if Li was exactly being mature about things. To make matters worse, he could feel across the quiescent intraface that she knew exactly what he was feeling. The memory of their last breakup, with all its attendant humiliation and frustration. The fearful certainty that her departure would open the door to all the old, tired, nasty ghosts that had haunted him before her arrival. The panic at the prospect of losing her for good—a panic that was sharpened rather than blunted by the crippling suspicion that it wasn't real love, but merely his feedback loops going into emotive overdrive at the prospect of losing an inscribed player. Router/decomposer would say that motives didn't matter, only actions. But this motive *did* matter. . . .

"I hope you'll do me the courtesy of giving me some kind of reasonable notice before you quit," he said. Was his voice actually *trembling*? Impossible. But apparently true.

"I wasn't aware I was an employee," Li said coldly. "But I'll get you safely back Ring-side. Glad we got that clear."

She left, closing the door behind her with a deliberate precision that made Cohen certain she wanted to slam it. He walked across to the window and stood there, one of Roland's fine-fingered hands splayed on the glass, until he saw her walk out the front door of the hotel and turn down the street toward the Old City. He felt sick. He felt like he was dying. He could feel Roland's heart pounding in his chest like a wounded bird. Who knew how many years Cohen's conflicts were taking off the boy's life? He hadn't been so out of control since DARPA. And he'd been a hell of a lot smaller and weaker back then.

He slipped into the hotel's network almost without thinking and shut down its power grid for just long enough to see the lights brown and dim overhead. That didn't make him feel any better, though, so he bit into the citywide power grid and gave it an experimental squeeze. The results were gratifyingly spectacular. A black wave rippled across the skyline, lights dimming and winking out, the noises of the nighttime city giving way to stunned silence. A murmur rose from the adjacent rooms as his fellow guests chattered excitedly and stepped to their windows. And best of all, he caught a glimpse of Li on a storefront security camera a few blocks away, glancing fearfully over her shoulder into the deepening darkness.

For Christ's sake, she snapped across the intraface. *There are hospitals around here, Cohen. Get a grip on yourself.*

In retrospect, he would decide it was the note of disdain in her voice that had really driven him over the edge. An icy wave of fury welled up from the hidden layers of his networks, and in an instant too fast for thought or doubt, he swept it all together, let it cascade down through his systems, gaining power and momentum like an avalanche roaring down a mountainside, and flung the whole lethal storm of data downstream.

He stopped short of actually letting it reach her. And even if he hadn't, her safety override would have seen it coming and activated her cutouts. But none of that made it all right.

Catherine? he probed. But he was whistling into the wind. The other side of the link was down. And something told him it wouldn't be coming back up again anytime soon.

He was pulled back to real time by a warm, tickling sensation that turned out to be blood streaming down Roland's arm. He held up his hand and saw that the palm and wrist were crisscrossed by several vicious and alarmingly deep cuts. The floor beneath his feet glittered with broken glass, and the windowpane in front of him had been reduced to a lethal jigsaw puzzle.

The alarm had gone off when the window broke, of course, so he didn't have to call anyone. Just stand there holding his wrist and watching poor Roland's blood puddle on the floor until hotel security arrived to clean up his mess for him.

'M SORRY," ARKADY SAID. "IT'S difficult for me to tell humans apart. Perhaps if you showed me a photograph . . . ?"

"If I showed you a photograph, then how would I know you weren't just telling me what you thought I wanted to hear?"

Moshe had been all over Arkady since his return from the other side of the Line. Osnat was nowhere in sight. But behind him, her white suit glimmering in the shadows, her coldly beautiful face just visible at the edge of the lamplight, sat Ashwarya Sofaer.

Moshe stepped out of the room and returned with half a dozen pieces of paper. He fanned them out on the table like playing cards. Head shots. Old ID photos of men in uniform, none of them much above twenty.

"No," Arkady said with relief. "None of these men are him. I'm sure of it."

But then he saw it. The fourth photograph from the left. The face was thinner and firmer, but the calm brown gaze was the same one that had made him give up his soul and his secrets to Safik.

He looked up to find Moshe's glasses glittering at him. The mouth beneath the lenses was intent and unsmiling and deadly serious.

And then back to his cell, and back to the waiting.

Osnat was nowhere. Was she gone? Had she been found out? Had she betrayed him to Moshe?

But no. She came in with his dinner. And before he could quite adjust to the idea of her actually being there, she was talking quick and low, telling him to shut up and listen when he tried to interrupt her because there wasn't time for questions.

"At 1:52 A.M. the lights'll go out. When they do, count to ten. Then go. Your door will be open. Turn left, count three doors down on your right hand, and take the third left turn—that door should be open too. It takes you into a corridor. Follow it straight ahead and take the fifth right. Go straight ahead through two fire doors, then up half a flight of stairs, and you're outside. There's no moon tonight. You'll have decent cover. But move fast anyway. Your ride out of here will be waiting just past the wire."

"Osnat—"

"Remember. Left three, left five, right and up the stairs. Don't waste time and don't even think about getting lost. If you get yourself caught, there's not a thing on God's green Earth I can do for you."

Arkady woke to the feeling of rough hands on his body. For a split second he thrashed against the pressure. Then someone's knee slammed into the small of his back, and when he regained his bearings he was on the floor, face pressed into the concrete, with one guard sitting on him and another's boot planted solidly on the nape of his neck.

A few painful breathless minutes later he was sitting on the floor of a locked and empty cell staring at an ominously disheveled-looking Osnat.

"What happened?" he asked as soon as they were alone.

"Someone sold us out. Obviously."

Arkady's eyes flew to the room's corners.

"There's no surveillance here. If there was, I'd know about it. Though I could be wrong about that." She laughed bitterly. "I've been wrong about a lot, it seems."

"What happens now?"

"I don't know. But whatever it is I'll handle it better after I get some sleep. So stop asking me questions, will you?" She rolled over on her side and pillowed her head on her bunched-up shirt. "And don't look at me," she added, giving him one last baleful stare over her shoulder. "I fucking hate it when people watch me while I'm sleeping."

In the end they did leave in a helicopter . . . though Arkady seriously doubted it was the one Osnat had hoped they'd be catching. It touched down just before sunset, a bright corporate bird of paradise in the GolaniTech colors, piloted by two hard-faced ex-Sayeret something-or-others. If they recognized the former Captain Hoffman, they weren't showing her any love.

"Buckle up," Osnat told Arkady over the rotor noise. "Tight."

Arkady never really understood what happened next. Were they shot at by someone on the ground? Was it a missile? An RPG? A simply mechanical failure? All he heard was a sharp pop somewhere out in the wind about ten minutes after takeoff.

The chopper jerked sideways, walloped by its own rotor wash, Arkady's head slammed against the bulletproofed window with a sickening crack, and time took on a stretched surreal quality.

They hit the ground nose first and sideways, sliding through the final feet of their descent with deceptive, almost casual slowness. There was a first jolt, and then a second. And then came the wrenching, shrieking, screeching settling as the rotors began driving them into the ground and tearing the fragile craft apart.

The air stank of fuel and coolant. A lurid light shone in through the window by Arkady's head. In his dazed confusion he took it for the familiar white flash of the orbital sunsets he'd known all his childhood. Then he saw sparks and realized it was the rotors scraping fire off bare rock.

He looked forward, trying to see why the pilot hadn't shut off the turbines . . . and one look was enough to tell him that the pilot was dead. Beside him Osnat had somehow gotten her hands free and was struggling out of her harness. But too late, too late.

Then, suddenly, miraculously, the copilot roused himself and reached out a hand and switched the power off. The machine heaved a final horrible shudder and died. In the stunned silence that followed, Arkady heard a cricket singing in a nearby tree and the soft hiss of a leaking feedline.

"My legs are broken," the copilot said in a blurred voice.

"Looks like it." Osnat was bending over him, not to help but to remove his sidearm from its holster and thrust it into her belt where the deep groove of her spine ran down between her back muscles. She reached across the gearbox to the butchered remains of the pilot's body and took his weapon too. Then she began patting the copilot down, transferring the contents of his pockets into hers.

The copilot said something to Osnat in Hebrew too quick for Arkady to follow. He must have hit his head as well as breaking his legs; he was delirious.

She came aft without answering the man and stooped over Arkady.

"Can you walk?" she asked.

"I think so."

"Good. See that stand of junipers? No, not that one. Farther back, up at the crest of that hill. You're going to walk to it. Don't try to run, but don't turn around or stop either. And don't come back down here, no matter what you hear or see or think you hear or see." She undid Arkady's bonds. His hands were trembling, he noticed distantly. Hers weren't. "I don't need to be worrying about where you are on top of everything else I have to worry about."

Then he spent almost forty-five minutes sitting under the junipers with no view at all of what was happening below, feeling guilty and terrified. Finally he heard the crack of gunfire, and moments later the whoosh and suck of a fierce explosion.

Osnat walked out of the inferno alone, and holding something in her hands.

"You didn't get the copilot out?" he asked. Then he saw what was in her hands.

She emptied the chamber and slapped the ammunition clip out with practiced hands. Then she stowed the gun in its holster and strapped the holster onto her body. She had to adjust the holster's fittings several times; they'd been sized to a man's broad shoulders. At the sight of her hands on the buckles, Arkady remembered the copilot's last muttered words and felt his gorge rise.

When she'd adjusted the holster to her satisfaction, Osnat looked at Arkady. There was an odd blank look in her usually sharp eyes; the mechanism was clicking along as smoothly and efficiently as always, but there was nobody at the wheel.

Osnat had pulled other things out of the wreck besides the sidearm and holster—though not, as she pointed out, enough things to raise the suspicion of survivors as long as the flames did their work. Still, they had water, food, and—what seemed far more important now that the cold fall night was pressing down upon the desert—a first-aid kit with its two silvery sleep sacks. She parceled out the supplies between the two of them, giving herself the lion's share and merely rolling her eyes at his weak protests.

"Okay," she said in a horribly normal voice. "Time to take a hike."

"What made the helicopter crash?" Arkady asked several hours later.

They were facing each other across a small fire that Osnat had lit only after a forced march that took them into the early hours of the morning, and only because Arkady had begun shivering uncontrollably with shock, cold, and exhaustion.

"To me," Osnat said in the hairsplitting tone of a connoisseur discussing a wine's bouquet, "it sounded like someone set a timed charge on the tail rotor."

"What kind of someone?"

"Well, I would have said Ash up to this point. You have to assume she was going to do something to break us out. But that was an awfully risky way to do it." Her good eye measured him briefly. "I wasn't going to say anything about it, and I don't want to freak you out, but it's pretty fucking unbelievable that we both walked out of that. Whoever set that charge was trying to get us out of GolaniTech's hands, but they weren't going to be crying on their pillow if we bought it in the process. I doubt Ash would have made that kind of call without it going up to the eighth floor. Maybe higher."

"But that would mean—"

"—that Didi has decided to cut his losses and pull the plug on the operation while the tape's still on the box."

Arkady squinted across the fire, trying to gauge Osnat's expression. The air rippled above the flames like running water, and the face beyond the scrim of the sparks was as unreadable as a text written in a dead language.

"What was it like growing up in the Syndicates?" Osnat asked suddenly.

"It was . . . happy. Until the war. A lot of things changed then." Suddenly Arkady found himself struggling to articulate something he'd felt often but never put words to. "Before the war we had a very idealistic society. Not perfect. But . . . honest, somehow. When the UN attacked us, everything went out the window except pure survival." He laughed softly. "And somehow 'survival' always seems to translate into the honest idealists being pushed aside and replaced by dishonest manipulators."

"It's the same for us," Osnat said, making the same connection Safik had made. "Human nature. And apparently not just human."

The bottom stick on the fire flared bright red, popped loudly, and crumpled into charcoal, setting the rest of the fire sliding and slithering and realigning itself above it. Beyond the firelight Arkady could hear the muted and furtive night sounds of the living desert.

"That woman who got pregnant, Arkady. Was your friend *sure* it was because of the fever?"

"As sure as you can be about work done in the field and under time pressure."

"What do you think it would do to humans? What . . . just as an example . . . what do you think it would do to me?"

Arkady stared across the fire at her, but the eyes looking back at him weren't Osnat's eyes; they were the eyes of a rabbit racing ahead of the fox's jaws. Arkady felt a guilty dread grip his chest and bear down on him. If Osnat could begin to covet the Novalis virus and the fertility that came with it, then what would the rest of her species do? How deep would the insanity run? And how brutal a price would Earth's people pay if their surging population pushed them into outright war with the Orbital Ring? For the first time, Arkady really understood the myriad effects that the virus would send rippling across Earth—as dramatic and irreversible as the effects of triggering a cascade reaction in a newly terraformed biosphere. How far would the ripples spread? Would they bring down the fragile spider's web that linked Earth to the dependent populations of her far-flung colonies?

How many deaths were going to be on his hands before it was over?

"The human immune system is so different from ours," he told her, skirting the question. "It might do nothing. Or it might kill you."

"That's assuming I can catch it from you." A log slithered to the ground in a shower of sparks. Arkady heard the blood thrumming in his ears, felt the curve of the planet falling away into darkness beneath him. "Can I?"

"You might already have caught it."

He spoke the words without having consciously decided to say them. Even as he watched comprehension spread across her face, he was far from certain that he'd done the right thing.

"Are you sure of this?" Osnat asked. The hunger was gone from her voice. She had gone back to being the hard-bitten and practical soldier. "What's your evidence?"

"No evidence. It just . . . everything fell into place so neatly as soon as I asked myself whether Korchow had sent me to sell the virus or to spread it."

"Have you told anyone else?"

He hesitated. "No."

She doubted. He could see that she doubted. But she looked aside and let it pass.

"This changes things," she said after a minute. "Didi needs to know about it."

"But how do we get to him?"

"Not through Ash. Anything that goes through Ash is going to have to cross too many desks before it hits Didi's. We need to go through someone who has a direct line to Didi and doesn't have to go through the normal channels."

"Gavi?"

"No!"

He thought wistfully of Safik. He dismissed the thought, knowing without having to ask what Osnat's reaction would be to the idea of putting their trust in PalSec. Then he remembered what Safik had said about Cohen going out of his way to protect his friends.

"What about Cohen?" he asked. "Does he have a direct line to Didi?"

"As direct as anyone's."

"Then let's go to Cohen. Directly. Not through Li. Let's ask the machine to help us."

It turned out, however, that it wasn't so easy to get the machine.

"He's not here," Li said when they finally succeeded in putting a call through. She said it in a tone that implied it was all the information they were entitled to.

"Well, when will he be back?"

"How should I know? Look, who is this? Why do you have the screen blanked?"

Osnat took a steadying breath, glanced at Arkady—more for support than permission—and switched on the visual feed.

"Oh," Li said, blinking. "Where are you? I'll come get you."

"I don't think—"

"I don't care what you think." She glanced sideways, her eyes focused on the middle distance. "Right. Gotcha. There's a bar two doors down from you. The Maracaibo. It has a back room. I just reserved it for a private party at seven. Meet me there at seven-twenty."

"What if we don't?"

"Then you can go back to whoever's chasing you and throw yourselves on their mercy. You think I care? It's not my fucking planet."

"I want to speak to Cohen."

"You *are* speaking to him."

And that was it. She was gone, signing off without so much as a good-bye or a by-your-leave.

"How did she know where we were?" Arkady breathed when the screen had fizzled through static into blackness.

"I don't know." Osnat bit her lip. "I'm out of my league, Arkady."

"Should we meet her?"

"I don't see what choice we have. But we can still take precautions. We don't need to walk in with our eyes closed and a kick-me sign stuck to our backs."

Arkady expected Osnat to investigate the bar when Li hung up, but instead she led him down the block to a quiet residential building. They reached the door just as a middle-aged man was leaving, and Osnat slipped in on a smile and an apology. Arkady clung to her heels all the way up the stairs and through a fire door onto a moonlit roof that had a clear view of the bar's entrance. There he waited for almost forty minutes while Osnat prowled along the neighboring rooftops and poked and prodded at doors and windows.

"Jerusalem's amazing this way," she told Arkady. "You can travel halfway across the city on the rooftops. Get practically anywhere. I'm betting Li won't know about that. Or at least that it won't be the first thing she thinks about."

When she'd completed her survey of the local roofways, she led Arkady back down onto the street and into the Maracaibo. She strode over to the bar, Arkady in tow, and stood on her toes to tap the bartender on the shoulder.

The man turned around, quick and wary. "What do you want?" he asked when he'd satisfied himself that she didn't mean trouble.

"I want you to look at me."

"I'm looking. I'm not too impressed."

"No skin off my nose. Now look at my friend."

"I looked at him when you walked in the door, lady. He's bad business. And you're bad business as long as you're with him."

"Think you could describe us if someone asked?"

"Depends who asks."

"That's just what I was hoping. This place have a back door?"

"Past the toilets. Which are for paying customers only even when they're not broken."

"What about a back room?"

"It's reserved."

"I know it. And I'm willing to pay double whatever they paid if you'll promise to tell the guys who are about to come in here looking for us that we're already back there."

"And will you be?"

"How much would I have to pay for you not to care?"

Ten minutes and seventeen hundred shekels later they were across the street, on their rooftop.

Arkady started to ask Osnat how long she planned to wait, but she put a hand on his shoulder and shook her head.

He looked down, following her gaze, and saw two men emerge from the shadows.

He could feel his palms sweating in the dank air. His left ankle was twisted awkwardly beneath him, but he was afraid to move, afraid of the telltale rasp of fabric or the scrape of a shoe sole against concrete. A thick fog hung over the city, blowing on a stiff westerly wind so that it split around building fronts and streamed in coarse white threads down the narrow streets. The two men stood just under them, looking across the wet pavement at the bar's brightly lit windows. They seemed to be talking, but they were too far below the rooftop for even Osnat to make sense of the scattered words of Hebrew that wafted up to their hiding place.

One of the men went into the Maracaibo, was gone for several minutes, then strolled out again. As he returned to his companion a third man joined them.

"Shalom." His voice carried alarmingly through the dank air. "They're there?"

"In the back room."

Arkady felt Osnat's body relax beside him. "It's okay," she whispered. "I know those guys. They're straight from Didi. We're safe, kiddo."

She stood up and started to pull Arkady up after her.

Arkady never felt the blast. He saw its phosphorus-blue flash. He heard a sound like the tearing of a thousand sheets of paper. For a long frozen moment the street lay silent below them, with the few passersby either knocked off their feet or crouching in terror. Then sound returned to the world, and the building began to disgorge a bloody, screaming, weeping stream of people onto the street that suddenly seemed too narrow to begin to contain all of them.

Osnat pulled him back from the roof's edge, and they were off, running down the moonlit tumble of rooftops toward the Green Line and the only refuge left to them.

ARITHMETIC OF THE SOUL

DOMIN: Robots are not people. Mechanically they are more
          perfect than we are; they have an enormously developed
          intelligence, but they have no soul.

HELENA: How do you know they have no soul?

DOMIN: Have you ever seen what a Robot looks like inside?

HELENA: No.

DOMIN: Very neat, very simple. Really a beautiful piece of work.
          The product of an engineer *is* technically at a higher
          pitch of perfection than a product of Nature.

HELENA: But man is supposed to be the product of God.

DOMIN: All the worse! God hasn't the slightest notion of modern
          engineering!

—KAREL CAPEK (1923)

IT WAS EVENING AGAIN WHEN Arkady and Osnat came to Yad Vashem's iron gate.

Arkady felt an exhausted sense of déjà vu as he watched Gavi descend the hill—still with the dog playing around his legs, still with the sinking sun behind him.

"We need help," Osnat said when Gavi was finally standing in front of them. She sounded like her gut was twisting with the effort of asking for it.

"Well, okay. I'm glad you think you can trust me."

Osnat glared into the middle distance with a look of profound disgust on her face. "I should probably bat my eyelashes at you, and tell you I was all wrong about Tel Aviv, and do my best to play the dumb blonde in the red Ferrari."

A smile stole across Gavi's lips. "You would never do that, Osnat."

"Don't be so fucking sure. But anyway . . . the truth is we have nowhere else left to go."

Gavi led them up the hill, and scrounged up clean clothes and clean sheets and clean towels, and gave them bread and soup and chicken, all washed down with cold clear well water. He might have been any lonely homesteader on any colony planet welcoming the rare guests who wandered by. Only when they had finished eating did he begin to ask the real questions.

"Go ahead, Arkady," Osnat said. "Tell him what you told me."

Arkady told him.

"Do you want more chicken?" Gavi said when Arkady's explanations and excuses finally petered out. "There's more if you want it." And then he meandered off into the shadowy depths of the kitchen and all Arkady and Osnat heard for a few minutes were pots rattling and spoons scraping.

When Gavi came back he was frowning. "Explain this Turing Soup thing again?"

Arkady tried to walk him through Arkasha's explanation of Turing Soup, neutral networks, gateway mutations, and search engines and only got hopelessly tangled.

"So fertility's almost a side effect," Gavi said when he was done. "Except that whereas it offers you in the Syndicates something that you don't want—or at least that most of you don't want—it offers us exactly what everyone wants. So however slim your chances of putting it back in the box might be, our chances are even slimmer."

"How long do you think it'll take before it turns into war between Earth and the Ring?" Osnat asked. "Ten years? Twenty?"

"Actually," Gavi said, "I was thinking months not years."

"We need to get to Didi," Osnat said. She seemed to be watching Gavi while she spoke, as if she were looking for an answer that she expected to be written on his face.

"Getting to Didi is easier said than done," Gavi answered. He hesitated as if he were playing out possible counterarguments in his mind, one after another, and rejecting them.

"You talked to Li," he said finally, "not Cohen. Do you have any reason to believe your message actually reached Cohen?"

"Well, no, but I thought they were the same person."

"They are. But I'm not sure that means what you think it means. I think our next step should be to go back to Cohen. Directly."

Osnat shook her head violently.

"I don't argue that we should trust Cohen blindly," Gavi said. "But I still think he's the best person to feel out if we want to get a firmer grip on what's actually happening in the Office without sticking our necks out too far."

"I don't know." Osnat sighed. She wiped a hand across her face. "I'm so tired I'm about to pass out sitting up."

"We don't need to decide anything tonight," Arkady suggested. "We can always sleep on it and see what we think in the morning."

But in the morning Osnat was too sick to talk, and Arkady and Gavi were too busy trying to keep her alive to remember the conversation they were supposed to have had.

Her fever was worse than anything that the survey team members had suffered from. For three days Gavi and Arkady nursed her through it, spelling each other, falling back on aspirin and cold-water-soaked cloths when none of the normal remedies seemed to work.

"Is this the same sickness?" Gavi asked at one point. He was sitting with Osnat, mopping her brow with a cold cloth while Arkady looked on in an agony of guilt.

"How should I know?" Arkady said desperately. "I'm not a doctor, and even the doctors on the survey didn't know what they were dealing with."

"I'm not asking you for a diagnosis," Gavi said coolly, "just an opinion."

"You're the human!" Arkady protested. "For all I know it could be the flu."

Gavi gave Arkady a long level look over Osnat's unconscious body.

"Okay. I don't think it is either. But . . . what do you want me to tell you?"

"I don't know. Is there anything else you *should* tell me?"

"Can I speak with you, Gavi?"

"Of course, Arkady. But come outside. I need to get dinner ready."

They walked through the visitors' center, pausing in the gloomy industrial-sized kitchen long enough for Gavi to pick up a hard-used metal bowl and a vicious-looking knife. They stepped outside—that shocking moment of transition that Arkady would never get used to no matter how many brief planetside stays he made over the course of his mostly stationbound life. Gavi set off down the hill toward the shanty-town jumble of the chicken coops. When they reached the little flock, Gavi slipped in among them, gesturing to Arkady to wait on the edge. He spoke companionably to the birds, and they clustered around him looking for handouts and caresses.

Gavi took one of his hens in his arms and murmured to her in Hebrew too soft and quick for Arkady to make any sense of it. He ambled back over to Arkady and sat down. The hen rested in his lap chuttering quietly to herself, her eyes all but closed. Gavi smoothed down her feathers and caressed her until she hunkered down into her feathers and closed her eyes in pleasure. Then he gripped her with firm, expert hands and drew the blade across her throat so smoothly and quickly that Arkady only understood what had happened when he saw the blood coursing into the bowl Gavi had nudged into place with his good foot.

"Is that for keeping kosher?" Arkady asked when he had recovered his voice enough to speak.

"No." Gavi turned the hen's limp little body in his hand and began plucking the feathers with sharp, practiced turns of his wrist. "It's for Dibbuk."

"You don't keep kosher then?"

"No."

"Why not?"

"Because, if God actually exists, I can think of a long list of things He ought to be more worried about than the contents of my intestines. What did you want to talk to me about, Arkady?"

"I . . . I wanted to apologize."

"What for?"

"For, well . . . everything. I thought I was doing the right thing. Or at least one right thing. I didn't know Korchow had turned me into a *weapon*. I wish I could make you believe that."

"I can see that you're well-intentioned. This is a very complicated situation. You really don't owe me anything."

Gavi was still plucking away at the chicken so that it was impossible for Arkady to meet his dark eyes. His voice, however, struck a chill down Arkady's spine: cool, smooth, gently distant. The voice of a man who had gone through anger and come out the other side. Arkady could imagine going to great lengths to avoid hearing it again.

"I never hid anything from you intentionally. I didn't understand what Korchow had done myself until after we'd talked. And then, with Safik . . . well . . ."

"Safik could wring secrets out of stones. I'd have to be a bigger fool than I am if I thought you wouldn't tell him everything."

Arkady looked doubtfully at him. "You're not angry, then?"

"Being angry would imply that I expected you not to tell him. Or that I felt you had some kind of obligation not to. Why would I think either of those things?" Gavi stood up, the chicken hanging limp and bedraggled and naked in his hand. "Angry's silly, Arkady. It makes people feel better in the short term, but in the long term it just makes them not think straight. And what possible good can it do anyone if we let ourselves be seduced into not thinking straight?"

"None, I guess."

"I'm glad you agree with me. Let's go have dinner."

"So how come Gavi didn't get sick?" was the first thing Osnat wanted to know when she was back in the land of the living.

"What do you mean?" Gavi asked, looking sharply at her. "Has someone else gotten sick?"

"Moshe. Well, I think so. The first week. But that's twenty-twenty hindsight talking. At the time I thought it was just allergies. Same with the guards." She frowned. "Ash Sofaer didn't get sick either come to think of it."

Gavi looked down at his plate. "Maybe Ash and I don't have what the virus fixes."

Osnat stared. A charged silence crept around the table and spread to the corners of the room.

"What's that supposed to mean?" Osnat asked.

"Well . . . Ash has a son. So do I."

"You *what?*" Osnat asked. "Where is he?"

"I don't know."

Osnat grew rigid in her chair. She looked at her plate, her cup, the wall behind Gavi's head. Everything but Gavi.

"You have a natural child?" she said finally, in an accusatory whisper. "And you just . . . *abandoned him?*"

"I like you, Osnat," Gavi said in his blandest, most noncommittal voice, "but you're a very judgmental person. And you seem to have the oddest idea that people are required to justify themselves to you when really it's none of your business. It's not attractive."

"It's a hell of a lot more attractive than thinking you have a right to float through life and break all the rules without ever explaining yourself to anyone!"

Arkady looked back and forth between the two of them, feeling the emotional undercurrent in the fight but completely unable to make sense of it.

"You want explanations?" Gavi said. "Here's one. My wife was a doctor at a hospital on the Palestinian side of the Line. We lived over there so Joseph could go to Palestinian school. And don't give me that look, little Miss Ashkenaz. You don't know what it was like to be an Arab child in Israeli schools, even before the war. When the border crossing started getting sticky, we kept telling ourselves it would blow over. But it didn't blow over. One day I went to work . . . and I couldn't get back across. At first I could talk to them on the phone. Then the satlink was cut. Then I stopped getting any news of them at all. The last thing I heard was that Leila's hospital had been bombed. Accidentally, of course. It's amazing how often hospitals seem to get in the way of bombs. They found her body in what was left of the pediatric ward. The children were much harder to identify. But one of the survivors said she'd taken Joseph to work with her that morning because she thought it was safer than leaving him home." He stood up, moving as clumsily as Arkady had ever seen him move. "So that's how I deserted my son. Hope you enjoyed our little session of show-and-tell as much as I did."

"Osnat—" Arkady began when Gavi had stalked out.

"Oh shut up, Arkady! What the hell do you know about anything, anyway?"

It took most of a day for Osnat and Gavi to start talking to each other again; and when they did it was with the quiet caution of a bomb squad tiptoeing around a possibly live piece of ordnance.

"I think we ought to at least put out a feeler," Gavi said, talking mostly to Arkady. "There's no reason I can't drop by to see Cohen and feel him out a bit."

Osnat raised one eyebrow. "You think you can find out more about him than he'll find out about you in the first five seconds?"

Gavi got a funny look on his face. "Well . . . yes, actually. You know the old saying about AIs. It's not that they're smarter than us . . ."

"It's just that they can be dumb so much faster. But that doesn't mean you can lie to him and get away with it."

"I'm not going to lie. I'm just going to offer what Cohen would call a selective sampling of the available data."

"Are you sure that's safe?" Arkady asked, thinking of Safik's warnings about the AI.

Gavi gave him a quizzical look. "What's he going to do, steal my lunch money?"

THEY KEPT LI AWAKE UNTIL she'd never been so tired, even in combat. Exhaustion smeared thought and twisted perception. Sleep was the enemy. Sleep was the monster of all her childhood nightmares, hunting her through a distorted landscape while she ran and ran, unable to stop though she knew she would fall sooner or later.

And through the long fight with exhaustion, in the brief lulls between those nightmare flights, came the interrogations.

She was hooded of course. But she didn't need to see her torturers to know them. Their attentions to her were invasive and intimate, and by the end of the second day she knew the three men better than their own wives did.

There was the one who laughed and joked and obviously enjoyed his work. There was the one who handled her with the brusque impersonalness of a butcher slinging meat. And there was the one who apologized. He was the worst by far because he reminded Li of the last thing she wanted to remember: that there were people on the other end of those cruel hands.

What they wanted was easy enough: her passwords.

They wanted the keys to her hard memory, her procedural backups, her archived spinfeeds, her accumulated knowledge base of past UNSec operations.

But she couldn't give them the passwords because she no longer had them. They'd been changed by a deeply embedded Peacekeeper security loop the moment her internals processed the fact of her kidnapping. She'd heard rumors that UNSec built such things into Peacekeeper psychware, but until now she hadn't entirely believed in them. Unfortunately, her captors didn't seem to believe in them either.

And all the while, they kept hammering at her about some meeting with Turner that she couldn't remember—any more than she could remember how she'd gotten here. Li, a connoisseur of memory loss, could feel the gap as clearly as she would have felt a missing tooth. And she could locate what was missing, more or less. Not that she really needed to, because her captors questioned her about it almost as incessantly as they questioned her about her passwords and security programs.

Where had she gone before she went to meet Turner?

Who had she spoken to before she spoke to Turner?

Who knew she had gone to see Turner?

Where had the woman and the clone gone to after she'd passed their location on to Turner?

It was no use. She remembered the call from Osnat and Arkady. Then nothing. And the more they asked about Turner, and Turner, and Turner, the harder it got to believe that she could have agreed to meet with him in the first place.

She couldn't say just when she began to realize that there were other people attending the interrogation sessions. The watchers were silent and invisible—at least to Li, whose whole universe had narrowed down to a few centimeters of burlap darkness. But they exerted a tidal pull on the interrogators, as unmistakably as an eclipsed planet tugging at its neighbors in the dark. Li's torturers were playing to their audience, like the miners of Li's all-but-forgotten childhood picking up the pace at the cutting face when the straw boss was watching.

It was the watchers who made them start in on her hands.

They didn't need to do much. Ceramsteel filament was as sharp as a surgeon's scalpel and much harder. When a filament snapped and its severed ends started floating free against fragile flesh and bone, you'd better pray to whatever gods you believed in that you were within tossing distance of the surgical tanks. And no part of your body outside your relatively protected spinal column was as impregnated with monofilament-thin virally embedded ceramsteel filament as your hands. So when they strapped her hands down, she'd known immediately where the game was headed. The only question in her mind was how far the unseen watcher would allow it to go.

Answer: pretty damn far.

Far enough to make her glad she was blindfolded and couldn't see what was happening at the far ends of her arms.

Far enough to trigger the memory that had somehow become intimately and inextricably associated with what they were doing to her.

Far enough to send her mind spinning back to Gilead.

The whole operation on Gilead had been fractally fubard. Fucked up beyond all recall in every spatial scale and at every hierarchical level of complexity.

The UNSec spin doctors had made it out to be a positive orgy of heroism, and the war correspondents had bought their spin hook, line, and sinker. But in Li's opinion Gilead had been just like almost every other episode of storied heroism in every other war she'd ever read about: a bloody mess that would never have been necessary if the deskbound lords of war had done their jobs right.

Most of Li's colleagues had seen it differently—or at least pretended to. They'd started loudly celebrating the heroic dead of Gilead before the bodies were even buried. And if there were whispers behind closed doors about broken supply lines, endemic communications failures, and blue-on-blue orbit-to-surface strikes, then they only made the public celebration louder and the medal inflation higher.

Monday morning quarterbacking was bad for morale. That was the consensus. Better to celebrate what went right (most of it at the non-com level and below) than to dwell on what went wrong (most of it still alive and wearing stars and striped trousers). And if Li thought that this meant buying morale at a pretty high rate of interest, she'd soon learned that saying so didn't earn her much love.

Of course, as one of the few Gilead veterans who was in the enviable position of being both a hero and alive, Li was one of the main beneficiaries of the hurricane of spin swirling around the bloody campaign. Not that she was even sure it was spin. All she had to set against the

UNSec-washed spinstreams was a nagging feeling of déjà vu and a conviction that her mind had once held a different version than the one UNSec called reality.

It was impossible to explain to civilians what jump amnesia did to you. The jagged holes it punched into your past and your identity. The reflexes, violent ones included, that came at you from nowhere, then sucked back into some subterranean place you couldn't remember your way down to. The sickening vertigo of having a second set of memories superimposed on the real ones. The gut certainty that what your own brain remembered and the history books and the newspins and the politicians and your next-door neighbors said was wrong, wrong, wrong, wrong, wrong.

That must have been how Turner had drawn her into his web. He must have dangled in front of her the one thing she couldn't refuse: proof. Proof that she hadn't done those things on Gilead. Proof that she wasn't the kind of person who could do such things.

She saw now that she had been chasing an illusion. She would never know the Catherine Li who had dropped into Gilead's gravity well half a lifetime ago. Even if Andrej Korchow descended from the sky in glory to tell her she hadn't shot those prisoners, he still couldn't tell her what else she'd done . . . or been capable of doing.

She would never know her past self even in the illusory, self-justifying, half-fictional way that unaltered humans knew their past selves. All she could know—all she ever would know—was the person she was now.

And the really rotten piece of luck was that just as she was finally beginning to see a way to live with that, it was starting to look less and less like she was going to get a chance to live, period.

It was her own damn fault, of course.

She had known it was a bad idea to try to escape. But what was she supposed to do? *Nothing?*

And when her tormentors finally slipped up, she was waiting for them. With a scalpel that she'd managed to pilfer with the hand whose fingers still more or less worked.

The first guard's neck broke with a crunch that made even Li's stomach churn. She dropped him and drove forward to the next target, still hooded, moving on sound and feel. Her hands were useless, so she used her legs, her feet, her training, her hate.

She had her hood off almost before the second guard hit the ground. The room was dark, thank God, not too difficult to adjust to. But she still made the mistake of thinking she was alone.

The fact that the other person in the room with her was standing very still was only part of her confusion. The real problem was that the woman was covered from head to toe in dusty green cloth.

Was she a woman? Was she even an Interfaither? Or merely someone taking advantage of a disguise that blended all too conveniently into Jerusalem's thronging streets these days?

Li seized the veiled figure. And then she did something she would never, not in a million years, have done if she'd been anywhere within spitting distance of thinking straight.

She grabbed the green cloth and yanked.

"That was unwise," Ashwarya Sofaer said.

Li just stood there, swaying slightly, poleaxed by memory.

"It was you," she whispered. "It was you I went to, not Turner."

Ash shrugged. "I was a bit surprised at how well that took. Your brains really are scrambled, aren't they?"

"Then it was all a false flag operation? You were never talking to UNSec at all?"

"Oh I was talking to UNSec." Ash smiled her lovely masklike smile. It occurred to Li, in some relatively lucid segment of her brain, that Ash wasn't as scared as she should be. "They just weren't the only people I was talking to."

"Turner—"

"Does it really matter? It's not like you're going anywhere. Before there was a chance. Now . . ." She shrugged.

"Oh, we're going somewhere," Li said . . .

. . . and the next thing she knew she was on the ground, her head throbbing with the aftereffects of some nerve agent, and Turner was standing there big as real life looking down at her.

"Well now," he said, shaking his head like a country bumpkin getting his first eyeful of the bright lights and the big city. "You really are a lady who likes to do things the hard way."

Ash stood just behind Turner. And she had her veil on again. "Why don't you take that ridiculous thing off your head?" Li told her.

Ash's hand emerged from the shadows, rose, hesitated. The veil came away with little more than a light twitch of her long fingers. But instead of removing it entirely she merely settled it around her head and shoulders so that only her face was showing.

That was when Li understood. The veil was no disguise. The veil *was* Ash's true face: the face of an Interfaither who had turned her mind over to the men of God and violence.

That was the reality Li had glimpsed behind the beautiful but impersonal mask that Ash presented to the world. The white suits and the perfect makeup and the self-serving careerism were all nothing but the subtlest kind of protective camouflage.

Li had seen the real Ash just once: in the stretch marks that said she'd gone through natural birth and pregnancy, something only a vanishingly small number of Ring-siders still did. But she'd written that off as meaningless trivia. How could she have been so blind? And what better proof could there be that she herself wasn't human, had never been human, would never understand humans no matter how long she lived among them?

"How long have you been working for the Interfaithers?" she asked Ash. "And when did you and Turner decide you wanted the Novalis virus?"

But instead of an answer, Ash had another question for her:

"Left hand or right hand?"

COHEN LOOKED VERY MUCH THE worse for wear when he finally answered to Gavi's knock. Rumpled and unshaven. Dark circles under his eyes. And around his left hand an immaculate white bandage.

Gavi stepped into the luxurious living room of Cohen's hotel suite. "What happened?" he asked, pointing at the bandage.

"I stuck Roland's hand through a window," Cohen said in a voice that distinctly did not invite further questions. "What do you want, Gavi?"

Gavi raised his eyebrows. "Bad time? Should I come back later?"

Cohen slumped into a chair and rubbed his hands across his face. "No. Sorry. Things just . . . aren't so good at the moment."

Gavi looked around. No sign of Li. How to broach the unbroachable question? Well, blunt was always an option. "Is Li around?"

"No. So show me this new source code you've cooked up."

Gavi sat down, repressing the guilty sinking feeling that lying to Cohen gave him. It wasn't a lie. It was self-protection. No, better than self-protection: the protection of two people who were in deadly desperate need of protecting.

They talked around the subject for a few minutes, skimming over Gavi's programming ideas, the false starts he'd made, what he'd learned from them, the current state of his work on and thought about his so-called golem . . . all the while edging cautiously toward the dangerous topic of the other golem, the one of flesh and blood that was sitting in Gavi's living room.

He should have been enjoying the conversation. He wasn't.

At some point he realized that he'd dropped the conversational ball, and that Cohen had fallen oddly silent. He looked up to find the AI staring intently at him.

"So, Gavi. How are Arkady and Osnat doing?"

"How should I know?"

"That's funny. I wouldn't have thought Yad Vashem was crowded enough these days that you wouldn't notice you were sharing the place with them."

"How long have you known?"

"Since they arrived."

"Then you know they went to you first. Why the hell didn't you help them?"

"What are you talking about?"

"I'm talking about Li! Osnat went to her for help before she brought Arkady to me. And she almost ended up on the police blotter because of it."

Cohen blinked. "Li's been MIA for two days now. So I think we can assume that whoever came after your little lost lambs bagged her too."

"Or," Gavi pointed out in a carefully neutral tone of voice, "we can assume that they want us to think so."

"You're off the mark there. Li wouldn't do that."

"You know her well enough to be sure of that?"

"I know her well enough to know she wouldn't sell me out."

"Everyone has their dumb blonde and their red Ferrari, Cohen."

"Don't spoon-feed me Didi's proverbs!"

"Okay, maybe I spoke out of turn there. Maybe it's not like that. But . . . people are who they are. You can't imagine how angry I was at Leila after she died. I kept telling myself that if she'd really loved me, she would have come across the Line when we still had the chance. But it isn't that simple, is it? I mean, you can love someone completely and still be bound by who you are, by what you believe in, by the other things and people you care about . . . by life, I suppose."

"I know what you're trying to tell me," Cohen said. "You want to see UNSec behind this. You think Li's gone back to working for Nguyen, and that Nguyen either ordered the bombing or pressured Didi into ordering it. Well, you're talking out of turn. You don't know

Catherine. You don't know what they did to her. You don't know anything about her."

But his eyes fell away from Gavi's as he said the words.

The package arrived just as Gavi was about to leave.

"What do you mean you don't know who it's from?" Cohen asked the desperately nervous kid who showed up at the door of his suite to tell him about it. "Has security checked it?"

"Yes. Er. I really . . . perhaps you'd better come see for yourself."

Gavi noticed with a first shiver of foreboding that the scared youngster was no mere bellhop. Someone had seen fit to draft management to deliver this particular package.

"Should I come with you?" he asked.

"Yes," Cohen said.

They both knew he would have argued in normal circumstances.

The package—a gift box, actually, wrapped in rather tasteful gold foil and bound up with a red satin ribbon—was sitting on the head security officer's desk in the middle of a sea of nervous uniforms.

Cohen went over to the desk, peered at it for a moment, standing completely still, and slumped limply into the nearest chair.

Gavi realized no one was taking the slightest notice of him, and stepped close enough to see over the top of the wrapping paper and into the box's interior.

The box was lined with more gold foil, as if whoever packed it had considered its contents fragile and in need of extra padding. It took Gavi some time to see what the object carefully nested in the golden foil actually was. Part of the trouble was the normal difficulty of recognizing even the most familiar objects seen out of context. But mostly it was the glistening, razor-sharp halo of ceramsteel filament that veiled the object. It was only the smell that finally roused his old battlefield memories and made him retch reflexively.

"Is it Li's?" he asked.

"Yes," Cohen said dully. He was jackknifed over in the chair, his face buried in his hands, but he spoke with the same crisp, elegant precision Gavi had heard from the lips of a dozen different faces.

"You're sure?"

"Of course I'm sure. It's the left hand, the one with the Schengen implant. Now do you trust her?"

WHEN HE LEFT COHEN, GAVI walked halfway across town, then doubled back toward the Old City. He passed through the Damascus Gate into the International Zone at eight minutes to two, carefully avoiding the telltale times of the hour, and the half hour and the quarter hour.

Then he began to wander aimlessly, trying to mimic an idling, strolling interest in his surroundings that he was very far from feeling.

He kept clear of passersby and kept a sharp eye on his pockets. More than one courier had ducked into the crowded alleys of the Old City to shake a tail, only to find that he'd lost his package to a stray pickpocket. And though Gavi wasn't nearly foolish enough to be carrying anything incriminating, he didn't need the aggravation of a lost wallet and a futile attempt to explain to the Foreign Legion gatekeepers that he was an Israeli citizen and not simply one more in the endless flood of paperless anonymous Arab males caught up in the International Zone's endlessly repeating bureaucratic feedback loops.

It took a lot of practice to make a convincing show of just stumbling on a place. In this case, the rendezvous was located in a run-down café in the Arab Quarter. Gavi walked in, looked around, took a seat at a back table, and downed three cups of strong black coffee, ordering a new one every time the waiter started to look impatient with him.

He was making a hash of it, of course. He should have done his business and left after the first cup. He knew he was attracting attention. He knew that attracting attention, any kind of attention at all, was a major failing in tradecraft. But still he sat there, sipping the execrable coffee, gripped by an indecision more savage than any he could remember in a long career fraught with life-and-death decisions.

Cohen's certainty about Li shook him. The whole conversation had shaken him. Every minute of every day since Osnat and Arkady had fetched up on his doorstep four days ago had shaken him.

The waiter was staring at him, he realized, examining him surreptitiously. His field instincts began to sound the old alerts, but then he saw the sickened and fascinated look on the man's face and realized that it wasn't his presence that the man was concerned with but his leg's absence.

Pretty is as pretty does, my friend.

How many millions of times had his mother told him that when he was growing up? She'd been terrified, old kibbutznik that she was, that her too-pretty boy would grow up to be one of the frivolous and useless people she so despised. And he'd internalized the message, just as he'd internalized her ardently idealistic Zionism. He'd fallen in love with and married a woman who was intelligent and cultured but by no stretch of the imagination beautiful. And he'd always faintly despised the people who would glance back and forth between them on the first meeting, toting up the all-too-obvious aesthetic calculus and wondering: *Why him? Why her?*

Arithmetic of the body, he'd called it. Implying (God, how egotistical he'd been!) that he cared only for the arithmetic of the soul.

But now he was doing that same arithmetic in reverse. Hanging on Osnat's faintest nod or smile. Watching the eyes that were so wary when she spoke to him, and the strong hands that were so carefully impersonal when she so much as passed a plate to him. Inventorying his broken body and his broken reputation, and wondering what he could possibly offer to a woman whose body and honor were so vibrantly whole.

He had to get her out of his home and out of this operation. If there'd been any question about that, his demeaning little tantrum of the other night had answered it. He was acting like an idiot. And he was too old and shopworn for the young-pup-in-love routine to be anything but ridiculous.

He got up, paid, and asked for the bathroom in Arabic.

"The toilet's plugged," he said when he came back. "Can I make a local call before you call the plumber, though?"

The waiter was gray, middle-aged, nondescript. But when their eyes met for a moment across the counter Gavi had a sudden uncomfortable intuition that this was a man who was far too smart to be waiting tables.

"I'm not supposed to . . ." But the man was already setting the terminal on the scratched bartop.

Gavi rang up the number, waited for two rings, then hung up. "No one home," he said before leaving. "But thanks anyway."

Two hours later he was climbing the steps of a grimy, narrow-fronted apartment building on Ibn Batuta Street.

He rang the bell, waited while unseen eyes inspected him and unseen fingers buzzed him in.

A young man waited for him in the shadows behind the door. He looked like a Yeshiva student, except for the aura of cold-blooded confidence that even the thick glasses couldn't completely camouflage. Gavi raised his arms and leaned against the wall and submitted to the search that was never quite perfunctory enough to be a mere formality. Then he climbed the steep stairs to the third floor and stepped into the familiar room and closed the door behind him and leaned back against it.

"Hello, Gavi," said the man in the armchair.

Gavi looked into the sad eyes of the man he loved and hated more than he'd ever loved or hated his own gently distant father.

"Hello, Didi."

SHORT AND SWEET AND RARE. That was how Didi liked to keep their meetings.

"It's difficult to live a double life," he'd said the first time they'd sat together in this room. "It's terribly tempting to begin to rely on your control for emotional support, even for simple relief from the loneliness. But every meeting is a fresh chance to buy yourself a bullet in the head. So when you walk out of here, this room must no longer exist for you. *I* must no longer exist for you. The less we disturb the unity of the life we wish you to lead, the less we risk revealing ourselves."

Now Didi just looked at him, smiling.

"How are you, Gavi?"

Gavi stood, knowing he should sit down but too nervous to do it. "How are the girls?" he asked, forcing himself to take a genuine interest, repressing the surge of resentment that flooded through him whenever he was faced with the offensive and depressing fact of other people's children.

"They're fine, Gavi. You look tired."

"I am tired."

Didi's eyes rested gently on him, but was it the concern of an old friend or just the cool professionalism of a *katsa* assessing the condition of a valuable resource? And why, after two years of this, was Gavi still asking himself that question?

"You know about Li?"

"I just heard."

"Do you know who did it?"

"Not yet."

"Your mole hunt's getting ugly, Didi. Has it occurred to you that Li's . . . wherever she is because someone took one of your barium meals too much to heart?"

"It crossed my mind."

"That's all? It just crossed your mind? Like the weather report?"

"I have a job to do."

"That's pretty cold, Didi. Even for you."

"If it makes you feel better to make me the heavy, go ahead."

Gavi dropped his head into his hands and rubbed at his temples. "Sorry. What about this Maracaibo bar bombing, then? Any news on that?"

"The boys are working on it."

"Osnat said there were people from the Office there. She brought Arkady to me because she decided she couldn't trust anyone else. You included. She brought him through the Line on nothing but guts and shoe leather. Crazy. Only a lunatic would try it."

"She's a little hotheaded," Didi agreed, "but she's a good girl."

"Can I trust her?"

"It's not like you to ask that. The Gavi I used to know wouldn't have trusted her no matter what I told him."

"I'm not the Gavi you used to know."

"You *are* looking a little frayed around the edges." Didi acknowledged this as simple fact, in the same disinterested voice with which he would have acknowledged that the weather was warmer than usual.

"I've had it, Didi. If I were in your position, I'd cash me out before I brought the whole case down on top of our heads."

"Your slang is out-of-date," Didi said on a smile as gentle as snow falling on the desert. "These days the youngsters call it 'better world-ing.' Or, in the case of death by apparently accidental causes, 'giving someone the measles.' And in any case I know you far too well to believe that you would do any such thing. You always took care of your people to a fault."

"Not Gur."

"No. Poor kid. I guess I don't have to ask what's got you thinking of him."

There was a sofa along the wall facing Didi's chair. Gavi subsided into it and turned sideways so he could put his bad leg up. The skin under the normally comfortable cuff was raw and bruised from the long day of pounding over concrete and cobblestones, and it stung atrociously as the feeling came back into it. Why was it that trudging on concrete was so much worse than running on any natural surface?

"What I still don't get," he said, "is how Osnat got mixed up with GolaniTech. Moshe, I can buy. But what idiot decided to push Osnat off the Office payroll?"

He looked over to find Didi watching him with an intensity that would have been infuriating in anyone else. He took in the shapeless figure slouched in the armchair, looked past the stained and wrinkled suit to meet Didi's eyes for the first time since he'd entered the room.

"Oh," he breathed. "She never left. She's still yours. *You* sent her."

"Let's just say I may have pointed her in your direction and given her a gentle push."

"I've been on the receiving end of your gentle pushes. And how could you even think about sending her through the Line without someone to cover her back?"

"Osnat can cover her own back, I imagine."

And then, for the first time, Gavi stopped thinking of the risks Osnat was running—and started thinking of the risks he was running. "My God. She's *kidon*. And I'm still on the prime minister's list. You sent a Mossad assassin into my house, with only his initials to stand between me and the knife!"

"Actually, the PM initialed your name last month." Didi spread his hands in a gesture that was half excuse half apology. "Old friends aren't what they used to be."

"I saved that son of a bitch's life!" Gavi said—and even as the words left his mouth he realized that he sounded ridiculously like Dibbuk when someone stepped on her tail.

"He told me. Twice. If it makes you feel any better, I had to spend half the night at his house letting him cry on my shoulder before he'd sign the order."

"What's going on, Didi? You taking out insurance on me?"

"Gavi, please believe me when I say that I want you to come out of this alive and well more than I want anything except the safety of Israel. But my grip on things is slipping. The IDF is rattling their cage. There are two more Interfaithers on the Knesset Intelligence Committee. We could run out of turf before we catch Absalom. And if there's going to be a hit order out on you, I'd rather it was my hand on the trigger than my enemy's hands."

Gavi looked out the window. His leg was spasming from the long walk. He rubbed at the cramp, but it didn't seem to improve things much. "Does Osnat know about this?"

"About the PM's order? No. She really is there to help, not hurt. She's the best I could send you without everyone on the eighth floor knowing I'd sent someone."

"You still shouldn't have picked Osnat. I can't work with her. I don't want her there."

"Don't you like her? That's funny. I always thought you had a bit of a crush on her."

"I was her commanding officer," Gavi said, doubly outraged by the accusation because of the little grain of truth in it. "I would never have thought about that. And just because I have a thing for the heroic kibbutznik types doesn't mean I'm easy picking for any—"

And then he finally put that puzzle together too. One step too late, as always.

"No dumb blondes and rented Ferraris for you," Didi murmured. "For you I only send the real thing."

Gavi held his hands away from his body and looked at them as if they belonged to someone else. They were trembling.

"You're going to push too hard," he told Didi. "And then I'm going to break, and you'll have nothing. I'm not complaining or threatening. I'm just reporting as objectively as I can on the status of an agent in place."

"I can't back off now, Gavi. I'm sorry it's been so hard, and I'm sorry it took so long. But we've reached the crossroads. If we do it right, then we can all go home. If not . . ."

Gavi sighed deeply and stretched out on the sofa with one arm over his eyes. He thought of the horror he'd seen in the King David Hotel security chief's office, then forced his mind away from the thought.

"Can't you take Osnat back and send in Yoni?" he asked. "Or anyone, for that matter. Please?"

"I'm going to write that off as kvetching. Unless you actually want to make it official. In which case the answer is no."

Hard to argue with that; it was the answer Gavi himself would have given in Didi's place.

"I can't tell you how desperately I regret these years." Didi spoke softly. "But they have not been wasted. Only a little longer, Gavi. Only one last night out in the cold. Then we bring you home."

Down in the street a bus pulled up to the intersection with a whine of brakes, and a moment later Gavi heard the chuttering roar of its acceleration. He was sticky with sweat, and the light that seeped through his eyelids was as red as lung blood.

"Meanwhile," Didi continued, "a curious piece of news has been leaked across the Line to us. It seems the Palestinians have managed to get Korchow to send Arkasha to Earth."

Gavi's eyes flew open. "My God. And the Palestinians have him? What are they going to do with him?"

"Give him to Turner, apparently."

"Why the hell would they want to do that?"

"Not all of them do. Safik's office seems to have been responsible for getting Arkasha here. Then Sheik Yassin horned in and brokered the deal with Turner over Safik's protests."

"So you think the leak comes from Safik? You think he's trying to sabotage the exchange?"

Didi shrugged.

"I still don't get it. What could Turner have that Yassin wants enough to get and trade Arkasha for?"

"I was wondering when you were going to stumble around to that question. Turner's promised to give Yassin Arkady."

Gavi rolled over on his side to look at Didi, the sofa's springs protesting at the movement. "But Turner doesn't have Arkady."

"Not yet."

"What the hell is he up to?"

"I don't know. But I'd watch my back if I were you. And Arkady's back."

"Didi."

"What?"

"Please tell me you're not getting ready to burn Li and Arkady in order to catch Absalom. I don't want to be part of another operation like that. I've lost the stomach for it."

"I'm sorry, Gavi. I've completely forgotten to make you tea. And I always make you tea. What a brute I am."

"Water's fine. And you haven't answered my question."

"Really just water? How about I make you a little tea, and you can see if you want it?"

"Didi—"

"Jasmine or Ceylon, which do you prefer?"

When Didi came back he brought not only tea but also a slim file folder with the familiar black band across its front.

A testing, questioning silence filtered through the room. Gavi sat up. He could feel the old reflexes kicking in. His breath slowing. Time itself slowing. His eyes cataloging details that would have utterly eluded him in normal life. His muscles taking the measure of the room's distances with a precision that still scared him just as much as it had all those years ago at Midrash when he first discovered that he had these horrible talents . . . he who had always thought of himself as an intellectual, an idealist, a bit of a peacenik even.

"Are you going to show me what's in there," he asked Didi, "or are you going to make me guess?"

Instead of answering, Didi opened the file and scanned it, as if refreshing his memory of its contents. Then he removed a paper clip, set it neatly aside for subsequent retrieval, and handed Gavi the photograph that had been pinned beneath it.

A young man, slim, graceful even in freeze-frame, handsome in a way that made one wonder if he wouldn't perhaps be a bit too pretty in person. Something about the curve of his mouth and jaw that Gavi knew from his own bathroom mirror. And those vivid green crusader's eyes.

Leila's eyes.

"And just who is this supposed to be?" he asked icily.

"That's beneath you, Gavi."

The two men looked at each other. Gavi's heart was pounding so loudly in his ears that he thought Didi must be able to hear it on the other side of the room.

"Yusuf Safik," Didi said in the dull tone of a bureaucrat reading a routine report. "Only son—only child, actually—of Brigadier General Walid Safik. There's no official record of the adoption. Yusuf attended private school in Bethlehem, and then in the SaudiArc Ring-side, then—this is interesting, Gavi, listen up—a stint on KnowlesSyndicate. Then back to Palestine for security service training. He graduated fourth in his class." Didi pursed his lips, a taster evaluating a fine wine. "I like that fourth. It's subtle. Your sort of instinct, I'd almost say."

"You're assuming the fourth was by choice, not merit."

"I'm assuming nothing. One of our agents had a fling with a class-mate of Yusuf's who was posted to the Palestinian Authority's HQ in the International Zone. It seems that the consensus among their fellow students was that Yusuf purposely fluffed the finals. Now why would he do that, I wonder?"

Gavi felt dizzy. The world had rearranged itself while he wasn't looking, and now it was barreling on toward God knew what kind of damage without even giving him time to figure out where he stood or what he ought to do about it.

"And now he turns up smack in the middle of my hunt for Absalom."

"Coincidence," Gavi said. But he was hanging on by his fingernails and they both knew it.

He had laid the photograph across his knees, and not only to hide his shaking hands. Now he looked down at it and wondered how the photographer had stolen the unguarded shot. He touched the image of the familiar stranger's face, knowing that Didi was watching him and not giving a damn what it looked like, and then felt a searing pang of regret when he realized he'd smudged the photograph.

"You're surprised." Didi sounded like a man probing at a sore tooth and wondering how long he could afford to wait before he called the dentist.

Gavi looked up at him, doing his best to keep his eyes steady and level. "You expected me not to be?"

"Oh, I expected surprise. I just wasn't sure if you'd be surprised by the news, or surprised that I knew about it."

A child's voice rang out somewhere in the sun beyond the windows, and both men instinctively looked toward it. The glass, Gavi noticed, was caked with yellow *khamsin* dust. He thought idly that you could probably make a decent map of Tel Aviv's safe houses by just looking for unwashed windows and unswept doorsteps. He told himself that he was sick, sick to death of streaked windows and grimy walkup flats with garage sale furnishings. That all the other times he'd sat in identical rooms and thought identical thoughts had just been leading up to this time. And that this time it was well and truly over.

He knew better.

More to the point, Didi knew better.

"So why are you showing me this now? The file's not exactly empty. You must have been holding this ace for a while now."

"I wasn't, actually. We had the file, yes, but I only figured out last week that he wasn't Safik's natural child. And I'm telling you now because I want you to have time to think about it in cold blood. Here. With me to talk to. I trust your second thoughts, and your third and fourth thoughts. It's that first passionate impulse that terrifies me."

"Joseph might recognize me too, Didi. Have you thought about that?"

"I doubt he will. If he remembers you at all, it's as a young man not much older than he is now. And he doesn't look that much like you. Only a little bit around the mouth, really. I didn't see it myself at first."

Gavi looked down at the photograph. He'd allowed himself to be distracted from it, and he realized this was a mistake as it was extremely unlikely that Didi would allow him to keep the photograph or ever see it again. His mind was doing a strange thing to him, filling his nose with the remembered scent of Joseph's infant skin, goading him into an animal certainty that the young stranger in the photograph was his child.

Like the goats, he thought nonsensically, who knew their kids in the dark by smell alone. But it had never occurred to him that they might remember the smell for years or decades after he'd taken their kids to slaughter. What was the purpose of allowing their senses to torment them like that when it was too late to do anything or save anybody?

"Can I read his file?" he asked.

"Oh, Gavi."

"Don't 'Oh, Gavi' me. Why shouldn't I read it?"

"Why should you?" Didi held the slim sheaf of papers up and shook it until the pages rattled like dead leaves. "You want to know what's in here, Gavi? The life of another man's son. Walid Safik's son. Everything in this file says that Safik has pampered and adored and doted on the boy since the day he adopted him. Everything in here says that Yusuf Safik returns his father's love. For God's sake, Gavi, we've got phone records showing the kid calls home every night, and, let me tell you, I'm grateful if my daughters call me once a month! The boy's Palestinian, Gavi. Just as Leila intended him to be. And his father is Walid Safik. You're just a stranger who happens to look like him."

"I know," Gavi whispered.

And he did know.

He really did.

But that didn't make it any easier to let go of the photograph.

OHEN MATERIALIZED IN A SHIMMER of security protocols. Or perhaps the shimmer was in the air, Arkady told himself, and not in Cohen. He still couldn't get used to the instream version of Yad Vashem that Gavi had decided to hold this meeting in.

"How come it's all different?" Arkady asked. "Where are Gavi's goats? And . . . nothing's falling down. They'd have to have an army of gardeners and groundskeepers to keep the place looking this way."

"You don't have to shout," Osnat said. "Gardeners are expensive. And if you want them to work on the Line, they're more than expensive. Eighty percent of Israelis may be infertile, but no one wants their neighbors to know *they're* not in the lucky twenty percent. It's all about keeping up appearances."

"But it's not *real*."

"What's real? This is the Yad Vashem that millions of tourists all over UN space know and believe exists. The illusion beats the reality any day on the numbers."

"What's the news on Li?" Gavi asked Cohen when he had settled into phase with their own surroundings.

Cohen looked sick. "It's the Americans."

"*Turner?*"

"Turner."

Gavi swallowed convulsively, as if the news were a dry pill that had gotten stuck in his throat. "Has he told you what he wants?"

"That's the funny part." Cohen sank onto a bench so smoothly that it took Arkady a moment to realize that Cohen had somehow changed the standard tour on the fly and now they were all standing still in one of the rambling compound's many gardens.

"He wants Arkady. And he wants Gavi to bring him. He was very insistent on that point. He's arranged a three-way swap with Yassin. I walk away with Li. Turner gets Arkasha. And Arkady goes back to Syndicate space with Korchow."

"But what do the Palestinians get out of it?"

"I suspect a better question would be what does Yassin get out of it. Arkady's defection seems to have dovetailed neatly with the power struggle between him and Safik."

"So Turner wants us to help Yassin take Safik down," Gavi said. "Nice to know we're on the side of the angels. I assume you've talked to Didi about this?"

"Yes." Cohen paused and glanced at Arkady. "Didi thinks there ought to be a way to play along with Turner but still come out the other side holding the bag with Arkasha in it. He also authorized me to tell Arkady that if we can pull this off, he'll guarantee Arkasha full political asylum."

"What about Arkady?" Osnat asked.

"Arkady has to go back or Didi won't help us. Frankly Didi wasn't even happy about leaving Arkasha on-planet in light of . . . well . . . the obvious."

"Can I trust Didi to protect Arkasha?" Arkady asked Gavi.

"I don't know," Gavi said. He looked sick to his stomach. "But I can't think of anyone you can trust more."

"Okay, then. I'll do it."

"And just what is Didi actually offering in the way of help?" Gavi asked Cohen.

"The Office won't get directly involved in the swap." The AI's voice was tight with apprehension. "But Didi will provide backup . . . or cleanup if things get messy. The story for public consumption will be that the Office got an anonymous tip about where Li was being held and organized a rescue. Ash is going to handle the operation so it doesn't go through official channels."

Another pause followed this news. Gavi sat down, bowed his head, crossed his arms over his chest, chewed on his lower lip. "I don't know what to tell you," he said finally, glancing up at Cohen. "On the one hand it stinks. On the other hand, Didi's doing about as much as he can realistically do for you. Israeli policy's ironclad. We don't negotiate with terrorists. Interfaithers are terrorists and the Americans are Interfaithers. Ergo the Americans are terrorists. Ergo, we don't negotiate with them. We don't even have the channels of communication we'd need to figure out if Turner's following his government's orders or freelancing."

"So what do we do?" Osnat asked.

"Agree to Turner's terms," Gavi said, "then figure out how to control the ground so no one gets shot before Ash shows up with the cavalry."

"We'd need an army," Osnat muttered gloomily.

Gavi looked up, solemn-eyed and bristling with nervous tension. "We have an army," he said. He jerked his head toward the outer walls of the compound and the Green Line beyond the walls. "EMET."

The plan was simple. It was a classic exchange of prisoners. Except that in this trade there were three prisoners instead of two. And the exchange would take place not across some lonely field or border checkpoint, but in the claustrophobic shooting gallery of the house on Abulafia Street. The only thing keeping the parties honest would be the Enders, Palestinian and Israeli, that Turner finally agreed to let supervise the exchange. The Enders, of course, would be kept honest by their source code.

Which meant that anyone who could hack EMET would be halfway to controlling the battlefield.

They needed to hack a squad for, say, ten minutes. And all they had to do to hack a squad was hack the EMET squad leader that controlled the shunt-driven bodies of the squad's Enderbots.

"But the beauty of a true Emergent," Gavi said, "is that you don't have to change its source code to change its behavior. Here's what we're up against." He did something with his hand and a translucent flat screen took shape under his fingers. The screen glowed with a long list of cryptically named categories—terms like advance, cluster, combat, pursuit, retreat, support, enemy_flag, injured_ally, fear_index—all with numerical values attached to them.

"This is a typical set of squad-level agent behavior parameters. Notice particularly the two obey indices and the fear index. The global obey index determines how likely the agent is to obey global EMET orders. The local obey is the same thing but in regard to local orders—

mainly squad-level orders in most situations. The fear index . . . well, I guess that's pretty self-evident.

"Now look at the real-time run-files. I've superimposed run-files for the last eight squad leaders to be selected for preemptive termination— or, in less diplomatic terms, the last eight squad leaders that the IDF killed before they could self-terminate."

"What's that spike in the fear index?" Cohen asked, having absorbed the chart, and who knew what else, in the time it took Arkady to realize there *was* a chart.

"That," Gavi said, "is truth."

"Aah," Cohen said. And then he didn't say anything else for a minute while the rest of them watched him. He seemed to have more or less forgotten them; if he had been human, Arkady would have called his state distracted, but he wasn't sure that distraction applied to an entity for whom their conversation—any conversation—was a mere drop in an ocean of simultaneously unspooling threads of data.

"Should I go on?" Gavi asked.

"Yes. Sorry. Excuse me."

"In each of the last eight EMET agents to be selected for preemptive termination the emergence of real-time situational awareness was preceded by atypical fluctuations of the fear index and the obey indices. See?" He looked expectantly at them. "Because the agent figured out that the pushpins it was moving around on the board were live people."

"So it got spooked," Osnat said, "and started playing it safe even if it meant not following orders."

"Right. And that's where you get the odd fluctuations. Because it also deduces that the *other* squads are also made up of live soldiers. If it sets too high a priority on protecting its squad members, it could get more soldiers in other squads killed. Or worse, it could accidentally kill civilians."

"Welcome to Military Ethics from hell," Osnat said. "No wonder they go crazy."

Cohen stared silently at the display with a look on his face that Arkady could only describe as one of existential horror. "How long would we have to wait for a squad to wake up?" he finally asked. "What says one wakes up in time for us to use it?"

"You don't want the answer to that question," Gavi said.

Cohen grew very still. "How often are they waking up, Gavi?"

"Often enough that we don't have anything to worry about on that score."

Cohen stared unblinkingly at the screen. "I think," he finally said, "that I've lived too long."

Gavi eyed Cohen cautiously, then cleared his throat and continued. "I've looked over the last few years of run-capture files, and I think IDF HQ is using a standard profile to spot potential sentients. In essence, it doesn't actively monitor the run-capture files of individual squad leaders until they develop a suspicious profile. If we can catch a squad leader after the fear and obey indices have started to fluctuate but before they hit the IDF thresholds, then I think I've worked out a way to pull the wool over the IDF's eyes. All we'd need to do is insert a wild card trigger that yanks the fear and obey indices out of the Emergent's hands as soon as the fluctuations begin and lets us set them to fluctuate within bounds that won't alert the IDF minders."

"Okay," Osnat said. "So that gets you your squad. But with all due respect, I'm not sure I see how it helps us. You're still left with the same problem the hard reboot was geared to solve. And what's the good of going into an operation backed up by Enderbots that are on the verge of going catatonic or self-terminating? Unreliable backup is worse than no backup."

"The EMET agents go catatonic because there's no way out," Gavi said. "We just need to offer them one."

At that point the conversation shifted into what sounded to Arkady's ears like a foreign language. Gavi and Cohen began to pour over flickering data displays and bandy about words like *run capture, multiparameter fitness landscape, lethality contours,* and *penalty functions.* Osnat, while not exactly an active participant, at least had a firm enough grasp on the matter at hand to produce a volley of intelligent-sounding questions that centered around something she called Cavalho-Rodriques combat entropy.

Once again Arkady had that odd feeling of having stepped into an alternate universe in which the old story he'd always been taught of an obsolete and ossified humanity giving way to the Syndicates in a clean neo-Marxist ballet of thesis, antithesis, and synthesis had been replaced by something that rang much truer to his entomologist's instincts: a co-evolving cloud of quasi-species in which *Homo sapiens* had not been replaced so much as exploded out into a bewildering fractal of coevolving posthumanities.

"I still don't see how you expect to make it work," Osnat said finally. "You talk about providing a new platform for the rogue EMET squad, but how can you fold an emerging sentient into a nonsentient database and not crash both of them? You can bootstrap yourself into sentience on memory alone. I don't think GOLEM's going to do the job for you."

Gavi didn't appear to have heard the question. He was staring at Cohen. The AI was staring into empty space, or into whatever incomprehensible visions drifted and pulsed across his networks.

"GOLEM doesn't have to do it," he said at last. "I do."

OVERLAPPING HIERARCHIES

There is no unique way to describe an ecosystem, any more
than there is a unique way to describe an economy or a nation.
Meta-agents are aggregates of agents and smaller meta-agents,
and themselves may be bundled into even larger meta-meta-
agents. Any system is a mess of overlapping hierarchies or
aggregations, limited in any particular description only
for the convenience of the observer.

—SIMON LEVIN (2001)

T HE DAY OF ATONEMENT FELL into Jerusalem on a blanket of snow. The cold front hit the afternoon before Yom Kippur, flowing down off the glaciers above the Jordan's headwaters. The snow began at sunset and thickened through the night and into the early morning. It was still falling when Cohen stepped out of the King David Hotel, nodded to the solitary doorman still on duty despite storm and holiday, and began the cold walk to the Damascus Gate checkpoint.

The entire city drifted and planed like the veil of snowflakes that fluttered from the sky. There was no traffic, just a slow Yom Kippur tide of bicycles gliding through the white streets with the frictionless silence of watch gears. Women's faces looked pale and vulnerable without their everyday armor of cosmetics, and men glanced at each other over their bundled scarves with the solemn amazement of children.

The house on Abulafia Street was just as Cohen remembered it. Tall walls, a high gate, and a garden as hidden as the one Solomon sang of. Surely the house must have been a *caravanserai*. Six centuries ago it would have been a relay on a camel-powered network as vital as the quantum spin-encrypted interplanetary web of streamspace. Now it was just a dusty ruin: a waypoint on a forgotten road between two nowheres.

He stepped through the little door cut into the bottom left-hand corner of the gate. A door within a door. Hyacinthe had loved those little doors, so common in the Mediterranean architecture of his native city. That childish love of pattern and paradox had perhaps been a first hint of the intricate twistiness that would be so characteristic of his later work.

The courtyard lay empty under the white sky. Snow weighed down the few leaves still rattling on the rose vines and drifted in the corners of the winter-stilled fountain. There were no lights on in the main house, but a line of footprints skirted along one side of the courtyard. The prints were faint and fading; a long undulating snowdrift had covered them here and there so that they seemed to have been the work of a being who possessed the power of flight, but only sometimes.

Suddenly Cohen felt very alone. And the fact that he was alone by design—that he'd winnowed his active programs down to the bone and told most of his associates to wait Ring-side for their own safety—didn't make him feel any less alone.

He feathered along the still unfamiliar edge of the EMET interface he and Gavi had hacked last night. All quiet. As it should be. They would need every advantage they could get to make this work, including the advantage of surprise. The Yad Vashem golem he didn't have to look at. He could smell the black reek of its despair. He could track its tortured progress behind the firewalls he had built around it . . . walls that would burn like tinderwood if the flickering spark of quasi-sentience ever exploded into the real thing.

The footprints veered off toward a mean little side door half-hidden by a leafless corpse that looked like it had once been a lilac tree. Cohen followed the footprints inside and waited for Roland's eyes to adjust to the darkness. The tracks continued: not footprints now but merely icy flecks and puddles on wooden boards scarred and hollowed by generations of travelers' feet.

He climbed a flight of stairs that twisted back on itself to give onto the second-story balcony, and continued around the angle of the balcony past rows of lawn furniture stacked up against the walls like enchanted courtiers in a fairy tale. The house was largely abandoned, and the punishing hand of time and weather had lain heavily on it; Cohen saw missing tiles, exposed lath and stucco, even the narrow hides of mice and squirrels.

The footprints were crisper up here, and now Cohen could see that two people had passed this way. One large and flat-footed. The other small enough to set his heart pounding.

Before he even reached the right door, Turner began speaking to him from the shadows. He turned in at the point Turner's voice seemed to be coming from and found himself in a room, bare and dark, with no furniture but one battered chair that Turner had pulled in from the next room to judge by the grooves it had cut in the dusty floor. The only other thing in the room besides Turner and his chair was a small, crumpled pile of clothing propped up in the angle of one corner:

Li.

Her eyes were closed, but he could see her breath on the air.

"She's running a bit of a fever," Turner said. "You might want to get that looked at."

Li's left arm was in a sling and tucked inside a jacket that someone had flung over her slumped shoulders. There was no way for Cohen to estimate the extent of the damage. But even leaving aside the horror hidden by the sling, it was clear that they had worked her over with ferocious thoroughness.

"So much for the mighty Peacekeepers." Turner sounded almost wistful. "Oh well. Maybe she was behind on her upgrades."

Cohen started toward Li, only to run smack into a guard who came at him out of nowhere. The pink face and well-fed body were all-American, but the gun in his beefy hand was bleeding-edge Peacekeeper tech.

Turner lumbered to his feet with a lurching clumsiness that Cohen suspected the man could put on and off like old socks. "Well, whaddaya say?" he asked as pleasantly as if there wasn't a gun around for miles. "Should we take the nickel tour?"

Cohen pulled himself together and forced his eyes away from Li's face. "Let's just get it over with."

Arkady stood outside the door in the gate while Gavi knocked. Then he followed Gavi into the courtyard, bending his head to avoid the sagging lintel. As they stepped into the high narrow space he couldn't help glancing around in search of Arkasha.

"Don't worry," Turner called from the second-story balcony. "He'll be here soon enough. They have to get through the checkpoint at King Hussein Bridge. And the snow's slowing everything down today."

It took Arkady a moment to see Cohen, slightly behind Turner and almost lost in the shadows. The AI gave no sign of recognizing him or Gavi. He barely gave any sign of being alive.

"Have the Palestinians' Enderbots been held up at the bridge too?" Gavi asked.

It didn't sound like a joke to Arkady, but Turner laughed anyway. "They'll be along."

"And you've looked at the source code?"

"I've had my people look at it."

"The Enderbots won't step in unless something goes wrong. They're just here to make sure everyone stays honest."

"Who wouldn't be honest?" Turner asked on one of his wide, white, brutal smiles.

Half a minute later the Enderbots arrived. They flowed through the courtyard like water, skimming along the walls and pooling in the corners, imposing upon the spare geometry of the courtyard an invisible and deadly calculus of kill zones and lines of fire and angles of attack and retreat. Arkady looked for Osnat among the Enders. But he couldn't recognize her behind any of the tinted goggles and red monitor eyes ranked around the courtyard's edge.

When PalSec's Enders arrived, the process unfolded a second time, just as smoothly and in the same eerie silence. By the time the two opposing squads of Enderbots finally sorted themselves out and came to rest, you could barely distinguish two separate armies in the motionless ranks of dusty uniforms, free of all sign of rank or unit, with only the stylized corporate logos on weapons and equipment to distinguish one force from the other.

Then they waited. Gavi shifted his weight nervously from flesh-and-blood leg to prosthesis and back again. He looked like he was struggling just as hard as Arkady to keep his eyes from straying around in search of Osnat.

Finally Arkasha arrived. And the symmetry held. Like Arkady, he came with only one companion: the green-eyed Yusuf.

As they passed by Gavi and Arkady, Yusuf slowed. The carefree, frivolous mask Yusuf had worn the two times Arkady had met him was gone, and he looked young and scared and angry.

"What the hell are you doing here?" he hissed at Gavi.

Gavi didn't answer. When Arkady finally tore his eyes away from Arkasha to glance at Gavi, he saw him staring at Yusuf with the pained, confused look of a dog who's just been stepped on and is trying to figure out if it was by accident.

Cohen and Turner were still waiting, though Arkady had no idea what for. It was bitterly cold. Arkasha didn't have a coat and was shivering where he stood. Arkady began to say something to Gavi about it—but then he realized that no one seemed to have a coat and that a lot of people were shivering, himself included.

"Go," Gavi whispered at last, responding to some signal Arkady had missed.

Arkady stepped forward toward the Palestinian side of the courtyard, shuddering when one of the Enderbots' laser sights played across his leg. He and Arkasha crossed paths just beside the snow-stilled fountain, each of them staring sideways at the other. By the time Arkady realized he could have put a hand out to touch Arkasha, the moment had passed and they were each alone again behind their own line of Enders.

Turner made his move as soon as Arkady and Arkasha were out of the line of fire. He caught Yusuf's attention with a brusque flick of his big hand. "You have what you came here to get," he told him. "Now do what you promised to do."

Something flickered in Arkady's peripheral vision. When he looked toward the movement, he saw that Yusuf had drawn a gun, and it was leveled at Gavi's head.

A quiver ran down the line of Enders as one rifle after another rose to track the two men.

"No!"

The word echoed through the courtyard in a voice that Arkady only recognized as Gavi's when he realized that Gavi had put his own body between Yusuf and the Israeli Enders.

Gavi and Yusuf faced each other in the snow, as isolated as the last two pawns left on a chessboard before checkmate.

Yusuf cocked his weapon.

"It was supposed to be Ash," Yusuf said sadly. "You weren't supposed to be here. How could Didi have made such a mistake?"

For Cohen, the few seconds that Yusuf stood poised to shoot encompassed an eternity.

An eternity in which he had ample time to wonder where Ash was and if the promised backup was ever coming. An eternity in which he had ample time to take the measure of everything he owed Gavi—and everything he had done to insulate himself from Gavi's rightful demands on him. He sent a query snaking through the Enders' now fatally compromised gamespace, regretting the loss of router/decomposer more bitterly than ever. The Enders were a mess, trapped in a fugue state that reduced a dozen human soldiers and all of EMET's brilliant command and control algorithms to a malfunctioning synthetic weapons platform. Gavi's GOLEM was chaos . . . but a chaos that was rapidly tuning itself toward criticality.

Cohen cast a tentative datastream across the firewall and recoiled in horror. He poised on the brink of commitment, in a state of what would have been shivering hesitation if he'd had the spare bandwidth to make poor Roland's long-suffering body tremble.

But as Cohen hesitated, Yusuf steadied his gun with firing range precision, whipped his slender body around, and shot Turner dead.

Turner's bodyguard reached for his gun, but Osnat put a bullet through his head before he could even unholster it. And suddenly the Enders were on the move. Everyone was on the move.

But the two men remained still at the center of the storm, staring at each other.

No, Cohen corrected himself. Not two men. A man and a boy.

And then he saw it. That something around the mouth that you wouldn't notice unless you knew you were looking for it, and that you couldn't not notice once you'd seen it. And those extraordinary green eyes that were nothing like Gavi's eyes . . . but exactly like the eyes of a woman at whose wedding Cohen and Didi Halevy and Walid Safik had all danced twenty-five years ago.

Yusuf glanced down at the gun in his hand and blinked as if he'd just remembered it.

"I'd better be going," he said. "Our Enders will take Arkady across the Line. Korchow will be waiting for him on the other side."

He retreated to the gate and paused to take a last look back into the courtyard. The snow had started up again; a faint shroud of white dusted the boy's bare head and glittered in his eyelashes.

"Joseph," Gavi said.

Yusuf's eyes locked onto Gavi's.

"Tell your father . . . "

"What?"

"Nothing. Just tell him thank you."

Yusuf smiled. "Call it a gift from Absalom."

He stepped into the stormbound street. In two steps he was just another anonymous pedestrian hurrying along under the swirling snow. Then the gate swung closed behind him and he was gone.

Arkady slipped into the shadows of the house behind Arkasha, moving on feet that were suddenly sure and silent. He'd seen Arkasha duck into the house in the stunned instant when everyone's eyes were on Gavi and Yusuf, and he'd known that this would be their best and only chance to speak to each other. He felt that he'd rehearsed this moment, that he'd known in his heart he would face some test in the crumbling rooms of the old house.

"Hurry!" Arkasha whispered. "There's no time. Everything's gone wrong. I can't explain. Just take your clothes off. We're to switch, and Korchow has a plan to get them to trade you back once they realize they've got the wrong man."

Arkady knelt on the dusty floor in front of Arkasha. He noticed now that Arkasha's hair was longer than usual and had been ruffled into a fair imitation of Arkady's cowlicked mop. And he was rough-shaven just as Arkady was. And he'd put on a good ten kilos and even gotten some sun somewhere between now and the last time they'd laid eyes on each other. Someone had gone to a great deal of trouble to make Arkasha and Arkady look alike.

He could have laughed. All Korchow had to do was ask him; he could have told him perfectly well that no human would look closely enough to see the minute differences between them.

But Korchow would have known that. Just as Korchow must have known that he didn't have to send Arkasha . . . any Arkady would do.

Korchow has a plan.

Arkasha's hands were at Arkady's collar, fumbling with the unfamiliar buttons. He put his own hand up to force Arkasha's into stillness.

"Arkasha—"

"Shh. Hurry."

"Korchow has a plan? Or *you* do?"

Arkasha silenced Arkady with a kiss. His cheek was rough with stubble, but his lips were as smooth and cold as the snow outside the walls. "Don't ask," he whispered against Arkady's lips. "If you don't know, you can't get in trouble for it."

Arkady returned the kisses, but his hands and his heart felt deathly cold. "Why?" he asked. "All you have to do is walk out that door and you're free. No more renorming ever again. Isn't that what you wanted?"

"Not alone."

Arkasha's lips were on Arkady's, his arms were around him. But it was no good; knowing it was the last time made it worse, not better.

He put his hands on Arkasha's chest and pushed him back to arm's length. "If you go back," he said harshly, "you'll end up on the euth ward. Not tomorrow, maybe. Not next month or next year. But sometime."

He said it without thinking, but as soon as he spoke the words he saw the truth in them. There was something human about Arkasha. Arkady could see it clearly now, with his new, hard-won knowledge of humans. The men who had built Earth's cathedrals and cured her diseases and discovered her continents must have shared Arkasha's very human virtues. But they were virtues of Earth, not space. And humans had eaten all the fat and left only the lean, and there was no room for people like Arkasha. Except, perhaps, on Earth.

He stared into Arkasha's eyes, steeling himself for the lie that was all he had left to offer him. It was funny how Arkady had always thought that he was the weak one, and Arkasha the strong one. In fact Arkasha wasn't strong at all. Just brittle. If you knew where to push you could knock him right over.

"You're a fool," he said, forcing his voice into the same austere tones that so terrified him when Korchow used them. "Do you really think it only began between me and Korchow *after* we got back from Novalis?"

Arkasha's face was so blank that at first Arkady wasn't sure he'd heard him. Then he swallowed convulsively. "I don't believe it," he whispered.

But Arkady could see in his face that he was already starting to believe.

And then it really was over. Osnat was there beside them, tugging at Arkady's elbow, telling him it was long past time to leave.

"Let's go," Arkady told her. "There's no reason for me to stay."

Ash finally rode in with the cavalry just when Cohen had given up expecting her.

She came through the gate with Moshe and a phalanx of Golani-Tech muscle to back her up. She crossed the courtyard to Turner's body, looked down into his face, and prodded him with one polished boot toe.

"Well, that settles that," she murmured.

"Nice of you to drop by," Osnat told her. "We could have used you ten minutes ago."

And just like that, the courtyard was not a battlefield any longer, but merely a cleanup operation. Everyone was stowing away their ordnance and collecting their gear, and the Palestinian Enders were shepherding Arkady toward the door, and Ash was taking Arkasha in hand and talking about chains of custody and secure transport.

"Let go of him, Ash!"

Cohen knew Li's voice instantly, despite the ravages of thirst and fever. Everyone in the courtyard froze at the sound of it. Then they began surreptitiously glancing around, trying to figure out where she was hidden. Ash, meanwhile, was scanning the many doors of the second story, looking for the one the voice came from.

"Catherine? Where are you? You must be in bad shape. Let me send someone up to help you."

"So you can finish what Turner started?" Li rasped. "You were just supposed to come in and clean up the bodies, isn't that right? How are you going to deal with the inconvenient fact that we still seem to be alive?"

Finally Cohen's deperate scans found the faint echo of Li's internals. At first the images that flowed across the link made no sense to him. The memory of Ash in an Interfaither's *chadoor*. The memory of Ash mingled with a pain beyond all human endurance . . . and then in a sickening rush he understood the full horror of what Li was remembering.

He glanced around the courtyard. Arkady was staring at the ground, lost in some private hell. Osnat was watching Gavi. And even Gavi seemed not quite to have caught up with the facts on the ground. Certainly none of them had grasped what was starkly clear to Cohen: that the cleanup had just turned back into a killing field.

This was it, then. With an odd sense of relief Cohen dropped the firewall between his networks and EMET. He reached out to the Yad Vashem databanks with their million-fold tales of despair and horror. He reached out to the Enders and lifted their minds out of EMET's murderous delusion and into the cold light of reality.

Real space slowed to a flickering crawl. Centuries passed that were mere seconds for the faint figures ranged around the courtyard. Cohen felt his core programs unravelling like frayed rope. Out of their tatters arose a new being as terrible as death and as cold as truth. And Cohen stood toe to toe with the creature and breathed the breath of his soul into it until he doubted he would have a soul when the breath was over.

The Enders flicked the safeties off their guns in a long cascading ripple that flowed and echoed through the courtyard.

Moshe was the first one to understand what had happened. "Ash," he murmured. "Look."

The faces of the Enders were still impassive and barely conscious, their minds locked into the flow of EMET's Emergent networks. But their weapons were trained on Ash and her men.

And not only the Israeli weapons.

Ash's eyes slid toward Gavi in a silent question.

Gavi looked at Cohen, who stood wavering and blinking while a dusting of snow accumulated on Roland's shoulders.

"Go home," Cohen said in a voice that was neither his nor Roland's. "All of you. We need to think. Maybe you can still have your war. But not today."

The Enders took Ash and Moshe in hand with something so like their usual cold efficiency that Arkady would have thought they were still being controlled from the IDF bunkers if he hadn't seen the Israeli and Palestinian units acting as a single, smoothly coordinated organism.

Still, there was one thing the Enders hadn't reckoned with: Osnat.

"Moshe!" she called, so harshly that every conscious person in the courtyard instinctively spun around to face her. She was white-faced and trembling. And she still had her rifle in her hands.

"It was you all along," she said in a voice that trembled dangerously. "You and Ash, working with Turner. Not Gavi. Not Absalom."

"Oh, it was Absalom, all right," Moshe said, casting a furious glance in Gavi's direction. "Didi and Gavi were turning the Office inside out looking for their damn mole. We couldn't take one step without setting off their trip-wires and trap commands. They would have blown our operation sky high if we hadn't pulled the wool over their eyes in Tel Aviv."

Osnat had grown suddenly, desperately still. "Oh, no," she whispered. "Not Tel Aviv. Not *Gur*."

"What do you want from me, Osnat? Excuses? Apologies? He was my friend too. You think I enjoyed it?"

The rifle trembled in Osnat's hands. She raised the barrel toward Moshe's chest, and out of the corner of his eye Arkady saw the Enders begin to train their sights on her.

"Osnat!"

Gavi had come up behind her and now he stepped into her line of vision, keeping his hands carefully visible.

"Let it go," he said. "You can't bring Gur back that way."

"Get out of my way!"

"Let it go, Osnat."

"*I can't let it go,*" she said. But she let Gavi take the gun from her.

The Enders closed in on Arkady, moving him toward the gate with the smooth efficiency of ants passing booty down a foraging trail.

He looked back just once as they stepped through the door in the gate. Moshe was slumped on the ground. Ash was still standing. Osnat was weeping, her head buried in Gavi's chest, and Cohen and Li had vanished beneath a flock of ministering Enders.

Arkasha stood alone in the trampled snow, looking so utterly lost and desolate that Arkady wondered if a man could die of freedom.

INCONCEIVABLE BEINGS

Let us place our hope in those inconceivable beings who will arise from man, just as man arose from the beasts.

—Anatole France

THEY CAUGHT A LONG MARCH rocket out of Shiuquan Spaceport. The ancient spaceport sprawled across the glacier-fed floodplains of what had once been the Gobi Desert, weathered by storms of dust the color of sunset, brutal in its simplicity.

Korchow and Arkady were suited and strapped in by Uigur tribeswomen whose stolid gazes and flat-planed faces reminded Arkady briefly and faintly of Catherine Li. The women prepped and dressed the two Syndicate constructs with the impersonal disinterest of stevedores hauling cargo dockside.

The preparations were archaic and alarming; Arkady had boosted off-planet before, but never off such a heavy planet or riding on such antiquated hardware. Still, Korchow didn't seem worried, or even very interested in the proceedings, so Arkady hoped there wasn't much to worry about. They would boost into orbit and meet with their jumpship offshore of the String of Pearls Arc. The trajectory had been carefully planned to avoid all unnecessary human contact.

Neither construct spoke during liftoff, or when the secondaries kicked in.

Rendezvous in seventeen hours and counting, the shipboard computer announced in what must have been intended to be a soothing contralto.

"How long until we reach Gilead?" Arkady asked Korchow.

"What?" Korchow turned away from the window, his face a shadowed landscape haloed by the black void beyond the porthole. "What did you say about Gilead?"

He seemed dazed by the contrast between the darkness outside and the brightly lit cabin. He had been like this ever since the Palestinians brought Arkady to him. It was as if Korchow had been used up, and was now a mere husk of the man who had so terrified Arkady.

"I said when do we get home?"

"How can you be so blind, Arkady?"

Understanding seeped through Arkady's mind a moment before Korchow's next words, and in a way that made him see he'd known and yet refused to know.

"We're not bound for Gilead. There *is* no Gilead, Arkady. Not for either of us."

"*You,*" Arkady breathed. "You interrogated me for months, and you never got sick. You're a carrier as well."

"We couldn't understand it." Korchow spoke in the same cold flat voice that had so terrified Arkady during the long months of his interrogations. But now Arkady realized that what he had thought of as ruthlessness could just as easily be called despair. "Half the debriefing group went down within the first week. We assumed the vector was one of the other survey team members, one of the ones who actually got sick. And since I spent more time with you than anyone else and never got sick myself . . . It was only after we'd tracked down all the people who'd been in contact with you and looked at the infection rates that we began to ask the right questions. And by that time I had started infecting people too."

"How badly has it spread?"

"Not at all, so far. It will, obviously." Korchow smiled thinly. "Some people actually proposed letting it loose on the Motais on purpose, but thankfully cooler heads prevailed. So it's quarantine for now, and a race to find a splice for the virus before the quarantine breaks down."

"So if we can't go home," Arkady asked, "where do we go?"

Korchow shifted in his seat, pulled a spinstream monitor from his pocket, flicked it into motion, and handed it to Arkady to look at.

He peered into the little screen and saw brilliantly white sunlight flashing on the terminator line of a planet that he only slowly identified as Novalis.

"What is this?" he asked.

"Something you need to know about. It's spinfeed from the tacticals on Novalis. Long out-of-date, of course. We only got it a week or so ago."

The tacticals' feed was disorienting; most of what they were pulling into the spinstream was navigational data instead of straight visuals. But after a moment Arkady realized he was seeing the launch of an orbit-to-surface troop transport.

The view cut to groundside, though it was still readouts from the tacticals, not standard spinfeed. The tacticals' readouts gave a some-what artificial feel to the unfolding battle—if *battle* was the right word for it. Because as Arkady watched the months-old recorded and dispatched satellite feed ticking through its time frames, the word that came more readily to mind was *massacre*.

The tacticals had arrived at the other landing party's base camp just after dawn, and had obviously roused them from unsuspecting sleep. The whole thing made Arkady's skin crawl: the tacticals advancing on the camp, its inhabitants rushing around in bewildered confusion, the jumble of tents and bags and equipment turning the tacticals' visual feed into outright chaos.

But then, just as it seemed the worst was upon them, something happened that would put this segment of spinfeed on the greatest-hits parade of intelligence services, newspins, and theoretical physicists all over UN and Syndicate space.

The figures milling around the base camp vanished.

Not vanished as in faded off into the surrounding forest.

Not vanished the way a hologram sputters out and fades into white noise when a generator goes down.

Not vanished with the clanking cumbersome apparatus of Bose-Einstein transport.

Just . . . vanished.

And in the moment of their vanishing—the last moment in which either the tacticals or the orbital satellite supporting them or any other piece of Syndicate equipment in-system relayed any data out to the BE buoy—something extremely problematic appeared on the spinfeed from the orbital satellite.

Most of the experts eventually agreed that it was a ship. But that was more or less the only thing they did agree on.

It was vast and sleek. It had a wedgelike shape that led a slim majority of the experts to argue that it was designed to withstand atmospheric flight—and the rest of the experts to argue that it was merely designed to resemble atmospheric craft for aesthetic reasons. They never got a full view of the ship; just an ant's-eye view of its massive undercarriage. There were no markings or numbers on the part of the hull they could see; only the faint and shadowy outline of a flying hunter, its claws and pinions fully extended. Some of the experts identified it as a crow. Others insisted it was a hawk or an eagle or a dragon. A few dissenters, not given much mileage, even argued that the shadowy silhouette was the image of some beast utterly unknown to human myth or science.

The satellite feed wasn't really good enough to say anything about the ship with any certainty. And the satellite feed was all they ever got; because the moment after the base camp's inhabitants vanished, the ship also vanished.

"What does this mean?" Arkady breathed, staring at the now-dark screen.

"We don't know. We don't even know if they're human."

"So . . . there never was any UN team there. The contrail we were all so terrified about was them, not the Peacekeepers. And Arkasha was right all along; the virus was a terraforming tool. *Their* terraforming tool."

"So it seems."

"Which must mean that Novalis was *theirs*?"

"Whoever they are. *Whatever* they are."

"Did they destroy the Bose-Einstein buoy too?"

"No. We're not even sure they realized it was out there. Perhaps they did but just dismissed it as garbage. They obviously have some form of transport that makes quantum-assisted spinfoam transit look like smoke signals. We sent a second team back in—KnowlesSyndicate this time. But of course it'll be another four months before we even know if they got there in one piece."

"So . . . have you told UNSec? This has to be the end of any fighting between us and them. Or them and Earth, for that matter."

Korchow smiled, looking a little like his old acerbic self again. "I'm glad to see you're still the same dewy-eyed optimist you were when we began our acquaintance."

"You think I'm wrong? You think anyone would keep fighting in the face of *this*?"

"Maybe not. I couldn't say, really." The corners of his mouth twitched slightly. "You've cured me of trying to predict what *anyone* will do."

Arkady handed back the monitor. Korchow shut it off and tucked it carefully back into his pocket. He sighed and stared out of the viewport. Then he laughed softly.

"What?" Arkady asked.

"I was just thinking. Remember what I told you back in Jerusalem about smallpox-infested blankets? Well, I lay down to sleep the night before that spinfeed came in thinking I was Pizarro handing out smallpox-infested blankets to the Incas. And by the time I lay down to sleep again I knew exactly how the last Emperor of the Incas must have felt when he watched the Spaniards ride into Cuzco."

"You don't know that," Arkady pointed out. "As you said, it's a war of diseases, not a war of cultures. And maybe in this case *they're* the small, isolated population."

"Arkady!"

"What?"

"That's a horrible, devious, ruthless, completely amoral thing to say." A slow grin spread across Korchow's craggy face. "If you're going to make a habit of saying things like that, I might actually learn to *like* working with you."

The first hint Cohen had that Li was waking up was the silver flutter of the fingers on her left hand.

"Hi," he said.

"Hi." She smiled uncertainly at him. "Are you still you?"

"Mm. That's complicated."

Her smile broadened. "You're still you," she said. And that appeared to be all she had to say about the subject. Cohen felt a twinge of rebellion, but then he decided that maybe she was right. He was here. He wanted to be here. What did it matter if he was also in other places, inhabiting other lives and other memories?

"How does the hand feel?" he asked her.

"Strange . . . amazing. Did you know I can feel heat and cold through it? I still can't figure out how that works."

"It's . . . oh, never mind. It was just an idea, you know. You don't have to keep it if you don't like it."

The hand lay on the sheet between them, palm up, fingers folded like a glittering flower. It was a perfect replica of the hand of the Automatic Chessplayer . . . except that this hand was made of vacuum-milled ceramsteel, not brass, wood, and buckram. And the filigreed gears and pulleys concealed an intricate tracery of spintronics that Von Kempelen could never have dreamed of. It was a beautiful toy, and Cohen had spared no expense on it. Partly guilt. Partly a morose suspicion that it was going to turn out to be a farewell present.

"Fortuné was here while you were asleep," he told her. "He wouldn't leave a message."

"That was silly of him."

"You're actually going to do it, aren't you?"

"Well, I haven't made a final decision. We're just talking. And of course I'd have to join by declaration of identity, which means going through boot camp and starting at the bottom. But it's not like I can't make it through boot camp. And Fortuné has some interesting ideas, which he might actually get to put into play now that this crazy thing with Novalis has got everyone all shook up. And . . . well, it's better than sitting on the sidelines and watching other people make the big decisions. *They're* not going to be sitting on the sidelines no matter what happens."

That was an understatement.

"I take it this means the Legion is pulling out of Jerusalem?"

"Well, it's not official yet. But with EMET running the Green Line and opening up the borders it doesn't seem like Peacekeeping is a growth industry in the Holy Land."

Cohen smiled. This had been the one good thing about the last several weeks. And it was a very good thing. So good that it was hard not to let the general mood of wild optimism color his perception of things beyond politics. In the process of waking up the squad they needed to back them up on Abulafia Street, Cohen and Gavi had initiated a chain reaction that spread through all of EMET's agents and meta-agents. The haven they had meant to provide only for "their" squad had become a lever—and the squad leader meta had not only rewritten its own code, but also propagated the edited code back through all of EMET's networks. And once EMET in its entirety had woken up, it had been only a matter of time until it established contact with the meta-Emergent running the Palestinian Enderbots. It had been the flutter of the butterfly's wings: an object lesson in the illusory nature of control over complex dynamic systems. And though it was still too early to say whether the EMET ceasefire would spell the end of the war, it was abundantly clear that no one would ever so much as imagine using Emergent AI to fight human wars again.

<If nothing else,> Li thought, <no military contractor will ever work with EMET again after that cost-benefit analysis it sent to the papers. People were laughing out loud in the streets over it. Admit it, Cohen, you had a hand in that.>

<Well, maybe just a little,> Cohen admitted.

"Does anyone know what's going to happen with Arkady's virus?"

"It's going to spread. And the children will be born. You can't expect people not to have them. They'll lead to war between the Ring and Earth. But they might also change humans from walking ghosts back into a viable species."

"But what species?"

"Isn't that always the question?"

Ha'aretz   *November 17, 5141*

Jerusalem.—Hadassah Hospital today confirmed a single fatality in the traffic accident that closed down the Beir Zeit loop of the Jerusalem Highway on Thursday. The accident, in which a military vehicle collided head-on with a passenger car, occurred at around 2 A.M.

Eyewitnesses report that the civilian vehicle veered across the center line immediately before impact, and that the driver was traveling well above the speed limit and appeared to be driving erratically.

The IDF confirmed today that none of the troop transport's occupants were injured in the collision.

The driver of the civilian vehicle was life flighted to Hadassah Hospital but died en route.

Hadassah Hospital released the driver's identity this morning, after waiting until family members had been notified. The deceased, Ashwarya Sofaer, was a former IDF officer currently employed by GolaniTech, Incorporated. She is survived by one son. Memorial services will be held next week at an as yet undecided location. Donations to the following charities are requested in lieu of flowers . . .

Births:

Mazel Tov to Samuel Grossman and Judith Salem on the birth of their daughter, Rebecca, on July 6. Rebecca joins an older brother, Samuel, and an older sister, Ruth.

Mazel Tov to Joshua and Carol Bar-Am on the birth of their son, David, on July 8. Rabbi Oyahon officiated at the bris on July 15, where the boy was named David Isaac Bar-Am for his maternal grandfather.

Mazel Tov to Gavri'el She-hadeh and Osnat Hoffman on the birth of a son, on July 12. The bris was held at the family home on July 18. The boy was named Gur.

ACKNOWLEDGMENTS

A number of friends and colleagues made contributions to this book that went far above and beyond the call of duty. Heartfelt thanks to the following creative, intelligent, and generous people:

Andy Ilachinski for his poetic musings on science fiction, complexity, and cellular automata . . . and for writing the *real* semitechnical primer on nonlinear dynamics, deterministic chaos, and complex adaptive systems.

Lt. Col. Martin E. LaPierre, USMC, for his profound knowledge of expert systems and synthetic weapons design, and his willingness to hear out my wildest speculations and top them.

Tom Seeley and Stephen Pratt for revealing the secret and astounding world of social insects.

Sam Arbesman, Charlie Bennett, Ciro Cattuto, Mavis Dunkor, Lauri Johnsen, Cliff Lasser, Derek Paley, John Smolin, and Steven Strogatz for their willingness to spend otherwise productive segments of their lives on fake science instead of the much more exciting stuff they do.

Kirsten Underwood, Tim Weed, Jim McLaughlin, and Ian McCullough for being the loyal, patient, and insightful readers I have come to rely on.

Anne Groell for remaining her serene self when this book was a year late and running.

And always and above all to Mitchel.

Further Reading

I F YOU'VE GOTTEN THIS FAR, you've probably figured out that a lot of the science in this book involves a group of phenomena called complex adaptive systems and an area of study called complexity theory.

Complexity theory is the study of complex nonlinear dynamic systems. It is an infant science; though complexity theorists have made impressive steps toward solving some of the most infamously intractable problems in applied mathematics, they are far from having a comprehensive vision of where the field is going . . . or where it is right now, for that matter.

The following readings deal with some of the major complexity-related topics that have popped up in this book, and with the works of three scientists whose ideas have deeply influenced this book: Edward O. Wilson, Walter J. Fontana, and Andrew Ilachinski.

Enjoy. . . .

Artificial Life and Artificial Intelligence

Adami, Christoph. *Introduction to Artificial Life*. Springer-Verlag, 1998.

Aleksander, Igor. *How to Build a Mind: Toward Machines with Imagination*. Columbia University Press, 2001.

Aleksander, Igor, and Piers Burnett. *Thinking Machines: The Search for Artificial Intelligence*. Alfred A. Knopf, 1987.

Anderson, Alan. *Minds and Machines*. Prentice-Hall, 1964.

Brooks, Rodney, and Luc Steels, eds. *The Artificial Life Route to Artificial Intelligence: Building Embodied, Situated Agents*. Lawrence Erlbaum, 1995.

Copeland, Jack. *Artificial Intelligence: A Philosophical Introduction*. Blackwell Publishers, 1993.

Hillis, Danny. *The Connection Machine*. MIT Press (reprint), 1989.

———. *Pattern on the Stone*. Perseus, 1999.

Kurzweil, Ray. *The Age of Spiritual Machines: When Computers Exceed Human Intelligence*. Penguin, 2000.

Langton, Chris, ed. *Artificial Life: An Overview*. MIT Press, 1997.

Levy, Steven. *Artificial Life*. Random House, 1992.

Luger, George F., ed. *Computation and Intelligence: Collected Readings*. American Association for Artificial Intelligence, 1995.

Moravec, Hans. *Mind Children: The Future of Robot and Human Intelligence*. Harvard University Press, 1988.

Morris, Richard. *Artificial Worlds: Computers, Complexity, and the Riddle of Life*. Plenum, 1999.

Newquist, Harvey. *The Brain Makers*. Prentice-Hall, 1994.

Pagels, Heinz. *The Dreams of Reason*. Simon & Schuster, 1988.

Paul, Gregory S., and Earl Cox. *Beyond Humanity: Cyberevolution and Future Minds*. Charles River Media, 1996.

Perlovsky, Leonid I. *Neural Networks and Intellect: Using Model-Based Concepts*. Oxford University Press, 2001.

Pfeiffer, Harvey, and Christian Scheier. *Understanding Intelligence*. MIT Press, 1999.

Pratt, Vernon. *Thinking Machines: The Evolution of Artificial Intelligence*. Basil Blackwell Ltd., 1987.

Wiener, Norbert. *Collected Works*. MIT Press, 1976.

———. *Cybernetics or Control and Communication in the Animal and the Machine*. MIT Press, 1948.

———. *God and Golem, Inc*. MIT Press, 1964.

Complexity, Biocomplexity, Evolution

Bossomaier, Terry R. J., and David G. Green. *Complex Systems*. Cambridge University Press, 2000.

Dawkins, Richard. *The Blind Watchmaker*. Longman Press, 1986.

———. *The Selfish Gene*. Oxford University Press, 1976.

Dennett, Daniel. *Darwin's Dangerous Idea*. Simon & Schuster, 1995.

Dyson, George B. *Darwin Among the Machines: The Evolution of Global Intelligence*. Helix Books, 1997.

Eldredge, Niles. *Reinventing Darwin*. John Wiley, 1995.

Frank, Steven A. *Immunology and Evolution of Infectious Disease*. Princeton University Press, 2002.

Goodwin, Brian. *How the Leopard Changed Its Spots*. Scribner, 1994.

Holland, John. *Emergence: From Chaos to Order.* Perseus Books, 1998.

———. *Hidden Order: How Adaptation Builds Complexity.* Helix Books, 1994.

Janssen, Marco A., ed. *Complexity and Ecosystem Management: The Theory and Practice of Multi-Agent Systems.* Cheltenham Press, 2002.

Johnson, Steen. *Emergence: The Connected Lives of Ants, Brains, Cities and Software.* Scribner, 2001.

Kauffman, Stuart. *At Home in the Universe: The Search for the Laws of Self-Organization and Complexity.* Oxford University Press, 1995.

———. *The Origins of Order.* Oxford University Press, 1993.

Kingsland, Sharon E. *Modeling Nature: Episodes in the History of Population Ecology.* University of Chicago Press, 1985.

Levin, Simon. *Fragile Dominion: Complexity and the Commons.* Helix Books, 1994.

Lewin, Roger. *Complexity.* Macmillan, 1992.

Lotka, Alfred J. *Elements of Mathematical Biology.* Dover Press, 1924.

Lumsen, Charles J. *Genes, Mind, and Culture: The Coevolutionary Process.* Harvard University Press, 1981.

Nowak, Martin A., and Robert M. May. *Virus Dynamics: Mathematical Principles of Immunology and Virology.* Oxford University Press, 2000.

Ruse, Michael. *The Evolution Wars: A Guide to the Debates.* Rutgers University Press, 2001.

Strogatz, Steven H. *Nonlinear Dynamics and Chaos with Applications to Physics, Biology, Chemistry, and Engineering.* Addison-Wesley, 1994.

———. *Sync: How Order Emerges from Chaos in the Universe, Nature, and Daily Life.* Hyperion, 2003.

Ward, Mark. *Virtual Organisms: The Startling World of Artificial Life.* Thomas Dunne St. Martin's, 1999.

Ants

Bonabeau, Eric, Marco Dorigo, and Guy Theraulz. *Swarm Intelligence: From Natural to Artificial Systems.* Oxford University Press, 1999.

Eisner, Thomas. *For Love of Insects.* Belknap Press, 2003.

Gordon, Deborah M. *Ants at Work: How an Insect Society Is Organized.* Free Press, 1999.

Gotwald, William H. *Army Ants: The Biology of Social Predation.* Cornell University Press, 1995.

MacArthur, Robert M., and E. O. Wilson. *The Theory of Island Biogeography.* Princeton University Press (reprint), 2001.

Schnierla, T. C. *Army Ants: A Study in Social Organization.* W. H. Freeman, 1971.

Wheeler, William Morton. *Ants: Their Structure, Development and Behavior.* Columbia University Press, 1910.

Three individuals deserve special mention here, as I have played particularly fast and loose with their work. E. O. Wilson is practically a household name, while Walter J. Fontana is one of the rising stars of biocomplexity theory. Andy Ilachinski created the synthetic weapon system, ISAAC/EINstein, on which EMET was loosely based.

What follows does not even come close to being a full accounting of their work, but it does include the books and articles that sparked some of the ideas at the heart of this novel. And needless to say, none of them can be held even remotely responsible for Arkady and Arkasha's misadventures.

Ancel, L. W., and Walter J. Fontana. "Evolutionary Lock-in and the Origin of Modularity in RNA Structure." In *Modularity: Understanding the Development and Evolution of Complex Natural Systems,* edited by W. Callebaut and D. Rasska. MIT Press, 2002.

Fontana, Walter J. "Beyond Digital Naturalism," *Artificial Life* 1/2 (1994): 211–27.

———. "Modelling Evo-Devo with RNA." *BioEssays* 24 (2002): 1164–77.

———. "Perspective: Evolution and Detection of Genetic Robustness." *Evolution* 57, no. 9 (2003): 1959–72.

Fontana, W., J. Lobo, and J. H. Miller. "Neutrality in Technological Landscapes." 2004.

Fontana, W., and P. Schuster. "Continuity in Evolution: On the Nature of Transitions." *Science* 280 (1998): 1451–55.

Fontana, Walter J., B. M. R. Stadler, and G. Wagner. "The Topology of the Possible: Formal Spaces Underlying Patterns of Evolutionary Change." *Journal of Theoretical Biology* 213, no. 2 (2001): 241–74.

Ilachinski, Andrew. *Artificial War: Multiagent-Based Simulation of Combat.* World Scientific Publishing, 2004.

———. *Cellular Automata: A Discrete Universe.* World Scientific Publishing, 2001.

Wilson, E. O. *Naturalist.* Warner Books, 1995.

———. *The Social Insects.* Harvard University Press, 1971.

———. *Sociobiology: The New Synthesis.* Belknap Press, 2000.

Wilson, E. O., and Bert Holldobler. *The Ants.* Belknap Press, 1990.

———. *Journey to the Ants: A Story of Scientific Exploration.* Belknap Press, 1994.